The Guide of Rhodes Castle

The *Guide* of *Rhodes* *Castle*

PATRICK WETENHALL

authorHOUSE®

AuthorHouse™ UK Ltd.
1663 Liberty Drive
Bloomington, IN 47403 USA
www.authorhouse.co.uk
Phone: 0800.197.4150

Published by AuthorHouse   02/03/2014

ISBN: 978-1-4918-9135-3 (sc)
ISBN: 978-1-4918-9136-0 (hc)
ISBN: 978-1-4918-9137-7 (e)

CHAPTER ONE

Jim Sandy was giving a coach-load of tourists a conducted tour of those parts of the garden and grounds of Rhodes Castle which were open to the public. The fair-haired youth wore a badge in the lapel of his jacket which had "Rhodes Castle: Official Guide, James Sandy" printed on it. They had begun, as the conducted tours always began, by looking at Rhodes Church and at the vault where the former Earls of Saint Helens were buried, and at the little churchyard in the West Park; then they had all re-boarded their coach to travel the half mile back to the complex of buildings known as the Visitor Centre, where the driver had parked his coach in the large visitors' car park. Now Jim Sandy lead his party of tourists out of the car park to the crossroads by the Inner Lodge where, standing by the open white gate of the Inner Drive, he assembled his party into a rough semi-circle around him, while he prepared to address them. He was about to speak, but a man in the crowd spoke first.

"Well now, Mr. Sandy, I sure hope you're going to take us to see the Servants' Graveyard." The speaker was a middle-aged American tourist, dressed in a rather loud shirt, and baggy trousers. His bald head was concealed under an enormous Western-style cowboy hat, and hanging from a leather strap around his neck was his camera case, although he was carrying the camera itself, an expensive-looking piece of optical apparatus, in his hand, as if eager to use it. He had already taken a few pictures of the little church in the Park.

"The Servants' Graveyard is where we go next, as a matter of fact," said Jim. "It happens to be the next place on our route, although I sometimes omit the Graveyard from these tours. There's really nothing to see there, that I know of; but if you want to see it, we shall see it. But first—"

"Oh, that's good," interrupted the American tourist. "You see, I've been looking forward to seeing Mrs. Buxton's grave, which is in that Graveyard, as I've no doubt you know, sir."

"Oh yes," said Jim, who had never heard of Mrs. Buxton's grave, never having bothered to read the inscriptions on the tombstones. "But first, let me tell you people what we're going to see next—after the Servants' Graveyard, which we'll look at briefly—and I'll say a few words about the Castle itself. I'm not going to bore you with a long, dull, historical account of the place, but a lot of our visitors have expressed interest in the Castle's name. It is, in fact, named after the Greek island of Rhodes, and I'll tell you how that came about. You see, Julius Dalmane, the sixth Earl of Saint Helens, was a great traveller, and he had a particular liking for Greece and things Greek. Now, I should explain that at this time this castle was somewhat smaller than it is today, and it was called Leigh Castle—after the nearby village of Leigh. Well, around 1750 Julius Dalmane, who was still quite a young man— in his thirties—returned from a visit to Rhodes. To cut a long story short, when he returned here he at once put into operation a building programme to enlarge and modernise his ancient home— and at the same time he changed its name to Rhodes Castle; and that name has stuck."

"Well, now, you don't say!" said the American man. "Now, that's just what I heard—sorry, sir, I must let you speak." He quickly became silent again as the Guide frowned at him and made an impatient gesture with his hand, demanding silence.

"As I was saying," continued Jim a moment later, "the old name of the Castle has been all but forgotten, and the new name of Rhodes Castle has remained the name of this place since the seventeen-fifties. We'll go and look at the Castle after I've taken you into the Maze—and we'll go there when we've seen the Servants' Graveyard. You see, what Julius Dalmane in fact did was to have a new house built for himself and subsequent Earls of Saint Helens. You can see it from here: it's the south-east facing façade which makes up the whole front of the present castle." (He pointed up the drive towards the front door of the Castle). "Now, before 1750 the buildings occupied little more than three sides of the present square enclosing the Bailey; this front side was mostly ancient walls then, with an archway exactly opposite the other arch in the north-western wall—that's an archway which remains intact. We'll see it presently. So what happened was that the sixth Earl, Julius, gave orders that the south-eastern walls and arch were to be demolished, and they were demolished—no trace remains of them, but luckily we know what they were like as there are drawings kept in the Estate Office Library. On the site of those walls a new and elegant house was built, so as to complete a square of buildings and to give the Castle a new façade. Now, I'm afraid I'm not allowed to take you into any of the rooms in this newer part of the Castle: the Family lives there, and they're all private. Be quiet, sir, please, if you don't mind." (He again waved a hand impatiently towards that tiresome American, who was trying to say something.) "If you have any questions, you can ask them in a minute or two.

"But we <u>can</u> go into the old rooms, where the Dalmane Family used to live until the mid-Eighteenth Century extension was built. All that's left, though, is a shell of most of those buildings: you can walk about in those old rooms under the open sky, but as well as the walls, we can identify such interesting features as the old staircases, and fireplaces, and doorways, and so on. I'll show you the most interesting things there are there, after we've been in the Maze. You people are not due back to your coach until a quarter past four (he looked at his watch) and we're on time so far, but we can't afford to spend more than a minute or two at the Servants' Graveyard. Now, are there any questions, please?"

Jim had made this speech, or something very like it, hundreds of times before, but he had seldom felt so bothered before while addressing the tourists. There were occasional trouble-makers, of course, but people like this exuberant American tourist, who were tiresome merely by wanting to interrupt the smooth flow of his speech, had, mercifully, been very rare on these guided tours. The man asked him whether the Great Tower was private, and Jim said: Yes, it was: he was sorry that he could not take them up the Tower for the view. Jim realised that this American already knew something about Rhodes Castle, surprising though that fact was. He must have been here before, he thought, or how else could he have known about the Servants' Graveyard?

A minute or two later the conducted tour was on the move again. Jim Sandy lead the party through the drive gate, and then by a small path which lead off the drive between a hedge bordering the Inner Lodge garden and a narrow piece of lawn. Then they went through a gap in a dense wall of screening evergreen trees, and there before them lay a small rectangular area of ground layed out as a little cemetry. It was entirely flanked by trees, and so very well hidden from everywhere.

"Now, where is it?" asked the American tourist eagerly, as soon as he set his eyes on the rows of two dozen or so tombstones.

"Really, Jack," said his wife, who was walking by his side, "what you want to make such a fuss about seeing that Mrs. Buxton's grave for, I can't think."

"Why, Ella," said the man, "I told you about Beryl Buxton before, didn't I?"

"Yes, but why do you regard her grave as being so special?"

"I don't know about the <u>grave</u> being particularly special, Ella. But she was special herself, I'm sure. Like I told you before, it says in that book I was reading that her ghost is supposed to haunt the Tower of Rhodes Castle, because she killed herself by throwing herself off the top of it. Maybe you could tell us more, eh, Mr. Sandy?"

"I'm afraid I can't tell you much more," said Jim, "and probably nothing that you don't already know, sir. You see, I'm still rather new to this job of being the Official Guide for the tourists here."

"Oh yes? So you don't know nothing more about Mrs. Buxton?"

"I have heard of a ghost that's supposed to hang about the Tower rooms of the Castle, though I've never seen it, and I didn't know it was supposed to be a Mrs. Buxton. I thought the ghost (if it really is there) was only known as 'the Dark Lady'."

"Ah, that's right, Mr. Sandy," said the man, "but her name is known, they say, and, properly speaking, she was really christened <u>Sarah</u> Buxton, although she always called herself 'Beryl' latterly, and I daresay others called her that too. Ah! I think I've spotted her grave!" His eyes shone excitedly behind gold-rimmed spectacles, as he moved off towards a newish white marble tombstone in the furthest corner of the cemetery. His wife followed him through the tombstones, already looking bored with what she considered to be her husband's stupid obsession with a former servant woman of Rhodes Castle, and Jim Sandy rather doubtfully followed them, feeling that it was high time for him to move the whole party on to see the Maze before they all got bored with looking at graves.

"Yes, here we are: I've found it!" said the American man excitedly. "You see, she's called by her real name, Sarah Buxton, on the headstone, and nothing about 'Beryl', her assumed name."

As Jim Sandy saw for himself, the inscription on the headstone of the grave at which they were looking was a remarkably simple one, and the stone itself was not decorated in any way. The words printed on the stone were:-

SARAH BUXTON
DIED 6TH JUNE 1951
AGED 40 YEARS

"It's a rather sparse inscription, isn't it?" said Jim.

"Ah, but remember," said the man, "that she was a suicide. She is lucky to have anything at all more than just her name on the headstone. So you haven't ever read that inscription before?"

"No, I haven't. But I'd have thought, all the same, that they would at least have put her date of birth on the stone, as well as the date of her death; although clearly she was born sometime in 1911. And the tombstone looks odd, to my way of thinking, without any description of what kind of a servant she was here, and without the usual 'In Loving Memory of', or any kind of epitaph."

"But it identifies the place of her interrment," said the man, "and that's the main thing." He had been walking about while they had been talking, peering through the viewfinder of his camera. "And now for two shots of this grave," he continued, "with first, a close-up picture to show those words." He was squatting down near the ground now, his camera at his eye. He pressed the shutter release to take a photograph, and stood up again, beaming happily. "There!" he said triumphantly. "I've come a mighty long way, mainly to take <u>that</u> picture, you know! Next, I want one of the whole of this little graveyard, showing where <u>her</u> grave is in relation to the rest of it."

As the man was looking for the best place to take his second photograph, Jim Sandy was beginning to think that it was very odd that this foreign visitor was showing such an exceptional interest in an obscure English woman who had, until ten years ago, worked at Rhodes Castle. He's mad, he thought. But no, maybe he's related to her family. This chap and his wife are quite obviously from the States, and have come over to England to see their cousins, and to look for their ancestors. American tourists are always like that.

The American man took his second photograph, and strolled back to join the others.

"That's it, Mr. Sandy, two photographs should suffice," he said. "But I sure am mighty pleased to have had this opportunity to see that grave and to take those pictures."

"That's all right," said Jim, "but we must move on now, or there won't be enough time to do our whole tour before you're all due back at your coach."

"Right you are, Mr. Guide; lead on, and we'll follow!" said the man jauntily. There were murmurs of approval of the idea of moving on from the rest of the crowd of tourists, who were beginning to wander about aimlessly, tiring of looking at gravestones. As Jim Sandy lead the party back to the drive, the American tourist and his wife were walking beside him, the man still talking enthusiastically about Beryl Buxton. "I suppose there's no chance, sir," he was saying, "of you showing us around those rooms of the Tower? I would <u>so</u> much like to meet that ghost of Mrs. Buxton there, and have a chat with her, maybe."

"I'm sorry, sir," said Jim, "but I can't do that. Those rooms are in the newer part of the house, which, as I said before, is private."

"Ah, what a shame!" said the man. "I <u>would</u> have liked to look around inside the Tower Library!"

"You might be able to do that, perhaps, later this summer, if you're still in England then," said Jim. "I believe Lord Dalmane is considering the idea of opening the house, or parts of it, to the public."

"Oh, is he now? That might well be worth another trip here if those rooms are opened. But we're going back to the States in another week. We come from San Francisco."

"It's rather a long way to come back to Dorset in England from California, isn't it?" said Jim, "especially when you consider that very likely you would <u>not</u> see the ghost if you go into those rooms for the specific purpose of hoping that it would appear."

"Very true, Mr. Sandy, very true. But I didn't mean that I would pay a return trip to England later <u>this</u> summer if I got to hear of Lord Saint Helens opening those rooms. It would be next year at the earliest, but I'd certainly come if I thought that there was a chance of meeting Mrs. Buxton's ghost."

"You must have been related to this Mrs. Buxton, I suppose, if you'll pardon me for asking. Or is it that you're just very interested in the ghosts of English stately homes?"

"Well, sir, I'm certainly interested in <u>this</u> one. But I'm not actually related to these Buxtons. The connection was that my dad used to work here as a valet to the late Lord Saint Helens—I suppose that would be the Earl before the present one."

"Oh, how interesting," said Jim. "Was it Lord Andrew Dalmane who was the Earl of Saint Helens then?"

"Andrew Dalmane, yes, that was the name; he was the Lord Saint Helens my old dad worked for, and Mrs. Buxton used to be employed here as Nanny to the Countess—the previous Countess, I suppose; not, of course, Lady Susan Dalmane, the present Countess."

"You mean Lady Mary Dalmane, the Dowager Countess, who still lives here in her own apartments; she is the mother of the present Lord Dalmane," said Jim. "Now, you must excuse me, sir, but we've come to the Maze, and we'll go in; but first I'll just say a few words about it."

"Fine," said the American. "You tell us all about it, Mr. Guide."

The party of tourists spread themselves out in a roughly circular group on the lawn around their Guide, Jim Sandy, who began to tell them about the Maze. "We always include a walk through the Maze on these guided tours," he said, speaking now to the whole crowd of tourists; the American man and his wife were still standing as close to him as they could get, as the man had not yet finished talking about Beryl Buxton. "The Maze of Rhodes Castle is much smaller than the one at Hampton Court Palace, which some of you may know," said Jim, "and it was planted about two hundred years ago . . ."

A few minutes later Jim Sandy, leading the way, and the rest of the party had gone into the Maze. At the first moment when he had a chance to get a word in to the Guide, the American man started talking to him again.

"Can I ask you, Mr. Sandy, if you've heard of that famous jewel called 'the Great Beryl of Saint Helens', which, they say, was stolen by Beryl Buxton?"

"No, I've never heard of it," said Sandy.

"Well, that stone was an aquamarine, a blue beryl," said the man. "A very famous stone, that was, and it used to belong to the Countess." Speaking now and then, whenever he had a chance, he went on telling Jim Sandy a tale about that stone. Jim was very busy keeping an eye on the people in his charge, giving directions at every turn of the Maze, and making sure that no one got left behind and lost, so that it was rather hard for him to attend to the story the eccentric American wanted to tell him; but he gathered the gist of the man's story nonetheless. The Great Beryl of Saint Helens, he was told, had been an old heirloom of the Dalmane family; it was an unusually large stone, square-cut, and perfect in every way, and it was of a beautiful shade of pale sky-blue. The Dowager Countess, Lady Mary Dalmane, when she had been the Countess of Saint Helens, had had the stone set into the famous old necklace of the Dalmanes, "the Luck of Saint Helens", a necklace of small emeralds and diamonds. Young Sandy pricked up his ears on hearing of this necklace. Surely, he thought, Susan sometimes wears that necklace—I've seen it round her neck a few times, and she looks even lovelier wearing it. But then he remembered that Susan's necklace terminated with a large diamond. That's rather odd, he thought. Why would Susan change the main stone of her necklace—or are there, after all, two separate, similar necklaces? But he said nothing aloud, other than to issue instructions on which way his party should turn to find their way to the centre of the Maze. The American man then told him that Beryl Buxton had greatly coveted the big aquamarine: she had been a woman who was passionately obsessed with jewellery. Then a dreadful day had come when the old Countess had found the aquamarine missing from its terminal place on her necklace "The Luck of Saint Helens". It was indeed surprising that the thief had not taken the whole necklace, but instead only that one large stone, which had been removed carefully, so that the rest of the necklace was undamaged. On that same day Beryl Buxton was found to have vanished, and so it was naturally assumed that she had stolen the gem. Now that stone, the man told Jim Sandy, had been reputed to be one which brought bad luck to its keeper. The next strange twist in the story was that there came a morning some months later—the sixth of June, 1951, in fact—when Beryl Buxton was found dead, her body lying on the gravel at the foot of the Tower. Later, when the body had been examined by a pathologist, it was concluded that her death had resulted from a broken neck, concurrent with a fall from a considerable height. At the coroner's inquest a verdict of suicide had been recorded, as there had been no shred of evidence to suggest anything other than that she had taken her own life, although at first it had seemed that this strange death might well have been a case of murder. The motive for the suicide, it seemed, was obscure, but it had been supposed that she had been depressed at the time because her husband had left her at about the time of her disappearance from the Castle. After the theft, and again after the death, the police had been called in, but the stolen gem had never been recovered, so far as the American man knew.

The whole affair, the man told Jim Sandy, had left a number of mysteries unsolved. Where now was that famous stone, the Great Beryl of Saint Helens? And why had Beryl Buxton, having vanished at the time of the theft, suddenly re-appeared at Rhodes Castle in order, apparently, to throw herself off the top of the Tower? For in that way, it was assumed, she had met her death, presumably on the same day as the body had been found.

Since her death, a number of people had claimed to have seen the ghost of Beryl Buxton, mostly in one of the ground-floor rooms of the Tower. The American tourist's father, who was Lord Dalmane's valet at that time, had said that he had seen that ghost "many times" (in his words) in the Tower Library, which had a window right beside the spot where the corpse had been found. Andrew Dalmane, the Earl at that time, had also seen that ghost a few times. Even before Beryl Buxton's suicide he had been fascinated by things supernatural, and had enjoyed hunting for ghosts (and meeting some, by his accounts) in his ancestral home. Some of the lesser servants of the Castle had also from time to time come up with unverifiable stories about meeting a strange dark-haired lady, who did not belong there, in or near the Tower Library. Beryl Buxton had, in fact, firmly established herself over the period of ten years since her death, as one of the resident ghosts of Rhodes Castle.

The party of visitors with Jim Sandy, their Guide, had reached the centre of the Maze, and the enthusiastic American man, enjoying being the centre of attention, had been telling this story to everyone. The people crowded around him, becoming fascinated at hearing this tale of how a new ghost had emerged at Rhodes Castle, although the sceptics in the crowd dismissed it all as a fabrication designed to draw in the tourists. People began to question the story-teller on aspects of his tale: one man wanted to know whether the ghost had ever given any hint of the whereabouts of the stolen gemstone. "It's probably still got it hidden away somewhere," he said. But the American said that he doubted whether a spirit could possess such a very material thing as a gemstone, although perhaps Beryl Buxton's ghost <u>knew</u> where the stone was.

Jim Sandy looked at his watch and saw that he had to move the party on at once: they were getting well behind the appointed schedule by stopping to talk in the middle of the Maze. "It's a fascinating tale you've told us, sir, though somewhat macabre," he said. <u>I</u> haven't met Beryl Buxton yet, and I don't think I particularly want to; but it's getting late. We must go on at once."

He lead the way out of the Maze, and the coach-party went on with their conducted tour. The American man was feeling very pleased with himself. He had managed to hold everybody spellbound by telling that tale. Let the doubters believe that it was all nonsense, if they wanted to: <u>he</u> was convinced that the ghost his father had described was very much a reality.

CHAPTER TWO

Later that day, his work for the day completed, Jim Sandy was in his little room in the Castle, lying on his bed.

His room was a very small one, and had in fact been adapted as a little bed-sitting room from its previous function as a sort of large storage cupboard. It was oblong in shape, the window opposite the door, and the bed was between two angles of wall immediately to the left of the door, where there was just enough room for a bedside table between the door and the bed; and a calendar for 1961 with pictures of railway scenes hung on the wall just above this table. The adaption of the room to its new purpose had been very carefully done to make it a pleasant, homely place. A shelf had been added above the curtains of the window, and there were new bookshelves above a small desk which stood in the corner to the left of the window. In the corner to the right of the window was a small armchair, and immediately beside it, making the small room rather cramped for space, stood a polished oak chest, which had previously been stored in the room, and had never been removed in the re-furnishing process. On the wall to the right of anyone entering the room was a chest of drawers with shallow drawers; Jim used this for storing his clothes and all sorts of small things. There were pictures on the walls which belonged to Rhodes Castle but which looked appropriate in that room, a thick royal-blue carpet covered the floor, and the curtains matched it. The room was on the first floor at the front of the Castle. Seen from outside, its window was towards the left-hand end of the facade (which was the southern end); from indoors it was the last door which opened off a long passage which ran behind the front rooms on the first floor. From the window there was a pleasant view over the front garden of the Castle.

Jim had come into his room with some twenty minutes of spare time before he would go downstairs for his supper and so, as he was feeling rather tired and had nothing particular to do until supper time, he had pulled off his shoes and layed himself on the bed, having first taken off the bedside table a photograph of Susan Dalmane. He would spend a few idle minutes (or, as he preferred to think of it, a few minutes of pleasant rest) thinking things over and admiring Susan's strikingly beautiful figure and pretty face as revealed in that photograph.

He was still very much in love with Susan Dalmane. During the first few days in his new job he had been able to see her often, and those had been days of heady excitement for him. But since those early days of being at Rhodes Castle he had, on most days, seen less and less of her; however, his infatuation for her had not diminished; the excitement had gone out of it gradually as the novelty had worn off, but the infatuation had remained at a fairly constant level within him.

That evening, as he waited for his supper, he was admiring his own photographic skill as he looked at the framed colour portrait in his hands. He had taken that picture of Susan Dalmane, and five others with it, himself with his own camera. Susan herself had given him the camera on his last birthday (his nineteenth) in July of the previous year. She had told him that those pictures were to be strictly private for him to look at when he was on his own in his room; and he considered that he had been granted an astonishing privilege in being allowed to take them. She had found time to be Jim's photographic model while he had taken six pictures of her, some on the Private Lawn (which was behind the Castle, on the far side of the brook), and some indoors. The photograph now in his hand was the one which he usually considered to be his favourite of the six portraits. It showed Susan sitting on an elegant chair in the drawing-room, wearing a striking semi-formal evening outfit of clothes which Jim had never seen before: smart dark trousers instead of one of her more usual skirts, and a black blouse with a low-cut neckline, which was clearly designed (Jim thought) to draw a man's eyes towards her magnificent bust. Around her neck in that portrait was the lovely necklace, the Luck of Saint Helens, and on her head was a small tiara, a silver circlet of precious stones. Instead of her usual gold, cross-shaped ear-rings Susan had that morning put on for the photography session her best pair of ear-rings, which consisted each of a sparkling cascade of small diamonds.

For a little while Jim held the photograph frame in both his hands while he stared as if mesmerised into the entrancing dark eyes of Susan in the photograph. Then he drew out the piece of glass which protected the photograph from dust and, with very great care not to damage the picture, drew it slowly to his lips and planted a kiss on the lips in the picture. It had been nearly a year since the last occasion on which Susan had allowed him to kiss her, but what he could not often do in reality, he often did in imagination, sometimes kissing this photograph, and sometimes keeping the action entirely in his mind's eye.

Sue, darling, you're marvellous, he murmured to himself, now holding the picture a little way back from his own face so that he could continue to stare at Susan's beauty. You look so regal in all those jewels, Sue, he continued. That was true enough. Susan Dalmane in that picture might well have been a queen, rather than a countess, with that delicate circlet of diamonds shimmering with blue and white fire against her dark brown hair; and the necklace of piercing shades of green and white against the black blouse emphasised the regal graciousness that was apparent in Susan in that pose. Jim thought that it had been a brilliant idea of his to ask her to dress up in plenty of jewellery for that photography session.

Presently Jim's eye, as he continued to stare at the photograph, alighted on the brilliant-cut diamond on the end of the necklace; and immediately he remembered what that American tourist had said about the Great Beryl of Saint Helens, which had originally been the terminal stone of that necklace. That had been a very strange story which the man had been telling about Beryl Buxton and her ghost, and about that famous stone; and it had been on his mind, more or less, all that afternoon from the time when that enthusiastic but eccentric fellow had been telling his tale. Jim Sandy had been thinking over some of the more puzzling aspects of this affair when he had come into his room, but only in a rather absent-minded way: he was not really interested in the ghost of Beryl Buxton, or in the whereabouts of the Great Beryl. The big stone of Susan's necklace <u>must</u> be a diamond, he thought. At any rate, it certainly <u>isn't</u> a square-cut, pale sky-blue stone. I wonder what really has happened to that Great Beryl of Saint Helens? But Jim, as he lay on his bed, looking at his portrait of Susan, soon ceased to think about the ghost and the gemstone. He did not believe that he was ever likely to meet this ghost himself, if only because he never had any cause to go into the Tower Library, and, so far as he could see, that state of affairs was not likely to change.

He had not seen Susan at all for a week, which was about the longest spell he had yet worked through at Rhodes Castle without even one glimpse of that lovely woman to cheer him on his way. Looking at his framed photograph of Susan (amorously, not lustfully) was having the effect on Jim of making him realise that he was desperately longing to be really with her in the flesh, or at least to see her, even if he could not talk to her. Was she deliberately avoiding being in places where she might meet him? He had often suspected that Lord Dalmane, even though he had never given any signs of jealousy or disapproval of the obviously intimate friendship which had grown up between his wife and Jim, did nevertheless disapprove strongly of this friendship. Might he then not have told Susan that she ought to take more care to avoid meeting him? Jim now thought that quite probably this was what had been happening, not only over the past week but, indeed, over the past year or more.

Jim had seen little of Susan recently, but she had been away for a day and two nights in the past week, staying with her friend, Mrs. Beck. Mr. and Mrs. Beck, who had come down from the North on the train with him and Susan, had been living with Mr. Beck's parents at Tolmers, near Hertford; but Mr. Beck had now bought a small new house on the outskirts of Bournemouth, and a few weeks ago they had moved into it. They had made the Dalmanes promise to visit them in their new house and so, on the Tuesday of that week, Susan had gone down to Bournemouth on the train to accept Mrs. Beck's invitation. Lord Dalmane had not been able to go with Susan, as he had been in London all that week since Monday morning, and had only just come back: he owned a London house at Roehampton and sometimes lived there from Monday to Friday, instead of commuting every day between London and Sherborne. Lord Dalmane was much busier nowadays in his work as a politician than he had been two years ago when he had married Susan; now he was not only on various committees of the House of Lords, but was also a Junior Minister in the Foreign Office, which meant that he was included in the full Government, although he did not have to attend Cabinet meetings. On this particular Friday he had come home on the early afternoon train (the three o'clock train) from Waterloo, instead of the 6.5 evening train, as he had no important business on either in the House of Lords or in Whitehall. Jim knew that he had arrived back at home as he had happened to see him step out of his car as it drew up at the front door some twenty minutes earlier.

Lord Dalmane's back at home, he said to himself, and Sue must be here too, because I know she was coming back from

Bournemouth yesterday morning, so as to be back here in time to welcome the Padgates yesterday evening. Lord and Lady Padgate of Dallam, Susan's Uncle Geoffrey and Aunt Nora, had come to stay at Susan's invitation for a fortnight at Rhodes Castle, their first visit to Dorset. Susan herself had driven her car down to Blandford Forum to meet them off the "Pines Express" from Crewe when they had arrived on the Thursday evening, so Jim knew that Lord and Lady Padgate were now staying at Rhodes Castle, although he had not yet seen them. I suppose Sue must be pretty busy now having those two to entertain, he thought, and she's had very little time to get ready for them yesterday evening since she got back herself from the Becks on the 9.19 from Broadstone. (Broadstone was the place just outside Bournemouth where the Becks now lived; Mr. Beck had resumed his job as an engine-driver, and was now driving trains between Bath and Bournemouth.) So she hasn't got any time to talk to me because of her guests, even if she wanted to, thought Jim. But maybe she doesn't want to see me any more, or at any rate, not so often. Or else she <u>does</u> want to see me really, but thinks she <u>ought</u> to avoid meeting me when possible because <u>he</u> has told her to. Ah, but he doesn't know (not really) that Sue to me is the most important person in the world, and that I'm bound to be miseraole without her.

Jim Sandy had, of course, considered thoughts of this sort thousands of times before, but he had never entertained any thoughts of real bitterness or jealousy towards Lord Dalmane. It was, however, his most secret hope that one day—perhaps in years ahead, but <u>sometime</u>—he would have the opportunity to make love with Susan in some secluded, outdoor place (this idea seemed to him much more exciting than the thought of merely going to bed with her, either at Rhodes Castle or elsewhere). He had never breathed a word of this secret fantasy even to Susan, but he thought that probably she had guessed long ago what he really wanted with her. He knew, too, that a hope of this sort was nothing more than a wild, sexual fantasy and, moreover, something which was unlikely ever to happen in reality; nevertheless it was such a very pleasing fantasy in itself that he liked to keep it always alive in his imagination.

Presently Jim slid the piece of glass back into its place in the photograph frame, but a suspicion of a frown for a moment contracted the muscles of his forehead as he did so. Are we drifting apart? he said to himself. Don't you love me any more, Sue? Is that why I hardly ever see you nowadays? He suddenly sat up, put the portrait of Susan back into its accustomed position on the bedside table, glanced for a moment at his wrist-watch, and made up his mind to go downstairs to wait a while if he should find that Cook had not yet got the supper ready, as it was still rather on the early side for the evening meal, which he ate with Samantha and Jack, the butler, in the servants' common room (but the Cook went home after she had finished preparing the evening meal). Jim put on his shoes, stood up, opened the door, and at once saw Susan Dalmane, a dazzling apparition in gorgeous evening dress, approaching from the other end of the corridor, and he felt his heart quicken at the sight of her.

"Hello, Jim! You aren't busy now?" said Susan cheerfully the moment she saw him.

"No, not now," said Jim.

"Can I have a word with you?"

"Yes, of course," said Jim. "Come in, please." He was delighted to have her once again in his room, even if it was to be only for a few minutes. He knew straight away from the happy tone of her voice that whatever she wanted to talk about, it was not going to be any unpleasant subject.

"There are a few things to tell you about," said Susan. "I've been rather busy lately, but I thought I'd catch you now. I won't be keeping you from your supper, will I, if we stay here for ten minutes, or so?"

"Oh, no," said Jim, "that'll be quite all right: it isn't really time for that yet. Won't you sit down, Susan?" He pointed politely to the armchair.

"Thank you, Jim," said Susan, a smile sparkling around her dark eyes. She sat down. The necklace, "The Luck of Saint Helens "was around her neck, and the little diamond tiara was on her head; but for a moment Jim was reminded again of the story of Beryl Buxton and the stolen gemstone as he caught a sudden flash from the big diamond of the necklace.

CHAPTER THREE

Earlier that evening, Susan Dalmane and Lord and Lady Padgate of Dallam were standing in the State Drawing-Room of Rhodes Castle talking and looking through the windows onto the big lawn. They were waiting for Lord Dalmane to join them when he had changed from his working-day-suit into evening dress, and for the drinks tray to be brought in. The State Drawing-Room was a large, square, elegant room, its door to the right of the Great Hall as seen by anyone entering the Castle at the front door. The Dalmanes did not use it as their sitting-room, except occasionally when they had guests staying, and wanted to be a little more formal than was their usual custom in the evenings. That room, with its exquisite gold chandelier hanging from the centre of the magnificently carved, white ceiling, always had a feel about it which suggested a very cold kind of formality; and Susan did not, as a rule, feel comfortable sitting on the settee or in a gilded armchair in there, except if it was a sunny, summer evening (which it was) and she was entertaining guests. (The chandelier was not of solid gold but was, in fact, of gold-plated silver; and the plaster ceiling was richly decorated with a circular motif of carved flowers around the chandelier). Susan thought that the reason why that room always felt excessively formal, rather than homely and comforting, had something to do with the large amount of valuable china that was displayed in there, but she did not by any means dislike the room: everything in it, especially the huge fireplace, the carved ceiling, and the chandelier, had great elegance which was entirely harmonious with the design of the room as a whole. It was one of the rooms which the Dalmanes had decided to open to the public.

The three who had foregathered in the drawing-room were all wearing evening dress. The Padgates had arrived at Rhodes Castle on the previous evening, but Susan had decided that today, Friday, was the right occasion to use the drawing-room for drinks, and for evening dress to be worn; she had no intention of using it again on any of the other evenings of the Padgates' stay as she preferred them to be informal and comfortable. Susan's dress was a very beautiful creation of deep blue material, long, and with a low-cut neckline, and with it she was wearing plenty of jewellery: as well as the "Luck of Saint Helens" strung around her neck she had on her head the little diamond circlet or tiara. Susan's Uncle Geoffrey, Lord Padgate of Dallam, was in his forties, a man of about average build and average height, and with receding hair and a kindly-looking face. Lady Padgate, Susan's Aunt Nora, was about forty years old, fairly tall for a woman of that age but (what one mostly noticed) she was very thin and angular. The dress she was wearing only just covered her knees, leaving plenty of her long, stockinged legs visible, legs which were too thin to be really attractively shaped.

The butler came in with the drinks tray, which he set down on a low table in the middle of the room. "Will that be all right, my Lady?" he asked. Susan cast an eye over the labels of the many bottles on the tray. "Let me see . . . yes, I think that should be fine," she said. "But I'll ring if we need you again. Thank you, Jack." The butler retired from the scene.

The Padgates had for several minutes been busy admiring things, both the furniture and china in the room, the ceiling, and the view over the main lawn. This view through the window was particularly taking up Geoffrey Padgate's attention, whereas his wife, Nora, was mainly fascinated in looking closely at each of the many delicate objects of fine bone china. Most of these were arranged on the shelves of a long china cabinet along one wall, though there were one or two larger pieces standing separately from the china shelves. The shelves of the cabinet were open-fronted, and Nora Padgate found that she could not resist handling some of the teapots, cups, saucers, and other paraphernalia that were displayed in there, and even taking them out to peer closely at them. It happened that she considered herself something of an expert on porcelain and earthenware, and she was looking with interest at the marks underneath the various items, and realising that the Dalmanes had a much bigger and better collection of fine china than she had at their home, Dallam Hall.

"Now," said Susan when the butler had gone out of the room, "what will you have to drink, Aunt Nora? . . . Look here, let's sit down." She waved a hand towards the settee. "And what will you have, Uncle Geoffrey?"

"Just sherry for me, Susan, please," said Lady Padgate. "You've got a gorgeous lot of beautiful china in here, you know. Will this be one of the rooms you're going to let people into?"

"Yes, I think so," said Susan.

"You'll have to be very careful, then, to know just what you've got in here," said Lord Padgate. "I'll have a gin and tonic, thank you, Susan."

Susan handed her guests their drinks, and they all sat down to talk and enjoy themselves. Presently Lord Dalmane joined them in the drawing-room, and helped himself to a glass of sherry. A few minutes later, during a lull in the conversation, he said: "How are you getting on, Geoffrey, with having the public allowed into the front rooms of Dallam Hall? You know, we're meaning to try it here in Rhodes Castle, as apparently many of our visitors to the grounds seem to be very disappointed that they can't get into the Castle itself."

"Oh, we're managing well enough," said Geoffrey Padgate. "Mind you, at Dallam Hall we only admit people into four rooms altogether, two on the ground floor, and two unused bedrooms on the first floor. We need the rest of the house to live in ourselves."

"But you could do much better than that here, I'm sure you could," said Nora Padgate excitedly. "Rhodes Castle is ever so much bigger than Dallam Hall, and part of it is much older. Anyway Dallam Hall is really a very unattractive, ugly, red sandstone house, whereas I really do think your Castle here is a lovely, rambling old place: just the sort of house tourists like to wander around in."

"Yes, indeed it is," said Susan. "That's why John and I have decided to open the house to the public. Only we don't really want the visitors to wander around the place unsupervised. We'll have to insist that they can only be taken on conducted tours by our Guide."

"Quite right," said Lady Padgate. "And, you know, Susan, you've got so much <u>more</u> in your rooms to fascinate the tourists than we've got, so I'm sure it'd be wise to have a Guide to keep an eye on them. Take this room, for instance. <u>I</u> haven't got anything like so much beautiful china for people to admire in my sitting-room as you've got in here. Why, I could happily look through this stuff for hours! Of course, if people are going to be allowed in here, even accompanied by a Guide, you'll have to have a very careful note of every item of china in case of breakages."

"<u>And</u> in case of thefts," added Geoffrey Padgate. "People <u>will</u> steal the odd little thing that they think they can get away with when no one's watching, as we've found out to our cost—not that we've had anything really valuable stolen yet from the public rooms. But so far this year a few saucers and other small things from our china shelves have disappeared, together with two or three books and a few other odds and ends. But as we have <u>every</u> item listed that's in our public rooms, we do at least know exactly what we're missing. You ought to do the same here, John, before you open these rooms."

"Yes, you certainly should," said Nora Padgate. "But what's your Guide like? Is he a competent fellow?"

"Oh indeed, yes," said Susan. "He's a most excellent man, a very valuable servant. He used to be in the Police before he came to work for us as Guide and a Junior Security Assistant. But he's a first-rate chap to have in that sort of job. Nearly every day he spots the people who surrepticiously try to steal bits off the trees to take cuttings from, or those who pull up plants, or help themselves to unauthorised souvenirs from the shop or the cafeteria."

"Yes," said Lord Dalmane, "our Mr. Sandy is a real expert at all that sort of thing. Heaven knows how much would have been stolen from the gardens and the outdoor buildings if it wasn't for his watchful eyes! His police training in watching people means that he is absolutely invaluable to us in that way. Of course, he can't be everywhere at once, but we couldn't do better than to have Mr. Sandy watching people as they go from room to room in the Castle."

"Oh, he's very good at it," said Susan. "Do you know, the other day we actually brought a succesful prosecution for theft—when he'd caught someone red-handed shop-lifting in the cafeteria?"

"Then you're very lucky to have such a well-trained expert to keep an eye on your property when people are about," said Geoffrey Padgate. "We could do with someone like that at Dallam Hall, it seems to me. But you will, no doubt, also nave adequate insurance cover against possible losses by theft or breakage by the public?"

"But of course," said Lord Dalmane. "All the contents of the rooms we're going to open will be covered against theft by insurance policies."

"That's fine; but I'd urge you, John, to have <u>everything</u> listed all the same," said Lord Padgate. "Believe me, it's a precaution which really ought to be taken before you open to the public. You want to have lists made out of every item that's in those rooms—every single object which is not a fitting—individually described on an inventory. You'll need to have a record of the author and title of every book, the distinguishing marks on every piece of china in these cabinets, and so on."

"That's right," said Nora Padgate, "that's the way it should be done. You could get one of your servants to make out lists of everything that's in this room and the other ones. Why not get this excellent Mr. Sandy to do this job for you, if he's the chap who's to keep an eye on people when they're in here?"

"Yes, we could do that," said Susan.

"When are you thinking of opening the house?" asked Geoffrey Padgate.

"In about a month's time at the beginning of July," said Lord Dalmane. "That was what we had in mind."

"Well, then, you've got no time to lose! If I were you, John, I'd have that job done right away. You'd be well advised, I'd say, to get someone onto it tomorrow morning, if possible. It might take quite a long time to make out thorough check-lists for several rooms. It took our chap at Dallam Hall nearly a fortnight just to go through four rooms in that way, but then he's pretty slow and rather inefficient; he doesn't seem to compare at all with your splendid Mr. Sandy, whom I don't think I've met yet. I imagine that he's a mature man—married, perhaps?"

"Oh no, he isn't married—not yet!" said Susan. She felt a slight hotness on her cheeks as she said this, hoped that the others had not noticed her blush, and hurriedly continued: "He's only nineteen years old, but he's very skillful at watching people, as I told you, to see that they don't commit any crimes while they're in our grounds."

"Only nineteen!" Lord Padgate was looking positively aghast with shock at hearing such a thing. "Why then, he's little more than a mere child! Do you really mean to tell me that someone so young can really be responsible enough in such a job?"

"Oh yes, I certainly do," said Susan. "Jim Sandy is, in fact, nearly twenty, which I know is very young for him to hold such a responsible job with us; but with his basic police training behind him, he does make an ideal person for a job requiring vigilance over others. He was a police cadet before he came to us."

"Was he indeed?" said Geoffrey Padgate. "Then I wonder that he didn't decide to go on with the Police, having started with them."

"He didn't much enjoy the idea of being a policeman," said Susan. He found that he'd made a mistake in joining them. That's what he told us, wasn't it, John?" John Dalmane nodded his head, but said nothing. "Anyway, he very much enjoys his work here for us," she continued.

"Well, if he can do his job properly, I suppose that's all you want of a servant," said Geoffrey Padgate. "I must admit, he sounds like an excellent young man to have around the place. He could do this job for you, I suppose, the listing of your room contents? I should certainly advise you to have it done at once."

"Fine," said Lord Dalmane. "We'll take your advice on that point, Geoffrey. Don't you think so, Sue?"

"Oh yes, definitely: I'm all in favour of the idea," said Susan. "I could get Jim to start on the job tomorrow; or perhaps you'd better have a word with Ambrose first, John."

"Okay, I'll have a word with Ambrose, and have young Sandy start straight away on that inventory job, if he thinks fit to do that. I don't believe Jim has anything else particular to do on Saturday mornings until the grounds open to the public at midday. I'm most grateful to you, Geoffrey, for suggesting this idea to us."

"Good," said Susan. "That's settled. Will you have a fill-up in your glass, Aunt Nora? Another drink for you, Uncle Geoffrey? We may as well take our time over our drinks as Cook won't have dinner ready for quite a while yet although, if you'll excuse me, I'll just go and see now what's going on in those regions."

Susan got up to leave the room.

"Won't you have another drink yourself, my dear?" said John Dalmane.

"Not just now, thank you, John," said Susan. "I've just got to go and see about things in the kitchen. I'll be back in about fifteen or twenty minutes, and I'll have a quick second drink then. Please excuse me, Aunt Nora." She went out.

When she had closed the drawing-room door behind her, Susan did not head for the kitchen. Instead she walked across the hall and went up the stairs. What she had just said about having to see about things in the kitchen was a convenient excuse for her to leave the room at that point, while her husband was there to look after Aunt Nora and Uncle Geoffrey, and keep the conversation going while they had their second drinks. She was on her way to Jim Sandy's room as there was much that she wanted to talk to him about: she had not managed to see him at all now for over a week. She was going to tell him about the inventory job in the public rooms, as the Padgates had suggested should be done; but there was something else on her mind which she had been wanting to tell him about for some days, something which would be a very happy surprise for him, a very pleasant treat. She had been feeling very proud of Jim, her consciencious and hard-working Guide, while they had been talking about his job, and she felt that he well deserved a little unexpected reward for his good work. As for not telling her husband quite truthfully why she was leaving the room, she was acting on a sudden impulse which had prompted her to say nothing at all about Jim Sandy to John at that moment, but she would indeed look in very briefly at the kitchen to see that all was well there—but only after she had visited Jim, whom she expected to find in his room at that time of day.

CHAPTER FOUR

"You weren't thinking of doing anything in particular tomorrow morning, Jim, were you?" said Susan.

Jim Sandy turned the desk chair round so that he could sit facing her.

"No, I don't think so," he said as he sat down. "At least, I don't know of anything I'm supposed to be doing then in the way of work. Have you got a job for me, Susan?" He smiled at her hopefully.

"Yes, I think we have a little job for you to start on tomorrow morning, and to go on with when you've got time during the day—when you're not being the Guide out of doors. You see, we've decided we're opening some of the Castle to the public very soon— next month, in fact—and that will mean that an inventory will have to be written out of things that are in the rooms that are going to be opened."

"I see," said Jim. "I think you told me the last time you saw me that you were considering the idea of opening the house."

"That's right. Well, we've decided to give it a try, Jim." She went on to tell Jim in more detail the plan which the Padgates had been discussing with them about the making of inventories of property at risk of theft. She told him that he would be the Guide for the indoor parties of tourists, just as he was already the Guide for the Garden tours. She told him which rooms in the Castle they were proposing to throw open to the public; and when he heard that not only the Tower Library on the ground floor, but all of the Tower was to be included in the tour circuit, the story of Beryl Buxton once again crossed his mind. For one brief moment he felt an unsettling worry at the prospect of working in the haunted rooms, but that was gone in a second or two, as he told himself that he did not in the least mind that. Don't be absurd, he said to himself, I've been into all those rooms before, and I've never seen the slightest sign of any ghost! It's probably all rubbish about a ghost in the Tower—just because Beryl Buxton killed herself there, people suppose that it must be haunted. Of course, it makes it all the better to be able to tell the visitors that sort of tale while they're actually in the very rooms where the ghost is supposed to lurk! What was that? His thoughts had wandered for a moment away from what Susan was telling him.

"You'll get exact instructions tomorrow morning, probably, on how to go about the job," she was saying, "when John's had a word first with Major Ambrose. Did I, by the way, detect a sort of shadow crossing your face when I mentioned the Tower Library? You won't have been in there very often, but I don't suppose you'd mind if you happened to meet the 'Dark Lady' in there? You were thinking about that perhaps?"

"Yes, I was actually. But I wouldn't in the least mind meeting her—in fact, I think I'd rather <u>like</u> to see that ghost sometime, if indeed it does exist. Apparently she was meant to be someone called Beryl Buxton, who killed herself?"

"That's right, Jim, so they say. Her name used to be Beryl Buxton—no, but really it was Sarah Buxton, I believe. <u>I've</u> never seen her ghost, but John swears that he once met a strange dark-haired lady in the library who apparently answered to her description. But I don't suppose that it's really likely that you'll meet her!"

"Nor do I," said Jim.

There was a short pause during which Jim thought again of the strange story the American tourist had told. He could not now believe that the Beryl gemstone which had once been part of the "Luck of Saint Helens" could be something which the ghost of Beryl Buxton was deliberately keeping hidden in a secret place of its own. But his thoughts moved on to something else. My word, Sue, he said to himself, you do look lovely with the "Luck of Saint Helens" adorning your bosom!—and that diamond tiara sparkling on your head is simply incredible!

"Jim, my love," said Susan, her voice pleasantly breaking into Jim's thoughts, "what I really came to say to you was: How would you like a day out walking with me sometime? You well deserve a little treat, I thought." She smiled to see the look of happy astonishment that had come over his face.

"Why, I'd love to come walking with you," he said, his eyes sparkling.

"Or rather," said Susan, "I should perhaps say a night out with me and John; at least it will be a long walk in the evening to somewhere, and when we all get there, wherever it is, we're to camp there overnight."

"Gosh, how fascinating! You mean, it's being organised by the Rambling Society you belong to when you say 'all'?"

"That's right, Jim."

"But can non-members join in on this outing? I'm not a member."

"Oh, yes. Non-members are welcome to come, until all seats are taken up in the special train. The only difference is that non-members will have to pay more to join us: in fact there would be the full train fare to pay. Members are being offered seats in the chartered train at a reduced fare."

"But where are we going to on this outing?"

"Oh, we don't know. You see, the whole idea is that it's a sort of mystery tour to an unkown destination. They're going to charter a special train (if we get enough people who want to come), and we get in, and—"

"At Sherborne?"

"Yes, starting from Sherborne Station. We get in, and presently the officials in charge will tell us we're just coming to the station where we're to get out. It could be absolutely anywhere in England, they say, but it can't really be all that far away because the train is due to leave Sherborne at three-fifty and, you see, the idea is that there will be plenty of time to walk from the station where we get out to somewhere else where they've already put up a lot of tents for us to sleep in. There has to be time enough, of course, to do that walk while daylight lasts."

"But do we Know how far that walk will be?" asked Jim.

"Yes, about twelve miles, the Secretary said. Twelve miles walking through easy country, mostly not hilly."

"H'm twelve miles? That sounds quite a long way to walk in the evening."

"Well, you see, Jim," said Susan, "that's why I don't think we can really be going all that far in the train. They must have allowed plenty of time for us to walk that twelve miles comfortably—not having to be rushed—before it gets dark—which is late enough at this time of the year. Mind you, I wouldn't have thought that a distance of that sort would bother you: I know you keep yourself very fit, Jim. More likely I won't manage to cover all that ground without having to be carried!"

"Oh, I expect you'll be all right, Sue; and I don't think that a twelve-mile walk would bother me either," said Jim. He knew that Susan was only joking about the possibility of having to be carried, but the thought rather excited him when he imagined for a moment carrying her himself along some road near their camping site, wherever that was to be.

"They must be allowing us about four to five hours, I should think, to walk that distance before nightfall," said Susan, "so it can't be all that far from Sherborne."

"When does all this happen," asked Jim. "Soon?"

"Yes, quite soon: the afternoon and evening of June 24th, in fact, which is a Saturday, three weeks on from now."

"Oh, that's good!"

"So you definitely want to come? I can't remember off-hand what the train fare you'd have to pay would be—though I think it might be something in the order of two pounds return—but all those details are on a sheet of paper, together with the times and other arrangements. I haven't got one with me now, but I could let you have one tomorrow, and I could tell the Secretary tomorrow to reserve you a seat on the train."

"Yes, please do, Susan. I'd love to come."

"Fine, then you shall come with us. You can have Saturday afternoon and Sunday off work that weekend, Jim, of course." Jim normally did a full day's work on each of those days, and had a day off on Tuesdays.

"Oh, thank you very much, Susan."

"Look here, Jim, I must go at once," said Susan. "I've already stayed with you longer than I meant to, and they'll be beginning to wonder in the drawing-room where I've got to."

"Good-bye, Susan, and thank you again for asking me to come on this outing."

"Good-bye for now, Jim. I'll see you tomorrow evening to let you have a type-written sheet on the mystery walking tour." She got up quickly from her seat, smiling, and planted a kiss on Jim's cheek, to his great delight. He had also risen from his chair at the same moment. But Susan was gone from the room almost in a flash, giving him a cheery wave of her hand as she went through the door.

As she walked quickly away down the corridor Susan was mentally chastising herself for her momentary lapse into inadvisable behaviour by kissing Jim. She knew that it had been ages since the last occasion on which this had happened; in fact, she remembered that this last occasion had been on Jim's nineteenth birthday in July of the preceding year, when she had given him the camera. That was a risky thing to have done too, she said to herself now. I must have known that he would use it to photograph <u>me</u>—and thereby encourage his infatuation with me! She knew that it had not been due simply to chance that during the eleven or so months since that last birthday no opportunities had arisen in which she might have kissed him, or he might have kissed her. It had been her deliberate policy, not quite to avoid meeting Jim Sandy altogether when that was not strictly necessary, but to keep the relationship with him at a rather distant level. At first she had been surprised to find how hard it was for her to hold herself aloof from Jim in this way: indeed it had been very upsetting for her, whenever she had thought about it, to know that she was deliberately denying Jim many opportunities to be in her presence. But she had been very determined for her husband John's sake, and for the love that was between them, that she would succeed in turning off the intimacy that she thought had developed too far in her friendship with Jim. In this matter she had received very little direct, verbal encouragement from John. He was indeed the very best and kindest of husbands, and had never shown any signs of jealousy even when, during the early days of Jim Sandy's appointment to the Castle staff, he must have known, Susan thought, that her relationship with Jim had gone well beyond what could reasonably be described as being "just good friends." So Susan had thought that she owed it to John to see that Jim could not become too familiar with her; and now, even as she left his room, the thought came to her that she had slipped up badly by giving him a quick kiss on a sudden and most unexpected impulse.

Oh, what nonsense! she said to herself as she came to the stairs and began to descend to the ground floor. That kiss was absolutely nothing. Just a little sign to show him that we're still friends. He couldn't possibly get really excited over a trivial little thing like that! But in her heart she was not at all sure about this; and on top of this doubt was the feeling that she was also being unwise in inviting Jim to join in the mystery walking and camping trip. Oh yes, she said to herself, but there'll be lots of other people walking with us, and anyway John's coming too. It'll be quite all right as far as <u>that</u> goes. Anyway, he'll enjoy it, so why shouldn't he come? And with that thought Susan tried to make herself feel that the matter was settled. Jim <u>would</u> come with her and John on the trip. And I'm really looking forward to that day, she said to herself, as she walked down the passage which lead in the direction of the kitchen.

When Jim went into the Tower Library the next morning to start work on the inventory job he was quite expecting that he would have met the ghost of Beryl Buxton before the morning's work in there was over. He was feeling very cheerful, however, thinking of the walking and camping expedition to come, and the thought that he might see a ghost did not at first make him feel at all nervous. But Jim had no encounters with ghosts that day. Indeed, the only unusual thing which happened while he was in the library was that he presently chanced to find a beautiful blue gemstone.

It was very quiet in the library. That morning both the Earl and the Countess were away from home: Lord Dalmane had gone up to London on the early morning train, and Susan had gone shopping in Sherborne immediately after her breakfast. The two maids who came in to clean the Castle were not working that day, and Samantha was busy in and around the kitchen, and had no cause to go anywhere near the front of the Castle, and so, when Jim walked into the library, he soon realised that he was working in a temporarily deserted part of the Castle: the Padgates were staying, but they too were out, having gone out for an after-breakfast walk. Jim very soon found that the library that morning was an almost frighteningly silent place. Outside it was a perfect June day, warm and sunny, as Jim could see for himself by looking through the large, lead-lined window (which he could not open); but the closed window shut out very effectively the songs of the birds and the other outdoor sounds. There was not a sound in the library which he did not make himself. The effect on him of the absolute quietness was decidedly upsetting and, remembering the unlikely tale of the American tourist—it had seemed improbable enough while that man had been telling it—Jim kept on feeling that the ghost of Beryl Buxton had appeared, or was about to appear, behind him; and several times he turned round sharply, expecting to see a shadowy figure; but none appeared.

After about an hour and a half of steady work listing the books of the library by authors and titles the job in that room was nearly done, and Jim sat down at the desk by the window to complete his cataloguing. On the top of the desk there were only a few objects: an electric reading lamp, a wooden letter rack, a silver ink-holder and pen tray, and a silver box. These and a few other items were to be added to Jim's inventory. He noted the lion hallmark on each of the silver items, denoting sterling silver, and then opened the lid of the box. This box was like a biggish snuff-box, and was of solid silver, and stood on four silver legs; and the lid when opened revealed a smaller box inside it. Jim, beginning to be interested in what he was doing, took out a little blue jewel-box, opened it, and gasped audibly in surprise. "Heavens, it's the Great Beryl!" he murmured aloud, seeing a big, sky-blue gemstone sparkling on its little white cushion in the box. He immediately picked up the stone and looked at it carefully. It was square-cut and translucent and, when Jim put it on the open palm of his left hand and held it up to the light—strong sunlight was streaming into the room through the window behind him—many fascinating inner lights of the stone were revealed. It's very beautiful, he thought, but of course it <u>can't</u> be the Great Beryl: that stone was supposed to have vanished without trace, presumed stolen by Beryl Buxton. What then was the stone in his hand? A replica of the Great Beryl? A paste stone made of blue glass? Jim looked at it wonderingly for some time while many questions passed through his mind.

When he left the room, the library inventory completed, Jim was carrying the blue gemstone in its jewel-box in a pocket of his jacket. He went straight to his bedroom, looked again at the stone, and then put it away in a drawer. He meant to show it to Susan at the earliest opportunity, in case it was, against all probability, the genuine Great Beryl; but, in fact, he did not even tell her about it until some months later.

CHAPTER FIVE

The special train pulled away from the platforms of Walton-on-Thames station, heading in the direction of London, having set down a party of about twenty-five walkers. It was the fourth stop which the two-carriage diesel railcar had made to set down passengers. The little train had been chartered from British Railways by the North Dorset Ramblers Society, of which Lord Dalmane was the President, and the organisers of the outing had divided up the passengers, many of whom were not members of the Society, into groups of about twenty-five people each; the event had been widely publicised, and was open to anybody willing to pay the fares. At Walton and at the three previous stops, which were also in Surrey commuter country, one of these groups of walkers had been detailed to leave the train. The plan was that these four groups of people would spend a pleasant evening walking, from their respective stations of disembarkation, and would all meet again later on at an agreed meeting point (Effingham Junction station) to return, changing at Surbiton, on the last service train of the day to Dorset. Only the final group of twenty passengers still aboard the special train were going camping. They knew that they would get out of the train at the last stop and walk with their leader, the Secretary of the Society, to the place where the tents had been pitched on the previous evening by a small group of organisers. These passengers had still not been told where they were to get off the train, or how far away, or in what direction their camping place lay.

Susan and Jim Sandy were sitting side by side in the special train. Lord Dalmane was not, after all, with the party. A message from London had come for him on the previous evening. He had arrived home for the weekend, only to find that he was urgently summoned to return to London on the very next morning (Saturday) for important Government business. He had been requested by his boss, the Foreign Secretary, to join him, the Prime Minister, and other Cabinet Ministers for a working lunch at Chequers, and for urgent discussions on the current crisis involving the super-powers. Lord Dalmane had been surprised that he, only a Junior Minister as he was, had been summoned to be present at these talks, but he knew that the request amounted to an order to head straight back to London on the early morning train. He had done this, cursing his bad luck that the P.M. had seen fit to ask him to come to Chequers for the Crisis talks: his plans for the weekend were now ruined. He had been very much looking forward to the train trip on the Special, the walking, and the camping with Susan; but, of course, he had to obey orders, which meant that there was no way out for him: he could not go on the excursion. Probably he would be away from home for the whole weekend.

"Well, Jim," said Susan, "wherever can they mean <u>us</u> to get out, I wonder? If we're not told to get out soon we'll be in London—in the outskirts at least! We practically are already. They can't mean us to go walking through the jolly scenery of Surbiton or Wimbledon, or to camp somewhere in suburbia!"

"I'm sure they can't," said Jim. "Do you know what the next station is, Sue?"

"No," said Susan, "I don't know about these suburban stations. The ordinary trains up to Waterloo from Dorset don't stop at them, but there must be lots more stations before Waterloo anyway. We can't be going <u>there</u>."

"To transfer to one of the other London termini, you mean?"

"No," said Susan, "we can't possibly be going on to Kent, or Essex, or Hertfordshire, or somewhere else. That wouldn't leave any time for walking. Our station <u>must</u> be one of these suburban Surrey stations."

"Yes, I suppose it must be."

The Secretary of the Ramblers Club, Captain Clark, who was going to head the last party of walkers to the camping site, came through the gangway from the rear carriage. They saw that he had an announcement to make. "Can I have your attention, please, ladies and gentlemen," he began, and went on to say that in a few minutes they would reach Esher Station, which was were they were to leave the train and start their walk. He reminded people that there was a walk of about twelve miles before them, over easy country.

"H'm, twelve miles," said Susan thoughtfully. "It does sound an awful long way to walk, now that I hear him say it."

"Well, they must reckon that we can walk it before night time," said Jim.

"I suppose so, but it's a quarter past seven now. There can't be any too much time."

"I say," said Jim, changing the subject. "Look at that! It must be going to rain!"

"My word, yes, it does look like it," agreed Susan. "Yes, it's beginning to rain now; there are a few drops on the windows."

They looked anxiously through the train windows at a threatening mass of dark cloud all over the sky ahead of them. The day had been fairly pleasant for a June day, although the weather was a little unsettled. It had been mainly sunny, but rather cloudy at times, and in the morning there had been a shower before they had left Rhodes Castle. However, Jim and Susan could see that it looked very much as if something more than a mere shower was about to pour down.

"The forecast did say that there could be thunderstorms in the South-East this evening," said Susan. "I heard that at five to one on the wireless."

"Gosh, it looks as if we're going straight into one!" said Jim.

"Bother it! It's raining properly now, and I'm sure we can't really afford to waste time sheltering from the rain."

"But I think we'll have to." Jim noticed that Susan seemed to be a good deal more bothered than he was about how the time was going to work out for their walk.

About a minute later they saw that they were passing Sandown Park Race Course, which lies beside the railway line at Esher. People were getting up and gathering their baggage together, ready to get out. A few moments more, and the train was slowing down. Jim and Susan had their knapsacks on their backs, and were standing up with the rest of the passengers. "Phew, look at that!" murmured Jim. The sky had grown even darker, and now there came a bright thread of lightning. Then, as the train pulled into Esher Station, there was a loud roll of thunder, and the rain suddenly poured down really heavily.

When the train stopped the passengers made a general run for the waiting-room, as the platform was not sheltered by an awning. The small room, almost empty half a minute before, became suddenly crowded with walkers. "That's right, Lady Dalmane, come and join the merry throng!" called Captain Clark, the Secretary. "It's a bit wet while this shower's on, so we'd better all wait a few minutes before setting off."

"A <u>bit</u> wet?" said Susan in surprise. "Good heavens, I call this more than just a shower! But don't you think, Captain Clark, that we might not have enough time to walk to the place where our tents are if we have to waste much time sheltering here?"

"Don't you worry about that, Lady Dalmane," said Captain Clark. "I'm sure we'll have plenty of time for the walk without having to be hurried so long as the rain eases off soon—"(he looked at his watch)—"say, within the next quarter of an hour, or so; and it looks to me as if it will."

"Does it?" said Susan doubtfully, looking through the window at the wet platforms and at the rain which was still pouring down. She knew Captain Clark fairly well, and knew that he was always inclined to take an optimistic attitude to any problems. He was a captain in the Royal Navy, and based at Portsmouth, where he spent most of his time, although his family lived at Sherborne, which meant that they were virtually near neighbours of the Dalmanes. He was by no means bald, but at only forty-two years old his whitish hair was becoming rather thin on the top of his head; and he was a very big man, but his temperament inclined him to light-heartedness, at least when he was off duty. Susan had earlier in the afternoon been talking to him in the train when she had explained to him how it had happened that her husband, John, the President of the Society, had had to be left behind, to his considerable regret.

"Now, let's have a look at my map, Jim," said Susan a little later, "now that we know where we're to start walking from." Captain Clark had moved on to talk to someone else.

"But how did you know which map to bring?" asked Jim in surprise, as he saw Susan bring out of her knapsack a map of Surrey. "You didn't know we were coming here, did you?"

"I didn't know we were coming to Esher, but I knew that it was likely to be somewhere in Surrey. I bullied Captain Clark into at least telling me that much when I was talking to him a few days ago, and I said that I wanted to know which map of my own to bring—I have a few sheets of parts of the South of England—at least, they're mostly John's maps. Look, here's Esher Station." She put a finger on the map at the right place.

"Let's see . . . yes, that's interesting," said Jim. "I suppose we'll walk somewhere more or less south, to head away from London, rather than towards it—when the rain stops. It's getting less now."

"Yes, it's getting brighter, and I think it <u>is</u> easing off."

"What did you bring the map for, Sue?" asked Jim. "We shan't really need a map, will we, with Captain Clark to lead us? I suppose it is more fun, though, to have our own map."

Susan looked suddenly serious. "It wasn't that," she said, "it was just so that we wouldn't be altogether lost if we should somehow happen to get separated from the leaders—although I really can't see how that might happen, but it's as well to be prepared . . . and anyway, I don't know the country around here very well in spite of having lived in London for a few years before moving down to Dorset; but it was mostly the other side of London where I knew the country, Middlesex and Hertfordshire particularly."

"Around Knebworth, for instance?"

"That's right: you were with us that night I brought you to Great Aunt Alice's house at Knebworth."

"The rain's stopping," said Jim.

Captain Clark and the other leaders of the expedition were having a last hurried look at their large-scale map of the country around Leatherhead and Dorking in preparation for setting off. The rain had almost stopped, and the sun was coming out again. It was nearly half past seven; they had not been quite ten minutes in the station waiting-room. There had been no more thunder after that one rumble at the onset of the rain. Captain Clark lead the party out of the station and off by a road which ran southwards to join the main Portsmouth Road.

Now that they were really setting off on their long evening hike through the Surrey countryside, Jim Sandy had a great feeling of good adventure ahead and high spirits; and he felt energetic enough (he thought) to walk twenty miles, if necessary. He had felt that a weekend of good adventure lay ahead when they had left Rhodes Castle some hours earlier to go by car to Sherborne Station for their special train, and this feeling had certainly been heightened by the very welcome discovery that Lord Dalmane had not been able to come. As they were only two from Rhodes Castle, instead of the originally planned three, Jim had reckoned that it would be not only natural for him to sit beside Susan in the train, but very much the right thing to do under the circumstances. Susan Dalmane obviously needed a man to be her companion on the outing, and since her husband could not be the companion, it was clear to Jim that this role was meant to fall to him. They had not talked a great deal to each other during the hours sitting in the train, but each had felt quite at ease in the other's company. Now Jim reckoned that he would really enjoy himself on the long walk at Susan's side, chatting pleasantly with her as they went. He was struck by the unexpected brightness as full sunshine re-appeared, shining dazzlingly off the wet road. The last drops of rain stopped falling.

After a few minutes of walking the party arrived at the main A3 trunk road, which they had to cross. Captain Clark had planned the route carefully with the result that they did not have to walk along this noisy, busy road at all, but only to cross it. He lead the way along a minor road which turned off to the south across Littleworth Common.

"It's very pleasant here," remarked Jim.

"Yes," said Susan, "and it looks to me as if it should keep fine now for the rest of the evening, with a bit of luck. And I suppose we didn't have to waste very much time after all in that station waiting-room. But there's a long way ahead of us . . ."

"Well, I don't see that that matters much. I think this is great fun; and, what's more, I think it's going to turn out a nice, sunny evening now that the shower's over."

Susan looked up at the sky. There were still big clouds up there, but there were now large breaks of blue sky, especially towards the north-west, where there was clear, full sunshine. "The wind's gone down too," said Susan (there had been a fresh breeze with the recent heavy shower). "Yes, I think you're right, Jim: it should stay sunny now."

"There are houses ahead of us," said Jim. "I thought at first that we were really out in the country. But I suppose this is Esher?" He waved a hand in the direction of an estate of modern houses on the further side of the Common, a little way ahead of them.

"It may well be that, Jim," said Susan. "But I don't know for certain where it is, and I can't very well be stopping now to get my map out. But if this is Esher it must be getting on for a mile away from its railway station."

In another minute their road had taken them into the built-up area of new suburban houses. It might have seemed a disappointment to see street lights, pavements, and houses again after the walk across the common, where there were none of these things, but Jim was in such a jolly mood that this did not affect him in the least. The party of walkers was tramping along the road at a good pace, passing some splendidly kept gardens of the houses in that newer dormitory region of Esher. At this early stage in the hike the walkers had not spread out very much, but already Susan and Jim were trailing behind most of the others towards the rear of the line. Jim Sandy, of course, cared about nothing but to keep pace with Susan, and was prepared to walk as fast or as slow as necessary in order to remain beside her. For her part, Susan was beginning to relax and enjoy the walk as she gradually forgot her nagging worries about the time and the long distance still to be walked. She was walking no less observantly than Jim, looking at the neat, little gardens as she passed each one, and particularly admiring the many shrubs and small trees, several of them flowering, which hung over the pavement from so many of the gardens. Jim also noticed them with pleasure; he was no gardener, but he had learned a few things in the course of his job at Rhodes Castle. It also pleased him to notice that there seemed to be hardly anyone about, barring the walkers.

"What lovely things people grow in their gardens around here!" exclaimed Susan involuntarily; the sight of a well-kept garden always pleased her.

"There are lots of rowans: they seem to be very popular in suburbia," she continued, talking aloud to herself. "And cherries, of course—it's a pity the cherry blossom is over—and the rhododendrons are more or less finished, but look at those azaleas in that garden: they're rather fine!—and there's a fig tree in the next garden." Susan's botanical instincts had been thoroughly woken up by the sight of many fine, oranamental garden trees, and she did not notice that they were now at the end of the column of walkers, and gradually getting left a little further behind. Jim noticed it, but was careful to say nothing about it.

About half a minute later Susan saw something which interesed her so much that she stopped for a moment. "Why, look at that, Jim!" she said. "I believe that's a tulip-tree flowering there: that one with big greeny-yellow flowers on it. They're a North American tree, you know, and you don't often see one of them over here in England; but I wouldn't mind taking a cutting from it to try growing one at home. Rhodes Castle has many unusual trees, as you know, out as far as I know, we haven't got a tulip-tree." She looked carefully around for a moment, and then added: "There's no one about: no one—except you—would notice if I broke off a little branch from it for a cutting." This remark reminded Jim how often in his work he had stopped someone from doing what Susan now proposed to do.

"I shouldn't do it, if I were you," he said quietly. "You wouldn't be able to put it in water, you know, until we get home tomorrow."

"And it would be dead by then," said Susan, smiling at him. "Yes, that's a tactful way of telling me not to steal it. But look, Jim, we'd better get a move on! Those people are beckoning to us—we're rather left behind!"

About two hundred yards ahead Jim saw a couple at the rear of the party of walkers turn round and beckon to them. Bother! he said to himself. Just when we were getting nicely left behind on our own!

"We'd better run for a bit to catch up," said Susan.

They jogged along the pavement until they had more or less caught up with the rest of the party. Soon they came to a cross-roads where a sign indicated a road to Esher to the right and a road to Claygate Station to their left, but their road ahead was unmarked. About half a minute later they saw that the road was coming to an end. The proper, metalled surface ended, and they were walking along a rough, muddy track, the big hollows in it still full of water after the recent heavy rain. In places they had to skirt around deep-looking puddles of rainwater. It was noticeable that the houses along this stretch of road were very much more recent than the other ones: most, indeed, were so new that they were not yet completely built. Blackbirds were singing in the new gardens; and overhead the sky was now mostly clear of cloud. The low evening sun cast long shadows of poplars and other trees across the rough road from right to left (for their direction was always roughly south).

"I wonder where this road leads to," said Susan. "Presumably it goes beyond these new houses."

"It doesn't really look like a road to anywhere," said Jim.

"Just so: it looks like it turns into a country lane. See, that's the last of these new houses, Jim."

"Oh good, we're out into the country at last! I say, it's all the more fun not knowing where this track leads to—but perhaps it just fizzles out and doesn't lead anywhere."

"It may do that. But it doesn't look to me as if it would go right on for miles until it would reach another town."

"What town do you think that would be, Sue?"

"Oh, I don't know: Leatherhead, perhaps, or Guildford . . . I can't remember just what the map looks like. But there's the sun away over to our right, so we must be heading roughly south. I suppose we'd reach the North Downs if we went far enough . . . but that might be an awfully long way."

They walked on in silence for a while, looking appreciatively at the country. Later, when Susan had an opportunity to look at the map, she saw that thereabouts it was called Arbrook Common, and a little further on, Esher Common. The rough, unsurfaced road they were following was little more than a country lane, and now that they had left the last of the new houses behind them, they met no traffic on it and few other pedestrians. The lane had high hawthorn hedges, interspersed with many wild roses, all in full bloom, and many flowering blackberries, and, here and there, a young ash or sycamore growing as part of the hedge. There were taller trees also, mostly oaks and ashes, meeting overhead in places, and some tall Lombardy poplars.

"Hello, some of our walkers have stopped," said Jim presently, seeing a group of people waiting a little way ahead.

"A main road must cross here," said Susan. "Did you see a car flash past just then?" Another car went past across the line of their sight, where the others were waiting to ensure that the stragglers went the right way.

"Good work, Lady Dalmane," said Captain Clark as they came near the leaders. "Not tired yet, I hope?"

"No, I'm not tired yet," said Susan.

"Then we'd better press on, and stop for a proper rest and refreshments when we've covered another three or four miles." The leaders of the expedition were already walking on.

"You're not tired, I suppose?" said Susan to Jim.

"Not a bit," said Jim. "I'm <u>really</u> enjoying this!"

They came to the main road, which crossed their lane from left to right (but not quite at right angles), and saw that the others were already walking along a smaller and narrower country lane exactly opposite to the one from which they had just come out. Jim and Susan were still walking at the rear of the line. Susan, although she was not yet really tired or footsore, felt little energy or inclination to try to walk any faster, and as they were not getting seriously left behind, she felt that to walk at her own pace was quite adequate. Besides this, she thought that the country was far too beautiful on such a glorious summer evening as it now was to allow its beauty to be wasted on her by hurrying. As for Jim Sandy, he felt that he could, if necessary, have walked at twice Susan's speed; but he only wanted to remain beside her.

They had walked for barely five minutes down this lane from the place where the main road crossed, when they saw in front of them a fence across it and a stile in the fence.

"Is this the end of the lane?" asked Jim.

"Looks like it," said Susan.

"There's a sign beside that stile," said Jim.

When they came near enough to read it, they saw that the sign had "Public Footpath to Fairmile" printed on it; but this did not help them to know where they were as Susan had no more idea than Jim had of where Fairmile might be. They crossed the stile and saw that indeed the lane ended there. Ahead of them stretched a field of ripening wheat, but they could see that their foot-path was a well-worn track skirting the edge of the field. The walkers were well spread out in ones, twos, and small clusters ahead of Jim and Susan along the path. The field was long and narrow in shape; only a short way off to their right were trees, almost a small wood, but the trees were not really thick enough on the ground to make a wood: what they saw was more like wooded parkland. The narrow field looked as if it widened towards its further end, where there was more wooded country to the left. Susan noticed that the woodland was mixed, mostly deciduous; but, rather surprisingly, there were some Scots pine trees amongst the other trees.

Jim and Susan marched happily along the narrow path between the handsome heads of wheat and a wire fence on the left dividing off the wooded country.

"Beautiful, isn't it, to be able to walk through a cornfield on such a lovely evening?" said Susan.

"It certainly is," agreed Jim.

"What could be a nicer way to spend a mid-summer evening?" said Susan dreamily, not as if she expected an answer. Jim did not answer aloud, but the thought in his mind was: Only one thing could be nicer: for me this would be perfect if we were walking here alone! But there was as yet no sinister design in his mind in his desire to be alone with Susan, no thought of trying to seduce her: he simply thought that their mutual company would have been that much more enjoyable had they been doing that hike on their own.

The field was a very long one, but at the further end of it their path crossed a fence by another stile (again with an arrow in their direction marked "Public Footpath to Fairmile"). Then they found that the footpath, having joined a cart-track which came in at the fence, ran straight on across open, wooded country. As before, it was park-like country with trees spaced randomly; and there were patches of coppice with dense undergrowth of foxgloves, brambles, and other colourful weeds. Again there were pine trees in these thickets, and when they passed them, Susan and Jim noticed a delightful smell of pine resin in the still, warm air. They walked past a pond which lay just to the right of their track and was partly covered in the large leaves and yellow flowers of waterlillies.

"I suppose they call this place a common or a heath," said Jim presently.

"Probably they do," said Susan, "but we'd better not stop to look at my map now. Gosh, there's a gorgeous fragrance of pine resin when we pass near these pine trees! My word, John would have enjoyed walking here with us."

"Yes," said Jim, "it's a pity he couldn't come."

Susan turned her head sharply and for a moment looked straight at Jim. He had said: "It's a pity he couldn't come," so coolly that it almost sounded as if he meant what he had said, but Susan saw in his face that this was mere polite bluff. Really he was extremely happy because her husband was not with them; Susan knew this, but she wisely decided not to pursue the subject further, and to allow herself to forget that she had mentioned John's name aloud. Jim for a moment felt annoyed that Susan had spoken to him about her conveniently left-behind husband, but this, in fact, affected him very little, and he soon forgot about it. Bother Lord Dalmane! he said to himself. It wouldn't be anything like so much fun if he were here! Thank goodness he had to go up to London for the weekend.

About half a mile on after passing the pond they reached a crossroads. They noted from the signpost that Fairmile was a village a little way off by the road to the right, that the road to the left lead to Oxshott and Fairmile Station, and that their road straight on was signed to Church Cobham and Stoke d' Abernon.

After passing the crossroads on the Common the route they were following again became a properly surfaced road, although a very small one. Susan noticed that the next pair of walkers in front of them were a long way ahead, and made the effort to walk slightly faster; and after that she and Jim lost no more ground for a while. She also noticed at about that stage in the walk how low in the sky the sun now was: it was, indeed, almost down to the northwestern horizon. Heavens! she thought, the sun's nearly setting. She looked at her watch and saw that it was five minutes to nine. Oh well, there can't be all that much further to walk, she thought. She was beginning to feel a little tired as she trudged along the small country road with Jim Sandy at her side, passing now through fields, and here and there seeing houses by the roadside. It was very quiet walking along that minor road. They had met hardly any traffic on it when it suddenly came out onto a main road. Here they found that they had to turn left and walk along the main road. Presently they passed a milestone at the edge of the road with "Leatherhead 3 Miles" written on it.

"We're coming to a place," said Jim: "a village called Stoke d' Abernon. What an odd name!" He read the name off a sign about a hundred yards ahead.

"It looks a rather pretty village," said Susan. "Ouch, my feet are beginning to feel pretty sore, Jim, with all this walking! We <u>must</u> have come about ten miles by now. How about you, Jim? How do you feel?"

"Well, I feel a <u>little</u> footsore, but nothing too bad, and I'm not tired yet." Susan did feel tired by that time, but she did not say so. "We must be nearly there by now, I should think," continued Jim. "Look, Sue, the sun's gone down."

"So it has; at least I don't believe it's really set, but it's below our horizon now," said Susan. "That means it will only be light enough for walking for about another hour, and it's a quarter past nine now."

At the end of the village, which straggled along the main road for a fair distance, Captain Clark lead his party of walkers by a smaller road which branched off to the right where the main road to Leatherhead bent round to the left. Susan looked back over her shoulder a few times to see the sunset colours in the north-western sky. She could not be sure whether or not the sun really had set, although it had certainly disappeared from their sight. There were no clouds in the sky now except for a few small ones over towards the sunset: puffy white clouds, and some long, streaky clouds, all tinged with a fiery red glow from the sinking sun, but the sky around them was pale and greenish. It's very beautiful, she thought, but I hope we don't have to go much further! Then, looking away ahead of the walking party into the southeast, she caught a glimpse of part of a distant town, where there were already lights showing against the dark background of hills behind it. The sky over there was already beginning to darken; looking carefully Susan noticed that a single point of white light, a bright star or a planet, had appeared in the deep blue sky; but there was the moon also, well up in the sky, and not far off the full. It won't be a dark night anyway, if we have to go on walking: that's one consolation, she said to herself.

About ten minutes later, Jim and Susan rounded a bend of the road and saw that the whole party had come to a halt. All eighteen of the other walkers were sitting down on the low stone parapets of an old bridge over a river, and they soon saw that Captain Clark had called a major resting halt for refreshments; knapsacks were being opened to bring out flasks and sandwiches.

"Hurrah!" shouted Jim. "They've all stopped for a rest. Come on, Sue, let's hurry on and sit down with them."

"Certainly!" said Susan thankfully. "I could do with a good rest, and we've still got some tea left in our flask, and there are some biscuits."

"Good," said Jim.

A minute later they too had sat down on the wide stone parapet on the western side of the bridge over the slow-flowing River Mole. Susan took off her knapsack, opened it, and brought out a flask containing tea and two plastic cups.

"Are we nearly at our camping place?" enquired Jim.

"Well, no, not exactly," said Captain Clark. "But we're about half-way now to it." Susan put the flask down on the wall.

"<u>What</u>!" she exclaimed in horror. "Do you mean to tell me, Captain Clark, that we've still got many miles to walk?"

"Oh no, Lady Dalmane," said Captain Clark, smiling at her affably. "I wouldn't put it exactly like that. You're not tired yet, are you?"

"I am rather, if you must know. How many more miles are there to walk?"

"About another six miles, Lady Dalmane. I hope you're going to be able to make it, or you won't be able to lie down at the end to rest in a tent."

"<u>Six</u> more miles!" said Susan wearily. "Oh dear! . . . but I daresay I could plod along again after a rest." Even Jim Sandy at her side, she noticed, was looking somewhat dismayed at the prospect of another six miles to cover. "We'll have our tea anyway, Jim," she said. She poured out two cups, and handed him one.

"Thank you, Susan," said Jim. "How long are you going to allow us to rest here for, Captain Clark?"

"About another ten minutes from now will have to do; then we shall have to be on the move again—at about twenty to ten."

"But it's going to be dark long before we reach the camp!"

"I shouldn't worry about that, Mr. Sandy. There'll be plenty of moonlight, and I think you'll find it a grand night for walking: and we should all be there by—"(he broke off, looked at his watch, and considered a moment)—"between eleven thirty and midnight. Lady Dalmane, I am very sorry if you think it's too far for you, but there's nothing I can do about it now."

"Oh, it's all right," said Susan. "It <u>will</u> be a beautiful night to be walking in the country, but I'd like to be allowed to look at your map before we start again, Captain Clark. Perhaps by now you could reveal the whereabouts on it of our secret destination?"

"Certainly, my Lady; I'll show it to you."

For several minutes Jim and Susan, and most of the others, sat on the bridge refreshing and resting themselves; luckily no motor traffic came past to disturb their peace. The sun had by now definitely set, and the twilight was growing very slowly darker, although when they set off again at the end of ten minutes rest, there seemed to be hardly less light in the sky than there had been when they had first sat down. It was a warm evening, and although sitting down on the bridge parapet did not feel as warm as walking no one felt cold. Jim Sandy was amusing himself as he drank his tea by looking down over the bridge at the dark water of the river, trying to see fish in it. The water looked deep and flowed slowly away from the arch without the slightest sound; rings of ripples kept appearing on its smooth surface, but for some time Jim failed to definitely identify any fish. Then, catching a sudden silvery gleam from a slowly moving shape down there: "There's a fish! It's a trout, I think," he cried. Susan looked quickly round and managed to see a fish which might have been a trout where Jim was pointing, but in another second it had gone.

Before they started off again, while Captain Clark had his map spread out, Susan and Jim and some of the others took a good look at it. "That's where we're aiming for: Ranmore Common up on the North Downs above Dorking; it's not really all that far from here," said Captain Clark. "Our tents are pitched on the Common fairly close beside that road, just a few hundred yards beyond where that church is marked on the map—close to where those two roads divide. See it everybody?" Then he outlined briefly the route they had followed so far from Esher Station, and ran his finger along the route they were about to follow to Ranmore Common. Susan attended carefully as he explained the route. "And as most of us are getting rather tired," added Captain Clark, "we'll start by taking a short cut. If we walk through the grounds of the big house, Bookham Lodge, which is just along the road here, we could save about a quarter of a mile. Look: we could walk straight through there—and cut off that loop of the road. Of course it will be trespassing, taking a short cut through that garden, but well worth it; we'll only need to go quietly and keep to the bushes, and the people who live there won't see us. Well, Lady Dalmane?"

"I don't like it," objected Susan. "If the people here haven't given us permission to walk across part of their garden, I think we're taking an awful risk by doing it; and I don't think that we need to anyway, as it doesn't look to me as if we'd be saving enough distance to make the short cut worth taking."

"Lady Dalmane, I don't think you quite understand the risk," said Captain Clark. "I have been past this garden in broad daylight more than once, and so I've seen what it's really like. I'm not proposing, of course, that we do anything as stupid as to walk across the lawn in full view of the house. But at the other end of the garden is a big area of very dense undergrowth with lots of bushes and little trees crowded together, and it comes right up to the edge of this road—you'll see it in a moment. Anyone could slip into that sort of jungle and be completely hidden from the rest of the garden. And so the risk of being caught in there would, I think, be very slight. But what do other people think? Perhaps, after all, we'd better go the long way round, keeping to the road?"

"No, no! The short cut!" said several voices.

"Oh well," said Susan, "if most people are willing to risk taking this short cut then I'll say Yes to it as well. But I don't like it."

"I think it'll be all right," said Jim, "if Captain Clark thinks so." It was finally agreed that they would walk via the short cut through the thicket in the grounds of Bookham Lodge.

The walkers gathered up their baggage and were on the march along the road again. About two minutes later Susan, having looked up and down the road and carefully all around her, found herself furtively climbing over a wire fence on the right-hand side of the road to get into the thicket of bushes, small trees and undergrowth which there lined the road. People climbed over the fence in different places up and down that stretch of the road to lessen the risk of being seen breaking into the private property. Jim Sandy had just climbed over the fence a few yards further back. There had still been plenty of dusky daylight on the road, but Jim and Susan found that, as they had expected, it was much darker in amongst the dense leaves and branches of the thicket. Jim was being careful to keep as close as possible to Susan's side for fear of losing her in that tangled place where one could not see very far and had to move slowly and with care. They saw glimpses of a lawn and a large house beyond the lawn, but were trying to head away from there, in roughly the same direction as the road (but the road curved away to the east, and then back again: this was the curve the walkers were aiming to eliminate).

"My goodness," said Susan quietly to Jim, "we'd have done better not to have taken this short cut! It may take ages to get through here, and it's already hardly light enough to find the right way!"

"It is going to waste time," agreed Jim. "Still, we've only got to follow the others through here until we come out onto that bit of common marked on the map, but, you know, it <u>is</u> rather fun groping our way through here, trying not to be seen. They couldn't possibly see us from that house anyway."

"That's true," said Susan, "but it also makes it difficult for us to keep the others in sight."

As the walking party combed its way through the bushes and undergrowth its members were becoming considerably fragmented. Susan and Jim were trying to follow about fifty yards behind the pair of walkers in front of them, but they kept losing sight of them amongst the many tree trunks and branches. Then, as they came to a small clearing, they were startled when a biggish bird came gliding past only a few feet ahead of them on perfectly silent outstretched wings; they saw it land in an oak tree quite close to the place where they were standing.

"That's an owl," said Susan. This opinion was confirmed a moment later when the bird gave a long hooting call, answered straight away by another owl somewhere further away. "Well, night is drawing on, I suppose," she continued; "at least, it's dark enough in here, and dark enough for owls to be out hunting."

"Look, Sue, it's just there, quite close to us, sitting quietly in that oak tree," said Jim. "It can't have seen us." He and Susan were talking to each other very quietly, little above whispering in volume.

"Yes, I see it, sitting on that fork of the tree-trunk. I say, what a beauty he is! I haven't ever seen one at such close range before."

"I haven't either."

"Maybe we could get a little nearer to get a better view," said Susan. "So far we can't have made enough noise to disturb him. I think we could creep up very quietly to that tree, and maybe he wouldn't fly away. Shall we?"

"Oh yes!" said Jim eagerly. "Let's try it."

"Right, perhaps we'd better move one at a time. Shall I go first, and you follow when I wave my hand?"

"Okay, Sue."

It seemed to Jim that Susan must have forgotten for the moment about the other walkers as she set off, being as careful as she could in the dusky half-light, to tread silently through the long grass and the tangled weeds. For about half a minute Jim remained where he was, watching her. It had not escaped <u>his</u> mind that by stopping in this way to stalk an owl they had probably already been left well behind the rest of the expedition, but he did not think that mattered at all: they had their own map, and now Captain Clark had told them which way to walk. It would be much more fun to be left well behind the others to walk just with Susan! He noticed with admiration how skillfully she was managing to stalk that bird, being careful as she set each foot down not to tread on a stick that would snap loudly. But suddenly he heard her give a gasping cry of pain, and saw her fall to the ground. She did not get up straight away, but remained lying where she had fallen as the seconds passed. Jim's heart missed a beat: what could have happened to her? He hardly noticed the owl flying away as he bounded forward to come to Susan's aid.

CHAPTER SIX

Susan was as surprised as Jim Sandy was when she suddenly felt an excruciating jab of pain through her left ankle, and at the same time found that it had twisted itself sideways as she fell down. By bad luck that foot, carefully set down onto what appeared to be solid ground, had met a hole completely covered over by the long grass. The ankle was badly sprained, but no more than sprained: it was not broken. Susan, however, could not at first imagine what had happened to her; she had seen no hole in the ground, but realising that she had somehow tripped over some irregularity of the ground, she thought: Oh heavens! Is it broken?

"Sue, what's happened? Are you all right?" asked Jim, at her side a moment later.

On the spur of the moment some thought prompted Susan at once to pretend that her injury was worse than she thought it was, although clearly it was bad enough in all truthfulness. In fact, she wanted to know what Jim would do with her if she were unable, or almost unable, to move any further. So for a few seconds she did not answer him at all, but lay where she had fallen, full length on the ground, her eyes tightly screwed shut; and her breath she let come in laboured gasps, as if she were in dire pain; although her pain was indeed real.

"Sue! What is it?" Jim, very alarmed, knelt down beside Susan and looked anxiously into her face.

"My ankle!—left one!" gasped Susan, opening her eyes.

"Oh Sue! You haven't broken it, have you?"

"Don't know."

"Can you move your foot at all? But perhaps you'd better not try."

"Yes, I'd better try it." Susan seemed to make a considerable effort to turn her left foot slightly from the ankle, closing her eyes again for a moment as a spasm of pain shot through the ankle. "Ouch! Yes, it does move; I don't think I can have broken any bones—just sprained it badly, I suppose."

"May I see it?"

"Just a moment, Jim; I'd better raise myself up a bit first."

"You'd better not try to stand up yet."

"No, I'll just sit up."

"I'll give you a hand."

Jim put his hands behind Susan's shoulders, and helped her to raise the upper part of her body carefully to a sitting position. As he touched her he felt a sharp thrill pass through him and became aware of a pressure on the front of his trousers, and knew that he had an erection. The thought entered his mind that here was the woman he loved totally at his mercy, sitting on the ground unable to escape from him: the circumstances were ideal to rape her. There's no one here to see us, the thought seemed to say to him, and in these bushes in this semi-darkness we couldn't really be seen anyway, so I could make love to her. But on the instant he rejected that thought angrily. What! he thought, I <u>never</u> would do such a thing—without her consent! I couldn't think of doing anything to hurt Sue—and especially not at a time like this when she's already injured and in pain.

"Oh!" said Susan suddenly, "my left arm's all bruised too from the elbow upwards where I fell on it."

"Oh, poor you!" said Jim kindly. "Do you know what you tripped over, Sue?"

"There's a wretched hole in the ground here, quite hidden under all this long grass and other stuff, and my foot must have just gone into it, and turned over on its side." She carefully pulled down her left sock as far as her shoe, revealing her injured ankle; she was wearing short socks. The ankle already showed signs of swelling and bruising. Jim very gently ran his fingers over the damaged area, ostensibly to check whether any bones were broken, although really he could not have determined that by touch and superficial inspection.

"Oh dear!" he said, "it looks like it must be beastly painful."

"It is!" said Susan.

There was a moment's pause. Jim looked into Susan's face, and she smiled back at him.

"But what are we going to do, Sue?" he asked. "Do you think you're going to be able to walk on it with care?"

Susan very slowly and carefully moved her left foot forwards and backwards from the ankle, notwithstanding some excruciating pain from the ankle.

"Yes," she said presently. "I daresay I shall be able to walk a little—with assistance from you, of course!—but only after I've given it a bit more rest."

"Then we'll have to try it; but if you find that you can't walk, after all, then I suppose I'd have to leave you here and try to bring help—fetch a doctor from somewhere. But we can't just go on sitting here!"

"You can't, you mean, Jim: I may have to, although I expect I could manage to hobble along somehow. You realise, of course, that by my foolishness in trying to stalk that owl, we've succeeded in getting ourselves left well and truly on our own! The other walkers are bound to be at least a mile ahead by now, and probably more. But you won't mind that, will you, Jim, you naughty boy? I expect this is just the sort of thing you were wanting to happen . . . isn't it?" They were sitting side by side on the ground now, which there was perfectly dry, as if there had been no rain at all that day. Susan's words made Jim feel uncomfortable for a little while: what she was saying showed clearly how much (he thought) she could read of his private fantasies, so that it was almost as if she were scolding him, only he knew that it was all said more or less in fun, with a smile on her face, and a hint of laughter in her voice. "Isn't this the sort of thing you'd hoped would happen?" asked Susan again a moment later when Jim had not answered her.

"Well—yes," he said doubtfully.

"What!" said Susan. "So this <u>is</u> just the sort of thing you'd wished for: me in dreadful pain with an ankle badly sprained! You're glad I've injured myself with only yourself at hand to help!"

"Oh no, Sue, of course I'm not pleased at all that you've hurt yourself and that you're in great pain. But what I meant when I said "Yes" was . . . yes, I am absolutely thrilled that I—that you—" He hesitated, and then was silent a moment, uncertain of Susan's real mood at that strange time.

"That I am <u>what</u>?" asked Susan, after waiting a moment for Jim to continue. She put a hand on his shoulder and drew his face closer to her's. "Say it, Jim: go on, say what's really on your mind."

"That you're with me, and that we're absolutely on our own!" said Jim in a sudden rush, finding that Susan had given him the courage and prompting necessary to say this.

"So?" whispered Susan. Their faces were almost touching now. Jim suddenly felt bold, his passion for this beautiful woman being considerably inflamed by her nearness to him. Instead of answering her with words he clasped her firmly to himself and planted a luscious kiss on her lips. Immediately it was as if a dormant passion was awakened in Susan. The pain in her ankle and the pain in her bruised forearm (neither of which places really hurt her very much) were more or less forgotten together with the walk and the fact that they were left well behind as for about a minute they embraced each other tightly and kissed urgently. Susan writhed about in a sudden flood of uncontrolled excitement as she kissed Jim, until a sickening jab of pain reminded her of her sprained ankle, and made her break away from their mutual embrace with a jerk. During that embrace some emotional barrier within her thoughts had been flung down, and she had felt a heady infatuation for the handsome, fair-haired youth, much as he had felt for her.

About ten minutes later they managed to find a small gate leading out of the thicket of bushes onto Great Bookham Common immediately beyond it. They were making very slow progress, Susan managing to limp along using a large stick held in her left hand to take some weight off her sprained ankle. In spite of the gathering darkness, before they had gone more than a few yards, Jim had managed to find under the trees a piece of broken-off branch of a size suitable for use as a walking-stick, but it was an unwieldy staff, rather too large for comfortable use; and they had not bothered to break off all the little twigs and leaves which were still growing out of it. Altogether it was not, perhaps, particularly useful as a prop for walking, but Susan found that just to have such a stick to hold in her left hand made her feel that she could walk more easily. They had experienced some difficulty because of the darkness in finding the way out of the garden through the only gate in the south side of the thicket; Susan had assumed that it was now impossible for her to climb over the wire fence.

When they came out of the thicket onto the Common, they found that it was, as they had hoped, more open country, although it was still wooded. A vague path could be seen leading away across the Common, but they stopped for a moment to look around.

"As we thought, Jim, there's not a sign of any of the others," said Susan. "They must be all a long way ahead."

"We can't possibly catch them up because of your ankle," said Jim. "But it doesn't matter. We know roughly which way to go, having checked the route on our map. Do you think we should try following this path, Sue?"

"We might as well. It looks as if it must go roughly in the right direction—somewhere near south—which should take us to that railway line we've got to cross."

"What if there's no bridge?"

"Oh, I don't know: we're sure to find some way of crossing it. Come on, Jim, let's be getting on again. My goodness, it's nearly half past ten."

They set off again, trying to follow the path at first, which was difficult, because it seemed a very vaguely defined track, and because there was now little more than moonlight to guide them on their way; but presently they decided that the path was leading them in the wrong direction.

"I think we're getting too far over to the right," said Jim. "Look, there are lots of lights over there." He pointed to the south. "Isn't that the village of Great Bookham?"

"We want to head that way if it is," said Susan. "Just a sec, Jim; we'd better have another look at the map." The map was brought out of Susan's knapsack and consulted again; they had already spent a few minutes studying it in the thicket at the place where Susan had sprained her ankle. "Yes, those lights must be Great Bookham, and that's the way we were told to go. We might as well head straight towards them, and see about that railway line when we get there."

Susan's map showed them that the south side of the Common was bounded by the railway line from Leatherhead to Effingham Junction, and they had seen that this had to be crossed before they could come to Great Bookham and the road which lead southwards from there to their camping site on Ranmore Common. The daylight had by this time virtually disappeared except for a faint reddish glow in the north-western sky behind them, which was hard to see because of the yellowish glare over the north-eastern part of the sky, marking the outer suburbs of London. However, the moon, a few days short of full, was giving plenty of light from a cloudless sky. To the south, against a backdrop of rising ground, lay a mass of lights, yellow street lights, and a great many points of white light marking houses: the lights of Great Bookham, Little Bookham, and Fetcham. As is always the way when looking at distant lights at night, Jim and Susan got the impression that they were looking at the lights of a fair-sized town, rather than a big village adjoining two other villages, for there seemed to be too many lights for a village-sized settlement. However, they made a welcome sight as something to aim for, and Jim and Susan could see that they were not far off—in fact, only about a mile away, as the map had showed them.

Soon after they had left the path on the Common they came to a fence which clearly marked the edge of the railway line. The light was quite good enough for Jim to see, between two small, shrubby trees inside the fence, a shallow cutting at the bottom of which a short stretch of the railway lines was dimly visible where the lines reflected the moonlight.

"Bother!" said Susan, who had been looking up and down the fence for a break in it, and not seeing one. "How am I to get over this?" The fence consisted of several strands of wire stretched between wooden posts, with a line of barbed wire on top. It was perfectly clear that Susan with her injured ankle had not a hope of climbing over it.

"We'll just have to walk along it until we come to a gap," said Jim. "As for the railway itself, we can just walk across the tracks if we can't see a bridge handy. You could manage to get down and up those gentle slopes, Sue?"

"Yes, I think I could; but I must tell you, Jim, that I'm not going to be able to get much further without resting that ankle properly for a while."

"Oh dear! Is it awfully painful walking on it?"

"I'm afraid it is. Look here, Jim, could you carry me for a bit? Because if you can't—if you think I'd be too heavy for you to carry on your back—then probably I shall soon be able to go no further. You'd have to lay me aside and go on by yourself."

"Oh no, I can't do that!" said Jim, horrified at this idea, but eager to try carrying Susan. "But I'm sure I could carry you on my back, at least for some of the way. But perhaps it would be best, Sue, to try to get over this railway first—before I pick you up."

"Oh certainly, if we can find a way through this fence without walking miles. The sides of that cutting are not very steep, but I don't think you'd better try having me on your back until we're on level ground and away from the railway."

"Right," said Jim, "which way shall we try: to the right or the left?"

"Let's try going to the right. There's a station marked on the map in that direction, if I can get as far as that, where we're <u>sure</u> to find a bridge over the line—unless, of course, we find a way across nearer here—and I hope we do! I don't intend to go one step further than is really necessary!"

The choice of walking along the fence to the right proved lucky. Almost as soon as they set off again they saw a place where the fence had been broken down, perhaps by vandals, and not repaired. All the wires had been slashed between two posts and lay on the ground. They walked through the gap, being very careful in the uncertain light not to trip over the wires or to tread on the barbed wire.

"Stop!" said Susan suddenly, just as Jim was starting to work his way down the side of the cutting. "We're through <u>this</u> fence all right, but what about the one on the other side? There's sure to be another, and if we can't get out, is there any point in going down to the railway lines?"

Jim thought for a moment. "I'll tell you what we could do, Sue," he said presently. "We might as well go down here, as we've got through this fence, and cross over the lines. Then, if we find that we can't get out through the fence on the other side, we could walk along beside the tracks, right into that station—Bookham, I think it was called—and get out there easily enough onto the platform on the other side. It's so late now that there would be little risk of meeting a train, and being run down by it."

"Okay, I think that's fair enough," said Susan, "only I hope we don't have to walk as far as the station platforms at Bookham." She opened the map, which she had not put away, but was still holding in her right hand. "Yes, it must be a good half mile into Bookham Station from where we are now." Jim peered at the map, which was difficult to read in the moonlight; but he found that after a few seconds he was able to see the relevant details. "Oh well," continued Susan, "on we go, down to the tracks!"

As they made their way slowly, slantwise, down the side of the cutting (which was shortish grass) they still had not seen the real danger which lurked at the bottom right beside the tracks. Jim held Susan firmly around her middle so that if she slipped he could catch her and hopefully prevent any further injury to the damaged ankle. They moved very cautiously, step by step, and there were no accidents.

"Oh heavens, look at that!" said Susan suddenly, when they had nearly reached the bottom of the cutting.

"What is it?" asked Jim, who had been carefully watching how Susan planted her feet on the grassy slope.

"Why, this is an electrified railway," said Susan, "as we might have guessed, being so near London. There are ground third rails."

"So there are," said Jim, looking at the conductor rails which were laid alongside each of the pair of running rails. "Oh dear, what are we to do now? But perhaps they turn off the current at night after the last train has gone past—only it may not have gone past yet."

"A quarter to eleven, it is now," said Susan. "How can we tell whether the last train has gone past, or not? And perhaps they don't switch off the current in the live rails at all. I know nothing about it, but perhaps we'd better go right down to the lineside to see if we can see anywhere else where we could get across safely."

In another moment Jim and Susan stood beside the gravel of the trackbed at the bottom of the cutting. There, beside the rails which carried the trains, glinting brightly in the strong moonlight, were the ominous, duller rails which carried the high voltage traction current. For all they knew, death might be lurking in those rails if they stepped across them clumsily; yet, equally, there might possibly be no current at all in them. But to Jim and Susan, wanting only to step across the rails and get away from the railway line, they presented an extremely menacing sight. They looked up and down the line as far as was possible in both directions, which was not far either way as they had struck the line on a long curve, but saw no signs of any welcome footbridge. Their eyes were by now well accustomed to the moonlight which, although it was bright, nevertheless played some tricks with what could be seen of the surroundings of the railway line because of the areas of deep black shadow cast by the lineside trees. They were particularly disappointed to see no sign of the station, looking westwards along the line; that way they saw only a signal post with a green lamp on it beside the signal arm, and there was another one, also showing a green lamp, at the edge of their vision in the other direction.

"I don't believe those green lights necessarily mean that a train is coming," said Susan thoughtfully. "They probably just leave them like that when there's nothing happening. I don't think we'd get run over, anyway, if we stepped across."

"But what are we to do, Sue?" said Jim. "Shall we not scramble back up the cutting and walk on until we come to the station?"

But Susan shook her head. "No," she said, "<u>I'm</u> certainly not going to go all that extra distance. My foot's nearly done for, and I'm jolly tired by now anyway."

"Well," said Jim, "I really daren't try carrying you on my back while stepping over those third rails."

"No," said Susan, "for heaven's sake don't try it. One slip, and we'd both be killed, probably. After all, it's dangerous enough, so far as we know, just to step across these rails without having to carry another person on your back. I'm going to try stepping across here under my own power, what's left of it, and you'd better do the same, Jim. Come on, we're wasting time: let's make up our minds to it. We've only got to step <u>very</u> carefully, and the danger will be safely behind us. Unless you'd rather stay behind, and perhaps find some safer and much longer way round."

Jim thought that there was nothing to be said in answer to that. If Susan could dare to step over those deadly rails, he would have to do the same. The thought of funking it, and leaving his beloved to face such a danger on her own, and with her injured ankle making the danger of a slip even worse, was too much for him. Come what might, he was not going to desert Susan now. But there was a strange mixture of emotions within him, as he felt Susan clasp his hands in a firm embrace.

"Come," she said quietly, "let's get it over: we can be over those rails in half a minute. It's as easy as easy, really. We only have to place our feet deliberately and carefully—and hope that my weak ankle won't let me down at the wrong moment!"

"Right," said Jim, "I'll go first, and I'll keep a tight hold of you as you step across." He held onto Susan with an outstretched right hand as, with a deliberate action he stepped across the first conductor rail and running rail onto the sleepers between the up pair of rails, being careful to step unnecessarily high over the live rail, so that there could be no possibility of the current reaching him by sparking. "That's it," he said, turning to face Susan, and grasping her firmly by both her forearms. "Move your good foot first, Sue, with a wide clearance." It was done, and for a moment Susan was straddled over the live rail. "Now the other one. Ready?" "Yes," said Susan firmly, and a second or two later she was standing beside Jim safely over the first dangerous hurdle.

"Good," said Jim. "So we've made it half-way across, but what if a train came tearing round the corner towards us now? I suppose we'd both die together!" He found it somehow rather pleasing to say that.

"Well, let's get a move on then, instead of stopping to talk!" said Susan rather sharply.

When the second pair of rails and its conductor rail had been crossed in the same way as the first pair, without any mishaps, Susan, feeling a great sense of relief, let go of Jim Sandy, and sank exhausted onto the grassy bank of the cutting on the south side of the railway line.

"Thank heaven that's over!" she said wearily. Jim was just going to sit down beside her when she stopped him. "No, Jim," she said, "we don't want to waste any more time. Let's get away from this damned railway line as quickly as we can; but first I simply <u>must</u> rest my bad ankle for a bit. Couldn't you go on ahead, and find where's the nearest place I could get through the fence on this side?"

"Of course I could, Sue," said Jim, already beginning to walk up the side of the cutting. "What a relief to have got across those third rails safely! I say, it could take me five or ten minutes, or longer, to find a gap in the fence."

"Never mind!" called Susan after him. "I'll be quite all right sitting here. See you later, Jim." He was off, scrambling quickly up to the top of the cutting.

Minute after minute passed while Susan sat at the lineside waiting for Jim to return. The pain in her ankle quickly eased to nothing more than a gentle throbbing now that she was no longer working it, but both her feet were feeling somewhat sore, and she was beginning to feel cold sitting still for so long in the cool night air. It was about eleven minutes after Jim had left her when Susan heard him, and saw him coming back.

"Sorry I've been so long," he shouted as soon as he was near enough for Susan to hear him. "I had to go nearly as far as that station to find a place where you could get through the fence, but then I found a gate in it, so that should be all right. I say, what's the matter?" He had now come right up to her, and had noticed an odd look about Susan, as if she were not listening to him, and he also noticed that she was shivering. "Are you cold, Sue?" She nodded to him. He quickly sat down beside her and put an arm gently around her neck and shoulders, and felt that her skin seemed to be very cold at the back of her neck where it was not covered by her jumper. "Sue, darling, you're shaking!" he exclaimed in some alarm, the word "darling" slipping out without conscious thought; but Susan did not seem to mind it at all. If she was shaking it was, in fact, not only because she was cold after sitting for a while at the lineside, but also because she was tired and experiencing an involuntary nervous reaction after the perilous crossing of the live rails.

"Can you warm me a little, my love, before we go on?" she murmured.

Well, thought Jim, what an extraordinary invitation! "I'll do what I can," he said softly. What she had just murmured was all the encouragement he needed at that moment to act boldly; yet he felt full of real concern for Susan and guessed that she was suffering in a way he did not really understand. Clearly her tiredness was not mere pretence, and the pain in her sprained ankle must, he reckoned, be genuine enough. His arm was already around her shoulder, and at a touch of gentle pressure on her cold skin, pulling her face towards him, he felt that at that time he could have done almost anything with her that he liked to do: she seemed to melt to his touch like a doll that has no power to resist. At any rate, she made no effort to resist him as Jim gently kissed her on the lips, shifting his hands round to the back of her shoulders in order to press her body tightly against his own to warm her. He felt that her shivering had stopped. "Do you feel warmer?" he whispered. "Yes!" she whispered in reply. "But don't stop, Jim; go on warming me for a little longer!" He pressed his chest into the full, round outlines of her breasts, and knew that his own intense excitement was being communicated to her through this firm but gentle contact, and through the touch of his hands, lightly moving over her back. For a minute or two neither spoke, but Jim saw the soft, dream-like smile in her dark eyes, shining in the moonlight. Then he felt Susan clasp him around the neck in both her arms as she layed a cheek against his forehead; he lowered his own hands to the small of her back, and they kissed urgently. "That's lovely—lovely!" she whispered. This time Jim was all but unaware of the powerful throbbing of his erection: there was nothing in his mind but an overwhelming love for Susan. They spontaneously loosened their mutual embrace, but still held each other. Neither of them remembered now that a live conductor rail was only about two to three feet away from them on the ground, or that a train might appear on the scene at any moment; but nothing happened to disturb their intimacy.

"I could lend you the spare pullover I've brought with me, if you like," said Jim. "It's in your knapsack, but I don't need it myself."

"All right," said Susan, "I'll have it." She let go of him and began to raise herself slowly to a standing position, assisted by Jim. "It's time we were going on again," she added in such an ordinary voice that he knew that she was deliberately concealing the excitement he had just felt aroused in her.

"Will you manage to walk now?" asked Jim as Susan put on his spare pullover. "I could carry you for a bit, if you like."

"Not just now, Jim; I'll walk. You can carry me later on."

"How does your sprained ankle feel?"

"The pain's much less now."

"Well, look: it would be much easier walking if we kept along the bottom beside the railway lines until we come to the place where that gate is."

"Did you find a path there?"

"Yes, and there's even a path up the side of the cutting leading to the gate, and a wooden level crossing for pedestrians—private, with a notice which says you mustn't cross—and then it looked as if the path went on across a bit of field towards a row of houses, and perhaps to a road."

"A level crossing!" said Susan. "Well, fancy that, after all our trouble to cross here! If we'd only kept to that other path across the Common when we came out of that thicket it probably would have lead us there! I bet Captain Clark lead the others by that way. But never mind, we can walk along here until we come to this crossing and gate."

"You're not too tired now?"

"No, I feel much better for that rest—now that you've warmed me!" Jim grinned happily, and Susan squeezed his hand gently in hers. "Come on," she continued; "lead me, Jim, and I'll go with you where you will. Here, just a minute, you can have the map."

She gave it to him and, holding hands, they set off. Luckily there was a gap like a narrow path between the edge of the gravel which made the trackbed and the bottom of the grassy slope of the cutting, a path which could be used by men working on the railway line. They were just far enough away from the conductor rail on their side of the line not to feel menaced by its presence so, as the railway was level, (more or less), the walking was as easy as it could be. Jim, in fact, thought that his progress along that path was more like floating than walking—as if his feet were hardly touching the ground as he moved—so blissfully happy was his state of mind. When they came to the crossing marked with notices which read: "Passengers must NOT cross the line except by the footbridge "and the usual warning about the live rails, they saw the platforms of Bookham Station a few hundred yards further on and a footbridge over the rails. The electric lights on the platforms were all switched on, but the place seen from the railway in the moonlight looked oddly deserted: if there were any passengers waiting there for a late train they were not on the platforms. They saw that the wooden crossing seemed to be provided for the signalman's exclusive use: it was adjacent to the signal-box.

"A footbridge!" said Susan. "So <u>that's</u> where we ought to have crossed. No doubt the others did."

"Well, here's our gate anyway," said Jim, pointing to a little wicket-gate in the boundary fence of the railway property. "There's a path on the far side of it which seems to go straight towards the village."

"Good. Lead on, then, Jim," said Susan.

Hand in hand, as before, they walked slowly up the slope on a gravel path, and so they left the railway, passing through the wicket-gate, and finding a path which, as Jim had said, headed towards a line of lights less than half a mile ahead. As they walked across a piece of park-like country, they heard behind them the unmistakable sound of a train rattling past and a squeal of brakes as it pulled up briefly at the station.

"Gosh!" said Jim, "that must be the last train of the day."

"We <u>have</u> been lucky," said Susan. "If we'd met that thing while we were down beside those rails, I don't suppose we'd be walking along here now!"

It was nearly half past eleven when Susan and Jim came into a well-lit village street. They were making slow but steady progress, Susan having refused another offer of being carried on Jim's back, and saying that she felt reasonably warm, not too tired, and that her bad ankle was really not all that painful. At first as they walked up that street there seemed to be nobody about, but when, a little later, they reached a cross-roads, they saw an inn just around the corner to the left and some men talking on the pavement outside it.

"Shall we go in there for a quick drink?" said Jim eagerly.

"It <u>can't</u> be open as late as this," said Susan. "I'm not sure when closing-time is, but it's almost half past eleven which is sure to be after closing-time. However, we might as well just see . . ."

They had already turned the corner and were walking towards the pub. They found the front door open, and went hopefully in, but a moment later they met the landlord who asked them politely to leave, saying that as it was the end of drinking-up time he was about to close: he was very sorry that he could not serve them in the bar. Then Jim Sandy, who had an idea in his mind and was not to be put down too lightly, explained eloquently that they had walked a long way, and still had some way to go to their destination, and that they were desperately in need of a little refreshment from a bottle. Before they had gone in, he had said to Susan: "Let me buy you a drink here," and she had said: "All right;" and now she seemed quite content to let Jim do all the talking. The landlord then agreed somewhat reluctantly to sell him a miniature bottle of whisky to take away.

"Thank you, sir," said the landlord as Jim paid for the whisky. "It's a beautiful night for walking."

"Yes, isn't it?" agreed Jim.

They took the bottle and packed it in the knapsack, meaning to have a drink a little further on. Then under a street light they consulted their map, and noted that the road to Ranmore Common, where their camp was, looked perfectly easy to follow. They walked on along the same road on which they had come into the village, passed another cross-roads, and kept straight on. They passed one or two people in the street, but mostly the village seemed to be already asleep. When they came to the end of the houses (and they had found that it was a big village), having failed to find a convenient bench, they sat down on the grass at the roadside. Jim had remembered when he had bought the small bottle of whisky that they still had some water in a bottle, so that they would be able to mix the two to obtain a warming drink (for he was still thinking in terms of "warming" Susan). They mixed a drink in the one cup they had brought, and then toasted each other happily, and both drank from it in turns. When they had consumed about half the contents of the whisky bottle they both felt very much revived and ready to walk on a few more miles.

"That was very refreshing," said Susan. "I feel less tired now, and there hardly seems to be any pain in that ankle. Thank you, Jim."

"Do you feel warm enough now, Sue?" asked Jim, grinning at her mischievously.

Susan laughed. "Oh yes," she said. "I don't need you to warm me again!—at least, not yet. Let's go."

They walked on once again. Their road was a small one, tree-lined, and it climbed gradually up a shoulder of high ground, an outlier of the Downs. Cheered by the whisky they were both now in good spirits, and were both very much appreciating the romantic side of their adventure: the bright moonlight on themselves and the surrounding scenery, and the solitude. They held each other's hands and trudged slowly on, mostly in silence to appreciate better the beauty of the night. Their solitude was indeed now perfect, for they met no one, either on foot, or in vehicles, once they had left the village behind. Jim did not put his thought into words in his mind, but he was thinking: What could be more romantic than to walk hand in hand with my lady-love in the moonlight on a lonely road at midnight, and in beautiful country too?—for the moonlight now lit up the whole country round about them, a country of low, rolling hills rising to a distant ridge ahead which was the main watershed of the North Downs.

The time reached and passed midnight, and still Susan and Jim were walking slowly hand in hand along that lonely road. At frequent intervals they passed through patches of deep shadow cast by a long line of ash trees on the left-hand side of the road. The road was climbing, but not steeply, now that they had left the village, and for about a mile they passed these ash trees. Where the road was not in shadow it seemed remarkably bright, for the sky was clear except for some small, puffy clouds ahead of them in the south.

Susan was feeling the romance of their situation at least as keenly as was Jim. She was only dimly aware that she was being attracted strongly to Jim; and this infatuation was almost certainly due at least in part to the alcohol she had consumed and to the fact that she was too tired to deliberately push aside these amorous thoughts. She was thinking of his handsome features: his comely pale hair, his large and beautiful blue eyes, his tallness and well-balanced stature, and (as she imagined it) his undoubted sheer strength of muscle; also she was by now more than well impressed by his courage and his kindness and considerateness to her—it had been his idea to buy her a drink. Susan had become a little light-headed after drinking her whisky on a nearly empty stomach when tired, after the nerve-racking experience of crossing the live rails, but she did not know that she was a little intoxicated: she only knew that but for Jim's outstanding bravery and coolness she would never have had the courage to step over those awful conductor rails. As well as that, she was thinking that he was the most handsome-looking man whose company she had ever known, and that John, her husband, seemed positively dull by comparison with Jim. She wanted, however, to feel, and enjoy feeling, his strength, so presently she stopped and said that she was too tired to walk any further.

"So Jim, my darling, could you very sweetly manage to carry me for a bit, like you said you would, on your back?" she said. "Or are you too tired?"

"Of course I could carry you," said Jim stoutly, although by now he was beginning to feel decidedly tired himself.

"The knapsack's almost empty, so there's hardly any more weight there—there's not much in it except the whisky bottle and the water bottle—so we might as well finish that drop of Scotch now, don't you think?"

When Susan had a drink in her hand (it was only about a mouthful of spirit diluted with water) she paused before drinking and said: "Do you know, Jim, when we went into that pub together to buy this stuff they must have thought that we were husband and wife! We look about the same age—we <u>are</u> almost the same age—so anyone could see that you couldn't be my son." (Susan was now twenty-three years old, and Jim was nineteen).

"Well, I suppose that's true," said Jim.

"So that landlord must have assumed that I was your wife!"

Oh heavens, thought Jim, if only that were true! Susan . . . my wife!

"Oh—perhaps not your wife," he said a little shyly.

"No, perhaps not, but he must otherwise have thought that we were engaged, or at least that I was your girlfriend!"

Jim blushed slightly, and for a moment looked away from Susan, and said nothing. Susan swigged her small mouthful of drink, and then laid a hand on his shoulder to attract his attention, and handed him the cup.

"Thank you, Sue," murmured Jim. He tossed down the remaining liquid in a gulp, and saw how Susan was smiling at him.

"I <u>am</u> your girlfriend, aren't I?" she said quietly. "That's how you think of me?"

"Yes, of course it is."

"You're naughty, Jim!" she said mockingly. "That's very naughty indeed to think of me that way!"

"Is it?" Jim was thinking quickly how best to answer her. "But am I not your boyfriend at this moment?"

"Maybe." There was a short pause; but Jim was not sure whether Susan was smiling at him or not. "No!" she added as Jim made a move as if to kiss her. "We've done enough kissing for one night. You're being naughty, Jim, you are." Jim, who was feeling rather light-headed himself, began to understand that the drink had rather gone to Susan's head. She stood up slowly and a little stiffly, and seemed to sway slightly for a moment before getting her balance right. "Now, you're going to carry me, aren't you? But maybe I'll be too heavy for you." She did not notice that she was repeating herself.

"I'll try whether I can lift you," said Jim, and he did it, after many false attempts, during which Susan and he laughed so much that he began to think that it would never be managed; but in the end he managed to rise to a standing position with Susan carried on his back, her hands clasped around his chest. Although she made a very heavy load for him to lift, he found that she was not really as heavy as he had expected (he had expected to find it impossible to lift her, but it was a case of eleven and a half stone— his weight—lifting about nine stone, her weight). He was being careful, too, to try not to hurt her sprained ankle any more.

"Gosh, Jim, can you really manage it?" she said. "Don't drop me, my love!"

"All right, Sue, I shan't; but I don't suppose we'll be able to get very far like this!"

"Well, you must be careful not to hurt yourself," she said. "Don't try to do too much, Jim."

After the first few staggering steps under the weight of his beautiful burden, Jim soon managed to get into his stride. Luckily they had almost reached the top of that hill when they had stopped, and after a minute or two Jim found that he was walking downhill; but he was already wondering how soon he would have to put Susan down. The answer to this thought came to him in an unexpected way about a minute later. Suddenly they realised that there were some other people about: voices were heard in the distance, and then they heard the sound of brisk walking along the road, and saw some pedestrians approaching them. At first they could not tell how many these other people were, but presently three people were seen, who appeared to be men, but they could not be sure in that uncertain light whether they were men or women.

"Fancy meeting other walkers at this unlikely hour!" exclaimed Susan. "Just a minute, Jim, I think I'd better get down. I could manage to walk a bit now."

They stopped, and Susan was very carefully set down onto the ground; and by the time that was done the other three had all but arrived. They saw Captain Clark and two of the other men of their expedition, evidently on their way back to look for the missing two. The rescue party was carrying with it a small tent which could be used, if necessary, for a stretcher. It did not take long to put Captain Clark and his men in possession of the facts they needed to know: that Lady Dalmane and Jim Sandy had been unintentionally left behind because Lady Dalmane had fallen down and badly sprained her ankle.

"We thought something like that might have happened when we discovered around midnight that you two were missing," said Captain Clark. "I suggest, Lady Dalmane, that you should complete the journey lying on this stretcher we've brought: I thought it might be needed. If we hadn't found you before we'd got back to Great Bookham we were going to let the police know that you were lost, but luckily now we don't need to."

The small tent was opened out on the ground like a stretcher with wooden carrying poles, and Susan was thankful to be helped to lower herself into it. It's a mercy they found us before they stirred up the police, she thought as she lay down on the stretcher, otherwise the word would have been sure to have reacned John that Jim and I had got lost, having been walking by ourselves. Gosh, he mustn't find out too much about what we've been up to tonight!

Jim was wishing that Captain Clark's rescue party had thought of bringing along <u>two</u> stretchers with it. As he plodded along beside the men carrying Susan on the improvised stretcher he was beginning to feel really tired. He had gathered that they still had about two miles to go to the place where the camp was pitched on the top of the North Downs. The road had dropped down to a little valley; but when they came to the place where it began to make the main climb to the higher ground, Jim, for the first time that evening, began to feel heartily tired of that long walk and to wish very much that it would soon be over. The hill was both long and, in part, on a steep gradient. As he trudged more and more wearily round bend after bend of that hill he felt his feet and legs aching and crying out to be rested. He was longing to see the tents beside the road at the top of the hill; but at the same time he was exulting in his mind at the way that things had turned out. It had certainly been one of the happiest days of his life, and he knew that the memories of his walk with Susan on that June night would for years afterwards be stored in his memory as pictures to be cherished: particularly his stumbling along the moonlit road with Susan carried on his back, and the time a little earlier in the evening when he had warmed her cold body in a loving embrace. Best of all, he sensed that this evening's adventures had brought about a change in Susan's feelings for him; he thought he had woken up a passion in her which was not merely something temporary, due to alcohol and unusual circumstances, but something which would develop and continue and be the beginning of a new crush in her on him. If he were right about this, it might well mean, he reasoned, that she would want to see rather more of him in the future, and that she would even want to be alone with him on occasions.

Such happy thoughts as these gave Jim Sandy sufficient strength and incentive to plod onwards up the hill in spite of his tiredness. At length the road stopped climbing; they passed a church and a road junction, and they saw a road running on ahead across fairly level ground, and to the right on the common, about a hundred yards or more back from the unfenced road, they saw a group of white tents, gleaming in the moonlight. It was their camp. At last their walk was over: the time was twenty-five minutes past one when Jim finally walked into his tent for the night (he had to share it with three other men who were, of course, already lying there asleep). They had been given cups of hot cocoa and biscuits when when they had come into the camp, and so they were able to lie down for sleep feeling somewhat refreshed. Little had been said by anybody on the last two weary miles of the walk while Susan was being carried on the stretcher, but Jim did have the chance to say "Good-night" to her when they had their refreshments at the camp site. He knew, of course, that he would not be sleeping in the same tent as Susan. Each married couple had been allocated a small tent for two, but as Susan had, at short notice, come on the expedition without her husband, Captain Clark, as organiser in charge of the camp, had re-allocated her a place in a tent with another (single) lady. There were eight women altogether in the party of twenty, all of them (except the one sharing Susan's tent) married women who had come with their husbands. But Jim retired to his tent tired enough to care about nothing except going to sleep, and knowing that he should sleep well, which he did.

Sunday morning dawned bright and sunny, but was already becoming cloudy by breakfast-time, which was not early. After breakfast the camp was struck, and they prepared to leave. Nearly every member of the party had sore, blistered feet, and many had aching legs, and the general concensus of opinion was that Captain Clark had made them walk too far. Susan still felt pain in her sprained ankle although the injury was certainly on the mend, and Jim was not surprised to find that he had woken up with pain in his back as well as in his shins, and sore feet. But everyone was feeling pleased that the arrangement was that they were all to be driven back to Esher Station in a minibus; the walk had been generally enjoyed, but people were agreeing with each other that enough was enough. The sky had clouded over, it was cooler than it had been the day before, and as they left the camp site in the minibus it began to rain: not much more than a drizzle, but it was enough to be a reminder that they had been very lucky with the weather on the walk. Although he was sitting beside Susan in the minibus, and on that account enjoying himself as before, Jim knew that the magical feeling of romance which had been his and Susan's the night before was now over. The cloudy weather and the fact that it was now broad daylight, not dreamy moonlight, had something to do with this, but the main thing was that he and Susan were no longer on their own. Soon they were back at Esher Station waiting for the train which would take them back home.

CHAPTER SEVEN

Susan was lying in her bed at home going over in her head the details of an exciting new idea. On some suitable occasion she would take Jim Sandy out with her in her car for a private picnic, and this little outing was to be kept strictly secret, something to be done while John, her husband, was away from home. A week had passed since the camping expedition to Surrey, and on this particular Sunday evening Susan, who had said that she was feeling rather tired, had retired to bed early, well before her husband, whom she had left watching television. Once she was in bed, however, it was as if her tiredness had melted away, so she took up her book and tried for a while to read it, but with little enthusiasm and little success. Susan always enjoyed best reading a novel when she had reached the point in it where the action in the plot really got moving, but in this particular book she was still reading the early chapters, had not reached a point where the story became easily readable, and began to doubt whether she would ever persevere long enough to reach that point. After about ten minutes she closed the book, feeling that she had taken in practically nothing of it. Her mind wanted to think about Jim Sandy and to look into the details of her new plan for a private picnic, but it did not want to read a book—at least not a dull one so, although she considered for a moment the idea of getting out of bed to look for a more exciting book to read, she decided instead to stay where she was. She was comfortable and could not be bothered to move, so she was happy enough to lie and plan for herself an arousing adventure.

The great thing is, she told herself, to take Jim out while John is staying for a few days in London so that he won't find out anything about it: for really he must <u>not</u> know anything about this! Now, when might we get a chance? This week? No chance: I'm tied up every day with things to do. Perhaps before we go away? The Dalmanes were going away for three weeks holiday in the North of England, starting as soon as August Bank Holiday Monday was out of the way, so that there were about another four weeks before the starting date for the holiday. Susan thought it over, but soon came to the conclusion that there were likely to be no opportunities to try her plan during this period. Then she thought: What about when we've come back?, and suddenly she remembered something. Why, so he is! she said to herself. John's got that conference on in the last week of August, and he told me he'd have to stay in London all that week, and perhaps longer! And I've got <u>no</u> engagements that far ahead. Splendid! We could go and enjoy ourselves one day that week, probably . . .

The bedroom door opened and in came Lord Dalmane.

"That play was no good," he said. "It was trash."

"So you turned it off?" said Susan.

"I did. I wasn't enjoying it, so I turned the old telly off, as there's nothing else on the box worth watching tonight. I'm for bed. I'll be with you soon, Sue."

"Good. I thought that play would be trash."

Lord Dalmane sat down on a chair, untied his shoe laces, and began to pull off his shoes and socks. As he took off a sock he was suddenly reminded by the sight of a foot that Susan had recently sprained an ankle. "By the way," he said, "how's that bad ankle of your's, Sue?"

"Fully recovered," said Susan. "I'd hardly know by now that anything had ever happened to it."

"What <u>did</u> happen to it, anyway? You've never told me properly about that, Sue—only that you'd somehow fallen down on that long walk, and that that friend of yours, Jim Sandy, had helped you to go on walking until you got to your camp site. You've been rather close, don't you think, about what you've divulged so far about what you and he were up to?"

"John, darling, <u>must</u> you really know more about that? I don't know what you mean either when you say: 'what we were up to', but if Jim hadn't been there to help me up after I'd fallen and sprained that ankle I don't know how I could have got any further."

"But how did you happen to fall?"

"We were in a wood, and it was dusky so that there wasn't much light under the trees, and all of a sudden that foot went down a hole that was completely hidden under the long grass, and of course that twisted the ankle. It was jolly painful too after that for the rest of the walk."

"No doubt it would be. And Jim Sandy just happened to be with you when you sprained the ankle, I suppose?"

This remark, by its implication that it was no co-incidence that Jim Sandy had been with Susan when she had sprained her ankle, annoyed her, but she did not show it, and only answered quietly: "He was with me."

John Dalmane wisely did not press the subject any further as he had no wish to be offensive in anything that he said. For a minute or two he went on with his undressing, while Susan again picked up her book, and pretended to be reading it, and neither spoke. Then Lord Dalmane in his pyjamas and with bare feet, walked across the bedroom to collect his bedroom slippers from their place under his dressing-table. He noticed a piece of paper lying there just before he trod on it, apparently some piece of paper which Susan had dropped on the floor, and he bent down and picked it up. He saw that it was, in fact, a little paper booklet of glossy colour pictures of bicycles.

"Eh, what's this?" he said. "Bicycles? You're not thinking of buying yourself a new bike, Sue? I thought your present one was okay."

Susan put the book down on the sheets. "Not a new bike for me," she said.

"What? You don't mean, surely, that you're getting me a new bike?" John Dalmane had a bicycle, but hardly ever found time to ride it, but Susan liked cycling, and was often to be seen on her bicycle on the roads around the Castle, and occasionally as far afield as Sherborne.

"Oh, John, dear," she said, "don't pretend that you don't know about it. I told you before that I was buying a bicycle to give it to Jim for his birthday—you know, when I asked you if it could be from both of us, and if you were willing to contribute towards it. That's what that catalogue is."

"Oh, I see. And have you chosen one from it?"

"Yes, I'm getting one of those with a picture on Page Three of that thing. They've got one in of that model, the right size, at the Bike Shop in town, so I've got it reserved until tomorrow, and I'm going shopping in the morning, and I'll pick it up and pay for it. So are we going to give him this present from both of us, or shall it have to be from me alone?"

"Sue, my love," said John gently, "what I told you before stands: I haven't changed my mind. I am taking no part in this birthday present for Jim, so I'm giving no money towards it. You can give him this present yourself, if you like—although I think that you're being very unwise in this—but count me out of it."

"John! What a nasty, mean attitude—just because you don't approve of him being friendly with me!"

For a few moments John Dalmane did not answer Susan, but he came and sat down on his side of the bed. "Sue, darling, don't let's argue over this," he said. "I'm sure it isn't worth it. But, as for my not approving of the very obvious friendship between you and Jim—"

"Well, you don't! Go on, John, you might as well admit it!"

"All right: indeed I don't approve of that freindship, but only because I—"

"Because you're jealous of Jim Sandy: you don't like to see him loving me!" Susan knew, in the back of her mind, that she was being unwise to interrupt her husband with remarks which might well provoke a nasty arguement, but she somehow felt impelled to do this.

"Sue, darling, I am <u>not</u> jealous of Jim Sandy: really and truely I'm not," said John, getting into bed as he spoke. He leaned over to his wife and kissed her; then, holding Susan in a close embrace, he said: "Don't you see, my dear? When I hold you in my arms it's a matter of total irrelevance to me that Jim is in love with you. Jealousy doesn't come into it. I love you, and I'm faithful to you; and I know in my heart that you love me, and that you're faithful to me—yes, faithful to <u>me</u>, in spite of a very close freindship between you and Jim. What do you say about it, my darling?"

Susan felt greatly moved at hearing her husband make this passionate speech (which he had made very calmly and quietly), but for a little while she made no other answer than to embrace him tightly. It was obvious to her that he genuinely believed that what he had said was true: he <u>did</u> love her, she <u>did</u> love him, and he was indeed not jealous of Jim Sandy. Most important of all, even as she remembered how she and Jim had kissed and cuddled by the railway line in the moonlight only a week before, she still felt that it was right for John to say to her: "you're faithful to me." Yes, she said to herself, I <u>am</u> really, in my heart—what Jim and I did that night doesn't really count, and anyway, we'd never get another chance like that again.

"John, darling, of course I'm faithful to you, and I'm sure I'll continue to be," she said. "Being friendly with Jim doesn't really come between us, does it? I don't see why it should. He's not my lover: only you are. Then why should you disapprove of our friendship? Why shouldn't you participate in giving him this bike for his birthday present? No one else will give him any proper presents, and you know that."

John Dalmane found it difficult to know what to say in answer to this. He certainly meant to stick to his principles, and to be seen to be giving his wife no encouragement in this matter of her friendship with Jim Sandy, and that meant that, according to this principle, he could not give any money towards this present. But he did not at all want to argue with Susan over it, for that would only tend to create bitterness and division between them.

"I should think that Jim Sandy <u>will</u> receive some other birthday presents," he said evasively. "For one thing, we know that the Padgates have left him a book token for us to hand over to him on his birthday; and probably his father will send something in the post, like he did last year."

"Yes, but Jim's father is not at all well-off, and won't be able to afford much in the way of a present for his son; and his mother, of course, will send nothing as she cares nothing about what happens to him. So, you see, it's up to us—or at least up to me, <u>in loco parentis</u>, to give him a decent present. Come, John, why not change your mind and give him the bike with me? Even if you only want to pay for a tenth of the price, or less, it would be so much nicer if it was from both of us."

But still Lord Dalmane was determined to stick to his principles and refused to change his mind.

"I'm sorry, my darling, but I really can't be persuaded on that score," he said quietly.

"Why not? You know I'm only playing the part of his mum by giving him this present because his real mother takes a beastly attitude towards him."

"Oh come, my love, don't exaggerate: his real mother merely ignores him."

"Well, that's pretty beastly of her, isn't it? I mean, it's as bad as if he hadn't got any mother living at all. So why shouldn't I be his mum?"

"Oh yes, you might as well be his mother, my dear. Only don't expect me, please, to play the part of his father and give him birthday presents. He doesn't need me to be his father: his real father in Cumberland will still do his bit about presents."

"But last year on his birthday you gave him that camera with me," said Susan. "What's the difference this time?"

"My dear, the difference is that now I know that I made a serious mistake last summer in sharing with you that camera as a joint gift. It should have been from you only, just as this bike should be, if you insist on giving it to him."

"I do! I tell you, John, I'm only acting like a decent mother for him, in place of his real mother. Why must you be so awkward about it?"

John sighed and shrugged his shoulders. "Awkward?" he said. "No, my love, I'm not being awkward. But I don't think you've really understood me. If it was only a case of you acting the part of his mother there really wouldn't be much for me to object to. But there's more to it than that: you know there is." He paused.

"What do you mean?" said Susan.

"Why, I mean, of course, that the boy, Jim, is very infatuated with you—and has been, I believe, ever since the day you first met him. We've talked about this before, my love, so you'll know that I know about this. Well then, from his point of view, the relationship with you is more than that as between a son and his mother. To put it bluntly, Sue, he's in love with you—he's dotty about you—he has a whacking big crush on you! But you've reassured me that you mean to remain faithful to me, so I won't ask you how you feel towards <u>him</u>. I don't want to know about that. But, however that may be, it seems to me that our position is not far short of a <u>ménage a trois</u>."

"Oh, John, don't be ridiculous!" said Susan rather crossly. "Of course we aren't a <u>ménage a trois</u>—he's not my lover—and, of course, I'm not going to let him go as far as that. We're just very good friends."

"But Sue, darling, what I meant was, your relationship with Jim—your friendship with him—might in time <u>become</u>—might turn into—"

"It won't," said Susan quickly. "It's not going to turn into a threesome. How could you suggest such a thing, John?"

There was a short silence, and then John said simply: "I'm sorry, Sue," and again there was a little pause. They were looking at each other as if each was trying to read the other's thoughts. John put an arm gently around Susan's neck and looked closely into her eyes. But Susan frowned slightly and remained silent, thinking about what John had been saying. Did she in her heart want Jim to become her lover? But if she were to allow that to happen then indeed they would be a triangle of lovers, a <u>ménage a trois</u>. Then Susan began to understand why John was not only unwilling to contribute towards the birthday present, but did not want her to give it either: it would be just the sort of action which might encourage undesirable rumours. If she were to give Jim the bicycle, might not the story get around that it was a special gift for her lover? Might it not begin to be rumoured that the Countess of Saint Helens was having an affair with her Guide? Was that inconceivable? No, it was not. Then Susan considered another aspect of the problem.

"John," she said, "I <u>want</u> to give him that bike, but perhaps I shouldn't. It would give him so much pleasure, you know, to receive a handsome present like that. But what are <u>you</u> going to do if I go ahead and give it to him?"

"What would I do?" said John Dalmane. "Oh, good heavens, Sue, I wouldn't dream of trying to stop you by force if you're set on giving this thing. I'll disapprove, but that's all."

"But why should you disapprove? We don't see each other often, you know. Surely I could give him a birthday present, but still continue for your sake, John, darling, to see that I hardly ever meet him."

"Except for several hours at a stretch on a long walk from Esher station to the North Downs!" murmured John.

"John! How can you say that, unless it's to tease me? It wasn't my fault that he walked beside me, or his fault either. As he was on that walk, and you weren't, how could he not have walked with me? Anyway, there was no harm done: he behaved very well with me."

"Yes, my dear, I'm sure he did," said John soothingly. "Don't upset yourself about it now." He saw that Susan's face had become somewhat flushed, either with shame or anger, and he noted that the tone of her voice was becoming slightly heated. Susan had hardly told him anything about the details of that long walk, and he was not too sure now whether she was being entirely truthful when she said: "he behaved very well with me;" but he did not want their discussion to degenerate into a nasty quarrel so he resolved that nothing more should be said on that point.

"I was telling you, John, that I'm taking care hardly ever to meet him," said Susan presently. "Anyway, I've scarecely seen him since we came back from Esher."

"Yes, it's probably wise for you not to see him when you don't have to."

"In fact, I've hardly seen Jim to talk to for nearly a whole year," added Susan; "that is, since his last birthday—except for just that one occasion last weekend. You see, John, I've deliberately tried to avoid him, for your sake—because I love you!" She smiled again.

"My darling, I appreciate that very much!" said John. "But about giving him this bike for his birthday present—I hope you'll at least think carefully about it before you act; then, if you're still determined to give it to him, I shall at least not hinder you in any way."

"All right, John, I'll think it over first before coming to any final decision on whether to buy that bike." But even as she said this Susan knew in her heart that, however much she might think it over, she would in the end give Jim that bicycle.

"Splendid, my dear!" said John. "Shall we talk about something else now? Have we fixed the date for when we go away?"

"August the 8th, I thought—that's the Tuesday just after the Bank Holiday. I put that date in my letter to Aunt Nora so, if she agrees, we'll be going up to Dallam Hall on that date."

"I see," said John. He also noticed that Susan had probably chosen that date deliberately so that they would be at home for Jim Sandy's birthday on July the 31st, but he said nothing about that.

Jim Sandy was delighted with his present of a new bicycle. Susan knew that he liked cycling; but he had not done much cycling while he had been at Rhodes Castle because the only available bicycle had been an ancient spare model that had once belonged to Lord Dalmane's father, but had been kept since his death to gather dust and to go rusty. That had not been a machine which Jim had enjoyed riding because, although it was large enough for him, he found it very heavy, cumbersome, and usually rather slow, although it was good enough down hills. Jim already owned a bicycle, but it was an old one which he had left at home at Cockermouth; he had not thought it worth the trouble of bringing it down to Rhodes Castle on a train, which would have meant a journey up North by train to fetch it and, because of Susan, Jim did not want to leave Rhodes Castle, even for a couple of days. The new bicycle, however, was light and delightful, and was clearly built for speed—unlike Jim's old one. Susan herself had handed the birthday present over to him. Jim saw a bicycle frame wrapped in bright gift-wrapping paper, and a label tied to the handlebars: "To dear Jim with much love from Susan on your birthday." He was more than pleased to receive that present, and the label pleased him to by having no mention on it of John Dalmane. Susan had told him that it was a gift from her alone, that her husband had asked to have nothing to do with it. Jim had been very pleased to hear that.

Susan had not spent a great deal of time agonising over the decision of whether or not to give Jim that bicycle. She soon had made herself believe that she was doing the right thing by giving it, as a mother to a son. Lord Dalmane had been as good as his word, and was ignoring everything to do with Jim's twentieth birthday. If Susan wanted to waste her money on expensive presents for that love-struck youth, then let her do that, he had decided; he hoped, however, that this episode would not further encourage the relationship between those two.

John and Susan had not discussed Jim Sandy and his birthday present any further after that detailed talk in the bedroom. They had reached an unspoken mutual decision that enough had been said on such a delicate subject. However, it was Lord Dalmane's hope that the over-amorous friendship between his wife and Jim Sandy would presently come to an end of its own accord as, sooner or later, Jim would grow bored with his infatuation and give it up. Once that began to happen, he felt confident that Susan would lose her unwholesome interest in the boy, so he was trying to be patient enough to let the passing of time bring that relationship to an end. He knew that this process might take a few years to complete, but he often told himself that all he had to do was to refrain from interference, by having nasty arguements with Susan about Jim Sandy, and, if possible, to ensure that neither Jim nor Susan did anything to actively encourage further mutual attraction. He soon began to understand that the giving of the bicycle, although it was an unfortunate and perhaps a regrettable incident, was not really important: Jim would soon forget who had given it to him.

Susan was still turning over in her mind every day her plans for a secret picnic with Jim on the first convenient occasion which would arise. It had been so very pleasant that evening when she had been alone with him with her sprained ankle, and he had behaved so gallantly towards her with such gentle, loving tenderness. Oh, she would think, we must let something like that happen again! We'll go to some really out-of-the-way place where we can be <u>really</u> on our own, and lie down together in the sun, and revel in each other's company! But how much will it be safe to let him do? He'll want to make love to me—he was dying to do it the other day when we were lying in each other's arms on the grass at the bottom of that railway cutting—but, of course, we really <u>can't</u> do that. I must think of John, and stay faithfully his wife. That's what he meant when he said: "you're faithful to me." And of course I wouldn't dream of being unfaithful to John. Jim and I are only going to have a little fun when we have this picnic—I think, perhaps, I might take off my bra and allow him to touch my breasts, or something like that—but we won't do anything really naughty—there'll be nothing to feel guilty about in planning this private outing.

But Susan <u>did</u> feel guilty whenever she thought about her planned picnic with Jim; nevertheless she remained obstinately determined that it was going to happen.

CHAPTER EIGHT

The Dalmanes were being driven by their chauffeur to Stalbridge Station to catch an express train to the North for the first leg of their summer holiday. This first leg was to be a trip to Warrington to stay for two nights and a day at Dallam Hall with the Padgates; after this they were going to take the main part of their holiday in the Lake District, before finishing by calling for a night on Lord Dalmanes's brother, who lived at Saint Helens. It was a warm, pleasant morning in early August and when, at about twenty minutes past ten, the Dalmanes stepped out of the car at the station in the little town of Stalbridge, they were both in excellent spirits, thoroughly looking forward to taking a good break from ordinary life at home. They had come to catch the 10.38 train to Crewe, the "Pines Express", which ran through from Bournemouth to Manchester; the Dalmanes had taken reserved first-class seats on the train for that day.

The chauffeur drove the car back to Rhodes Castle as soon as he had set down his passengers and their luggage; the Dalmanes planned to hire a car in the Lake District for local sight-seeing, as neither John nor Susan would have enjoyed the very long drive to the North, even with the journey broken at Warrington. The Dalmanes' car had no sooner been driven away when they saw the porter, a man who knew the Earl but had not met Susan before; he at once carried the suitcases onto the platform, setting them down near the front end of it to be handy for loading them into a first-class carriage near the front of the train. Lord Dalmane thanked him and gave him a handsome tip. They had allowed rather more time than they needed to wait for their train, but on that pleasant morning neither of them minded the waiting, especially when they heard the train in the distance approaching the station several minutes before the booked departure time.

Two minutes later the "Pines Express" pulled into the station and came to a standstill. John and Susan, with the porter's help, had estimated very well the correct place to stand to be adjacent to a first-class carriage; there were two of these right at the front of the train, immediately behind the engine and tender. John and Susan were about to move forward to get into the train when a voice called from the engine: "Lady Dalmane!" They looked round. As soon as he had stopped the train, the Driver, knowing that he had about three minutes to wait because he was early, had leaned out of his cab to watch the bustle of the passengers and their luggage boarding the train. The Dalmanes saw a slight-looking middle-aged man, not very tall, wearing dark blue overalls and the standard issue peaked engine-driver's cap, and recognized him almost at once in spite of the fact that they had not seen him before except in an ordinary suit.

"Why, it's Mr. Beck!" said Susan in considerable surprise. Lord Dalmane signed to the porter to place their two suitcases in the second carriage, and hurried after Susan up to the engine to have a quick word with Mr. Beck.

"Good morning, my Lady," said Mr. Beck politely, taking off his cap. "How do you do, my Lord? You must be off for a holiday? I saw your suitcases being loaded into the train."

"How nice to see you on the footplate, Mr. Beck," said Lord Dalmane. "Yes, we're setting off on our holiday." The Fireman turned round for a moment to stare at the two aristocrats whom the Driver, apparently, knew by name.

"What a surprise to see that you're driving us, Mr. Beck," said Susan. "Come on, John, we'd better get into the train."

"You'll be all right," said Mr. Beck. "We won't be starting from here for another two minutes as I've got in a little early. Started from Bournemouth maybe half a minute early, and gained a bit more on an easy run. Anyway, I promise I won't start the train until you're safely inside it."

"Oh good," said Susan. "But I had no idea you were driving the 'Pines Express' nowadays. I thought Norma said you were only on the local trains to Bath."

"I was doing that, but all this week I'm on the 'Pines'."

"But how far do you take us before someone else takes over?" asked Lord Dalmane. "As far as Bristol?"

"No," said Mr. Beck. "I'm driving all the way through to Manchester. We run non-stop through Bristol, not going into Temple Meads Station. Look here, you'd better be getting in now: it's nearly time for the 'off'." He had caught sight of the Guard, whistle and green flag in his hands, looking angrily at the two passengers who were talking to the Driver, as if they had no business to be doing such a thing.

"Just a moment!" said Susan quickly. "Could we have a word with you when we get off at Crewe?"

"Yes, by all means, my Lady."

They waved their hands to Mr. Beck, and ran back to the first carriage to get into the train through the first door they reached. Mr. Beck, watching them from the footplate, saw the door slammed shut behind them. They walked along the corridor into the second carriage, and presently found their compartment with its reserved seats and, as they found them, they heard the Guard's whistle blown. The train began to move.

"Good," said Susan, "our suitcases are here." She was looking up at the luggage rack where the porter had put their suitcases. They had two corner seats, one facing the engine and one back to it. Susan sat down facing forwards. "What a stroke of luck to meet Mr. Beck!" she continued as she watched the train pull away from the station platforms.

"Why do you say that, Sue?" asked John.

"Because I was going to write to them to ask them to come and stay with us. Of course, first we'd have to find out whether Nigel has a holiday sometime soon so that he could come with Norma."

"They can't come at least until September," said John. "You haven't forgotten, darling, that I've got this conference on in London almost as soon as we're back from our holiday."

"Oh yes, I hadn't forgotten that. I'm not asking them to come while you're away. But the great thing is that, as Mr. Beck is driving us, we can ask him when we get to Crewe when he is free to come, and perhaps get it all settled without having to write to Norma first."

"Of course; it'll save a lot of time and trouble."

Susan remembered that with her husband going away for a week or longer to that conference there would be, surely, an opportunity to have that secret picnic with Jim. We'll have our picnic on the Tuesday of that first week after I'm back at home, while John's away, she thought, as Tuesday's Jim's day off work. The thought reminded her that Jim was going to be living at Rhodes Castle without her for quite a while. It's a good thing, really, for him to be separated from me for a bit, she said to herself. But in the back of her mind she did not really believe this. She thought that behind her more immediate thoughts—of looking forward to her holiday with John—there must still be a longing to be with Jim. And Jim? No doubt he must be longing for another occasion when he could go out with her. For a minute or two Susan noticed nothing of the countryside to be seen through the carriage window as she thought about Jim. She wondered whether he would feel very lonely until she returned home, and thought that he probably would, although he saw very little of her even when she was at home.

They had a very comfortable and reasonably punctual journey by the "Pines Express" by way of Bath, Gloucester, and Birmingham. It was just before a quarter to four, only a few minutes late, when the express pulled into one of the long platforms of Crewe Station. The Dalmanes had nearly an hour to wait there for a connection which would take them on to Warrington, but as soon as the train stopped they were ready to get out, so that they could hurry forward to the engine, knowing that there would be only a few minutes in which they could again talk with Mr. Beck before he had to take the train on to Manchester. Mr. Beck told them that he had two weeks holiday in September, and would be delighted to visit Rhodes Castle, but first, of course, he would have to consult Norma, his wife, about it. Then, when they had watched the "Pines Express" go on its way without them, Susan said to her husband: "That's all very satisfactory, if Norma agrees that they can come to us in September. Look here, John, we've still got ages to wait for the 4.40 train; we might as well go into the Refreshment Room and have tea to pass the time."

That evening Jim Sandy was feeling a little depressed. He had finished work for that day, had his supper, and gone up to his room, having felt, as usual, reasonably cheerful throughout the day while he had been keeping himself always occupied with doing something. Now, however, he was suddenly aware that some vital element was missing from the heart of the Castle's life. Such was the effect on his spirits when he remembered that Susan had gone away, not to return for two and a half weeks. The feeling was like a kind of vacuum in his own life—as if a part of himself were missing. It surprised him very much.

The Dalmanes left Warrington very early in the morning on the Thursday of that week to travel on northwards, having spent the whole of Wednesday there. They had made their exact itinerary plans the evening before with the help of their host, Lord Padgate, who, as a Director of British Railways, turned out to be quite knowledgeable on some useful timetable details.

"We'd like to get to Cockermouth by around midday, or at least by one o'clock, in time for lunch, if that's possible by train," said Lord Dalmane.

"It won't be possible, will it, from so far away as Warrington?" said Susan. "We're booked in for tomorrow night at the Lakes Hotel,[1] but it would be good if we could lunch there, and then look for a car-hire garage."

"I think it should be possible for you to get to Cockermouth in ample time for lunch," said Lord Padgate. "I've got all the timetables, and I'll look it up for you presently. But I know you could get to Penrith by the early train from here at about nine something—and then you'd be able to get a connection onwards. But the snag is, if you are going with 'Lulu' it will mean a very early start in the morning."

"I beg your pardon?" said Lord Dalmane.

"Who's Lulu?" asked Susan.

Lord Padgate chuckled. "'Lulu' is the local name for the early train from Warrington to Carlisle," he explained. "Don't ask me why it's called 'Lulu': I haven't the slightest idea; but that's what the engine drivers call it."

"Oh yes, I see," said Lord Dalmane. "But just how early does this 'Lulu' leave?"

"It starts from Bank Quay Station here in Warrington at six a.m. Is that too early for you? I don't in the least mind running you to the station in time for it."

The Dalmanes looked rather doubtfully at each other. "Well, that's very kind of you, Geoffrey, to offer us a lift at such an unearthly hour of the morning! But what do you think, Sue?" said Lord Dalmane.

"I think we should take Geoffrey's offer, and take the early train, 'Lulu'," said Susan. "It's very nice to be up and moving really early on a sunny summer morning, and I think it would be rather jolly to be travelling in that train past houses where many people are still asleep. But perhaps it won't be a nice, sunny morning?"

"I've had the weather forecast," said Lord Padgate, "and I gathered that they think that it probably <u>will</u> be mainly sunny at first, here at least, and gradually get more cloudy. But they say that further north, in the Lake District—where you're going—there may be a little rain by midday."

"Oh, bother it!" said Susan. "But if it's sunny first thing, I think it <u>would</u> be very jolly to be off by the early train." She looked doubtfully at her husband.

"My dear, that's hardly the point, whether it's sunny or not," said Lord Dalmane, taking a practical view of the problem. "Surely the point is that we <u>can't</u> get to Cockermouth by lunchtime <u>unless</u> we travel on this 'Lulu' train. That's right, isn't it, Geoffrey?"

"Yes, I should say it is. The next train from Warrington would, I think, be too late for you to arrive at your destination by lunchtime, if that's what you want to do. Look here, I'll look it up for you now, and we'll be sure about this." Lord Padgate got up out of his armchair and took a fat red paperback volume off the mantlepiece, where he had left it to be handy in case they needed to consult the timetable. While he was turning over the pages of the timetable, Lord Dalmane said: "Mind you, darling, I daresay you're right all the same about how pleasant it is to travel at an early hour." In his heart, however, he did not believe this. Inwardly he groaned at the idea of having to get up at five o' clock in the morning, or earlier, while he was on holiday, but, as usual, he did not want to argue about it so he decided to agree with Susan. Presently Lord Padgate looked up from the pages of his timetable and confirmed that only by the early train 'Lulu' could they reach Cockermouth in the Lake District by the middle of the day. "The connection from Penrith will get you there, in fact, by as early as a quarter past eleven, whereas if you waited for the next train from Warrington it would be half past two when you got there. Mind you, it looks as if 'Lulu' must be a pretty slow train: it seems to stop at practically every station."

"Oh, we won't mind that," said Lord Dalmane. "We won't, after all, be in any great hurry to get there once we've managed the early start from here—if we <u>do</u> manage it!"

"We will," said Susan; "and if there are a lot of stops it will be all the better for seeing things."

"No doubt it will be." Really John Dalmane was already looking forward to a ride in this early morning slow train, even though the thought of getting up very early did inspire a certain dread in his mind.

"Well then, let's call it settled that we're going by the 'Lulu' train if Aunt Nora could manage to give us a little breakfast at that time," said Susan.

"I should think my wife could . . ." began Lord Padgate, but at that moment Lady Padgate came into the drawing-room, and the discussion moved on to the topic of an early breakfast for the Dalmanes.

The journey by the early morning stopping train, "Lulu", turned out to be comfortable enough and by no means irksomely slow; in fact, the train moved at a good, brisk speed between some of the stops which were not close together. They had somehow expected to see a rather grand-looking train at the platform at Warrington, forgetting that the name "Lulu" was strictly unofficial; and so they had been a little disappointed to see only a shabby-looking affair: a not very long train, hauled by a very large and very dirty black engine; but the train did at least have two first-class carriages, in one of which the Dalmanes took their seats. At first the morning was sunny and almost cloudless, as had been promised, and the suburbs of Warrington and the other South Lancashire places through which they passed—Golborne, Bamfurlong, and Wigan— looked almost attractive bathed in the warm early sunlight soon after dawn. However, it soon became clear that the clouds were gradually encroaching over the sky. By the time 'Lulu' reached Lancaster there was a heavy cover of lowering grey clouds overhead; and when the train began to climb up to Shap Summit it became misty: low cloud swathed the fells, and they were now in it, rather than underneath it. As they stopped at Shap Station it began to rain: little more than a misty drizzle at first, it soon increased to a good steady rain. The Dalmanes changed at Penrith and sat in a dingey, dark waiting room in order to keep dry until the train for the Keswick Line came in from Carlise, while outside the rain continued to fall steadily, as it very often does in August in the Lake Counties. When the local train came in John and Susan had time to look into the cab to see whether Susan's friend, Mr. Ruddock, was driving it; but he was not there.

"Perhaps Mr. Ruddock's retired," said John as he stepped into the train behind Susan.

"Oh no, I don't think he would have retired yet," said Susan. "He said in that letter that he was doing three more years driving, so he's still got about one more year to do; then he'll be sixty-eight, and he'll have completed fifty years of service with the Railway." Of course, we don't know which of the trains he drives: we only know that he works on this line."

"Anyway," said John, "here, at last, is my opportunity to travel this line, which I've wanted to do ever since that day when I had to be left behind in Cockermouth. But it <u>would</u> have to be raining, just to spoil things."

"Ah, but remember that we've still got the journey to make in the other direction, when we come back, and it may be fine then. I say, there's the Guard; he isn't Mr. Blencow either." They saw a man in guard's uniform talking to a passenger.

"Mr. Blencow?" said John.

"He was our Guard that time when I travelled in the cab with Mr. Ruddock," said Susan. "But I suppose those two always work together. Ah, good, we're off."

The Guard had waved his green flag, the Driver had sounded a short two-note blast on the horn, and the little diesel unit was moving away from the platform on its way to Keswick, Cockermouth, and Workington. As the journey through the Lake District progressed they were both suitably impressed, in spite of the poor weather, but they were pleased to notice that by the time they reached Keswick the rain had eased to no more than a drizzle, the low clouds over the fells seemed to be lifting, and the sky began to look a little brighter. The excitement of both Susan and John was mounting as the train neared Cockermouth. They had not seen the little town since that strange day when Susan had set off from the station there to travel to her Great Aunt at Knebworth, and John had been arrested by the local police in mistake for a murderer for whom they were hunting. This time the Dalmanes intended to visit Mr. Sandy, the father of Jim Sandy, who had first met Susan also on that day, as Susan now remembered.

The train was about to reach Cockermouth, and the Dalmanes stood up and took their suitcases towards a door to be ready to step out at the station, but they were busy looking out of the windows recognizing again the landmarks of that earlier adventure.

"There's where they arrested me at Bridge Number Eleven."

"And there's the Cemetry."

"And the town."

Moments later the train was slowing down as it rattled over the concrete bridge spanning the river and through the points of the sidings. The drizzle had stopped, but the sky was still overcast. The train pulled up at the west-bound platform.

When the Dalmanes had stepped down from the train onto the platform they looked around to see whether anything had changed noticeably since their last visit to Cockermouth station; but everything looked just the same as before. About a minute after it had stopped the train started again from the station to continue its run down to Workington, and the Dalmanes were then able to get a better view of the opposite platform, which had been the place where they had spent most of their long wait on that previous occasion.

"Nothing much seems to have changed," said Susan. "Look, there's the bench we sat on while we were drinking tea with Mr. and Mrs. Beck—before you and Mr. Beck went off on that walk up the line."

"That ended with me being arrested," said John. "Heavens, what a fiasco that affair was! But look here, Sue, hadn't we better be moving on? Where shall we go first? Where does that Mr. Sandy live?"

"In Lorton Road," said Susan, remembering the address she had written in her diary. "But we don't want to start by going to visit Jim's father. Anyway, he wouldn't be in at this time of day, so we'll go and look him up one evening when he comes home from his mine—we'll have plenty of days here if we want to stay in the town. Let's start by going into the town to look for our hotel: it'll probably be about lunch time by the time we've found it, and seen our room."

"Right, but the stationmaster's coming along to say something to us." The stationmaster had been talking to a small group of people near the end of that platform, but he had seen the Dalmanes standing on the platform looking, he thought, lost; so now he came along to offer to be of assistance. The porter, he knew, was still busy moving some crates of merchandise which had been loaded off the train, so he (the stationmaster) would carry those peoples' suitcases himself.

"Good morning, sir; good morning, madam," he said politely. "May I carry those suitcases for you?"

"Oh, thank you very much," said Susan. "Take them out of the station, if you like, but I think we can manage them ourselves after that."

"Have you a car coming for you, madam," asked the stationmaster, "or are you, perhaps, intending to walk to somewhere in the town?"

"We're booked in at the 'Lakes Hotel' so we thought we'd walk there," said Susan. "I don't suppose it's far to walk?"

"Oh no, you haven't far to walk: about half a mile, perhaps, at the most. Is this your first visit to Cockermouth?"

"No, we've been at the station once before, but we've never seen the town properly. Can you direct us to the 'Lakes Hotel'?"

"Certainly, madam," said the stationmaster. "I'll just carry these cases for you as far as the road, and set you off on the right way." They had been standing on the platform talking, but now the stationmaster lead the way out through the subway and the booking hall to the yard outside the station. He put the two suitcases down beside the War Memorial statue where the station yard adjoined the public road. "Here you are," he said, it'll be no more than about ten minutes walk, I should think, to the 'Lakes Hotel' from here. You just walk down this main road, and you'll find yourselves at the top end of Station Street, which you can see from here at the bend by the junction of Lorton Street, just beyond the cinema." (He pointed the way). "Then keep on down Station Street to the junction of Main Street at the bottom of it. You turn left there, and walk along Main Street—it's a wide tree-lined street—past the Mayo Statue and past Wordsworth House, and then you'll see your hotel on the right-hand side of the street, just before you come to the Catholic Church." The Dalmanes attended carefully to these directions, thanked the stationmaster warmly for his kindness, picked up their cases, and set off walking down Station Road as the stationmaster went back to his office.

"I say, John," said Susan, "we could have asked him about Mr. Ruddock. He's sure to know him as he still works on this line."

"To ask the stationmaster <u>what</u>, my dear?" said John.

"To ask him which are the trains from here that Mr. Ruddock drives," said Susan, "so that, if possible, we could choose one he's driving and go back on it ourselves when we return to Penrith. I'd so much like to have a chance to have a word with him again."

"I'm afraid we'll have to take a chance on that, my dear," said John. "We really can't pick and choose which train we'll depart on, you know; it'll depend on the rest of our plans because of the connections southwards."

"Yes, I know it will. But perhaps he'll be driving the 10.8 train, the same as he was before. We might as well go by that train, don't you think?"

"If we're going straight up to London, without stopping off at Saint Helens, then I'd say, yes, we'll take the 10.8 train from here—if it still runs at that time. Otherwise, if we're going to stay a night at Saint Helens with my brother, then I should think we might do better to leave here on the early train, the seven something, isn't it? Look here, perhaps we'd better sort this out this evening. I'll ring Dick again this evening." Dick Dalmane (Sir Richard Dalmane, Baronet) was Lord Dalmane's younger brother who lived at the family's ancestral home at Saint Helens in Lancashire. Jonn and Susan had rung him up the evening before from the Padgates' house, Dallam Hall, and had got no reply. The idea was that they would make a courtesy call on Dick Dalmane and his wife on their way home, not because they wanted to (Lord Dalmane rather disliked his brother, and Susan found him ostentatious and disagreeable), but simply because it would be diplomatic to make such a call. But now they began to think that Dick and his wife must be away on their holidays.

"I think they must be away," said Susan. "Do you think, John, if we again get no reply when we ring up tonight—"

"Yes," said John. "They're not expecting us. We'll forget about going to Saint Helens if there's no reply again. That would leave us free to go direct up to London, starting on the 10.8 from here."

"I say, John, what a small town this seems to be! I suppose this wide street here is the Main Street—we seem to have come to the bottom of Station Street?"

"We have. I walked up and down these streets a few times when I was here that other time—you know, when I had four hours to kill while waiting for the Sergeant to give me a lift in his police car to Carlisle. I had a very slow morning coffee and a lunch at the Globe Hetel to put in time—that one's the Globe, over there to the right."

"But you didn't find the 'Lakes Hotel' that time?" asked Susan.

"No I didn't; but I didn't walk much further down Main Street that time than that statue." He pointed to the left down the wide street to the place where the statue of Earl Mayo stood in the middle of the street. "He was some Irish Earl, I gathered, the Earl of Mayo, I believe, but I forget his name."

"Well," said Susan, "let's cross over by that statue to be on the right side for our hotel; and we can have a closer look at Lord Mayo."

They crossed Main Street by the statue, pausing there to read the tablet on the pedestal, from which they gathered that the name of the imposing stone figure gazing down the street was Richard Bourke, who had been the sixth Earl of Mayo and a Viceroy of India. Then they walked slowly on along a pavement rather crowded with shoppers and presently saw the "Lakes Hotel".

When Lord Dalmane telephoned his brother that evening he was answered by a housekeeper who told him that Sir Richard and Lady Dalmane were on holiday in Switzerland, and would not be back until September 6th. "So that settles that," he said to Susan afterwards. "We don't have to go to Saint Helens, thank goodness."

"Good," said Susan. "So if we leave here on the twenty-fourth, as we planned, we could spend that night in London, couldn't we—seeing we didn't plan to get back home until the day after at tea-time?"

"I don't see why not," said John.

For the next fortnight the Dalmanes enjoyed a very pleasant holiday in and around the Lake District. They had hired a car on the afternoon of their arrival by train at Cockermouth, and toured around locally visiting Buttermere, Wasdale, Eskdale, Keswick and

Borrowdale, Ullswater, and many other places. During the first week of this part of their holiday they stayed at night at the "Lakes Hotel" in Cockermouth, but during the second week they moved further south and stayed at Windermere and at Coniston. They returned to Cockermouth on the last day to hand over the hired car to the garage from which they had hired it. The weather was kind to them for most of this period, and although there were a few rather cloudy days there was little rain, and they had plenty of sunshine on most of the days. John and Susan gave themselves plenty of time for walking on the fells and by the lakes, as well as doing sight-seeing by car. During all this time Susan felt that she was just an ordinary tourist like anyone else, and was happy to be just herself on holiday, as was John. They knew that their holiday was of an unconventional kind for the titled classes, but enjoyed it all the more for the informality they had chosen.

They stayed their last night in the Lake District at the "Lakes Hotel" again, and on the next morning they went up to the station to catch the 10.8 train. When it came in they were very pleased to see that Mr. Ruddock was driving it. There was just time for a quick word with him while they stood on the platform and Mr. Ruddock leaned from the window of his cab; then they boarded the train, and so travelled up to Carlisle. Susan found the journey much the same as her trip that way of two years ago, although this time there was, of course, no question of her going into the driver's cab in order to see the scenery better. But she thought that, as this time John was with her, the journey was even more enjoyable than last time, even if she could not again have an unimpeded view of the line ahead.

There was a short wait on Platform Four of Carlisle Station until the 12.5 train to London, the "Thames-Clyde Express", came in from Glasgow. It had been Lord Dalmanes's idea to travel by this train, instead of by the "Royal Scot", so that he and Susan could enjoy a trip up to London by a different route from their usual one. As they left Carlisle on this train the Dalmanes were in high expectation of an impressive run through the scenic part of the route, the Carlisle to Settle section of the line, as the day was, by good luck, hot and sunny, but with some small white clouds in the sky: excellent weather for seeing the high Pennines in all their glory. Just after the train had passed through Garsdale station, and was heading for Rise Hill Tunnel, John said, almost casually: "Wouldn't it be a pity if they were to close this line some day? It has been rumoured, you know, that British Railways have <u>thought</u> of doing that, although nothing like that is likely to happen for some years yet."

"What!" said Susan. "It would be a disaster if they closed this beautiful route! I'm sure the local people want it."

"Yes, that's just what I think," said John.

The express train brought them to Saint Pancras station in London soon after seven o' clock that evening. From there they took a taxi to Lord Dalmane's London house in Roehampton. Their holiday was all but over, and it was a measure of how much Susan had enjoyed it that she had hardly ever given Jim Sandy a thought since she had left home. It was getting on for four in the afternoon next day when the car drove up the main drive of Rhodes Castle and Susan noticed Jim busily directing a party of tourists around the grounds. I wonder whether he's missed me much, she thought, and then: Our picnic . . . yes, we'll go next Tuesday.

CHAPTER NINE

What a gorgeous day it is, thought Jim Sandy, looking out of the window of his room in Rhodes Castle. It was a Tuesday morning, and the sun was shining in a cloudless sky. And it's my day off work, said Jim to himself. What luck! I think I'll go off somewhere on my bike: it looks just the day for it, although it may get very hot later, unless the day turns more cloudy. Then the thought crossed his mind how very pleasant it would be to go for a bicycle ride with Susan, but he had to dismiss this idea as an idle fantasy. At the back of his mind he knew very well that Susan would never agree to accompany him on a ride on her bicycle, and especially not if there were no one else riding with them. He had an idea that, after the exciting adventures of that long walk in Surrey, Susan was being more strict with herself in not allowing any situation to arise in which she would be alone with him. All the same, he thought, with Lord Dalmane away all this week at that conference in London, there <u>ought</u> to be some opportunity, some occasion when we can at least meet.

Four days had passed since the Dalmanes had come back to Rhodes Castle after their holiday, but all Jim had seen of Susan had been a brief glimpse of her as she had stepped out of the car at the front door on that Friday afternoon of her return home. Similarly, he had only glimpsed Lord Dalmane since the holiday on that same occasion; in fact, if he had not happened to see the Dalmanes stepping out of their car he would not even be sure whether they had returned, or not. As for their holiday, Jim knew nothing at all, as Susan had never said anything to him about it before she left, so he did not know even where they had been, except that it was somewhere "in the North of England" (that much he had heard from Major Ambrose). He was not particularly curious to know any more, but rather hoped all the same that Susan would find some opportunity presently to tell him something about it.

While he dressed, Jim was turning over in his mind where to go for a ride on his new bicycle. Somewhere I haven't been to before, he thought. And I ought to make a round of it, rather than there and back over the same road. Yetminster? Yes, that would do for a start, but then where? I've been on the Yeovil road from there before, and the Chetnole road. Where else could I go from Yetminster? What about Netherton? And Closworth? But would I have time to go any further? Isn't there a road south from Closworth, towards the Downs? What about that way.? I must look at my map. He finished dressing, sat down at his desk, and opened a map of Dorset. He pored over this for a few minutes, and was just thinking of folding it up to go downstairs to have some breakfast, before making a more detailed study of the map afterwards, when he was startled by a knock at his door.

He had heard no one moving in the corridor outside his door, and anyway it was most unusual for anyone to knock on his door so early in the morning—it was not yet eight o' clock. "Come in," he called, wondering who it could possibly be; but when Susan came cheerfully into his room, he could only, for the moment, exclaim in joyful surprise: "Susan!"

"Hello, Jim," she said. "I'm sorry to call on you so early, although I thought I might find you in your room now. I hope you don't mind me coming here?"

"Not at all!"

"Jim, as it's your day off, and as I've nothing in particular to do today, I wondered whether you'd like to come out with me? But perhaps you'd planned to do something else today?"

"But I'd simply <u>love</u> to come out with you today!" said Jim, trying not to sound quite as excited as he suddenly felt.

"Are you sure?" asked Susan. "I see you've a map spread out there. Hadn't you planned to do something else? Would you have gone out on your bike if I hadn't asked you to come out with me?"

"Well," said Jim, "I was thinking of doing that. But I hadn't made any definite plans yet of where I was going to. But what did you have in mind, Sue—to go out in the car, or on your bike? Perhaps we could ride somewhere together? Won't you sit down, Sue, while we talk?"

"Thanks," said Susan, and sat down on the end of his bed; Jim sat down again in his desk chair. "I think," continued Susan, "that maybe it would be best for us to use the car this time—that is, if you'd like to come with me. I was thinking of a picnic. It's a nice enough day for a picnic, but I wasn't thinking of going very far."

"Oh well, distance doesn't matter very much, does it? But I'd love to come with you for a picnic, if you want me to come!" He could hardly believe that what he and Susan were saying to each other about a picnic together could be real: he almost wondered whether he was still dreaming, and had yet to wake up (he had dreamed about Susan that night, as often before).

"Fine. Then you can come with me in the car; but we won't be starting until nearer lunch time, as we're only taking a fairly local trip."

"Had you a place in mind?"

"Yes—roughly; I thought we might go up into the Downs, somewhere Hillfield way perhaps." She paused a moment and glanced at Jim's partly spread-out map. "No, look here, I'll tell you later where we're going," she added. "I haven't much time now, and I don't want to keep you from your breakfast."

"What time would you like me to be ready for?"

"Oh, I think about twelve o' clock would be soon enough to start for a lunch picnic. You'd better meet me secretly somewhere in the grounds just after twelve, and I'll pick you up with the car. So if you're not doing anything else, Jim, you see there'll still be time for you to go cycling somewhere first."

"Yes, I'll do that; thank you, Sue."

"Now, look here," said Susan, speaking now more confidentially. "I want to keep this a closely guarded secret that I'm going out somewhere with you in the car. We must be very careful that no one gets a hint of what we're doing . . ." She went on to outline to Jim her carefully thought-out plans to allow the two of them to slip quietly away from Rhodes Castle unnoticed by anyone. Then, having given Jim precise instructions on where in the grounds he was to meet her at about five minutes past twelve, Susan said Good-bye to him and hurried away; and Jim went happily and thoughtfully to his breakfast. It certainly promised to be a pleasant day in more ways than just the weather.

It was a few minutes before twelve noon, and Jim was lying low in a dense thicket of bushes beside the rough track which lead from the Castle to Lewes Farm, while he kept a sharp lookout on the roadway for Susan's car. Susan had told him to wait for her in the bushes just short of the gateway where the track lead out from the Castle gardens (where there was a cattle grid instead of a gate as outside the track was unfenced, and ran across the parkland towards the farm). It was a way out to the public road which the Dalmanes hardly ever used as parts of it were too rough and full of potholes for comfortable motoring; but Susan reckoned that she was less likely to be noticed driving that way than if she were to go by the main drive, which ran past two lodges. Jim remembered that a little further down that track was a place where it divided into two tracks, one of which ran into the farmyard and was a dead-end, while the other went on until it lead out into the road, so luckily by going that way they would not need to drive past the farm buildings. If it had been necessary to drive through the farmyard someone, thought Jim, would almost certainly have spotted him being driven with Susan in her car. He was not at all sure of where they were going to aim for as their picnic place: Susan had been rather vague in saying simply "somewhere Hillfield way", and he did not know exactly where Hillfield was, although he thought it was a village which lay somewhere to the south of the Castle.

Suddenly he remembered that he had that map of Dorset with him. Jim took a careful look along the track in the direction of the Castle, but could see no sign of Susan's car, so he opened the map. He found the little village of Hillfield roughly where he had thought it was. I see, he thought, Sue's going to leave the Castle by a very round about way so that, if anyone <u>does</u> see her driving away from home, he'd think she was heading towards Sherborne, whereas really we're going to be heading almost exactly the other way once we're out onto the main road. Sherborne lay some seven miles to the north of Rhodes Castle, but Hillfield nestled in a hollow just below the Downs, about south from the Castle.

Jim was beginning to feel impatient for Susan to arrive at the secret rendez-vous. He had been so anxious not to be late that he had been there since just before ten minutes to twelve. After breakfast he had gone out for a quick bike ride, more or less on the line of his original plans; but Susan's early morning visit to his room had changed the whole feel of the day for him, so that eager anticipation of the picnic with her had taken away some of the pleasure of a bicycle ride by himself. He had cut down that ride to a much shorter outing than anything originally envisaged as clearly what mattered most for him now was to be waiting where Susan had told him to wait in good time. As he had ridden to Yetminster he had taken in virtually nothing of what there was to be seen, so busy was he thinking about the picnic to come; until he had come to the little station at Yetminster on the line from Yeovil to

Weymouth, which he had glanced at as he passed. He had looked down at the pretty little River Wriggle in the village as he passed over the bridge, and had continued on his way to the smaller village of Netherton, again not noticing much of the scenery because he was too busy thinking, and that in spite of the fact that he was now riding over a road new to him. He had gone a little further than Netherton, and had stopped for a few minutes to look without much interest at the water in the reservoir, which was like a little ornamental lake; and then he had decided that he had better go no further, although he would have liked to ride on through Closworth on the road which lead up into the North Dorset Downs around Chelborough and Uphall. He had bicycled back via the same roads, and had arrived back at the Castle, very hot and slightly breathless, having ridden very hard for fear of being late; but the whole ride had taken him less than an hour, and still he had plenty of time to spare before the appointed time for the secret meeting with Susan.

It was very hot for Jim lurking in the dense thicket of bushes in the strong midday sun of late August, although he managed to keep more or less in the shade. He did not think it wise to move from his place of concealment as it had now gone twelve o' clock, and he knew that Susan's car ought to appear at any minute. Although he felt hot, he was not really uncomfortable waiting there; he did not mean to move until the car drew up beside him, when he would step quickly into it. Five past twelve, he said to himself. Sue ought to be in sight by now; and a moment later: Good, here she is! The car had come into sight being driven slowly, cautiously, and as silently as Susan could manage, as it approached the clump of bushes where Jim was awaiting it.

A few minutes later Susan and Jim in Susan's car had left the Castle grounds and were driving south along the A352 main road as if they were bound for Dorchester.

"So where, exactly, are we going?" asked Jim who, to lessen the risk of being seen in Susan's car by anyone who knew him, was sitting in the back seat.

"We'll go through Hillfield, like I said before," said Susan, "and then up to Batcombe Hill, which is just a mile or two on the other side of the village. Have you been that way on your bike yet, Jim?"

"Not yet," said Jim, "but I will soon: I'd like to explore all the small roads around here."

"It's very nice up on Batcombe Hill, as you'll soon see," said Susan. "I've been for a picnic up there once before with John, when we found a very pleasant, secluded little spot near the road, but not too near: an ideal place for a picnic, and with a good view too."

"And that's where we're heading for?"

"Yes, that's our place for today. We'll be in the shade of the trees there, which may be just as well, as full sunshine might be a bit overpowering today."

"Yes, it's getting very hot."

It certainly was becoming very warm, but in the car with the windows fully wound down while Susan was driving fast along the main road they were in a strong draught, and felt quite cool enough. It began to look, however, as if the sun would presently be obscured by clouds, which were rapidly rising in the sky from the south; but they were puffy, white, fine weather clouds: there was as yet no hint of rain in the sky. For a few minutes neither spoke, and then, as they approached a certain crossroads, Susan slowed her car down and turned off the main road to the right. Jim looked at the signpost which had "Hermitage" printed on it, pointing in their direction. He opened a few folds of his map of Dorset in order to see where this new road, a very small one, would lead them to.

"Good," said Susan, seeing the map. "I'm glad you've remembered to bring that map: I think I may need to stop to look at it to be sure of our way."

"Now?" enquired Jim.

"No, not yet," said Susan. "This is the right road for Hillfield, going through Hermitage, although it might have been a little quicker to have gone further along the main road and to have turned off for Batcombe Hill at Dogbury Gate."

"Yes, I see," said Jim a moment later, finding the place on the map. "But I expect this small road is much prettier?"

"It is; and as we're not particularly in a hurry now that we've got properly away from home, I thought we'd go this way. But I'm going to pull up when we get near Hillfield and have a look at your map, if I may. I'm not certain which road to take beyond there, as there are several small roads branching off, and I can't remember it properly as it's some time since I was last this way."

While she was speaking, Jim noticed that the small road, which twisted about a good deal, was beginning to rise towards higher ground. "The road's beginning to climb already towards the Downs," he observed.

"A little, yes," said Susan, "but it climbs really steeply after Hillfield. You'll see. There are the Downs, just ahead of us, and Batcombe Hill is somewhere over there." She pointed vaguely ahead through the windscreen. "Going up from this side is almost as steep, I should say, as some of the hills we found in the North."

"Oh!" said Jim, suddenly being reminded of it, "How did you enjoy your holiday? You haven't told me anything about it yet."

"We enjoyed it very much indeed, thank you."

"Were you in the Lake District?"

"Yes. We started with two nights with the Padgates at Dallam Hall, and then went up to the Lake District for the rest of the holiday. We stayed in your old home town, Cockermouth, for quite a bit of the time, and we met your father and your two sisters for dinner one evening. We talked with your father for quite a while, which was interesting."

Jim suddenly looked worried at the mention of his father. "Oh," he said shortly as Susan had paused as if she expected him to make some remark. There was a short, awkward silence while Jim was wondering what the Dalmanes had said about him to his father, and while Susan was recollecting an idea which had first occoured to her while she had been having that talk with Mr. Sandy. She had thought then that some time, and probably not in the too distant future, she would be forced to give Jim his notice of dismissal from her service in the Castle because, naturally, the story was sure to get around that they were having an affair. As she remembered that idea again now she suddenly frowned, for it jarred painfully against her present carefree, happy mood. But here I am, she thought, taking a private, furtive outing with Jim: doing the one thing, in fact, which John would definitely <u>not</u> approve of. If he should get to know about it . . . oh, but he mustn't! But even so, sooner or later, someone is <u>bound</u> to say something to John about us having an affair . . . and Jim will have to be sacked. Well, I don't want to think about it now. She saw the worried look on Jim's face, and guessed something of the thoughts that were passing through <u>his</u> mind. She smiled again, not realising that Jim had seen the sudden frown on her forehead a moment earlier, and was anxiously wondering what it meant.

"Don't worry, Jim," she said with deliberate cheerfulness. "I know what you were thinking. You were wondering what sort of things I'd said about you to your father, weren't you? Particularly whether we'd dropped any hints that your one fault is that you are far too friendly with me!"

Jim blushed. "Yes, I was wondering whether you'd said anything about that," he said.

"Well, we didn't, so you can cheer up on that score! If you want to know what sort of things about you we <u>did</u> talk about, I can tell you that I told your dad what an excellent worker you are, and how very well you're getting on in your job with us."

"Oh, thank you very much, Sue; that was kind of you," said Jim, very relieved to know that his father had not been told anything he did not wish him to know of what really went on at Rhodes Castle nowadays between himself and Susan, when they had a chance, as at the moment. He saw how Susan was smiling at him and smiled himself, never guessing that only moments earlier Susan had been thinking about his possible dismissal.

"And another thing," said Susan. "Your dad asked us when you would be having <u>your</u> holiday, and whether you'd be going home for it; so we said that, if it's all the same to you, you could start your holiday the last week in September."

"Thank you," said Jim again. "Yes, I might as well go home for a fortnight from September 25th—I think that's the last Monday in the month." He had forgotten about his own holiday arrangements and was not particularly pleased to be reminded about them when he was about to have a private picnic with Susan because it would mean a further period of separation from her. He had talked a few weeks earlier to his immediate boss, Major Ambrose, about his holiday, and Major Ambrose had afterwards spoken to Susan, but no decision had been reached on the dates for his holiday. This was not a prospect which interested Jim very much anyway, since he could not take Susan with him if he went North, and so he had given the matter little thought.

Then Susan pulled the car up, seeing a convenient wide place in the narrow road by a field gate. Jim handed over his map, already opened at the correct folds for reading the country marked on it around Hillfield. They had stopped about half a mile short of the village of Hillfield because even here, although they were about five miles from Rhodes Castle (as the crow flies—it was much further than that by the devious route they had taken) Susan did not want to take the risk of some busybody who might recognize her seeing her in the car with Jim Sandy. She knew that this risk would have been even greater if they had pulled up in the village, where there might be people about, than in the countryside; but even before the car stopped both Susan and Jim looked warily around, including in the adjacent fields, to be sure that no one was there to notice them—but they saw no one. Jim was just as much aware of the implications of the danger of being seen together with Susan as she was, although they had said nothing to each other about this since he had got into the car.

They went on a minute or two later when Susan was sure of which road to take to reach her intended destination. Jim noticed that the village of Hillfield was only a tiny place; he and Susan saw no one in the road as they passed the few houses and took the road which runs past the Friary and up to Batcombe Hill. As the car went on its way, and presently began to climb the steep hill, Susan, who seemed to have resumed her carefree, easy mood, continued to chat to Jim about how her holiday had been spent. She told him something about the train journeys she had made with her husband, about meeting Mr. Beck and Mr. Ruddock, and about some of the places they had visited in the Lake District.

"This is our way," said Susan a little later, interrupting her narrative for a moment, as she turned the car suddenly to the right onto an even narrower road than the ones they had thus far followed. It was a minute road, hardly suitable for motor cars and only just wide enough for Susan's car to pass along it: a road almost more like a farm track than a road, with many pot-holes and, in places, grass growing along the middle of it. It ran along the top ridge of the Downs before winding its way down to a narrow valley which opened out towards the south. They came into an area thickly wooded on either side of the road, and Susan stopped talking and seemed to be carefully looking for some place she would recognize.

"Here we are: this is the place," she said cheerfully as she saw a wider place where a grassy track through the trees joined the road. She pulled the car well over to the side of the road to leave room enough for another vehicle to squeeze past it, if necessary, stopped the engine, and opened the driver's door.

"Just stay where you are a moment, Jim, while I scout around to see if the coast's clear for you to get out," she said as she stepped out of the car.

"Okay," said Jim.

The green track through the trees was not marked as a Public Footpath, and as Jim watched Susan climb neatly over the fence across the opening of it (there was no gate or stile) he thought that it must be a private path and that, strictly speaking, they would be trespassing by walking over it; it looked, indeed, he thought, as if the farmer who owned the land must at some time have taken out a stile or a gate there to block up the entrance to the path to keep trespassers out. Well, what does it matter if it's trespassing, so long as we don't get caught doing it? he thought. Sue and I were trespassers on that other walk—we all were—when we took that short cut through that dense thicket that was part of somebody's garden. Then we trespassed again by walking on that railway line when we stepped over the live rails.

Susan had quickly disappeared from his view into the trees, and it was several minutes later when she re-appeared from a different direction.

"It's all clear," she said quietly when she had come back to the car. "You can get out now, Jim. I've had a good look round, and there's not a sign of anybody either in our picnic place or anywhere around here."

"Good," said Jim. "Then we can take the things out of the car. Shall I carry the basket?"

"All right, and I'll carry the rug," said Susan.

"It can't be far to walk from here, is it?"

"Oh no; you can't see it from here because of the trees, which makes it all the better, but it's hardly a hundred yards away up that track. It's a nice place for a picnic, as you'll see—it's where John and I had a picnic soon after we were married."

"Oh. But do you think that track is really a private path, Sue? It isn't marked as a footpath."

"I don't know whether it's really private: there are no notices telling people not to trespass. But it doesn't look to me like a public footpath either, which is all to the good."

"Yes, of course. We want a bit of privacy, don't we, Sue?" He grinned meaningly at her.

"Indeed we do! Well, you'll see, trespassing or not, it's a private sort of place where we can sit down together . . . or lie down together—and, hopefully, not be disturbed. Come on, Jim, this way!"

They clasped each other's hands for a moment, and then climbed over the fence one at a time, passing over the heavy baggage they had brought with them. Then Susan slung the large rug over her shoulder, and they walked hand in hand slowly up the steep slope of the grassy lane, Jim carrying the picnic basket in his free hand. As he walked he felt his excitement mounting almost step by step. They were only holding hands now, but he knew that very soon they would be embracing and kissing.

"Well, Jim," said Susan, "it seems we've been lucky so far in not being recognized. I think we got away from the Castle without anyone noticing us going away together; in fact, I'm pretty sure we did. And, so far as we know, no one has followed us, and there's no one around here."

"It's a jolly good place because it's so out of the way: not the sort of place most people would even know about," said Jim, looking around him and wondering exactly where the place was. It must, he thought, be very well hidden from that little road. "Hardly a hundred yards away," Susan had said, but he reckoned that they must have already walked about half of that distance. "And I was very careful about not being seen when I was getting into my hiding place in the bushes," he added. "I don't believe anyone saw me on my way there."

"Good," said Susan. "Let's not worry about that any more now. We're in a really out-of-the-way place here, so let's relax and enjoy ourselves. Now, where's that overgrown path got to? Ah, this must be it. We go this way now, Jim." She turned suddenly to her left and lead the way along a little path which was so overgrown that it was hardly a path at all. It was, in fact, more as if Susan and Jim were pushing their way through a dense thicket of branches and briars, but a few seconds later they came out into Susan's private picnic place.

Jim saw at once that it was a perfect place for lovers to enjoy outdoor privacy with each other. He set the heavy picnic basket down on the short grass at his feet. They were standing in a little grassy hollow of the chalk downland, a roughly circular hollow which was only a few yards in diameter. The hollow was on the side of the hill so that it had a general slope downwards in the same direction as that of the green lane up which they had just walked. It was covered only with short grass, perfectly dry, so that their rug was not going to be really necessary; and in the grass there were small chalk-loving downland wild flowers growing, mostly harebells and yellow vetch. The little grassy hollow was almost completely shut in by a dense screen of thick and tangled vegetation, except where the overgrown path came into it on the east side, and another point on the perimeter where there was a slightly larger gap to the south. Above the lower leaves and branches of the undergrowth, which hid the place so effectively the branches of the taller trees hung well over the hollow, casting a dappled shade over it. From inside the hollow one could not see out except where the larger gap in the undergrowth on the low, south side of the depression gave a spy-hole view down to the road and beyond it, well down the course of the narrow, dry valley of Sydling Saint Nicholas (this village was a few miles further down the valley).

The sun had come out from behind a cloud, and strong shadows of the tree branches were cast on the ground. The place was fairly well sheltered from the wind, a fresh breeze from the south-east, as the first part of the valley below them ran down towards the south-west, so that there was sheltering spur of higher ground immediately to the south-east. It had felt pleasantly cool a moment earlier with the sunlight occluded by a cloud, but now Susan and Jim felt the air suddenly become hotter again.

"What a gorgeous place this is," said Jim. "It's beautifully well hidden by these trees and bushes, and yet there's this lovely view as well when you look through that gap. I say, Sue, this grass is so dry that we could sit on it without bothering about using the rug."

"Yes, I know," said Susan, "but we may as well use the rug seeing that we've brought it." She had spread it on the ground, and now they both sat down on it beside their picnic basket. "It is a splendid place for us," she continued, "but, my word, isn't it hot now that the sun's come out again? I think, maybe, I'd feel more comfortable if I were to take off a layer . . . You wouldn't mind if I took off my blouse, Jim?"

"Not a bit!" said Jim enthusiastically.

Susan, of course, knew that by removing her blouse she would be greatly encouraging and increasing the excitement of her companion, but in her present carefree mood she felt that it would be a good thing to do that. She peeled the green and white garment slowly off, and saw that Jim was carefully watching her do it without making it too obvious that he was very interested. He noted with delight that the upper part of her body was now exposed naked to his view except for her breasts which were still concealed within her bra. Almost he decided to take off his shirt so as to be the same as Susan, stripped to the waist, but when he had undone the buttons he felt a little shy, and decided that he would not do this until Susan took off her bra; and he had high hopes that she would do this in due course. Her mood, in fact, surprised him very much. He interpreted her present gaiety as being carefree almost to the point of being <u>careless</u>, or even reckless—with apparently little regard for the consequences of exciting him so much—and it made him wonder in the back of his mind why she was acting as she was. It had been surprising enough that she had asked him to accompany her on this furtive, secret picnic, but he thought for a moment that for her to start undressing with himself there to watch everything was a really surprising developement. Did it mean that she was deliberately acting provocatively, encouraging him to have ideas of having sex with her? No, he thought, it did not mean that: she must, of course, know that there was an element of provocation necessarily involved in stripping off some of her clothing but, after all, it <u>was</u> hot, and no doubt she was going to feel cooler and more comfortable with less clothes on. Really, he thought, it meant no more than that; but, of course, it was very exciting all the same. Heavens! he said to himself, those bra cups must hold in place a large, round pair of lovely breasts!

"That's right," said Susan a moment later, as she dug about in the basket, looking for the bottle of wine, "take a good look, Jim! Just for once, I'd <u>like</u> you to have a good look at me, and enjoy it—and I promise you I won't mind a bit, even if you want to stare at me! Perhaps later on I'll take off my bra and let you see what my breasts really look like. But let's get on with our picnic first." She had a bottle of red wine in one hand and a corkscrew in the other. "Shall we have a drink first, Jim?"

"Yes, let's," said Jim. "Shall I open that bottle, Sue?"

"All right." She handed over the bottle and corkscrew. "A little alcohol will help us to lose our inhibitions, and help us to relax, act naturally, and enjoy ourselves. Sit <u>really</u> close to me, Jim, my love, when you've pulled that cork out, and we'll have a good time!" Jim had stood up to use the corkscrew to draw the cork from the wine bottle. He had found this reasonably easy, and now he put the bottle carefully down in the basket, where they would not accidentally knock it over, and as he sat down again beside Susan on the rug, he decided that she was right that they should enjoy each other's company fully while they could. The wine, he knew, was going to help him to slip into a mood as relaxed and carefree as Susan's already seemed to be, so he decided there and then to let himself be swept along into whatever adventures were going to happen. But at first he put an arm rather shyly around Susan, a little afraid to take the lead in the matter of showing his love for her. He noticed that her body was already well sun-tanned, so he knew that she must have been doing plenty of sun-bathing in private at home, and he wondered whether she took off her bra when she was doing this. Her body struck him by its beauty, clad just as it was in only her bra, a pair of shorts, and with red ankle-socks and white gym shoes on her feet. The shorts, he knew, were a very unusual garment for her, and he guessed rightly that they had been especially selected for today for his benefit. Susan rarely wore any kind of trousers, as she preferred to be seen in more feminine garments, either skirt or dress.

Susan responded straight away, as Jim had hoped that she would, to her lover's shy embrace around her waist by clasping him in her arms and kissing him on the cheek. "Sue, my darling, you're <u>so</u> lovely!" murmured Jim in reply, as he kissed her gently on the cheeks. He had read her signals correctly: she clearly wanted him to make loving advances towards her, so he was more than happy to oblige. But it was hard for him to believe then, and it became even harder as the afternoon wore on, that Susan had not for long been his girlfriend. As they held a kiss for a few long seconds of ecstacy he somehow felt as if he had been used to knowing her intimately like this every day in the past for months, or even years. The truth was strangely hard to grasp: that he had not kissed her since that June night two months ago, and before that, perhaps not for nearly a whole year. But he was strongly reminded now of how they had kissed in the train on his very first day with Susan.

"Sue, darling," he said, "this makes me think of that lovely day when I met you for the very first time, when we kissed in the 'Royal Scot' on our way from Carlisle to London."

"Does it put you in mind of that day, my love? Yes, that was very delightful, I remember. With you it was love at first sight, wasn't it? You've been madly in love with me ever since that day, I know. Come, let's have a drink, and then we'll eat something."

Their mutual embrace broke apart. Susan had brought two glasses in the picnic basket, carefully wrapped up in a tea towel so that they would not be broken; she now unwrapped these, stood them on the rug, and poured out some wine. They clinked the two glasses together, beamed lovingly at each other, and drank.

"That was a really memorable trip we had in the 'Royal Scot' that day," said Susan thoughtfully a little later. "You know, I like nearly all the journey by that line, not just the pretty bit over Shap. I enjoy going through South Lancashire that way and seeing Preston, Wigan, and Warrington; I suppose, because there are such different things to see around there—I mean different from the Shap moorlands. And then it was so pleasant when we got past Rugby to see the big, rolling fields of the South, so different from the little fields with dry-stone walls in the North."

"I thought that part of the journey through the hilly country around Tring and Berkhamstead looked rather like it does round here," observed Jim.

"The Chilterns are chalk country, the same as it is in this hilly part of Dorset," said Susan, "so it's not surprising that around here looks somewhat similar to that country to the north-west of London. I know the Chilterns quite well around Berkhamstead from when I lived near there."

"When you lived on the north-western fringe of London, you mean? Where exactly was the place?"

"Hatch End, it was, between Harrow and Watford. That was a nice house and almost as good as living in the country."

"Yes, I remember you telling us in the train that we were passing within a mile or two of your old house."

"I can't say that I really know the countryside of Dorset yet like I got to know Hertfordshire," said Susan, "but then I didn't know Hertfordshire well either, except around Knebworth—I didn't really know it as I know the lovely country around home—I mean my parents' home, Soken Hall, by the Walton Backwaters in north-east Essex. I'd like to take you there sometime, Jim, to meet mother and father, and to go boating on the Backwaters. But I suppose this ridge of chalk hills we're sitting on now must be a continuation of the South Downs westwards . . . or perhaps of the North Downs. I can't remember how the map goes." Susan took another sip of her wine and then said: "Right, Jim, let's start on the sandwiches. Are you hungry?"

"Yes," said Jim, suddenly feeling hungry at the mention of sandwiches, which reminded him that it must be time for lunch. Until then he had been too infatuated by Susan's close presence to him to remember anything about hunger, but he had been interested by what Susan had just said about her old home. Yes, I'd like Sue to take me there and show me those Backwaters, he said to himself.

"I've brought two kinds of sandwiches for us," said Susan. "Which would you like first: chicken or cheese? We had some cold roast chicken over from the other day so we've put it into the sandwiches, but we made some cheese sandwiches as well." She took a large paper package, which contained two smaller packages inside it, out of the basket, put it on the rug, and began unwrapping sandwiches, while Jim wondered for a moment who she meant by "we". Did someone in the Castle kitchen know that Susan was taking a picnic somewhere?

"I think I'll start with a chicken sandwich, please," he said after a thoughtful pause. "Thank you, Sue." He beamed a radiant smile at her as he took a sandwich off the top of the pile of sandwiches she held out to him. Susan, who did not feel particularly hungry, took a cheese sandwich. But after eating a few mouthfuls of his, Jim said: "I say, Sue, there wasn't any awkwardness about preparing these, was there? I mean, surely someone else must have been in the kitchen with you when you were making them, and would realise that you must be taking sandwiches out on a picnic?"

"I don't think you need worry about that, Jim," said Susan. "One of the reasons why I chose today for the picnic was that Cook is away today. She might well have found out everything if she'd been there. And Samantha is off for most of the day. Only young Sandra, the kitchen maid, was with me in the kitchen, helping to make the sandwiches and prepare the other things, and of course I told her absolutely nothing about what I wanted all these things for, and she didn't ask any questions about it. Anyway, I always regard Sandra as being a bit stupid—and she _is_ a bit thick, you know—so whether she would guess that I was going out in my car for a picnic, I don't know, but I doubt it. But she'd never think that I was going out with <u>you</u> in my car. After all, I've never done such a thing before today, and we've taken great care today to ensure that no one would know that we've gone out <u>together</u>. So I'm sure that's all right, Jim; really, I am."

"Yes, I expect it is," said Jim. But in fact, although he did not like to admit it to himself, he did not feel altogether convinced that their escapade together was going to remain undiscovered and unsuspected. There was another short silence as they both continued to eat sandwiches, while Jim's eyes were resting mainly on the beautiful outlines of Susan's breasts under the cups of her white lace brassière. Susan, however, seemed unaware of Jim's gaze. She was trying to convince herself that they had got away from the Castle so carefully, and were going to come back so carefully, that no one was going to have any cause even to guess at what had happened, much less to find any concrete evidence that she had gone out in her car with Jim to a lonely outdoor place. Suddenly, as she bit into a second cheese sandwich, she began to wonder whether what she was doing, and what she knew in her heart they were about to do when they had finished eating and drinking, was something very foolish—even if it should remain undiscovered. She had for days been telling herself that this picnic was going to be a delightful treat both for herself and for Jim. Also, she had felt a little depressed over the last few days, and so had been all the keener to go out with Jim to some quiet corner of the countryside, there to indulge in a little "fun" of a harmless kind to chase away the rather flat feeling of despondency which had come over her on returning home from her holiday. It was not really depression, and it had not seriously bothered or surprised her. The return to ordinary life at home after all the enjoyment of the holiday in the Lakes had simply come as a slightly unpleasant shock, although Susan knew that such a feeling was to be expected, and that after a few days it would probably disappear of its own accord. However, she had been thinking of her slight feeling of depression as an excuse to go ahead with the picnic quickly. I had to chase away those home-from-holiday blues, she argued to herself. But, after all, are we being foolish by being here on our own? Are we going to be foolish in what we're going to do? Surely I'll forget all about my worries and my holiday blues when he makes love to me! Gosh, will he really do that? Can I afford to allow it? Oh, but I want him so badly, I want to feel him inside me . . .

With that thought Susan pulled herself together and remembered that Jim was sitting close beside her on the rug, full of love for her. During the past minute or two she had been lost in her thoughts while silently eating, but now she slipped quickly back into her former lively, happy mood of expectation.

"Have another sandwich?" she said.

"Yes, thanks," said Jim, and took one. He had guessed from Susan's recent silence that she had something on her mind which was troubling her, but now he saw that she was thrusting her worry aside, whatever it was. I suppose she's worried that someone will discover us here, he thought, and perhaps somebody will. But I can't be bothered about that unless, or until, it happens.

"Do tell me more about your holiday, Sue," he said. "Did you come back on the 'Royal Scot' this time, like we did that other time?"

"No," said Susan, "this time we travelled on the 'Thames-Clyde Express'. It was a beautiful journey—at least, the first part of it was, up in the Pennines." She went on to tell Jim more about that journey, and as they were talking the thought crossed her mind that it was almost as if he were not at all interested in her sexually; but she saw where his gaze kept focusing, and the excited gleam in his fine blue eyes, and knew that this was not so.

Presently Susan offered Jim more to drink. "We may as well finish up that wine," she said.

"Yes, I'll have some more, thanks. What's in that flask, Sue?"

"Coffee."

"Oh. Shall we have that to finish with?"

"I thought we would. What would you like to eat next, Jim?"

"What else is in that basket?"

"Digestive biscuits and some fruit cake—it looks a very good piece of cake, although it was bought, not home-made. I didn't bother to bring any cheese and biscuits, as I thought there would be enough without them. And there are two apples to finish with, and the coffee, and chocolate." Susan brought out the slab of cake and partly unwrapped it so that Jim could see what it was like.

"That cake looks first-rate," he said. "I'll have a piece now, please, then some biscuits; and then my apple. Susan took a knife from the basket and cut two large slices of cake, one for herself, and one for Jim. They continued their picnic, chatting happily about inconsequential things.

When they had finished the picnic apart from drinking mugs of coffee and eating squares of milk chocolate, both Jim and Susan felt that they could give more attention to enjoying each other's company. The day remained very pleasant: hot and sunny most of the time, which made them glad of a little shade for their heads from the overhanging branches; but every now and then a cloud would pass in front of the sun, and for a little while it would be cooler and much less bright until the sun shone out again. There was an occasional rustling of the beech leaves overhead when a gentle breeze blew through the hollow, but they were well sheltered from the wind, and most of the time it was very quiet. They were not talking much now as they both found that the warm, drowsy summer silence was too pleasurable to spoil with too much unnecessary talk. They were sitting on the rug, Jim with an arm around Susan's waist, while she had an arm around his shoulders. The road, seen through the gap in the foliage, seemed to be almost deserted. They had seen only one car go past while they had been there, and they had not noticed any cyclists or pedestrians.

"This is perfect," said Jim as he finished his last piece of chocolate. "It's a lovely place, gorgeously private, and a perfect day—and, best of all, we're really alone here."

"Yes," murmured Susan dreamily.

There was silence again for a few minutes. Jim sensed that Susan did not want to hurry things, and so he was quite happy, for the moment, to do nothing except to revel in her nearness while he experienced the almost soporific effect of the place on that warm afternoon. He was all but certain that they would soon be making love, but he was not thinking about that now; he was lost in a happy dream as he stared into Susan's enchanting eyes which, he thought, were like two pools of very deep, calm water, so dark were they. At the same time he marvelled anew at how well her perfect eyelashes and delicate eyebrows complemented those eyes. She was indeed in Jim's eyes a girl unique in her beauty, a priceless treasure, and he had never felt so much in love with her. They spoke no words but, as Jim's lips moved towards her's, he saw the light in her dark eyes as she smiled at him, and he knew that she was vibrant with excitement and perhaps as much in love with him as he was with her. Their lips met; for a minute or so they remained locked in a loving embrace. Then, withdrawing her lips slightly from his, Susan whispered: "I like love to be like this."

"Out of doors, you mean?" asked Jim. "In a lonely place like this?"

"Yes," said Susan softly. "What could be more romantic than this? A lovely place, a perfect lazy summer day . . . and just you and me together."

Jim did not answer her. Susan did not want any answer in words, but he leaned forward and kissed her again. Almost he felt that he ought to pinch himself, or ask Susan to pinch him, so that he could wake up from this blissfully happy dream—if it was a dream. He was tempted to believe that what he and Susan were doing could not be real, that he must somehow be asleep. But if I'm asleep, he said to himself, why bother to wake up? Why spoil such a heavenly dream? Ah, no! (he pressed Susan's face close against his). This is no sleeping dream: we really are as close to each other as this . . .

Time passed, but neither Susan nor Jim had any idea of how much time—it might have been five minutes, ten minutes, or an hour—until Jim suddenly heard Susan saying in a quiet voice: "Take it off, Jim." They had been sitting there, and then they had been lying down together on the rug, facing each other while they had embraced, but they had been saying very little to break the drowsy silence so, when Jim heard Susan say: "Take it off, Jim," he was puzzled for a moment.

"What?" he whispered, looking enquiringly into her eyes which, he saw, were sparkling at him almost as if she were repressing a laugh. But the next moment he had understood what she meant. He was a little surprised to find that he was fingering the cups and straps of her bra.

"Take it off!" she said again. "You want to see what I've got underneath them, don't you?" Jim nodded. "Right, we'll have it off, and you can have a look at my breasts, if you're going to take off your shirt. It <u>is</u> very hot, you know, and I think we'd both feel more comfortable on top with nothing on. That's right." Jim was already flinging aside his unbuttoned shirt. "Good. Now <u>you</u> can take the bra off me. Just unhook it at the back and slip those straps over my shoulders and it should fall off." Jim unhooked the fastening of the brassiere and put his hands to the straps which went over Susan's shoulders, and then hesitated, hardly able to believe that she meant him to take the thing off. "Go on!" she said. Jim slipped the straps over her shoulders, and as the brassière fell off her he gasped in amazement and excitement.

"Sue, they're gorgeous; they're magnificent!" he breathed when he had stared at the delectable sight in silent wonder for several seconds, while Susan smiled at him with laughter in her lovely eyes. Susan's breasts, as he now saw them in their naked beauty, were not really all that big but they were well rounded and hung rather low on her chest. He saw the paler marks where her smooth skin had been covered up by the brassière, and he noticed that her nipples were small and the areolae surrounding them hardly any darker than the remaining part of each breast. He also noticed, however, that Susan seemed to be greatly amused (or was she simply flattered?) by his obvious interest in her breasts.

"You like them, my darling?" she said, checking her impulse to laughter as well as she could so as not to hurt his feelings. Jim nodded again, smiling as he met her eyes. "Well, they measure thirty-eight inches when the tape measure is put around me up there," she continued, "and if you'd like to know all my measurements—my 'vital statistics' as people call them—I'm 38—24—36, and I'm five feet six inches tall! So now you know!" She said this with not a little pride in her voice. Susan was proud of her fine figure, and particularly she enjoyed having big breasts, although she often wished that they were less rounded and more pointed at the nipples; however, to have them admired by a genuinely admiring lover was pleasurable indeed. But Jim's attitude of wonder was, she thought, so great that, in a strange way, it put her in mind of a very animal reaction: like the look of a faithful dog gazing lovingly at his mistress; and that was what she had found so amusing in the way he was looking at her.

Susan leaned forwards and kissed Jim again, and as they held a tight embrace he became intensely excited by the feel of her full breasts pressed warmly against his own bared chest.

"Come on, Jim," she whispered, "let's make love!"

"Oh, Sue, my darling!" murmured Jim.

"I'm ready for it now."

"Oh yes!" And then Jim's tone changed slightly. "Only—would it be safe?" he asked cautiously.

"Safe? How do you mean, 'safe'?"

"I mean, er—if we make love, I mustn't make you pregnant, must I?" said Jim awkwardly.

"Oh, I see. I thought you meant that you didn't want anyone to see us—and let's hope no one does. But you needn't worry about that side of it, Jim. You see, John and I don't want to start a family just yet, so I take a contraceptive pill."

"Oh, so it would be safe to make love?"

"Quite safe," said Susan, unbuttoning the top of her shorts as she spoke.

But Jim thought that the inflexion of her voice belied what she was saying. So Sue doesn't think that it's really all that safe, he said to himself. But if she doesn't care, I certainly don't! But now what was happening? Susan had stood up; she was pulling her shorts down, and taking them off; and now she was pulling her knickers downwards, revealing to Jim's excited gaze a triangle of dark and curly pubic hair between her plump thighs. The atmosphere of their picnic was changing. Gone now was that soft, dreamy feeling they had experienced earlier, as their need for each other's love now became a much more insistent force; yet the background to their lovemaking remained soothing and soporific in the quietness of that warm afternoon, and this gentle background was not lost on Susan and Jim: on the contrary, they were relishing it.

Jim suddenly became aware of a pleasant sensation as he felt Susan's fingers lightly stroking the bulge in the front of his trousers; then she unzipped the trousers. "My darling!" she whispered huskily in his ear. Jim seemed to spring to life with surprising suddeness as he instantly pulled down his underpants and savagely flung them aside. "Let's lie down," said Susan urgently as they met in a naked embrace. Jim could by now definitely feel her excitement. She was trembling all over in eager expectation and seemed, indeed, hardly able to continue to stand up. They sank down onto the rug. "On top of me, Jim, my darling!" she panted urgently.

They made love, but such was the measure of Jim's excitement that in less than two minutes he had come to his climax. Then they rested quietly for a while, lying now facing each other on the rug, both naked except for their shoes and socks. By now they neither knew nor cared whether anyone was watching them: they were aware only of each other.

"I'm going to have <u>everything</u> off," Jim announced presently with decision. "It's hot, isn't it, now that the sun's come out again?"

"But not too hot," said Susan. She lay where she was, watching him, as he sat up and pulled off his shoes and socks. For some time the direct sun had been obscured by cloud, but now, as Jim had said, it had come out again: they were bathed in warm sunlight, but there were dappled tree shadows over their bodies.

Jim lay down again on the rug beside Susan.

"Sue, darling, you have the most marvellous breasts!" he said with gentle feeling as he kissed them, one after the other.

"But the only thing is that they are rather heavy," said Susan in a matter-of-fact sort of way. "I sometimes like to wear no bra underneath my blouse, you know, but usually I do wear one."

"You need to wear a bra, do you?"

"I do." Susan propped herself up on her left forearm, while with her free right hand she guided Jim's left hand onto her left breast and cupped it underneath that organ. "Heavy, isn't it?" she continued. Jim's eyes sparkled in agreement. "So, you see, my boobs need to be supported by a bra so that they don't sag and loose their shape."

"Of course. They're very beautiful, Sue. I love them!"

"Indeed you do!" said Susan, and laughed. "You're a real breast-fancier, you are, Jim!"

He continued to kiss and pet her for perhaps another quarter of an hour, and then he mounted her again and they began to make love for the second time. But only a few seconds later Jim paused in his movement.

"What did I do wrong last time?" he asked.

"Wrong?" whispered Susan. "Nothing. Nothing at all, my darling. But don't stop, Jim—don't stop doing me!" Jim started again, slowly, to thrust into her. "We were just too tense last time, that was all . . . This time it'll be better!"

It was. They made love more leisurely and more slowly, but Jim soon felt that they were moving smoothly together almost like a single body. The thought went through his mind: I bet Sue had this in mind when she first planned this picnic! and he grinned happily at the idea. That afternoon, anyway, she had given herself totally to him, and there she was underneath him, utterly his own. The rest of the world had melted away, and there was only his beloved Susan. He kissed her warmly on the lips and stared again into her dark eyes which were alight in rapturous pleasure. They began to increase the tempo of their mutual movement until Susan gasped in ecstatic delight as she experienced a most satisfactory climax, which was followed seconds later by Jim's climax.

Then again they rested, lying in each other's arms on the rug.

CHAPTER TEN

"I suppose it's time we were thinking of moving," said Susan much later. She and Jim were still lying on the rug, their arms around each other's bodies. "You're not asleep, Jim?"

"No," said Jim, opening his eyes. "I was just rather dazzled by the sun, lying on my back, so I had to close my eyes." As he spoke he was raising himself to a sitting position so that he could again look at Susan.

Susan, in spite of what she had said, felt a great reluctance towards the idea of moving. It was partly, perhaps, a matter of slothfulness, she told herself, but it had been wonderfully pleasant lying there with Jim so she decided to give herself a few more minutes of pleasure. When she decided that she had to move she slowly raised herself up on one arm, and then, rather stiffly, she rose to her feet. She had just looked at her watch and seen that the time was now ten minutes past three, and that, she knew, meant that it was high time to bring her delightful private picnic with Jim to its close. She had reckoned that to be safe she ought to be back in the Castle before four o'clock; if that could be managed there would be a good chance that no one would have missed her. Samantha had been out since breakfast time, but Susan expected her to return to the Castle between four and five o' clock, as she was due back on duty that day at five in the afternoon. Samantha was a good servant, and usually Susan shared all sorts of confidential matters with her, but today she did not want Samantha even to know that she had ever left the Castle: that way no awkward questions could be asked.

Jim, who by now was feeling a little tired, had again laid his head down on the rug.

"Well, Jim, my love," said Susan, standing just beside his head while she smiled down at him, "it's time, I fear, that we were packing up and heading for home."

Jim now found that he could look straight up at Susan without being dazzled by the sun. He did so, and saw her standing naked over him, except for her shoes and socks, and he broke into a relaxed smile of pure pleasure, but for a second or two he gave her no answer. Then: "Must we?" he said. "Heavens, it has been gorgeous!"

"Yes, I know," said Susan, "but we really <u>must</u> go home now." She bent down for a moment to pick up her under-clothes, and then began to dress herself. Jim, however, made no effort to move for a minute or two, while he smiled again as he watched Susan pulling on her panties and fastening her bra in its place.

"It's been unbelievably lovely, what we've done, Sue," he said dreamily as he somewhat unwillingly raised himself slowly to a sitting position. "I can't somehow think of going back to ordinary things after this, but I suppose we've got to."

"I'm afraid so, and as soon as we can," she said. "We don't want anything to go wrong at the end, do we, when everything has worked out so beautifully so far?" She held out a hand to help Jim to stand up. "My darling," she continued, "I understand how you feel. You've been an absolutely super lover, and I don't think I've ever enjoyed love so much before. That second time was really fantastic, wasn't it? But now we simply must be going back. You'd better start putting your clothes on, my love." She looked at him, her eyes shining with love for him.

"All right," said Jim. But even as he said it, he took her in an embrace and they kissed each other warmly. He was still thinking of prolonging the pleasure a little further, and he knew that Susan would also have liked to stay there with him in that very private leafy dell for a while longer in spite of her talk of the necessity to return home—which, of course, he perfectly understood.

"It's so beautifully quiet and lonely here," he murmured. "Oh, I <u>do</u> wish we didn't have to go home now!"

"Never mind, Jim, my love," whispered Susan; "perhaps some other time . . . what's that?"

Jim and she listened attentively and the next second they both distinctly heard from close at hand a sound that was familiar to them: someone was riding a bicycle along the little road. They heard in the still air (the wind had dropped almost to nothing) the slight regular squeak from a pair of pedals which needed a little oil and the small sounds of pebbles bouncing about as the wheels of the bicycle crossed the holes and ruts in the rough surface of the road. So far as they knew no one had gone past on that road either on foot or in any sort of vehicle, except for that one car they had noticed, in all the time that they had been in their picnic hollow. It sounded as if whoever was riding that bicycle was only moving very slowly, as anyone might on such a rough, hilly road. Susan and Jim looked anxiously at each other and then quickly looked again to the short stretch of road which was visible through the gap in the branches which made a spy-hole. They were holding each other tightly and silently. Whoever it was would appear in that spy-hole at any moment; and when, a second later, a young man with a rather red face riding an ancient-looking bicycle duly appeared to them, Susan gasped silently. She knew that man by sight, and knew his name too, although she hardly knew him apart from that: he was a labourer on a farm not far from Rhodes Castle. Susan and Jim froze as they saw the man get off his bicycle there and prop it up against the fence just behind the place where Susan's car was parked. They saw him standing there, clearly looking around to see whether the people who had parked a car there were close at hand. At one moment he seemed to be looking through the trees directly towards Susan and Jim, although they doubted whether he had noticed them through all the intervening branches at a distance of about two hundred yards, while they remained still as a statue of two lovers clasping each other in an embrace. Jim was silently cursing the stranger for his inquisitiveness in stopping where he saw a parked car, while Susan was thinking that the whole secret of their illicit love would be out if that man saw her now with Jim Sandy without a stitch of clothing on him. Would there be time to hide him if the man were to walk towards them, she wondered? But the man, having looked straight towards them for a moment, had turned right round to look the other way the next moment, as if making up his mind which way to go. For a little while as the man still hesitated by the fence, Susan had hopes that he was about to re-mount his bicycle and ride away, not having seen them, but suddenly they saw that he had made up his mind about what to do next. He was climbing nimbly over the fence just where they had climbed over, to come up the grassy track towards their hiding place. In the next instant he was again hidden from their view behind the trees.

"Quick! Under the rug!" hissed Susan. She had seen that unfortunately he had flung his clothes too far aside when he had undressed to be able to pick them up again instantly: hiding under the rug was going to be the only hope. Quick as thought Jim dropped to his knees, and in another moment had burrowed under the rug. Susan desperately rucked the edges of the rug into natural-looking creases, ridges, and valleys as well as she could in three or four seconds to try to conceal, as far as possible, the lump made by Jim's body underneath it; but she took care to see that he was not going to be altogether suffocated by this necessary concealing process. She heard that man's footsteps coming nearer up the grassy track, and heard him whistling little tuneless phrases in a casual way as if he were not intent on doing anything in particular. Susan looked frantically around. That intruder would push his way through the tangled overgrowth which partly obstructed the small path into their hollow at any second: he obviously wanted to see who was there, and she thought he must have heard something as Jim had dived head first under the rug. She decided on the instant not to try to put on either her blouse or her shorts. She was covered quite well enough in the interests of modesty in just her bra and her panties: there was not going to be time enough to put on another garment without being caught desperately trying to pull it on as if she wanted, at all costs, not to be seen in her underwear. No, it would be much better, she decided, to pretend to be calmly sunbathing in just her underwear. She took a very quick look at the way the rug was lying at her feet. The concealing of Jim under it had been done in such a desperate hurry that, she thought, they had not managed it very well. The long lump under the middle of the rug <u>did</u> look rather like a motionless human body lying on the ground, but the decoy bumps and ridges she had managed to introduce around it were really not bad: perhaps they would mislead the man when he looked down at the rug. Anyway, there was not another moment to do anything more to it, for just then she heard the branches overhanging the path into the hollow being pushed aside. The man had arrived. Susan dropped to a sitting position on a corner of the rug as quickly as if her legs had suddenly given way beneath her; and a fraction of a second later the rather red-faced farm labourer stepped out from the bushes.

"Oh, hello!" he said, checking his steps. "Why, it's Lady Dalmane! Well, fancy meeting you here, Lady Dalmane!"

"Good afternoon, Mr. Cottem," said Susan coldly, hardly bothering to look up at him.

"Having a picnic are you, Lady Dalmane?" returned the other. "It's a grand day to be sitting out of doors soaking up the sunshine, I must say. Really warm today, isn't it?"

"Yes." Susan's reply was so short that it rather took the young man aback, so that he was temporarily at a loss to know how to continue the conversation. But he was fascinated by what he saw of Lady Dalmane, and after looking for a moment straight at the odd-looking lump in the rug, his eyes automatically returned to stare at Susan as if he were mesmerised by her unexpected nearly naked beauty. Susan, watching him carefully, saw no change come over the expression of obsessive fascination on his face at the moment when she thought that he must be looking directly at Jim's hidden form. Thank heaven! she thought, it's worked! He doesn't know that Jim is under that rug. But the young farmer, forgetting his manners, continued to stare at Susan for second after second. He seemed, indeed, to have become powerless to shift his gaze to anywhere else, and his unwanted attention soon irritated Susan considerably.

"Don't just stand there goggling at me, Robin Cottem," she said. "If you've got anything to say worth saying, please say it, and then clear out. I don't like being stared at; nor do I see why I shouldn't be nearly naked to do a bit of sunbathing in this very private place. Haven't you ever seen a girl wearing a bikini before?" It seemed to her on the spur of the moment to be a good idea to refer to her white underwear as a "bikini" to remind him that she was thus scantily dressed on purpose for sunbathing.

Robin Cottem, the young farm labourer, turned even redder in the face as he heard Susan rebuke him for staring at her.

"Oh yes, Lady Dalmane; I'm really very sorry to have intruded on your privacy but, you see, I have my job to do, my Lady," he said.

"How do you mean?"

"Well, you see, Mr. Challice, my employer, is very particular about not having people trespassing on his land, and he always likes me to take a firm line with any trespassers as I find while I'm about my work. You maybe didn't know, Lady Dalmane, but the land hereabouts on Batcombe Hill—leastways on this side of it—belongs to Mr. Challice. We have sheep and lambs grazing on the Downs just above these trees."

It was now Susan's turn to feel a little awkward. She had had no idea that the land that she and Jim had been picnicing on belonged to Robert Challice, a near neighbour to Rhodes Castle, who had a farm on their side of Yetminster. The farm was, in fact, part of Lord Dalmane's estate, whereas the area of downland at Batcombe Hill, which was farmed by Mr. Challice, had been bought by him from Lord Dalmane. Susan's face showed just a slight hint of a blush as she answered Robin Cottem.

"I see: I'm sorry I'm trespassing but, honestly, I never suspected that the land hereabouts was anything to do with Summerhays Farm; but, of course, I'll leave at once if you like. You aren't working here today, though, are you? I've just seen you come up the hill on your bicycle from the Sydling direction."

"That's right, Lady Dalmane, it's my day off, you see. I was biking over to Sydling meaning to visit my girlfriend who lives there, but I find when I get there that she's out, so I turn round and start biking back again. Well, I'd noticed a car parked just here when I was riding over to Sydling, and I thought to myself: 'Trespassers there', but seeing as I was in a bit of a hurry to get over to Sydling (and as it was my day off) I decided to turn a blind eye and go straight on. And then later on, when I'm riding back, I see that same car still parked here, so I think I'd better stop and look around to see who it is on our land without permission. And then I find that it's you, Lady Dalmane."

"When did you go past on your bicycle the first time, Mr. Cottem, on your way to Sydling?" asked Susan.

"It would be about three quarters of an hour ago, maybe."

"Ah. Well, if you want to turn me off here, I'll go straight away."

"Oh no, Lady Dalmane, I'm sure it will be all right for <u>you</u> to remain here, if you want to. Your husband, the Earl, is a friend of Mr. Challice, isn't he? Then he's bound to have Mr. Challice's permission to come onto his land whenever he wants to. If it had been anyone else picnicing here, Lady Dalmane, I'd tell them to move on straight away, or else; but you're very welcome to stay here, as you're doing no harm anyway."

"Well, that's very kind of you, but I'm about to leave to go home in any case. Now, if you'll excuse me, I'll dress and go."

"Good afternoon, Lady Dalmane."

"Good afternoon, Robin."

Robin Cottem turned and walked off by the way he had come into the hollow. Susan felt an immense relief as he disappeared from her view and she heard him walking down to the road. She looked down at the lump under the rug (she had carefully stopped herself from doing this while the young man had been talking to her) and saw that Jim was taking no chances. There was no sign of any movement under the rug: Jim was not totally sure that the coast was yet clear, and was waiting for Susan to give him the "all clear". In about another minute Susan, peering through the spy-hole gap in the branches towards the road, saw Mr. Cottem pick up his bicycle from its place against the fence and, without a pause or a backward glance, ride away on it in the direction of Hillfield. For a few seconds she heard the scrunching of gravel under the cycle wheels, but she gave him about half a minute to get right away. Then she stirred herself. "Damn that man, barging in on us like that!" she muttered. She plucked at the rug. "All right, Jim, you can come out now; the coast's clear," she said. Jim emerged from under the rug and saw at once that Susan was looking serious.

"Well?" he asked. "Do you think it will be all right? I tried to lie absolutely still while he was talking to you."

"I know," said Susan. "You did that marvellously, Jim. He couldn't have seen the slightest movement from under there, but he may still have guessed that there was someone hiding under the rug. I don't like it. Even if he hasn't guessed about you, he'll probably go and tell Bob Challice, the farmer he works for, that he found me with most of my clothes off sitting on a rug sunbathing on their private property, and then, sooner or later, John will get to hear about it. He's a friend of Bob, you see, and a fairly near neighbour, and so sometime, when John's round at the farm, perhaps, they'll get chatting, and it will come out about me having a picnic here on my own and sunbathing nearly nude. And John will think, That sounds pretty odd, Sue having a picnic there on her own . . . Are you nearly ready to go, Jim?"

Jim had been hurriedly dressing while he listened to Susan, who had pulled her shorts on, and now put on her blouse. "Yes," he said, "but perhaps that chap won't tell his boss anything about finding you sunbathing here. After all, he said it was quite all right for you to be here."

"Yes, I know, but we can't <u>count</u> on our picnic here remaining a secret now," said Susan dully. "He may tell, or he may not, but in any case that's really spoiled the day, him finding me here . . . Oh well, come on, we'll go now."

Susan sounded so gloomy that Jim could think of nothing to say to her. Silently he picked up the rug, folded it, and flung it over his shoulder to carry it, while Susan took the picnic basket. Silently they walked away from their picnic place, squeezing through the overgrown path through the bushes in single file, Susan first, but walking down the grassy track to the road hand in hand, as before, except that Susan only gave Jim the ghost of a smile as she held out her hand to him. They had not said another word to each other when they stepped back into the car. But Susan had a further worry on her mind, and before she started the engine she turned to Jim and said:

"There's another thing, Jim. You heard me ask Robin Cottem when he went past on his bicycle the <u>first</u> time, when he was on his way to Sydling?"

"Yes. He said it was about three quarters of an hour before he came back, and stopped, and found you."

"Well? What do you think about that?"

Jim considered a moment, and then could not resist a smile at Susan in spite of knowing how worried she felt about Robin Cottem discovering her "sunbathing". "I know what you mean," he said. "It must have been while we were lying on the rug together making love that he went past that first time. My word, it's been glorious, Sue—it's been wonderful! You did think so too, at the time, didn't you?"

The worried look on Susan's face had vanished, and now she beamed a smile at Jim and gave him an unexpected kiss. "Yes, my darling, I did, and I still do think so," she said quietly. "But that's not quite the point I was getting at. Don't you think Mr. Cottem may have overheard something when he passed, or perhaps even seen us doing it?"

"I knew that was what was worrying you, Sue, but I don't believe he could have either seen or heard anything. He said that he never stopped that time, didn't he, because he was in a hurry to get to the place where his girlfriend lives?"

"Yes, that's what he said."

"Well then, surely he would have stopped if he'd heard anything, or seen anything, which gave him the slightest suspicion of what we were doing. Surely any man's curiosity would get the better of him under those circumstances, and he'd want to take a peep at a loving couple, even if he wasn't really sure of what was going on? But he went right past, Sue. He can't have suspected anything. It must be all right."

But Susan did not look at all as if she thought that it was all right. "Well, is it?" she said; and after a moment's pause she added: "He only <u>said</u>, mind you, that he went past without stopping. But we were much too busy to notice anything else going on around us. That might have been a lie: we've no way of telling whether he went past without stopping, or not. And another thing is this: I don't think that he saw <u>you</u> when he came back, before you dived under the rug, when we first saw him arrive on his bicycle and lean it against the fence—but he may have seen you then. We just don't know. But if he caught a glimpse then of a stark naked man with me—and me with most of my clothes off—then it's all up. Surely he would be able to put two and two together as well as any other man and deduce what we'd been up to? But I don't believe he knew anything about you being here, although I don't think it'll make any difference in the long run. He'll tell his boss something about me, and then John will get to know about it, and he'll guess everything about what I was really doing."

There was a short silence in the car after Susan had said that. They were holding each other's hands, but neither was smiling, while they were considering various grim possibilities which might be the end result of their unwise adventure of that day. Then, remembering that the time was going on, Susan started the engine of her car. "I can't turn round in this narrow road," she said as they drove off, "so we'll have to go on first towards Sydling to look for a place where I can make a three-point turn."

When Susan had turned her car round near the hamlet of Upper Sydling they set off on the road back to Rhodes Castle. Little was said by either of them for most of this journey. Jim was considering what would happen to him if Lord Dalmane were to find out about his affair with his wife, as Susan seemed to be very nearly sure that he would find out everything sooner or later. He realised then for the first time since his intercourse with Susan that in that event his punishment was certain to be dismissal from his position in the Castle. Whether or not Susan could be said to be to blame for what had happened, because she had deliberately lead him into it and urged him on, he had gone too far, he thought. To be sacked from his good job and to have to leave Rhodes Castle must be too high a price to pay for their supremely enjoyable act of love. Yet was it really so, he wondered? In his heart he could not at all make himself regret what had happened that afternoon. Why should he regret it?

He had that day, after all, experienced the fulfillment of the hope which had been in the back of his mind ever since he had first known that he was to live in Rhodes Castle under the same roof as his beloved Susan.

If I get the sack for this, he thought, I'll have to leave Rhodes Castle. And what then? I'll not be living with Sue any more. I'll have to say goodbye to her and leave her. I'll have to find somewhere else to live, and a new job, if I can, and perhaps it's even possible, if it comes to this, that I'd never see Sue again . . . but perhaps all this won't happen, after all. If only Lord Dalmane doesn't find out, it'll be all right. But if he does . . . why, I don't see how I can <u>possibly</u> be given any less punishment, or any other, than the sack.

Jim came out of his daydreams with a start when he suddenly realised that Susan was about to turn the car off the public road into the track leading through Rhodes Park to Lewes Farm and via the back way to the Castle. His day out with Susan was all but over: in another minute she would be putting him out at the same place where he had got in, by the bushes at the cattle grid.

"Here we are, home again," said Susan, breaking her silence. "Look here, Jim, I'm going to let you get out at the same place as you got in, so that we're not seen arriving together. Not that I think that there's much point in taking such precautions now after the disaster of that chap seeing me, but I suppose we'd better arrive separately, just in case. You don't mind waiting in those bushes just until I've driven away, and then walking from there?"

"Not a bit," said Jim. "But maybe that wasn't really a disaster after all, Sue. You said—"

"I don't want to talk about it now, Jim, if you don't mind," said Susan, interrupting him. "What will happen, will happen; so we'll keep our mouths shut, and hope for the best."

Susan drove the car down the rough road, veering to the left where the track to Lewes Farm branched off to the right. As they approached the cattle grid at the back entrance to the Castle gardens Susan slowed the car down almost to walking pace while she looked around very carefully, but there was no sign of anyone around the place. She pulled up alongside the dense thicket of bushes.

"I just don't know how to thank you for today, Sue," said Jim, as he saw Susan suddenly smiling at him. "I know it's been an awful pity about that chap turning up—but . . ." His words trailed off into silence as he could not think of a way of telling Susan how much he had enjoyed making love with her.

"Jim, my darling, I was in heaven while you were on top of me! Oh, you were so marvellous . . . !" Susan had put on the handbrake of the car, and now she let go of the steering wheel as she kissed Jim. He again felt his pulse rate speed up as they held each other in a tight embrace. "Now, if only Robin Cottem hadn't caught us with our clothes off—at least if he hadn't seen me with very little on—let's hope he never suspected that you were there—then it would have been a perfect day. It's been gorgeous anyway, but I can't help but worry about what may happen now." Susan kissed Jim again, and then let go of him. "Now, off you go," she said. "Good-bye for this time, Jim, my love!"

Jim stepped out of the car into the outer fringe of the bushes, which there leaned out towards the roadway. For a moment Susan leant right over towards the open window on the front passenger side. She stretched out her left hand, and Jim clasped it firmly.

"Good-bye, Sue!"

"Good-bye, darling!"

Their hands broke apart, and Susan blew Jim a parting kiss just before she again grasped the steering wheel and the gear lever, and immediately drove smoothly and quietly away in low gear. Jim stood in the edge of the bushes watching the receding car. There was not a sign that anyone else was near. Within a few seconds more Susan and the car had vanished round the next bend of the back drive.

CHAPTER ELEVEN

One evening when Jim came up to his room to go to bed he remembered the blue stone which he had found in the Tower Library when he had been making the inventory. Ten days had passed since the afternoon when he had come back from the picnic with Susan on Batcombe Hill, and he had been doing a good deal of thinking about it at various times when he was doing nothing in particular. That evening as he climbed the stairs and walked along the passage towards his door he was considering once again that vexing question on his mind since the picnic: would Lord Dalmane discover that he had been very directly involved with Susan on that day, or would he not? Clearly the future of his job at the Castle depended on Lord Dalmane discovering nothing about it.

In his room Jim presently opened a top drawer of the chest-of-drawers and, rummaging in it, looking for some photographs he had taken, he happened to come across the little jewel-box containing that blue gemstone. He took the box out at once and opened it. He had long ago forgotten all about that strange blue stone and the even odder story of the ghost of Beryl Buxton, which appeared to be linked with the stone (assuming that it was the Great Beryl of Saint Helens), but now that eccentric American tourist and his seemingly absurd tale flashed back into his mind. For a little while Jim forgot about the other matters on his mind as he placed the stone on the palm of his left hand and stared at it, holding his hand under the desk light. It was almost as if he were becoming mesmerised by the scintillating beauty of that gem when a sudden thought came to him, cutting short his other daydreams. Why, I must give this thing back to Susan at once, he said to himself. What else can it be but the Great Beryl of Saint Helens? But then a doubt came to him. Even if it was the Great Beryl, would it be wise for him to take it to Susan? He had seen very little of her in the days since the picnic, and when they had met they had done no more than exchange a nod, a brief smile, and sometimes a "Hello". Jim thought that, temporarily at least, Susan was trying to avoid meeting him. So ought I to take the risk of being seen talking with her? he wondered. But at once, like a flash of inspiration, the answer came to him. The blue stone now in the palm of his hand provided him with a wonderful excuse for going to see Susan. It was her's, wasn't it? It had to be given back to her. Naturally he meant to talk to Susan, if he could see her tomorrow, about the important matters on his mind; but if anyone were to challenge him on what he was doing, he would say, quite truthfully, that he had found a gemstone which he believed was Susan's, and that he was returning it to her. Splendid, Jim said to himself, I'll take this stone to her tomorrow—yes, I'm quite determined that, somehow or other, I'll find an opportunity to get this thing to Sue tomorrow; and then, I hope, I'll be able to ask her whether she thinks everything's still all right about our picnic. His mind now resolutely made up on this line of action, Jim put the stone away in its box, and closed the drawer.

I'm going to see Sue today, thought Jim as soon as he opened his eyes in the morning. Although he had as yet no definite plan in his head for how to accomplish this meeting, he felt very certain that it was going to happen that day, probably in the evening. It was a cheering thought for him to rise with but as he dressed he again fell to wondering about the chances of his dismissal, if his part in that picnic should be found out.

As he left his room to go downstairs to his breakfast, the thought suddenly came to him: Maybe I could go and see her now. He thought that Susan was certain to be up and about at that time (about a quarter past eight), and that probably she would be having her breakfast with John Dalmane in the small east-facing room near the Library which they used as a breakfast-room. Of course, he would have to talk to her on her own, but he thought that maybe he would be able to get word to Susan now that he very much wanted, as it were, to arrange an appointment for a mutually convenient time that evening when they could talk—and, of course, he would bring that gemstone with him and hand it over to her. At any rate, there would be no harm in going round to the breakfast-room to see whether he could locate Susan there, or pass on a message via a servant that he had an important matter to be discussed with her.

Jim always ate his own breakfast in the common-room next to the kitchen, so that it was a thing quite unheard of for him at that time of the day to be walking, as boldly as he could manage, towards the front of the Castle and the private breakfast-room. As he was walking along the passage leading to the Great Hall he saw Susan's maid, Samantha Villers, carrying a tray; she had just come out of the breakfast-room, and was walking across the hall in the direction of another passage which lead to the kitchen. Jim immediately quickened his pace.

"Samantha!" he called out, not too loud.

The maid immediately turned her head and saw him. She stopped.

"Hello, Jim," she said. "What's up?"

"I want to see Susan," said Jim. "It's about something important."

Jim had always thought that Samantha Villers was a rather plain-looking girl, almost dull to look at, but somehow this morning he thought that she looked much more attractive than her usual self. It may have been partly due to the fact that she was more glamorously dressed than usual that he thought that she looked prettier, and perhaps it had something to do with his eager looking forward to seeing Susan. Samantha was wearing a pale blue, short-sleeved, light jumper with a low neckline, and with it a summery skirt of pale colours and a flowery pattern: an outfit which Jim had not seen her in before, and which he thought looked very becoming on her. Anyway, whatever the reason for it might have been, Jim saw her differently that morning. He saw that she was really pretty, and vaguely wondered why he had always thought of her as plain.

There had been a short pause while Samantha set down her tray of dirty breakfast crockery on a table at the other side of the hall. She had raised her eyebrows slightly on hearing that Jim wanted to see Susan about something important, as if she were a little shocked, or was pretending to be a little shocked, to hear him say such a thing.

"What!" she said. "It's rather early in the day, don't you think, for you to be seeing Susan to talk about love with her?"

"No, not about love! I tell you, I have something I need to discuss with her urgently."

"Oh, have you indeed? It sounds naughty to me, Jim!"

Jim knew Samantha well enough to realise that by her teasing remarks she was only poking a little fun at him harmlessly. Nevertheless, what she had said strongly suggested to him that she knew something about the special relationship between himself and Susan, and that surprised him, and irked him a little. He did not often meet Samantha either in the course of his duties or in his leisure time, and he had thought that she knew comparitively little about his love for Susan. Their eyes met for a moment: Samantha looked keenly at him with her greeny-blue eyes, while Jim looked appreciatively into her face. How lovely her blonde hair looks, he thought, resting in shining tresses on that pale blue top she's wearing!

"What do you mean?" he asked. "What do you know about my love life, Sam?"

"Oh, quite a lot, Jim," she said, smiling. "Oh yes, I know about you and Susan."

"You do? What do you know?" Jim was beginning to forget that he had meant to ask her straight away whether he might be able to have a word with Susan in the breakfast-room. He did not like the idea of going in there unannounced and unexpected. But this woman's banter about his love life with Susan annoyed him, as he sensed that any moment, if the conversation were not steered away from such a delicate subject, he might unwittingly let out some secret which he felt should remain unmentionable in public.

"What do I know?" said Samantha. "Why, <u>everyone</u> in the Castle knows about you and Susan—that you're in love with her, and that she has a crush on you. Oh yes, that's quite common knowledge, I'm afraid."

Jim reddened slightly. "Oh, is it?" he said; and after an awkward pause he added: "I want to have a word with Susan <u>now</u>. I'll go in. She's still in the breakfast-room?" He had walked over to the door of the breakfast-room, and now paused, hesitating, the knuckles of his right hand poised to knock on the door.

"Yes, she's there, and Lord Dalmane's there with her," said Samantha.

"Oh, bother! I thought he was away last night. If he's there I can't tell Susan—I mean, I can't say what I wanted to say."

"You mean, you don't want Lord Dalmane to hear what you've got to say to Susan?"

"Just so; I don't." He stepped back from the door.

"Look here, Jim, can I give Susan a message for you? She might say that she could see you later today if there's something you want to talk about privately. I'll ask her that now, if you like."

"Yes, please do," said Jim. "That's very decent of you, Sam—thank you very much."

"No, that's quite all right," said Samantha. "You're being very mysterious, Jim, but of course I'll pass on your message. Just wait here a sec, and I'll bring you back the answer."

Jim sat down in a rocking-chair with an ornately carved wooden back, while Samantha went back into the breakfast-room. Sam's a good sort, really, said Jim to himself as he waited a minute or so until the door opened again and Samantha re-appeared.

"Seven-thirty this evening in the sewing-room," she said. "Susan says that she'll definitely see you then, for about half an hour, if you like. Is that good enough? I should come and wait in the Green Drawing-Room at about twenty past seven, if I were you." (Susan's sewing-room was next door to the Green Drawing-Room, but did not open off it). "She says she's far too busy to see you now."

"This evening at seven-thirty will do fine," said Jim. "Thanks a lot, Sam." Samantha waved a cheery hand at him, picked up her tray, and hurried off in the direction of the kitchen, followed more slowly by Jim, on the way to his breakfast. He was feeling very pleased to know that he was going to have his chance to talk to Susan that evening, and to hand over the aquamarine, but already he was hoping that the intervening hours, until it was time for that meeting in the sewing-room, would not go too slowly.

When Susan was told that Jim wanted to talk to her about some important matter she immediately guessed that he was thinking about that picnic. Samantha's message rather worried her, and as soon as her maid had gone out of the room, and she had said "Seven-thirty this evening in the sewing-room", she began to feel that she had made a mistake. She certainly was going to be very busy that day; what with a shopping trip into Sherborne, and visitors expected towards lunch time, there was going to be no time to spare at least until the evening, but she thought that she ought to see Jim for a minute or two straight away to find out what exactly was bothering him. The visitors expected were her brother-in-law, Dick Dalmane, and his wife, Jane, who had telephoned late the previous evening to say that they meant to call in on John and Susan around midday that day on their way home between London Airport and Lancashire at the end of their Swiss holiday. "But we're not at all on their way between Heathrow and Saint Helens," Susan had complained when the telephone had been put down. "Coming to Rhodes Castle will mean they must be making a diversion of hundreds of miles just to see us for a few hours." "I know," John had said; "and we don't at all want to see them anyway, but what can we do about it?" Susan, in saying "Seven-thirty" as the time when she and Jim could have a private talk in the sewing-room, was taking a calculated gamble that her unwanted guests would have left by that time to continue their journey north. If, however, they were to change their minds, and stay the night instead of making a brief visit of a few hours, Susan knew that it could become very awkward indeed to keep her rendez-vous with Jim. If that were to happen, she would have to be very busy keeping her guests entertained all evening, and might not be able to leave them long enough in the Green Drawing-Room with John to slip away next door to talk to Jim.

Susan, who had been hurrying through her breakfast, had nearly finished it when Samantha returned to deliver Jim's message. Samantha had given the message in a very low voice, little more than a whisper, so that Lord Dalmane, who was sitting at the opposite point of the circular table, should not hear it. He, in fact, saw nothing unusual or sinister in the maid whispering something in his wife's ear, so he had not tried to overhear what was said. He was taking one of his rare days off work; Parliament was still having its summer recess, and that day he had no business at the Foreign Office, so he was looking forward to a moderately idle day at home; at least, it probably would not be very idle when his brother arrived with Jane, his wife, and needed entertaining. But for the moment Lord Dalmane was taking things very easily, and was nowhere near the end of his meal.

The door was closed as the maid left the room, the message delivered.

"John, I'm going to hurry off to Sherborne as soon as I can, so that I can be back before they arrive," said Susan. She crammed her last mouthful of toast into her mouth. To herself she was saying: I'll just go and see whether Jim's waiting out there in the hall.

"Yes, dear, that's much the best plan," said Lord Dalmane, "but I think I could manage to keep Jane and Dick happy for quite a while without you, if you do happen to be delayed."

"They really are very tiresome, if you don't mind me saying so, dropping in on us at such very short notice."

"Yes, but my brother, Dick, was always like that: thoroughly inconsiderate of other peoples' arrangements."

"How long do you think they'll stay?"

"Oh, I think they'll be on their way again before tea-time, probably no later than three o' clock. I believe they're meaning to motor back to Saint Helens this evening, you know, without arriving too late at night."

Susan swallowed the last mouthfuls of her cup of coffee, rose from the table, and went quickly to the door, blowing her husband a quick kiss as she went. She was just too late to find Jim waiting out there in the rocking-chair. Oh well, it doesn't matter, she said to herself. He'll have gone to the kitchen, I expect, for his breakfast, but I won't follow him there. We'll be talking this evening. Even if those others are still here, I must find out what's bothering him.

*

Jim had thought of remaining in the Hall until Susan came out of the breakfast-room, but had decided against it. He had gathered that she was too busy to talk to him at that time, so he realised that she was in a hurry for something, and that there might hardly be time to exchange more than a passing word with her. That would hardly be worth waiting for, when a time had been fixed for that evening, and anyway, Lord Dalmane might come out of the room first, even though it was his wife who was in a hurry. Jim had not seen Lord Dalmane since the picnic, and did not at all want to see him. Of course, if Lord Dalmane were to find out that he had been with Susan on that occasion, then very probably, Jim thought, he would be sent for to be questioned on what had happened on the picnic. He took the fact that so far he had not been sent for by the Earl as a very hopeful sign that he had found out nothing at all about it yet; consequently Jim thought that it would be wisest to avoid meeting him, and to continue for some time, if possible, to avoid him.

While Jim was eating his breakfast Samantha re-appeared briefly in the servants' common-room to tell him that Lord and Lady Dalmane were expecting visitors that day. Samantha did not know that Sir Richard and Lady Jane Dalmane were only likely to be at the Castle for a few hours over lunch time, so she simply told Jim that they were expected as guests that day. His spirits sank at hearing this news. He immediately saw his private date with Susan that evening threatened by the presence of guests staying at the Castle. It seemed to him that it was only too probable that Susan would not be able to tear herself away from the guests for long enough for them to have the pleasant, cosy chat in the sewing-room to which he was looking forward. But, if they only had a minute or two to talk in private, would that be long enough, he wondered, to hand over that jewel and explain how he had found it and, most important of all, to get Susan's reassurance that all was well, or seemed to be well, following their picnic? Would, say, five minutes be long enough for all that? He doubted it. But if Jane and Dick Dalmane were still at the Castle he would be lucky indeed to get even five minutes talk with Susan. However, the arrangement still stood for that evening, he gathered, so he would have to hope for the best.

It was quite soon after he had finished his breakfast when Jim accidentally met Lord Dalmane. He had just been to the Estate Office to look for his boss, Major Ambrose, and had been surprised to find him not in the Office. It was unusual for the Major not to be in the Estate Office at that time of the morning; but Jim needed to find him in order to recieve his orders for the day's work. The Estate Office was a large room on the ground floor of a wing of the Castle which had once been the Stables, but had been mostly converted into a series of store-rooms and a garage. This wing of the Castle formed the south-western side of the square of buildings surrounding the bailey, which was partly paved over and partly cobbled. The bailey could be entered in a vehicle through the arch in the north-western mediaeval wall, or on foot from any of various doorways opening into it from the surrounding buildings. One of these doors was a back door of the lived-in part of the Castle, and it was towards this door that Jim directed his steps as he came away from the empty Estate Office. He was thinking of entering there to see whether Major Ambrose was in a certain little room which he used as a second office. Unknown to Jim, however, Lord Dalmane was at that moment approaching that same back door from inside the building. They reached the door almost at the same moment. Jim was about to put a hand on the door knob when the door was opened from the inside. Both men looked startled for a moment, particularly Jim, who had to pull up suddenly to avoid a collision.

"Oh, I'm sorry, sir," he said awkwardly.

The Earl of Saint Helens quickly recovered his dignity after the momentary shock of being suddenly confronted with Jim Sandy at his back door. He took his after-breakfast pipe from his mouth. The Earl smoked a pipe when he had the chance to enjoy one.

"Hello, there, Mr. Sandy!" he said cheerfully. "An unexpected meeting, as you might say, eh?"

"Yes, sir."

"Well, how are you getting on with your work? I never seem to see you much nowadays to ask how you're getting on."

"Oh, very well, thank you, sir. I enjoy working here very much."

"I'm glad to hear that," said Lord Dalmane. He puffed again at his pipe for a moment, and then said: "I'm just on my way, actually, to have a word with Ambrose."

"He's not in the Estate Office, sir, if you were going to look there. I'm looking for him too, and I've just been there."

"Ah! So he isn't there, eh?" Lord Dalmane looked thoughtful for an instant, frowning slightly. "H'm, he may be indoors, in that little cubby-hole of his, perhaps," he continued. "But if we don't find him there I'll ring him at home. Something may have delayed him this morning, but I would like to have a little talk with him. You might as well come with me, Jim."

"Thank you, sir," said Jim. He hoped that it was not about himself that Lord Dalmane wished to talk to Major Ambrose. The Earl then lead the way along the passages as Jim followed him back into the "house" (as Lord Dalmane called the main part of the Castle, in which he and Susan lived).

"He's not there either," said Lord Dalmane, pausing a moment to look round the open door of the little room which was really no more than a large cupboard adjacent to his own Study. Major Ambrose had a desk in that little room, but that morning there were no papers scattered about on it to suggest that he had been in there and gone off somewhere else.

"Do you think he's still at home, sir?" asked Jim. He thought that never before while he had been working at the Castle had he known Major Ambrose fail to turn up by nine o' clock at the Estate Office: he was a stickler for punctuality himself, with his ex-Army experience behind him, and Jim had easily fallen into a pattern of keeping punctual times for working under his day-to-day instructions. But it was now eight minutes past nine and there was no sign of the Major.

"Could be still at home," said Lord Dalmane. Major Ambrose lived at the Inner Lodge, hardly a quarter of a mile away. "I'll give them a ring at the Lodge, and we'll see if he's there. Would you like to come into the study a minute, Jim, while I telephone?"

As they went next door, into his Study, Lord Dalmane began to explain why he wanted to talk to the Major. "It's about some land I'm selling to Mr. Challice, the farmer, who pays me a rent at the moment for some of his fields. Ambrose should by now have had a reply from our solicitor to a letter he wrote to start things moving; and if he's had a reply, I'd like to be put in the picture as to how long this business is likely to take."

Lord Dalmane sat down at his desk, took the telephone, and dialled a number; then he waited while the number was being rung. Well, thought Jim, I'm glad it's nothing to do with me, what he wants to talk to him about. He had sat himself down in an armchair to wait until Lord Dalmane had finished making his telephone call. It seemed to take a long time until someone in Inner Lodge answered the telephone: Jim could hear the number being rung. His gaze wandered absent-mindedly around the room, one which, not surprisingly, he hardly ever had cause to enter. It was a long room with two large, south-facing windows which were part of the facade at the front of Rhodes Castle. Jim thought that the oblong shape of the room seemed to be somewhat awkward because the desk stood diagonally across the further window, the desk chair behind it in the window recess, so that the Earl, when sitting there, had a view half towards the wall with the hearth in it, to his left, and half towards the view through that window, to his right, while he looked directly towards the door near the opposite corner of the room. The fireplace was cavernously large, but looked as if it were seldom used, as a screen stood in front of it with the coat of arms of the Dalmane family embroidered on it in fine stitch-work.

In front of the screen an electric fire was positioned within a large brass fender. The wall opposite to the windows, separating the room from the passage behind it, contained three bookshelves which ran between the corner of the room, near the fireplace, and the door; the shelves were full of Lord Dalmane's own books. Major Ambrose's little cupboard-study room lay just the other side of the fireplace wall. It's a good idea, really, having the desk like that, at forty-five degrees angles to those two walls, thought Jim, because of the shape of the room. If it were square, I suppose he'd have the desk in the middle. But then he'd have to face either the fireplace or the door.

This way he can more or less face both at once. Ah, someone's answered at last . . .

"Hello, that you, Ambrose? John Dalmane speaking," said Lord Dalmane. "Yes, that's all right . . . What? Your wife ill . . . ?"

The conversation on the telephone with Major Ambrose lasted perhaps a minute or two. Jim could not quite hear from where he sat what the Major was saying, but he gathered from Lord Dalmane's side of the talk that Mrs. Ambrose had been taken ill during the night, but that the illness was not anything serious. That, of course, explained why his boss had failed to turn up at work: he had been worried about his wife, and probably had some extra domestic duties to do before he could leave his house. Jim understood that the doctor had been sent for and was expected to arrive at the Inner Lodge some time during the late morning, but that Major Ambrose would not be waiting at home for him; he was coming very soon to the Estate Office and, when he had given Jim his instructions and discussed the topic of the sale of the fields with Lord Dalmane, he would be going back home to meet the doctor when he arrived.

Jim thought that this whole incident was a good stroke of luck for him. Less than one hour ago, while he had been eating his breakfast, he had been thinking of how he did not want to meet

Lord Dalmane lest he should hear that the Earl had found out something about that picnic. But it was only too clear now that he knew nothing at all about it. Jim was feeling immensely relieved to know that not only was he in no trouble with Lord Dalmane over his involvement in Susan's picnic, but here was Lord Dalmane in a good and friendly mood. I do believe it's going to be all right after all about our picnic, he thought. Obviously he knows nothing about it, and no one is likely to tell him anything now. That young farm worker must have kept his mouth shut about what he saw when he came across Sue "sunbathing" on the rug. He'll probably have forgotten about it by now, and so Mr. Challice won't be told anything. Now, if only these damned guests who are coming today don't prevent Sue and I from having our private talk in the sewing-room this evening, things look like working out really well.

Lord Dalmane replaced the receiver of the telephone on its bracket. "Well, Jim," he said, "Ambrose will be at the Estate Office in about ten minutes, he said, so we'll walk round there and meet him. You'll have gathered that Mrs. Ambrose is not very well—nothing serious—but that's what kept him at home."

The two men left the study and, going this time by way of the front door of the Castle, strolled round to the Estate Office, chatting together happily almost as if they were old friends. Jim felt particularly pleased when Lord Dalmane said: "I'm really pleased that you're getting on so well in your job here, Jim. Ambrose tells me that you are a marvellous worker and ideally suited, he thinks, to being the Guide for our tourists."

"Thank you for saying so, sir. I do my best," said Jim.

Time passed slowly for Jim Sandy that day, waiting as he was, impatiently, for half past seven in the evening. Half past twelve found him sitting on a wooden bench near the Visitor Centre eating a snack for his lunch. The day was very warm for early September, so Jim had thought that it would be pleasant to sit out of doors to eat there, as he had done many times during the summer. He had been into the Cafeteria and obtained his food free as a member of the Castle staff (the Cafeteria and the other buildings at the Centre were designed primarily to serve the visitors' needs: there were the Cafeteria, the Souvenir Shop, ladies' and gents' toilets, and a huge car park). Jim had gone down to the Visitor Centre because a coach-load of day-trippers from Bournemouth was expected at about one o' clock. He would give those people when they arrived about half an hour to refresh themselves at the Centre before setting off on the usual guided tour. He had authority to organise the itinerary and approximate timetable of each tour exactly as he thought best, but he had evolved a Standard Tour which he generally kept to, omitting parts of it only if time was pressing. Major Ambrose did not interfere at all nowadays with the way in which Jim organised this important part of his work, nor did he usually stand in for him as a Deputy Guide on his days off on Tuesdays, or when he was off work because of sickness or holiday: on these occasions the guided tours were "off" and the tourists were left to wander around the place more or less as they wished. Jim had a holiday coming up shortly but he had as yet given it little thought: he was to travel home to Cockermouth by train.

As he ate a sandwich sitting on that bench in the sun Jim was thinking about how frustratingly slowly the hours of that day seemed to be passing. Hurry on, half past seven! he kept saying to himself. There was no one about near his bench, which stood on an area of pavement beside the car park; behind him was a high hedge dividing off a lawn. The sun shone warmly down and it was very quiet apart from the occasional songs of birds: one of those calm, almost windless days which often occur in early autumn. Suddenly Jim heard voices coming from somewhere behind him. He stopped eating and for a moment sat still to listen. There were people on the lawn just on the other side of that high, thick hedge which screened the bottom of the Castle gardens from view from the area around the Visitor Centre. Jim listened attentively. Why, that's Sue's voice, he said to himself, recognizing her voice: a fairly low-pitched one for a woman's voice, but there was a certain softness of intonation which to Jim's ears was highly distinctive. Yes, that gentle voice is Sue's, and there's another woman . . . heavens, what a fearfully affected accent she has, quite ridiculously aristocratic . . . and that's a man's voice. They must be those other Dalmanes, Dick, John Dalmane's brother, and his wife—what was her name? Jane?—and that's Lord Dalmane. They must be showing those guests around the garden before they have their lunch.

"We won't go down to the Visitor Centre; there's nothing to see there, and you've been past it before, anyway." That was Susan's voice. "We might as well stroll back and have our lunch now."

"A bite of lunch would be very welcome, thank you, Susan," said the other woman's voice with the highly affected accent. "How nice your garden is looking!"

"Yes, you've got everything really tidy down here," said Dick Dalmane's voice, which was very like Lord Dalmane's, Jim decided, but a little more refined. "By the way, what is there over that way— up that path beside the narrow lawn and through a gap I can see in a row of little evergreen trees? I don't think I've ever been up there when we've been at Rhodes Castle before."

"There's only the Servants' Graveyard up there," said Susan's voice. "Not very interesting, but we'll just have a look at it, if you like, while we're here."

At this point Jim Sandy stood up. He had nearly finished eating his snack, but his curiosity was getting the better of him. He wanted to see what these guests looked like without being seen himself. The big, old hedge behind him would, he knew, screen him from sight from the other side if he were quiet and careful, so he hurried quietly up to it and found a place where he could peep through the dense mass of beech leaves, twigs, and branches.

"You have a servants' graveyard?" Dick Dalmane's voice was saying. "What an anachronism!"

Jim, peering through the leaves, which were mostly still in their summer green, saw a man who looked, at first glance, quite similar to Lord Dalmane; but he was a little shorter, and clean-shaven except for a small, neat moustache. Unlike his elder brother, the Earl of Saint Helens, this younger brother wore spectacles, but Jim saw that his brown hair had the same slightly reddish tint in it as Lord Dalmane's. He was wearing an extremely smart-looking dark suit with well polished black shoes, beside which the clothes Lord Dalmane was wearing, an old tweed suit of jacket and trousers, looked positively unkempt, although really they were perfectly clean.

"But you don't still bury your servants in a graveyard of their own, surely?" said his wife, Jane Dalmane.

"Oh no, not nowadays we don't," said Lord Dalmane.

"But the last servant to be buried there was interred quite recently: 1951, I believe," said Susan. "A certain Mrs. Buxton, it was. Come on, I'll show you, and then we'll go back for lunch."

"Well, fancy that; it was only ten years ago that this Mrs. Buxton was buried in this private graveyard!" said Jane. Jim, peeping at her, saw a woman who could have been in her early thirties, with longish blonde hair. His first impression was that she was remarkably ugly. Afterwards, when he had had time to think about it, he came to the conclusion that the features of her face were somehow too masculine to be pretty; certainly compared with the soft outlines and utter femininity of Susan's sweet face, this woman's large nose and mouth looked clumsy, most unattractive. And her hair! said Jim to himself, still peeping at her through the hedge. Anyone could see that it's been dyed. It's not a bit like Samantha's: her's is more of a golden colour and obviously a natural shade of blonde. I don't like either of these people; and I particularly don't like their artificial, ultra upper-class accents.

The party on the lawn seen through the beech hedge was now moving away, led by Susan. Jane Dalmane's strident voice carried well through the still air, and for a few seconds more Jim could still hear what she was saying. "Oh, Susan, we had such a <u>lovely</u> time in Gstaadt. You know, this was our first visit to the Alps in summer; we'd only been there before for the skiing in winter . . ." The party had crossed the drive and was walking up the path between the Inner Lodge garden and the narrow piece of lawn which was a part of the Dalmanes' gardens. A second or two more, and Jim could no longer hear what Jane Dalmane was saying. Then they disappeared through the gap in the trees. Jim returned to his bench to finish his lunch, thinking again of that American tourist who had been so madly keen to see Beryl Buxton's grave and to talk about her ghost. I reckon there is no ghost of Beryl in the Library, said Jim to himself; but I've got that blue stone she must have left there. Gosh, I hope these other Dalmanes go soon! Sue will be disappointed too if we can't keep to our arranged meeting time because of them.

CHAPTER TWELVE

It was just after half past seven when Jim knocked on the door of the sewing-room. He had hopes that the other Dalmanes, Richard and Jane, had left as he had seen no sign of them in the last few hours, but he was not sure of this, and would not allow himself to feel glad that they had departed until he knew for sure that they had. He had rather expected to find those two sitting in the Green Drawing-Room that evening being entertained in conversation by Lord Dalmane while they waited for eight o' clock, which was the hour when, as Jim knew, the Dalmanes normally ate their dinner, as they called their evening meal. But he had not found Jane and Dick Dalmane in the drawing-room. There was no need for Jim to go in there first, before going into the sewing-room as the sewing-room did not open out of the drawing-room but had its own door from the passage; but Jim had thought that he would take a quick glimpse into the drawing-room to see whether Jane and Dick Dalmane were there and then, if they were not, go on to the sewing-room door. He had looked round the door of the Green Drawing-Room, which he had found ajar (for it was still reasonably warm in the house), and had seen Lord Dalmane by himself sitting in an armchair reading <u>The Times</u>.

The Green Drawing-Room was so called because green was its prevailing colour: the walls were covered with a pale green wallpaper. It was the room which the Dalmanes used as their regular sitting-room: John and Susan usually referred to it simply as "the drawing-room," whereas they called the grander State Drawing-Room, "the White Room" or "the State Room" as in it white predominated in the colour scheme. Jim had determined beforehand that he would not go into the Green Drawing-Room, or get drawn into any conversation there, if he could possibly avoid it. He was aware that he was taking a risk by this manoeuvre of being questioned by Lord Dalmane as to whether he was looking for someone, and he had decided in advance that he would answer, if necessary, that he was looking for Major Ambrose. True, it was not very likely that Major Ambrose would have been sitting in the drawing-room at that hour, particularly on a day when his wife was ill at home, but Jim knew that he did occasionally sit with the Dalmanes in there before dinner time if he had something to discuss with them.

"Hello, sir," said Jim, seeing Lord Dalmane immediately raise his eyes from his newspaper when he put his head round the door. The Earl nodded to him and continued to read his paper. Jim quickly withdrew, leaving the door ajar as before, having noted with pleasure that the other Dalmanes were not there, and feeling very thankful that Lord Dalmane had said nothing. Then he thought: Perhaps I'd better just have a quick look in the State Drawing-Room to make <u>quite</u> sure that they're not sitting in there. He looked at his watch, saw that it was not quite half past seven, and walked briskly back up the passage and crossed the Great Hall to the door of the State Drawing-Room. Cautiously he opened that door and looked round it; but that severely formal room was empty, as he had thought it would be. The china on the long display shelves and the gold of the chandelier were gleaming in the evening sunshine, and all was quiet in there, but the feel of the room was, as usual, cold and unwelcoming. Jim closed the door quietly. Good, he said to himself, those two guests really must have left. And now for the sewing-room and Sue at last! With a jaunty step he once more crossed the hall and set off down the passage, passing in order on his left the doors of Lord Dalmane's study, Major Ambrose's cupboard-study, and the Green Drawing-Room. Then he tapped lightly on the door of the sewing-room.

"Come in, Jim," said Susan's voice from the other side of the door.

Jim entered and, even as he did so, groaned inwardly at the sight that met his eyes. Susan was there, sitting at her sewing table, evidently busy with making some garment, but Samantha, the maid, was also there. Jim was so shocked for a moment at seeing Samantha that it was as if cold water had been thrown in his face. The frustration of it! Why did Samantha have to be in that room just when it was so vital to him to find Susan on her own for their private talk? He felt a sudden surge of anger towards the maid for being, in a literal sense, in the way of his plans, but in an instant he regained his composure: he felt his momentary anger being swallowed up in a re-established mood of calm hopefulness.

"Hello, Jim!" said Samantha with, Jim thought, a mischievous glint in her eyes as she looked up. She was kneeling on the floor measuring a spread-out piece of cloth with a tape measure.

"That's right, Jim," said Susan, "come in, but mind you don't step on that dressing gown. I'm making it for John for his birthday, and Sam's helping me with it. Just sit down, won't you?" She took her hand off the sewing machine for a moment and indicated an empty chair. "We'll talk in a few minutes, but I'd just like to get these measurements finished."

"I'll go, if you want to talk in private," said Samantha, rising to her feet.

"No," said Susan. "Not yet. You were just going to measure the length to see if we've got it too long. We'll get that done first, and have it noted down on your piece of paper. You don't mind waiting, Jim? It won't take us more than a few minutes. Then I can go on hemming the belt while you're talking to me."

Samantha dropped again nimbly to her knees and began to apply the tape measure to the length of apple-green silk which was carefully laid out on the carpet.

"How do you think John will look in it when we've got it made into a dressing gown?" asked Susan.

"Oh, fine," said Jim, who had sat down in the vacant armchair. "That pale shade of green will look splendid on him, probably." Really he was not at all sure about this, and could hardly visualise Lord Dalmane wearing the finished garment over his pyjamas.

He had about five minutes to wait until Samantha, her part in the work finished for that time, got up to go. He had waited quietly in the intervening time while he had watched the two girls busily completing the measuring task. Samantha called out various figures and used technical expressions which Jim did not understand, and Susan made notes in pencil on a piece of paper, but Jim did not interrupt them by a word. Impatient though he was to begin his private talk with Susan, he appeared quite calm and relaxed as he sat in the armchair. In fact, in spite of his frustration at the delay, coming as it had at the very moment when he had thought that he and Susan were about to be alone together, he was deriving a good deal of pleasure from watching those two working together. Jim knew that Samantha was seven years older than Susan, which made her thirty years old, although she hardly looked as old as that, he thought. Though they were both pretty women, seeing them together made him realise how different they were in appearance. Samantha with her long, fair hair and greeny-blue eyes, and Susan with her short, dark hair and dark eyes: those were the oovious differences between their faces, but there was something else, something much more undefinably different about them: something which Jim could not put into words for himself, although he tried to.

When Samantha had closed the door behind her Jim immediately looked hopefully at Susan. The moment had come at last. But Susan spoke first.

"Well, what is it, my love?" she said gently. "You know that it's all right about our picnic—you know, about me being seen by Robin Cottem? John certainly knows nothing about it, so I think that will be all right now. Robin won't tell now, as he hasn't told yet."

"Good," said Jim. "He's probably forgotten about it anyway by now."

"We hope so."

"But Samantha knows we're having a private talk now," observed Jim, who had forgotten for the moment that the blue gemstone was his special pretext for meeting Susan.

"You needn't worry about Samantha," said Susan. "She won't say a word to anybody. Even if I thought that she knew that I'd taken you out for a lunch picnic by ourselves, I could trust Sam to keep her mouth shut about it. I'm quite sure about that, Jim; but then I'm sure she doesn't know about it anyway. How could she know, when we've been so careful to see that no one finds out anything?"

"That's right: she doesn't know anything about Batcombe Hill." Jim smiled meaningly at Susan as he saw the smile shining in her eyes.

"It'll be all right about Sam, and it'll be all right about Robin Cottem," said Susan. She looked thoughtful for a moment, and then added: "And there's another thing. You were worried, perhaps, that our love-making might have made me pregnant?"

"I was really."

"Well, you can set your mind at rest about that side of it. I'm definitely not pregnant, Jim, my darling. There are reliable signs, you know, by which a woman can usually tell when she's pregnant, but I've had no trace of sickness these last few days—or any other signs that a baby might be on the way." She paused, noticing that Jim was a little red in the face at the mention of this embarrassing subject. "You needn't look so worried, Jim, my dear," she added a moment later. "Remember that I invited you out that day: the picnic was all my idea—and you could say, I suppose, that I invited you to make love with me!" Again she paused, and Jim, looking at her face, could not be sure whether there was a hint of a blush on it, or not; but her eyes were radiant with love, and her calm, quiet voice had a very soothing effect on him. He felt that his own embarrassment and agitation were rapidly slipping away.

"Yes, I suppose you did," he said. There was another little break in their conversation. Susan held a thimble in her right hand and was fingering it absent-mindedly, for now she was not thinking about her sewing task at all.

"Was there something else you wanted to talk to me about?" she suddenly asked.

Jim looked at her carefully. Was she expecting him to make an advance towards her? Was she inviting him to kiss her? He was not sure, but he had remembered the blue gemstone and decided that now was the time to mention it.

"Yes, I found something of your's the other day, Sue. At least, I think it must be your's." He dug in a pocket for the jewel-box.

"Oh, really?" said Susan wonderingly. "A jewel-box?" she added as Jim brought it out for her to see.

"There's a blue gemstone inside. Look!" He opened the lid and passed it to her.

"My word!" she gasped, her eyes opening wider in surprise. "Good heavens! It looks to me as if this might be . . . the Great Beryl. But where did you find it, Jim?"

"In the Tower Library."

"The Tower Library? But how on earth—whereabouts exactly did you find it?"

"The jewel-box was inside another box. There were a few things on top of the desk, and I'd sat down there to finish the inventory by adding them to the list—and there was this silver box—I put it down in the inventory as a snuff-box—and when I opened the lid I found the little jewel-box inside it."

"Good heavens!" said Susan again. "Well, fancy that! We thought the Great Beryl of Saint Helens had gone altogether—stolen—but perhaps it was in there all the time! Maybe no one ever thought of <u>opening</u> a snuff-box to look inside it. Maybe . . ." She stopped, and seemed to be thinking of what Jim's discovery might mean.

"But perhaps it isn't the Great Beryl," suggested Jim presently. Susan had taken the stone out of its box and was examining it closely. "Perhaps this is some other stone that just looks like a blue beryl, but isn't. I remember thinking when I found it that it <u>couldn't</u> be the Great Beryl."

"Maybe," said Susan doubtfully, "but it certainly looks to me like my big aquamarine . . . oh, Jim, my darling, I can't thank you enough if you've found that lost treasure! It was on that day when you were doing the inventory job, you say?"

"Yes, that's right,"

"But that was a long time ago! Do you mean to say that you've been keeping this thing all that time? It was a day in early June, I remember, when you were sent into the Library on that job."

"Well, I'm awfully sorry, Sue, but I have kept it in my room since that day when I found it. You see, I put it away in a drawer in my room where it would be safe; and, of course, I meant to bring it to you, but I'm afraid I forgot all about it."

"Until when?"

"Until last night, when I happened to open the drawer where it was. And then, of course, I knew that I <u>had</u> to see you today to give it to you—and so that we'd have an excuse to talk together privately, Sue!"

"Indeed, yes!" Susan's eyes sparkled at him for a moment; but then she looked again at the aquamarine resting in the open palm of her left hand. "Beautiful little stone!" she murmured to herself, and then, addressing Jim in a rather puzzled voice: "But, Jim, how had this stone in its little jewel-box come to be hidden inside that snuff-box? I know the silver box you mean: it has four silver legs and the Dalmane Crest stamped on the lid."

"Yes, it was in that box. Presumably Beryl Buxton must have put it there herself—that is, assuming that it was she who stole it."

"H'm, I daresay you're right about that." A thoughtful frown furrowed Susan's brow for a moment, and then she added: "It seems that she may have had second thoughts about stealing that stone. She probably brought it back and hid it there on the night when she killed herself. We can't tell what was in her mind, of course, but John says that she was very depressed at the time."

"It was after her husband had left her, wasn't it?"

"That's right: Mr. Buxton had apparently deserted Beryl—found another woman, I suppose, so it's hardly surprising that poor Beryl became very depressed."

"But you never met her, Sue, did you?"

"Oh, good heavens, no," said Susan. "I'm only telling you what I've heard about her. You see, she died ten years ago in 1951, but I only came here first early in '59 when I married John."

"Yes, I see."

"You know, Jim, although, of course, I can't be certain, I'm inclined to believe that this stone <u>must</u> be the Great Beryl." Susan was again examining the gemstone carefully.

"Is there no way we could find out for certain if it's the real stone?" asked Jim.

"Why, yes, there is," said Susan, her face suddenly brightening in a smile as she looked up. "I'll take it to my jeweller in the West End and let him examine it."

"In London, you mean?"

"Yes, my London jeweller. I know a man who's a jeweller in Bond Street, an expert in a firm of very classy jewellers. And in any case I was thinking of motoring up to London on Monday for some shopping at Harrod's, so I could take this with me and call at the "Crown Jewels" in Bond Street—that's the name that the firm trades under—and have this chap look at this stone. If anyone can recognize the Great Beryl of Saint Helens, he can."

"Why do you say that?"

"Because it was he who actually cut the Great Beryl and set it into my necklace 'The Luck of Saint Helens'. I'm sure he could tell whether this is the same stone. But if he says it is—and surely it must be—I don't think I'd ask him to re-set it in the necklace. After all, the Great Beryl is supposed to bring bad luck to its keeper and, anyway, I've grown very fond of the big diamond we've put on the necklace in place of the big aquamarine."

"Then what would you do with this stone? Sell it?"

"Possibly I might," said Susan. "I really don't know. Perhaps, if this chap tells me he reckons it is the Great Beryl, the best thing to do would be to have it kept in the vaults of my bank in Sherborne."

Again Susan stared into the limpid blue inner lights of the stone as if she were falling under some enchantment emanating from it. For perhaps a minute she did not speak except to murmur, more to herself than to Jim: "No, maybe I'll keep it myself to admire it occasionally—pretty little aquamarine!" Jim watched her silently. He looked at the round outlines of her lovely breasts under the low-necked red jersey she was wearing. The jersey fitted rather tightly over her upper parts, and he guessed that this evening she was not wearing her bra. He also noticed the tape measure lying on the floor where Samantha had dropped it near Susan's feet, and suddenly a wild idea came into his head. She had told him what her measurements were on that memorable day of the picnic, but what fun it would be to hold that tape measure to her bust himself, to see for himself how many inches she measured around there! But could he dare to do it now?

Just then, as if she had come to a decision regarding the future of the aquamarine, Susan suddenly put the stone back into its jewel-box, snapped the lid shut, and set it down on the table beside her sewing-machine. She glanced at her watch.

"I say, Jim, it's about seven minutes to eight—nearly time for your supper, and our's," she said. "Don't you think that perhaps it's about time you were on your way? Thanks ever so much for finding that stone, and looking after it, and bringing it to me." She hesitated, and then added: "There wasn't anything else you wanted to talk to me about, was there?"

"Well, er, yes . . . at least, not exactly," said Jim awkwardly. He flashed a momentary glance straight at Susan's bust and then immediately lowered his gaze to stare at the tape measure, hoping that she would understand what was in his mind. Squinting at her face as he looked downwards he saw a decidedly puzzled expression come over it; but suddenly it disappeared, and a smile lit up her face. Filled on the instant with boldness, Jim picked up the tape measure.

"No, no, no!" said Susan quickly. "It really wouldn't be safe, Jim, dear, to have any fun in here; and anyway I told you the other day about my vital statistics—while we were having our picnic."

"I know you did," said Jim. "But—but I would like to measure you myself, Sue." He stood up and stepped towards her, smiling and holding the tape measure.

"Oh, Jim, it <u>wouldn't</u> be safe. What if someone were to come in and find me with my top off while you're putting the tape measure around me?"

"Well, I could measure you without taking off that red jersey. It'd be much the same thing and safe enough—we'll be able to hear if anyone's coming along the passage before they come in here. Go on, Sue, say yes!" Susan had also stood up, and was backing away from him towards the wall, but Jim could tell by the look in her eyes that she really wanted to feel the touch of his hands on her breasts. He cornered her, took her hands, kissed her warmly on her lips, and flattened her gently to the wall. Suddenly they were both becoming very excited: Jim could feel the rapid beating of her heart as well as that of his own. For a moment they held their embrace and kissed. Then, with her help, Jim carefully encircled Susan around the bust with the tape measure.

"Gosh, almost thirty-nine inches!" he breathed as he drew the circle of tape tight around Susan's chest. "Look, Sue!"

"Yes, maybe I'm a bit bigger than I was—I haven't taken my bust measurement for a long time—but I must measure slightly more wearing this red top than I would with bare breasts."

"No bra?" whispered Jim.

"No bra today."

Jim let the tape measure fall away from her and gently pulled open the jumper at the point of the V neck until he could see most of her breasts under the garment. He buried his face in her magnificent cleavage while she clasped him tightly to herself, her arms round his neck. He had forgotten all about caution, and she seemed to have forgotten also, but suddenly she stiffened, and then pulled herself sharply away from Jim; and at the same moment he heard footsteps rapidly approaching along the passage from the direction of the Hall. They froze, and waited, but the steps went straight on down the passage past the sewing-room door. Jim recognized female footsteps, and guessed that it was Samantha. It was just as well that she had not come in, although they were no longer embracing.

"You must go, my darling," said Susan quickly. She kissed him lightly on the cheek. "But come in here to see me again soon another evening, won't you?"

"May I really?" said Jim.

"Of course you may, and we'll talk again—preferably when there's no-one else about. Good-bye for this time, Jim, my darling—and thank you again for that gemstone."

"Good-bye, Sue."

Bother the gemstone, said Jim to himself as he closed the door and set off down the passage for the kitchen. That was super fun, well worth waiting for. And she said I was to come and see her again another evening!

But he would soon be off home on his holiday. The next meeting with Susan in the Sewing Room—if indeed they could manage more such meetings in the evenings—might well have to wait until after his return from Cockermouth, depending mostly on whether Susan could manage to be free when he wanted to see her. As Jim sat down to his supper in the common-room he realised with some disappointment that Susan's latest invitation to him was so vague that nothing at all could be said to have been definitely planned. Nevertheless, he was in a light-hearted and optimistic mood as he began to eat a large helping of macaroni cheese with a healthy appetite.

CHAPTER THIRTEEN

The train stopped, and Jim Sandy opened the door and stepped down onto the platform of Cockermouth station. It was a dark September night, and the dim lights on the platforms did very little towards the general illumination of the place; rather, there were a number of separate pools of weak light so that it was hardly possible for Jim to take in at once the various faces of people waiting on the platform to catch the train. However, he immediately looked warily around before proceeding towards the exit in order to see whether there was anyone there he recognized. But it took him only a few seconds, watching the handful of new passengers boarding the train, and checking yet again the other faces who had disembarked with him, to be sure that there was no one he knew there. He had been rather glad to find, when he had changed trains at Carlisle and boarded the little local diesel, that Mr. Blencow was not on duty in it as the Guard, and that the man in the driving seat was certainly not Mr. Ruddock. Jim had now arrived in Cockermouth not yet having met any of his former acquaintances from the Lake country. In his mind was the hope that he would not see or be seen by any of his old Cockermouth friends, especially any former colleagues in the police, at least until he reached home; and it was his intention to head there straight away. Jim had come up from Rhodes Castle that day at the start of a week's holiday. Travelling by train from the South had taken virtually the whole day, the last leg of his journey having commenced when he had boarded the 7.53 p.m. train from Carlisle to Workington. Now, at a quarter past nine, he had arrived at Cockermouth station. He had not seen the place since the day more than two years ago when he had suddenly left his home and his job to go off by train in search of work in London, and had met Susan instead.

It feels funny to come home, he thought, as he walked along towards the exit through the Booking Hall. I suppose it's because I've got so used to thinking of Rhodes Castle as home. But it's rather cold so I'll hurry on home.

It certainly was rather cold. There had been rain off and on all that day in the many counties of England through which Jim had travelled, and it had been mostly a grey, cloudy day, although there had been gleams of sunshine from time to time. Then, soon after passing Lancaster, Jim had seen a wet and stormy-looking sunset over the hills to the west, and not long after that, as it grew dark, there had been more rain. It had seemed to Jim in his well lighted compartment of the express from the South that the darkness had come down very rapidly that evening. Sitting inside the train at night it was, of course, hard for him to be sure what the weather was really like, but judging by the fact that the rain, driven by a very strong wind, was making horizontal lines of water along his window, Jim concluded that it was very heavy rain. When he had changed trains at Carlisle there had been a welcome break between heavy downpours, but there had been more rain as he travelled on in the Workington train through the Lake District. Now, at Cockermouth, Jim had stepped out of the warm, fuggy train into a stiff north-westerly breeze, decidedly a cold-feeling wind, sweeping over the old railway station, and bringing with it a few drops of moisture, hardly enough to be called drizzle or proper rain. Jim thought that he saw a wavering of the dim gas lamps of the platforms in the stronger gusts of the wind, like candle flames flickering in a fresh breeze.

He handed over his ticket to the porter who was waiting by the entrance to the Booking Hall to collect it. Autumn, he thought, as that strong, cold wind met him again in a damp blast as he came out into the car park in front of the station. Carrying a small suitcase in his right hand he walked briskly across the car park in the direction of the street and the stone pillar of the town's War Memorial (which has on top of the plinth the figure of a winged lady holding a laurel wreath). However, he walked mechanically in the right direction, hardly noticing the War Memorial or anything else while he allowed his thoughts to follow a natural reverie. I'd have done better to have had this holiday a month or more ago, as Sue did suggest to me, he thought. I reckon summer's over now, and this is the first real back-end weather of autumn. But on second thoughts it doesn't really matter what the weather's like, as I'd rather have stayed at home—at Rhodes Castle—with Sue; and the Castle <u>does</u> seem more like home than up here. But if only Sue could have come to Cockermouth with me—that would have been best of all.

Jim had come out onto the street and was walking down the pavement, heading towards Station Street and the town centre and not really noticing anything, when two figures on the opposite pavement walking slowly together suddenly caught his eye. Instantly and automatically Jim quickened his pace as he walked to pass by those two. They were two tall people, a man wearing a helmet, and a woman wearing a hat with a chequered band around it, and both wearing dark blue capes which looked simply black in the yellow glare of a street lamp as they passed under it. They were certainly two police constables on the beat. There were a few other people about, but only those two constables were strolling slowly, as if aimlessly, whilst such other folk who were out in the wind and the drizzle were to be seen only briefly, hurrying along purposely to get indoors again somewhere as quickly as possible; and this made the constables conspicuous in spite of the artificial light, so that it was hardly surprising that Jim noticed them in spite of his daydream. He thought that the policewoman must be W.P.C. Laura Apsley, but he had not seen the other constable's face, and he hoped that neither would recognize him. Anyway, he thought, another few seconds and I'll be round the corner into Lorton Street.

"Hey! You there, deserter! Think we haven't noticed you, eh?" The loud and strident voce of the policewoman came from just behind Jim. Damn! he said to himself, and stopped, and looked back; he had almost come to the street corner where he was going to turn right into Lorton Street. He saw at once that the man was his old friend and former colleague, Constable Nickley.

"Hello, Jim! You're a stranger here nowadays?" said P.C. Nickley.

"Hello," said Jim. "I'm just going home."

"Going home? Haven't you come to see us, then, your former colleagues before your desertion?" said Constable Apsley.

"Well, perhaps—but not particularly," said Jim. "I've just come back to Cockermouth for a short holiday, that's all."

"Are you working, Jim?" asked Constable Nickley.

"Yes," said he shortly, "in Dorset."

"Well, perhaps you'd better not show your face to Sergeant Koppel while you're here, if you don't have to," said Constable Apsley. "He was pretty mad about you deserting with never a word to us. Happen you're better off down in Dorset out of his way. So long!" With that peremptory farewell and a wave of Constable Nickley's hand the two police officers continued their stroll up the road, while Jim, without a backward glance, hurried round the corner into Lorton Street.

Jim did not see Sergeant Koppel during his short stay in Cockermouth; nor did he see policewoman Laura Apsley on the beat in the streets again, although he did at one time or another meet all of his other former colleagues when he was in one or other of the town's two main shopping streets, doing a little shopping. This, however, he rarely did; he argued to himself that he was not deliberately trying to avoid meeting his former friends, so much as simply going where he wanted to go, and during the daytime, when he was not at home, that was mostly on walks by himself in the country. Jim would have liked more opportunities to go out with his father both for walks and, perhaps, for trips in his father's car to see some of the fine Lake District panoramas which he had not seen for over two years; however, his father's company was not available for him except on the Saturday and Sunday of that weekend. From Monday to Friday Mr. Sandy put in long hours of work as Mine Manager at the mine in the fells near Keswick, where a small labour force mined barytes under Mr. Sandy's general directions (he was also geologist to the small private company which owned the mine, an old lead mine). As manager, Mr. Sandy did not nowadays take up his pick or don safety helmet, other than on exceptional occasions, or when on a tour of inspection of the levels; instead his work was in a little brick building on the site which was used as the office.

Arthur Sandy was a man of physical features broadly similar to those of his son, Jim: like his son he was a tall, fair-haired man. He and Jim got on well with one another; Jim's mother's desertion of the family had, if anything, strengthened their close relationship. The morning of the day after Jim's arrival at Cockermouth turned out to be fine, although rather cool, and so Jim decided to go with his father in the car after breakfast when he set off for work at his barytes mine. Then, while Mr. Sandy worked in his office or went around the mine supervising the day's activity, Jim spent most of the morning walking or climbing on his own in the surrounding fells. He could not help feeling a sense of loneliness while he walked on his own; and this, of course, had the effect on him of making him wish that it could have been possible to have brought Susan along with him for his holiday. He wondered what would be the outcome of his last private talk with Susan in the sewing-room at which she had taken charge of the gemstone. Would it turn out to be that

Great Beryl, or would it not? It now seemed to Jim that it could hardly matter at all: at least, not to him.

Jim's thoughts took on a different aspect as he began to pick his way up a steep part of the little footpath which ascended the fell behind the mine. Mostly following the path, but occasionally taking his own short cuts, he was heading for some rough heaps of stones near the top of the ridge. These stones were all that remained to mark the position of another mine, a long disused lead working. Jim had found some interesting mineral samples there before, and this time he was hoping to find a good piece of yellow fluorspar; he knew that there was supposed to be fluorspar lying about up there as well as the lead minerals, galena and cerussite, which he had found on earlier visits to that old working.

He found the piece of stone he was looking for accidentally and before he had started seriously to look for likely mineral specimens. Jim was moving cautiously up a stretch of loose scree—by way of taking a short cut—when in spite of his care he missed his footing and slipped. Luckily he only slid back a few yards down the scree and did not hurt himself, but when he came to rest he found that his right hand had closed on a loose piece of stone. He looked at it. Gosh, he said to himself as he turned it over, this is the very thing I was looking for! On one side of the stone were a mass of little, pale yellow cubic crystals, some of them appearing rather transparent: Jim recognized it as a good specimen of fluorspar. He slipped it into a pocket and climbed on.

Not long after that Jim came to a summit cairn on the top of the fell. He rested a few minutes by the little pile of stones while he admired the wide and splendid view in many directions. He was nearly a thousand feet higher than his father's mine from where he had started, but he could not see it: the mine tip heaps were too close in against the steep side of the fell to be visible from the summit cairn. The very fresh wind that was blowing was the same cool north-westerly breeze which had greeted his arrival at

Cockermouth the evening before, but up there on the top of the fell it felt very strong indeed, almost gale force, Jim thought. He soon started down again to get out of the wind; as on the upward climb the fell itself gave him shelter from the north-west. There was a good deal of cloud in the sky most of the time, but also plenty of blue sky and frequent intervals of sunshine; and so far it had kept fine. It was the sort of day when one would expect showers, but when Jim looked up at the clouds from time to time he noticed that they were mostly small and white, and that they were being blown very rapidly across the sky in the strong wind. But, although he noticed the fresh aspect of the sky with pleasure, he was soon engrossed again in a pleasant fantasy in which he was imagining that Susan was climbing with him, at his side. What a place this would be, he suddenly thought, for a picnic like the one we had on Batcombe Hill! And around here no one knows Sue, so even if we were seen making love it would be all right—or would it? Someone might well recognize <u>me</u> here. No, of course, that would never do. Anyway it's far too open around here for that sort of thing.

According to plan he was back shortly before half past twelve at the mine office building to share a picnic lunch of sandwiches with his father. Mr. Sandy was there with one of his miners, Bob Cole, his foreman, an older man than Arthur Sandy, and a man with long experience of work in the metal mines of the Lake District fells. There were, indeed, only six men employed altogether by the Leadthwaite Barytes Mining Company Ltd. as miners under Mr. Sandy, as manager, plus a handful of other employees—the company had one wagon of its own, and so needed one or two men qualified as Heavy Goods Vehicle drivers who could also turn mechanics when necessary. With such a small workforce under his command Mr. Sandy counted all the men his personal friends, but Mr. Cole was especially his close friend and adviser, and acted as Deputy Manager when his boss was absent for any reason. When Jim came in to the Office he found that the two men had already opened their packets of sandwiches and had begun to enjoy their lunch. Jim knew Mr. Cole and so did not feel at all shy at coming in to join their lunch picnic. He washed his hands at a small sink in a corner of the room, and then came over to the table where the lunch was spread out—cheese sandwiches laid out on pieces of greaseproof paper, mugs, and bottles of beer—a simple but appetising picnic.

"Beer, Jim? A bottle of lager?" said his father.

"Oh, yes please, dad; I'm jolly thirsty after all that climbing," said Jim; "and hungry too."

"Well, tuck in, then. Here's your lager." Mr. Sandy opened a bottle, and slowly poured out the contents into a mug for Jim. He pulled up a stool to sit at the table as there were not enough chairs: Mr. Sandy and Mr. Cole were already sitting on the only two rough wooden chairs in the room. Jim had noticed a desk in a corner of the room by a window, and a heavy, revolving desk chair pulled up to it, and had decided that it must be his father's special desk chair, not meant to be moved. He gulped down some lager, and then bit into his first sandwich. As he ate he looked around. The square room looked much the same as he remembered it from his last visit of several years ago. There were two doors: one lead in up a step from outside, and the other was marked "Toilet" and lead to the lavatory: the little brick office building consisted only of these two rooms. There was another, much larger building on the site which housed all manner of stores and machinery. Jim looked at the manager's desk and noted a typewriter, telephone, and two trays of papers on it, and put the question which came into his mind.

"Do you do all the typing yourself, dad?"

"I always have done until very recently; but not any more," said Mr. Sandy. "I've a secretary now who deals with all that sort of thing very efficiently, a Miss Rothwell—a very nice girl."

"Very!" added Mr. Cole in a surreptitious undertone to Jim; he was sitting beside Mr. Cole.

"Oh!" said Jim. "But I suppose she only works part-time?" He was looking at the empty chair by the desk.

"The firm can only afford to pay her for two afternoons a week," said Mr. Sandy. "Such is our precarious financial position, Jim—in other words, we're damn near bankrupt, and may have to go out of business soon, worse luck. But Jackie Rothwell is the only female employee on our payroll at the moment. You'll see her this afternoon, Jim. She generally comes in at about one o'clock to start work at half past one—so she could be here quite soon."

"Aye, you're in luck, Jim," said Mr. Cole. "If you'd come to visit us on a Monday, a Wednesday, or a Friday, you wouldn't be seeing Miss Rothwell, as she's only here on Tuesday and Thursday afternoons. Ah, but she's a very pretty young woman, Jim, is Miss Rothwell!" He caught Mr. Sandy's eye across the table for a moment with a mischievous glint in his own dark eyes. Mr. Cole, Jim thought, could have been almost any age between about fifty and seventy; he was short with black hair, slightly greying, brown eyes, and a clean-shaven face.

"Yes, I must admit she *is* rather attractive," agreed Mr. Sandy.

"Rather?" exclaimed Mr. Cole. "Why, Arthur, you absolutely adore her—although she's only been here for three weeks! You've a crush on her—you might as well admit it!"

"All right, then, I do admit it!" said Mr. Sandy. "And what's wrong with that?"

"Wrong? Eh, there's nowt wrong with that, if you fancy her that much."

"How old is she?" asked Jim. He was startled to hear of a pretty, young secretary at the mine office, and even more startled at Mr. Cole's revelation, but he noticed that his father did not seem in the least embarrassed in admitting a strong attraction towards his new secretary.

"Miss Rothwell is twenty-three years old," said Mr. Sandy. "And, though I call her 'Miss Rothwell', I should, perhaps, really call her 'Doctor Rothwell': Jackie is a science graduate from London University, a D.Sc."

"Oh!" Gosh, Jim said to himself, she's only Susan's age, but she's brainy as well as pretty. This sounds interesting!

"Have another sandwich, Jim?"

"Yes, thank you."

As he continued to eat cheese sandwiches and drink lager beer Jim kept looking through the window, hoping to see Jackie Rothwell arrive: apparently she lived in Cockermouth and drove her own car, a Mini. He saw the sky suddenly grow dark outside, and then, with little warning, it was raining. In another moment it was pouring down really heavily.

"My word, Jim, you were lucky not to get wet on your walk up the fell," said his father, staring at the water streaming down the window panes.

"Hello!" he added a moment later, "hailstones!" There was a loud rattling noise of big hailstones bouncing off the slate roof and the plate glass windows of the office building. Jim went to a window and looked out.

"The hail's lying on the ground like snow," he said.

"Shows how cold it is today," commented Mr. Cole. "But, of course, those hailstones will very quickly disappear once the shower's over, as it's only September—not winter yet."

"True," said Mr. Sandy, "but it won't be very nice for Jackie driving over the pass in this weather, if she's on her way now—as I expect she is." He looked at his watch.

"She'll be all right," said Mr. Cole. "It'll be over by the time she gets here, likely."

Jim and the two men went on with their lunch without hurrying over it: there was no need for any hurry, Mr. Sandy explained, as there was an hour allowed for lunch break for everybody, himself included, from half past twelve to half past one.

Within a minute or two they saw the hail revert to rain, but it continued to be wet outside while they ate.

"Convenient of it to be wet <u>now</u> while we're having our lunch, isn't it?" said Mr. Sandy. "Assuming, of course, that the shower will be over by the time we want to go out. Do you know, Jim, I reckon you've got a better job than mine here."

"Oh, I don't know about that, dad," said Jim. "After all, this is your mine, and you're the manager here; and in spite of what you were saying about financial difficulties, it <u>is</u> fairly prosperous, isn't it?"

"I wish I could say it was!" said Mr. Sandy with a laugh.

"Aye, what your dad means is that there's nowt much in t' way of prosperity in mines like this nowadays," said Mr. Cole. "And so what's your job then, Jim?"

"Hasn't dad told you?" said Jim. "I work down in the South for the Earl and Countess of Saint Helens." (He was pleased to hear a quiet gasp of amazement at this). "They live at a place called Rhodes Castle, in Dorset, which has huge grounds, usually open to the public. I'm employed as the Guide, and I live there."

"Phew!" exclaimed Mr. Cole. "So you work for an Earl at some great castle! I bet it's a well paid job you've got. No wonder you say, Arthur, that Jim's got a better job than what you or I have!"

"That's right," agreed Mr. Sandy. "You see, Jim, what you've got, being the Guide of Rhodes Castle, which we've <u>not</u> got working here, is job security. I don't see what's to stop you staying on at Rhodes Castle for years, if you're happy at your work there, as I believe you are, and maybe being appointed presently to some even better position in the Castle. You aren't thinking of leaving, are you?"

"Oh no, dad, certainly not! I'm very happy working for the Dalmanes."

"Yes, I gathered you were from your letters. Well, you've got a job with a future, a secure job, but you could hardly say the same of Mr. Cole and I, or our other workers here."

"Oh, I know what you mean, dad. You've told me before that this mine is hardly a viable business proposition. You must have nearly got to the stage where there's no more barytes left to be mined in this hillside, or else you simply can't get much more out—because it's too deep, or something."

But Mr. Sandy and Mr. Cole both shook their heads.

"No, it isn't like that, Jim," said his father. "It isn't a question of our not being <u>able</u> to mine the stuff for much longer."

"Precisely," said Mr. Cole. "And there must be any amount of barytes left in this hillside, enough maybe to go on mining it at the present rate for another ten or even twenty years—that's assuming that we'll find plenty more in unexplored parts of the veins, further down into the hillside. No, but the thing is, Jim, that it's all a question of economics, whether one can go on with a small, private venture like this. Capital expenditure's very heavy, and there's damn little profit in barytes nowadays."

"Too true, it's a question of economics," said Mr. Sandy. "And there's no doubt that this is an uneconomic mine. Now, if our small company is taken over by one of the big, international corporations—and there's a fair chance that such a take-over could, be in the offing—then I think we could be saved in the short term from a complete shut-down in the very near future. But, even if we are taken over, I should think that we'd only survive for a few more years at best—for reasons of simple economics—until someone in authority says: 'Leadthwaite is an uneconomic mine, and therefore it must close'."

"And then, there we are, out of our jobs," said Mr. Cole, "and on the dole, very likely. An old miner like me'd never get another mining job in this area—no chance. Mind you, when a mine or a pit does become uneconomic to work, I don't dispute the logic of closing it down, and the inevitability of job losses to follow. It may be a very pessimistic view, but that's the only sort of future I foresee for t' likes of me."

"You're right, Bob," agreed Mr. Sandy. "Worse luck, there's not much future in mining in these fells, as I see it—unless most unlikely discoveries of ore should be unearthed. But even then— mining prospects wouldn't look good."

"But why not, dad?" asked Jim. "Surely, if you discovered a new reserve of barytes nere, you'd mine it? Just suppose, for the sake of arguement, that tomorrow you find a new lot of barytes in a place underground where you'd never suspected there was any."

"H'm, some hope!" muttered Mr. Cole, and took another bite of his cheese sandwich.

"And you decide to do some prospecting at once," continued Jim, ignoring Mr. Cole's interruption, "to ascertain by scientific means the likely extent of the new discovery. And you find out, or it seems to you from your soundings, that what you've found is a vast body of barytes, probably occupying the whole inside of this hill. Surely then you wouldn't say that the prospects don't look good?"

"Ah, maybe not!" said Mr. Sandy, and dissolved into laughter at his son's wildly enthusiastic and unlikely assumption. Mr. Cole did not laugh, but there was a wry smile on his face at the all but impossible thought (as he reckoned) of their suddenly striking rich into some stupendous bonanza of hidden mineral wealth. "Maybe you should come into the mine this afternoon, Jim, to see for yourself just what there is where we're mining now, and to estimate the likeliness of what you've just described."

"I'd love to come inside, if I may," said Jim.

"Well, you can come into the New Level, and welcome. We've some spare safety helmets."

"Thanks a lot, dad. I was hoping you'd invite me in; it was fascinating underground in the level the last time I looked around, several years ago."

"Ah, but we've done quite a bit since then. Your last visit, Jim, was into Number One Level, if I remember right, where we'd nearly worked out the useful stuff. The New Level, Number Zero, hadn't even been started then."

"Is it Number Zero because it's lower down the hillside than Number One Level?"

"That's it."

"Well, I know where the entrance is," said Jim. "I saw the place this morning before I went off climbing up the fellside: it's that door into the hillside where a tramway leads in, and where you've put up a notice: 'DANGER. KEEP OUT'."

"Yes, that's the entrance to our New Level," said Mr. Sandy. "The notice is there to keep unauthorised people out at times when we've got the door open when we're working inside. Anyway, come in and have a look round when you've finished your lunch . . . Ah, here's Jackie."

At that moment they heard a small car drive up and stop just outside the office. Jim looked out of the window eagerly: he had been looking forward to seeing Jackie Rothwell after what he had heard about her. The driver, a brown-haired woman wearing a shiny black mackintosh, switched off the engine and windscreen wipers of her car, a Mini, stepped out into the rain, which was now easing off, slammed the car door, and made a short run for the office door.

"Hello!" said Jackie Rothwell as she came into the office. "That was a pretty nasty shower!" She began to unbutton her mackintosh, which was hardly wet, to hang it up on a hook behind the door.

"Hello, Jackie," said Mr. Cole.

"Hello, Jackie," said Mr. Sandy. "Yes, that shower was very heavy, but it seems to be nearly over now: there's the sun shining again. This is my son, Jim, who's come to visit us today to see what goes on in the mine. This is my secretary, Jackie Rothwell, Jim."

"How do you do?" said Jim a little shyly.

"How do you do?" said Jackie cheerfully, shaking hands with him. He was instantly struck by her beauty: perhaps he had not really believed in what Mr. Cole had said about Jackie being "a very pretty young woman". "You'll find it very interesting inside the New Level, if that's what you've come to see," she added.

"I'm sure I shall." said Jim.

For the moment, he could find nothing further to say to her; however, it seemed that there was no need to say anything further yet. Her jolly smile pleased him enormously and, without knowing it, he was smiling back at her. She went over to the desk and sat down in the revolving chair, turning it so that she sat facing the others.

"Coffee, Jackie?" said Mr. Sandy, who had stood up, and gone over to a small cupboard in the wall, and opened it.

"Please," said Jackie.

"And for you, Jim?"

"Yes, please," said Jim.

Mr. Sandy took from the cupboard various things for making instant coffee: three cups (Mr. Cole did not drink coffee), one saucer—there was only one, meant for Jackie—a jar of instant coffee, one of powdered milk, sugar and teaspoons. Then he switched on an electric kettle which was standing on a small adjacent table, having first checked that there was enough water in it.

Presently Mr. Sandy, Jim, and Jackie Rothwell were drinking their cups of coffee while they talked, and Jim was looking at Jackie admiringly; he was trying not to stare at her, but his eyes kept moving their gaze towards her whenever he tried deliberately to look somewhere else. Jackie was sobrely but smartly dressed: she was wearing a white blouse, open at the neck, and over it a dark navy-blue V-necked pullover, with a matching dark blue skirt. She had big, greeny-blue eyes which, as Jim had noticed, looked very bright indeed when she gave him a sparkling smile. Her eyebrows were dark and well-formed, and her hair was a darkish shade of brown, slightly curly; it reached down to the nape of her neck, where lovely brown ringlets caressed her smooth, white skin. Jackie was not very tall, at only five feet, three inches, and this, with a large bust, made her look not exactly fat, but almost, Jim thought, a little plump. Her breasts particularly delighted Jim. I believe she might almost be bigger than Susan in front, he thought. He was near enough to her to look closely at her fingers, which he did, scanning them for an engagement ring or a wedding ring, but he saw no rings at all on any of her rather short, fat fingers. I wonder, he thought, whether dad might eventually marry her, if she stays here long enough as secretary and, of course, if dad gets his divorce from mum. There's not really all that much difference between their ages. But then, it does seem unlikely, I suppose, that Jackie will be able to stay on as dad's secretary for long enough to get to know him well because of the company's financial crisis—perhaps the mine will have to close down next year. But what was dad saying about a possible takeover by a big international corporation? If that were to happen, would it make people's jobs here safe?

Jim was not expecting to hear his questions answered, but just then Mr. Sandy put down his cup of coffee on the table, and spoke in an almost casual way to Jackie Rothwell.

"Miss Rothwell, would you be interested in a possible full-time job here?"

"I'd be very interested!" she said.

"You like working here as my secretary?"

"I enjoy it very much, thank you, Mr. Sandy."

"Well then, there's a possibility—and, mind you, this _is_ only a possibility—nothing's certain yet—that we may soon be able to offer you a fulltime, Monday to Friday job as secretary and accountant. But it all depends on how our negociations with RTZ go on. If they <u>don't</u> take us over then, frankly, I see no future for our little company; but if the take-over goes ahead, as we hope it will, and we become a subsidiary company of RTZ, then we should be saved from the prospect of going into liquidation, and most, if not all, our jobs here should, we hope, be secure for a few more years at least. In your case, Miss Rothwell, with your geological training behind you, we could—as I hinted at your interview when we took you on for two afternoons a week—be thinking of a much more interesting sort of work for you."

"You mean, you might be asking me to do some field work as well as my desk work?" asked Jackie Rothwell. "Helping with prospecting, and that sort of thing?"

"Precisely," said Mr. Sandy. "We'd certainly want you to continue with the secretarial work, including, as I said before, work on preparing the accounts, and the balance sheet, and so on, as well as typing the letters. But then, from time to time—and this is assuming that you're working a nine to five, Monday to Friday job—I'd need a qualified assistant to help me out of doors with the various scientific instruments for prospecting. And that's where your knowledge of these things would come in very useful."

"I'd be most interested to do that sort of work sometimes, Mr. Sandy. I really would be."

"Then I hope you'll be able to. But remember: we can't count on any of these things actually happening. In the end it'll all depend on the RTZ shareholders when they put the take-over proposals to the vote."

"And their Board of Directors will recommend to them how they should vote anyway," said Mr. Cole. "I wouldn't like to speculate on the outcome of it. But unless they vote for the take-over we're sunk, as I see it—we'll all be out of our jobs. By the way, Arthur, didn't I hear you saying something the other day about them sending in some of their own geologists to do a bit of snooping around here?"

"That's right," said Mr. Sandy. "Any day now we could be seeing two or three RTZ geologists here doing a bit of prospecting, or 'assessing our reserves', as they put it in their letter—in other words they'll be trying to find out whether the Leadthwaite Barytes

Mine is <u>worth</u> taking over, or not, and reporting back to their Board."

"Aye, and I'm not too hopeful of what they'll find out," said Mr. Cole.

Ten minutes later the three men came out of the office building, all of them wearing on their heads miners' safety helmets, having left Jackie in the office to type a pile of letters. As they followed the rails of a narrow-guage tramway which lead to the entrance of the New Level, Jim was thinking of his position as Guide of Rhodes Castle in a new light. He had not joined in the conversation about the possible take-over of the company by the RTZ Corporation, and about Jackie's possible new, full-time job, but had sat listening while he drank his coffee. Even if the take-over did happen, he realised that his position at Rhodes Castle should be a much more secure one than his father's, or those of the other workers at the mine. His father had said that at best he did not foresee the mine staying open for longer than about another ten years. So by 1972, probably, or sooner maybe, there'll be nothing going on here, he said to himself. But what about me? Why shouldn't I still be the Guide at Rhodes Castle in 1972? I won't be dismissed now, surely, as Lord D. hasn't found out anything, but another time Sue and I'll have to be more careful.

They were walking along beside the tramway between high banks of loose stones when, on turning a corner, they saw the door into the hillside which was the entrance to Number Zero Level. Here they met the other miners who had also been having their lunch break; they had taken refuge from the rain in a small stone hut there, but close to the door there was a large, flat slab of stone on which the men were accustomed to sit on fine, warm days during their lunch hour. Mr. Sandy took from his trouser pocket a key which he fitted into the padlock on the corrugated steel door; it was set in a very solidly built doorway into the steep hillside, where stout wooden posts were being used as the door lintels, with a strong wooden beam over the top of the doorway.

When Mr. Sandy had opened the door, and the other miners had gone into the level, he turned to Jim.

"Ready, Jim? Have you checked your lamp?"

Jim switched on the lamp mounted on the front of his helmet, as he had been shown how to do it.

"It's working all right," he said. "But don't you have electric lights in there?"

"Yes, indeed," said his father, "we have mains electricity in the level, supplied by a cable from the office, and not only for lighting. The cutting machinery and the locomotive need electricity to power them. Couldn't do without it. You'll see, Jim. Now then, you follow me, and Mr. Cole'll bring up the rear. And watch your step, Jim, on the sleepers of the tramway. You'll have to walk between the rails, but you could easily be tripped up."

"All right, I'll be careful." Jim followed his father through the doorway into the newly-cut tunnel in the hillside. As he had expected, remembering his earlier visit to the Number One Level, he found it rather wet underfoot. A stream of water was trickling along beside the rails; it was flowing as there was a slight gradient to the tunnel. "It's what we call a self-draining adit," his father had explained to him.

The new tunnel did not go as far into the fell as Jim had expected it would go. He saw that the miners who had gone in ahead of him were already at work, loading newly mined ore into wagons standing on the tramway.

"Look at this!" Mr. Sandy, raising his voice to be heard above the din of an air compressor, drew Jim's attention to the wall on his right at eye-level.

"My word!" said Jim. "It's all solid barytes around here! We must be right inside the vein here?"

"We are, and luckily for us the vein is very wide where we're standing, and it contains a good deal of high-quality barytes," said Mr. Sandy. "It's not actually solid barytes, as there are impurities in it—galena and blende—which are impurities from <u>our</u> point of view, as it's only the barytes we're interested in. There isn't nearly enough lead or zinc ore to be worth bothering with. But if you look carefully you'll see where the ore occurs, in streaks and flecks in the barytes."

Jim peered more closely at the wall of the adit in the light from the lamp on his helmet. He ran a finger lightly over some crystals of the whitish mineral with a vitreous (glassy) lustre. Yes, it was all solid barytes. Or was it? Some of it was yellowish, but that was also barytes; but his attention was now caught by a dark patch of crystals which sparkled brightly in the light of his lamp.

"Yes, I've got it," he said. "Here's a good piece of zinc blende. I see what you mean about the ore occurring as impurities in a mass of barytes."

"The barytes, you see, is the gangue in which these ore minerals occur," explained Mr. Sandy. "But it's what we want. Now, the old men who worked the mine long before us found a good deal of lead and zinc ore in the upper levels, and we found more of them in Number One Level above here than we see down here."

"Oh. So the lower part of the vein is more gangue, and the upper part is mostly ore minerals, galena and blende?"

"Yes, that's more or less how it is; and they found other lead minerals with the galena in the upper levels: cerussite and stolzite. Have you got any stolzite in your mineral collection?"

"No, I haven't. What exactly is stolzite, dad?"

"It's lead tungstate—an ususual mineral."

"Gosh, I must try to find some for my collection. Is it rare?"

"It is quite rare," said Mr. Sandy. "You could try looking for it on the tip heaps outside, but I doubt you won't find any."

"I was going to comb those spoil heaps thoroughly anyway," said Jim. "I'd like to find a piece of stone which is a good sample of barytes, blende, and galena, all in one piece."

"You could easily find one like that out there."

Jim was fascinated by mineralogy. For him there was romance in mines and stones, and in the collecting of stones, particularly when they were beautiful or unusual mineral samples. He had quite forgotten Jackie Rothwell while he was in the level, just as he had forgotten Susan when Jackie had appeared in the office towards the end of the lunch break. The time he had spent in the level had been absorbingly interesting; he had even been allowed to use a hand drill under Mr. Cole's supervision. Then, when he had come out into the open air again, he spent a long time combing the mine spoil heaps, looking for mineral specimens good enough for his collection. It did not take him long to find what he was really looking for: a hand-sized piece of stone contaning roughly equal proportions of the three main minerals of the mine: barytes, blende, and galena. He had no luck in finding any of the rare mineral stolzite, but did not really mind, as he was pleased with what he had found. He could search again for stolzite another time.

When would his next visit be? His father said he was welcome to come with him to the mine as often as he wanted to. But Jim, when he thought about it, said to himself: I'd better <u>not</u> come on Thursday, which is Jackie's next day here. He sensed that too much of Jackie's presence would endanger his close and loving relationship with Susan. He could all too easily find that he was falling in love with Jackie. It would be better to avoid meeting her. Anyway, he thought, she seems to be dad's girlfriend! I won't come here on Thursday.

But Thursday found Jim back at the mine. The prospect of seeing Jackie Rothwell again proved an irresistible temptation.

CHAPTER FOURTEEN

Autumn at Rhodes Castle passed into early winter, not dramatically with any sudden cold spell, but gradually by insensible and quite unspectacular degrees. There were many dank, rather dark days, which were not really cold but only dismal, towards the end of October and in the first week of November. After that there was a spell of cool, fine weather with plenty of sunshine and a little frost at night sometimes, although it was never cold enough to be really like winter. Towards the end of November the weather turned more unsettled but milder, and it remained mostly like that until after the New Year.

There was less for Jim to do at the Castle in winter but, by a mixture of his own initiative and instructions from Major Ambrose, he managed to keep himself busy during working hours. The Head Gardener was the only gardener at Rhodes Castle employed on a permanent basis: usually other gardeners were taken on temporarily as necessary, generally from April or May to about the end of September, while at other times it was one of Jim's duties to assist the Head Gardener as required with the more menial outdoor tasks. The newly opened public rooms in the Castle were only open to the public in summer, but the grounds remained open to visitors all the year round, so that there was no season during which Jim's duties as Guide ceased altogether although, obviously, there were fewer visitors to attend to during the winter half of the year than there were in summer, and no organised coach tours. However, on most days there were a few people in the grounds, on whom Jim would keep a watchful eye, while he busied himself with some task such as sweeping leaves off the drive or chopping wood for fuel. But he was always ready to show any visitors who wanted to see it round the church, or to take them through the Maze and conduct them through the gardens.

In January the weather turned colder. By the beginning of the second week of the New Year there was the first snow of the winter lying on the ground, not very much, but it did not melt. It was the beginning of a prolonged spell of cold weather, much of it really wintry with severe frosts at night, and more snow from time to time, until a thaw began towards the middle of March. There were a number of false promises of a real thaw during the intervening weeks when mild air from the south-west would come in from the Atlantic Ocean, working its way northwards over the southern counties of England, and bringing with it a small thaw, until the mild air became displaced by the return of very cold easterly winds. During these lesser thaws the snow melted a little but never disappeared altogether. For days on end no visitors came into the Castle grounds, and Jim might have found that he had even less to do than usual, but he still managed to keep himself busy and very happy. When he was working on non-guiding jobs he usually managed not to feel bored by the routine nature of his circumscribed tasks; and when he was off duty he would meet Susan from time to time, sometimes by accident, but occasionally by arrangement, and when he met her by arrangement they would usually have an evening talk together in the sewing-room. From these talks it became overwhelmingly obvious to him that the affair of last summer's picnic on Batcombe Hill had never come to the ears of Lord Dalmane. Even Susan never mentioned it, unless to re-assure Jim briefly that there was still no trouble arising from their escape on that memorable day.

On the first occasion when they met in the sewing-room since Jim's holiday, an October evening, Susan surprised him by wearing the Great Beryl mounted in a new brooch. She had just received it back from her London jeweller, she explained. On her instructions it had been made into a brooch, and Jim, looking at it pinned onto the front of the black woolen jersey Susan was wearing, admired the jeweller's clever craftsmanship. He saw that the rectangular blue stone had been bedded into what appeared to him to be an oval nest of fine gold wires.

"Very pretty, isn't it?" said Susan. "That's twenty-two carat gold that the stone's set in. Mind you, it doesn't really look right on an ordinary jersey like this. But I've only put it on to show you it; normally I'd only wear it with formal evening dress."

"I must say, it looks very pretty, "said Jim.

Occasionally Jim would remember Jackie Rothwell, but now that he was back at Rhodes Castle his thoughts never lingered long with his father's secretary. When he pictured her in his mind he could not understand now how she had made such a great impression on him by her beauty. Yes, she was certainly pretty, but so were many other girls of around her age whom Jim had seen, and he was now inclined to believe that she was no great beauty. There's really nothing very special, or exciting, about Jackie's looks, he thought, although she is nice to look at. Dad certainly fancies her, though; you could tell that by the way he kept looking at her. And she seems to like being his secretary. Well, if this is the start of a relationship between them, I hope it blossoms.

*

"I'm going to walk to the farm after breakfast to see Bob Challice," announced Lord Dalmane one morning as he came into the breakfast-room to join Susan, who had already started her breakfast. "I'm going to let him have the deeds to his new fields now that the deal's all finished, but really that's just an excuse for walking that way over the fields on such a gorgeous morning. Why not come with me, Sue?"

"I'd love to John, but I can't," said Susan. "Remember that we've got Norma coming to lunch today. I must stay here to see that things are got ready."

"Oh yes, I'd forgotten about that. Is Mrs. Beck coming by herself, or with Nigel?"

"Only Norma by herself. I suppose Nigel must be working today, like any other day, although it's Sunday."

"Yes, I suppose so."

"But do go for your walk through the fields, John. It'll be lovely today in this warm sun, and I wish I could come, but really I mustn't. You'll be back by lunch time, won't you?"

"Oh yes, my dear, easily by lunch time, and probably by twelve o'clock, or soon after."

So it happened that on a morning of late March, a few days after the Spring Equinox, Lord Dalmane, wearing a short outdoor coat and, for the first time for several months, no scarf around his neck for outdoor walking, set off to walk to Summerhays Farm, which lay between Yetminster and the little hamlet of Chetnole. On the way he would be walking by a footpath through the very fields which Mr. Challice had just bought from him, the deeds to which Lord Dalmane would be carrying with him in a long brown envelope. He had every confidence that it would be a good morning for a country walk, of about two miles, as it already felt surprisingly warm out of doors when he set off at about half past nine through the back door of the Castle, and the bailey, thence passing into the rear parts of the garden through the main arch in the ancient wall of the courtyard. The long cold spell had come to an end some two weeks earlier around the eighth of March when it had begun, gradually, to turn mild. It had taken two or three grey, cloudy days of thaw, with relatively mild south-westerly winds, to melt completely all the lying snow. There had been a little rain and some foggy weather for several days as the warmer air rolled over the still frozen earth. Then there had been heavy rain, followed by days of changeable spring weather, remaining mild, with some sunshine and showers, or longer spells of rain at times. But on that morning of the 25th March there was no sign at all of any rain. Without doubt it was going to be the first really warm day of spring, with plenty of sunshine and only a light southerly wind; Lord Dalmane expected his outdoor thermometer to show around sixty degrees Fahrenheit by the time he returned home in the middle of the day. Indeed, he was not at all sure that he would not presently become uncomfortably warm walking in his overcoat, although it was only a light one.

Lord Dalmane walked down a garden path which lead to a small wooden gate for pedestrians; beyond this gate the path continued across the western corner of Rhodes Park and thence, as a public footpath, it ran south-westwards over the fields. But the gravel path on which he was now walking, and the gate which was just ahead of him, were public rights of way, as that part of the garden, to the west of the Castle, lay in the area open to the public. However, Lord Dalmane met no one that morning, and he thought that, on the whole, he was glad to meet no one as that way he could enjoy better looking at the crocuses in the rough grass to his left, and enjoy too listening to the manifest sounds of spring: the songs of the birds, and the buzzing of bees at the flowers. There were snowdrops and daffodils growing in that area of rough grass to the left of the footpath, as well as the crocuses, which were now at their best, and fully open to the warm rays of the sun; but the snowdrops were nearly over, and only about half of the daffodils were yet in flower. Lord Dalmane stopped, and then decided that he would turn aside briefly to have a closer look at the various bulbs which were showing in the grass. Close to him was a small metal notice at the side of the path: "Please keep off the Grass". Members of the public were invited to walk along that path, but the Head Gardener and, of course, the Dalmanes themselves, did not want to encourage anyone walking that way to take a short cut over that rough grass to reach the big West Lawn, which was only some thirty yards away, but which extended from there round the south-western corner of the Castle up to the Main Drive by the Ponds. Lord Dalmane put his feet down very carefully, meaning not to tread on a crocus by accident; some of them were hard to see in that longish grass. He stooped down and examined the exquisitely beautiful purple and white petals of a crocus, with its magnificent orange stamens and pistil. Ah, that must be a bee from the hives at North Lodge, he thought, as he listened happily to the drone of a bee, and saw it alight on the crocus close to his feet. My word, it really is spring, he said to himself.

Again treading carefully, Lord Dalmane returned to the gravel path. On the other side of it was a long flowerbed, a border full of bright flowers in summer, but at this time of the year, so soon after the ending of the cold weather, there was practically nothing flowering in it. Lord Dalmane looked up at a tall horse chestnut tree which stood just to the left of the gate. He noted with pleasure the swelling leaf buds. If the weather keeps as good as this for a week, he thought, those leaves will probably begin to come out. He went through the gateway and turned off the path to the right, where there was a grassy bank beside a ditch on the outside of the garden wall. Yes, I thought they'd be well out today, he said to himself. He knew that grassy bank as a good place in spring for seeing a fine display of lesser celandines, together with some violets and a few other wild flowers. He was already in a very light-hearted mood, but the sight of that bank of celandines, their starry yellow petals opened out as if to drink in the warm sunshine, cheered him and lightened his step even more.

There was a narrow strip of coppice which ran from north to south across the western corner of the Park, and the footpath from the garden ran straight across it at right angles. Being in the Rhodes Park this clump of deciduous trees was not bordered by any fence and, although there was a good deal of small undergrowth in the wood, the track of the footpath had been kept clear by the passage of many feet that way; consequently Lord Dalmane had no difficulty in following the path in among the trees and then, thirty or so yards further on, out again into the open Park. The Whitfield Copse, as the wood was called, was somewhat unusual for that part of the country in that it contained more silver birch trees than any other species, but there were also some poplars, aspens, willows, hazels, and other deciduous trees of the smaller sort; whilst in the northern end of the Copse there were also some pines and other evergreens, and near the path there was some squat, bushy holly. It was not easy to walk in the Copse off the path because of the dense undergrowth, so Lord Dalmane did not leave the path, but he walked slowly and paused to look up among the bare birch branches. He noted that these were in bud, like the horse chestnut he had just observed, although birch leaves normally come out later than early trees like the horse chestnut.

Presently Lord Dalmane came to Knighton Lane, the western boundary of Rhodes Park. Here he stopped by a stile in a fence to admire the view before proceeding further. Knighton Lane was a narrow but metalled road; on the Park side it was open, but on its other side a fence ran along it, dividing it from the fields of lush farmland which lay immediately beyond it. Lord Dalmane cast his gaze over the huge field which was extended before him, a sweeping expanse of bright, young green from the lane all the way down to the Leigh Brook, at the far end of the field, about four to five hundred yards away. The young grass, if it was grass seed that the farmer had sown there (Lord Dalmane was not at first quite sure about this) looked velvety smooth, and with the gentle downward curve of the field towards the distant stream it made a prospect which pleased his eye considerably. This was still one of his own fields, although his neighbour, Mr. Challice, farmed it for him. The public footpath ran in a straight line right across the middle of the vast field. This was, perhaps, a nuisance from a farmer's point of view, but this fact had come about because the Whit Field, as it was called, had once, long before Lord Dalmane's time, been two fields separated by a hedge along the muddy line through the middle where nowadays the footpath lay. In those days, as Lord Dalmane knew from the old writings about his property, the footpath had lain alongside the hedge at the edge of the right-hand field (as seen from Knighton Lane): that had been a reasonable course for a footpath across arable land although nowadays, the hedge having been removed a century or more ago to make a bigger field, the course of the path through the middle of the field looked slightly ridiculous. It was, of course, a broad track, combining the width of the old hedge and the old footpath and, what was more, it was often a very muddy track to walk on, as Lord Dalmane soon found out that it was on this very pleasant spring morning, after the recent rains. But he had been expecting mud on this country walk, and had set out well prepared to trudge through it; on his feet were black Wellington boots. Lord Dalmane kept carefully to the middle of the footpath, where there was a good, solid bottom to the track, and found that it was not as muddy as he had feared that it might be. Bob Challice had always pestered him for permission to have this tiresome footpath fenced in between two wire fences—it was tiresome from his point of view—in order to prevent or deter people from walking on whatever crops he might be growing on the field. But Lord Dalmane had always refused his permission to this idea on the grounds that fences, however simple they might be in construction, would spoil the appearance of that handsome field as seen from the top end by the lane, looking down across the green slope to the little, sluggish brook.

The Whit Field, mused Lord Dalmane as he walked across it. Of course, it must have been called "The White Field" once, and the name has become corrupted to "Whit" over the centuries. Fields are quite often called "white" as in "White Lea" or "White Meadow", but I've never really seen the point of it. Maybe this was once a White Field because it used to be covered in daisies or some other white flowers? But who knows? Anyway, it looks beautifully <u>green</u> today, a really vigorously growing colour, a velvety shade of green. It was all ploughed up the last time I saw it, last back end. And now, what has Bob sown in it? Is this grass and clover, or has he put in just plain grass seed? I really can't tell which, but it's marvellous to see how quickly it's greening up in this warm weather, after the rain.

Then Lord Dalmane noticed a bird standing on the field some way off. He extracted from the pocket of his coat a small, easily portable pair of field-glasses which he had brought with him and applied them to his eyes. He saw that the bird was a lapwing and, noticing another one sitting on the ground near it, surmised that the pair had a nest there. Lord Dalmane had heard that Bob Challice took any lapwings' and plovers' eggs which he found in his fields to eat them; he maintained that they were a tasty delicacy, but Lord Dalmane deplored the practice of taking any birds' eggs from their nests for any reason. Well, if there are any lapwing's eggs laid in this field they're mine, rather than his, he said to himself. Bob has no right to take them—not that he'd be deterred by that consideration, I know.

Lord Dalmane walked on down the big field. Before he came near the small stream which ran at the bottom of it he heard skylarks singing high above him in the calm, clear air, and he also heard the distinctive calls of curlews in flight. He was reluctant to leave that delightful place, as it was that morning, but pressed on, nevertheless, and soon came to the little footbridge over the Leigh Brook, which was nothing more than a brick-built arch over the small stream. Lord Dalmane looked down at the brook; it had more water in it than he had expected to see, and was flowing quickly enough to be just audible, although it was usually a silent, sluggish stream. Above the bridge a large area of dark green leaves down at the water's edge was a fair sized patch of marsh marigolds. Lord Dalmane thought that their large yellow flowers would be out in about another month, and made a mental note to take another walk down there to see them.

Almost immediately after crossing the brook, the footpath intersected a rough, muddy lane; but beyond this a stile took it on into the fields, the approximate direction of the path being indicated to pedestrians on a fingerboard bearing the legend: "Public Footpath to Chetnole". At this point in his walk Lord Dalmane came onto the first of the fields which he had just sold to Mr. Challice. He looked at his watch and decided that he ought to try to walk a little faster. If I don't, I'll take all morning to reach Summerhays Farm at this rate, he thought. Certainly he had been taking his walk at a very leisurely pace thus far, and although he now began to walk a little more briskly he was still looking keenly about him, enjoying enormously everything he saw.

He came to the Yetminster to Rhodes Corner road, crossed it, and reckoned that he had come about half way from the Castle to Summerhays Farm. All the fields through which the footpath passed on this western side of the brook had been his own fields, but had now been sold to Mr. Challice. Soon he came to a bridge over another little brook, and here he turned aside from the public right of way on the footpath, and walked down the stream to the right for a few hundred yards; he did not doubt that Bob Challice would never object to him walking where he would on his fields, since they had previously been his own. He stopped when he came to a boggy place in the corner of a field, down beside the stream. This swampy corner rejoiced in the name of Summerhays Marsh, just as if it was a place large and significant enough to feature on Bartholomew's Half Inch Map of Dorset—which it did not. However, it occupied quite a large part of one low-lying field, about a quarter of an acre in extent. Lord Dalmane hoped that Mr. Challice, as the new owner, would not be too quick in deciding to drain that field properly, as he had always found that marshy corner an attractive place; besides, Lord Dalmane was a great believer in trying to maintain a good ecological balance in the countryside by the application, where possible, of natural methods of farming. He was, in fact, somewhat ahead of his time by being in favour of what is now called "organic farming"; thus he opposed the use on farmland of unnatural chemicals for fertilizers, and the unnecessary drainage of swampy and boggy corners of fields, knowing that such places are the exclusive habitat of many creatures, particularly of some species of marshland birds. Unlike many members of the English nobility Lord Dalmane was by choice no sportsman: he had never handled a gun in his life, and had never given his permission to any other sportsmen to go shooting game birds on his land. However, he knew that Summerhays Marsh was a good place to go with binoculars to see certain kinds of birds in their natural environment. He began cautiously to work his way into the edge of the marshy ground, picking each step he took with care, trying to avoid putting a boot into one of the pools of brackish water between the lumpy tussocks of rushes. As he advanced slowly he noted a number of small birds which he thought might be reed buntings, flying out from amongst the reeds which flanked a stagnant pool in the middle of that marsh. It was certainly a fascinating place; in summer that pool tended to be covered over by slimy green waterweed. Then Lord Dalmane, in a momentary lack of concentration, put a foot wrong, and narrowly escaped losing his balance and falling over, as one boot sank right up to the top into oozing black slime. "Good heavens! What on earth am I doing going right into this bog?" he said aloud. He heaved mightily at his right boot and with a great sucking noise managed to drag it out of the mire with his stockinged foot still inside it. "A fine fool I'd look if I fall over here and have to turn up at Bob's plastered from head to foot in mud!" he muttered as he began to stagger back to firmer ground. But at that moment he all but fell over again as, very close to him, a brown bird which had been lurking unseen in a tall clump of rushes suddenly flew up with noisy wingbeats, emitting as it rose from the marsh a harsh note of alarm. It was a snipe, as ne saw for himself clearly when he managed to focus his binoculars onto it.

However, Lord Dalmane did not intend to cause any more than minimal disturbance to the birds and other wildlife of the marsh, so he decided to continue his walk without further delay. Soon he came to a gate which opened onto a farm lane. The footpath continued through another gate opposite this one into another field on its way to the hamlet of Chetnole, but the lane lead to Summerhays Farm, and Lord Dalmane's way now lead to the left up this lane. He was nearly there; the farm itself was only just out of sight round a corner, about three hundred yards away. Lord Dalmane shut the field gate behind him, and was about to walk on when his eye chanced to alight on the grassy bank of the right-hand hedge bordering the farm lane; that bank was bright with many small flowers. He went over for a closer look. There were many celandines there, but he thought he had noticed something else. Yes, he said to himself, that is a primrose. One clump of primroses was in flower, although only one flower was fully out. How marvellous, he thought, to find a primrose out so soon after the ending of that cold spell. But maybe I'll find some more. This bank is in the sun, a warm place, and well sheltered.

He began to walk along the lane, looking out for more primroses, but a moment later, just as he noticed another clump in flower, the peaceful quietness of the morning was suddenly shattered by the roar of the engine of a farm tractor. Someone was driving a tractor at speed out from the Summerhays farmyard down the lane towards Lord Dalmane. The lane was so narrow between its two nigh hedges that he knew at once that there would be very little room for him to get out of the way. He squeezed himself into the hedgebank by the second primrose clump, and a second or so later saw the tractor as it rounded the bend. The loud roar of the engine diminished sharply as the driver noticed him and promptly eased off the throttle. It was not Bob Challice himself driving the tractor, but his farm hand, young Robin Cottem; he was towing an empty trailer which banged and rattled as its wheels bounced over the stones and potholes of the lane. Lord Dalmane had expected to see Bob in the driving seat, but when he saw that it was Robin in charge of the tractor, he felt that he did not care about having a talk to him: he regarded Robin as something of a half-wit, a creature of very low intelligence, not someone worth spending much time with in conversation.

Robin Cottem waved an arm from the tractor seat in a gesture, making as if to touch a cap he was not wearing, which indicated that he recognized the pedestrian as the Earl of Saint Helens. Lord Dalmane briefly waved a hand to him and squeezed himself a little closer in to the hedge to allow Robin to drive the tractor and trailer past him. But Robin brought the tractor right up to Lord Dalmane, and then switched off the engine so that he could talk without having to shout.

"Hello, Lord Dalmane! It's a grand morning."

"Hello, Robin. Yes it is," said Lord Dalmane.

"Are you keeping very well, my Lord?"

"Yes, fine, thank you."

"And your wife, Lady Susan?"

"On, she's very well, thank you."

"That's good. You know, sir, I haven't seen you for quite a long time. And I haven't seen your wife since that day last summer when I met her having a picnic by herself on Batcombe Hill."

"A picnic?" queried Lord Dalmane, puzzled. "What picnic?"

"Why, sir, it was a hot day last August, and I was down Sydling way on my bike when I happened to meet your wife. There was a rug on the ground, and a picnic basket, and your wife said she was just doing a bit of sunbathing—with very little on—I mean, she was just wearing her underwear, if you understand me, sir, because—"

"What?" interrupted Lord Dalmane. "What is all this you're telling me about my wife having a picnic and doing some sunbathing? I don't understand it at all. Did you say that you met just Susan by herself? Was there no one with her sharing this picnic?"

"Well, sir, at first I thought there was no one else there; but then, when I looked a bit closer like—closer at the rug—well, I reckoned that maybe she wasn't alone."

"Whatever do you mean?" asked Lord Dalmane rather angrily. A sudden sense of alarm and suspicion had come to him on hearing this farm labourer's strange tale of meeting his wife one day last summer "doing a bit of sunbathing in just her underwear".

"Oh, sir," said Robin Cottem awkwardly. "Well, er . . . well, it isn't important really, sir."

"Yes, it is," said Lord Dalmane. "I want to hear the end of this tale, Robin Cottem, seeing that you've started telling it." He knew that Robin's sudden awkwardness meant that he had realised, too late, that he had blurted out something which might have been better kept secret; but now that his suspicions had been aroused that something untoward might have occurred and, perhaps, been "hushed up", he decided to get to the heart of the matter, if he could. "Look here," he continued, "what did you mean by you 'reckoned that maybe Sue wasn't alone'? Was there someone hiding there?"

"Yes, sir, I'm inclined to think that there was. It looked like there was someone hiding underneath that picnic rug. There was a shape, like it were a body under that rug, a human body, sir, lying underneath it, hidden."

"Are you sure it was a body? Might it not simply have been another basket under the rug?—or some clothing, perhaps? I think you said that my wife didn't have much on . . ."

"Well, sir, I can't be positive about what was hidden under that rug, but it did look to me very like the outline of someone's body. I don't think it was just clothes. When I looked close, I could see slight movements, like it was breathing, whoever or whatever was underneath."

"H'm." Lord Dalmane frowned and was silent for a moment. "Why should there be someone hiding under Sue's picnic rug while she was picnicing on Batcombe Hill—or sunbathing, or whatever she was doing?" he muttered, speaking not to Robin, but aloud to himself. "Most mysterious. Perhaps I'd better ask her about it . . . But look here, young Robin (here his voice changed and became crisp again as he addressed the farm worker) I must get on. My purpose in walking out here this morning was to see your boss, Mr. Challice. Will I find him in if I go on to the farm?"

"Oh yes, sir. He was in the house a few minutes ago when I left. You'll find him somewhere about the place, sir."

"Thank you; then I'll be going. Good-bye, Robin."

Lord Dalmane was hardly listening as Robin said "Good-bye, sir," and started his tractor engine, but he waited a few seconds longer until the tractor and trailer had been driven past him. Then he resumed his walk at once. But this time he had forgotten about looking for primroses. The sun was still shining, and it was still the same envigorating spring day, but Lord Dalmane was now too worried by what he had just heard to notice the beauty of it any longer. And when, about half an hour later, having had his chat with Bob Challice and handed over the deeds, he set off to return home by the same route, he hardly noticed anything of the sights which had so recently fascinated him.

CHAPTER FIFTEEN

Jim came into the Castle bailey through the mediaeval arch in the massively thick outer wall of the old courtyard, and as he walked he was quietly humming to himself a jolly little tune. The harsh calls of jackdaws came to his ears, and he looked up to the top of a crumbling pinnacle of ancient stones at a jackdaw's nest on the pinnacle. It was a broken shape which had once been a turret on the top of an old tower, but most of it had fallen down long ago. All those old walls and towers on the left of the bailey, the shell of the old Castle, were in a structurally dangerous state, as Jim knew, and some of the old staircases had been bricked up at their entrances to prevent visitors from climbing up towers of crumbling masonry, and perhaps having serious accidents. The pinnacle on which rested the jackdaw's nest was one such tower. Jim had seen the nest, an untidy collection of twigs and sticks, many a time, in its lofty, uncertain position; indeed he had often watched one of the jackdaws, or both of them, working at making it. Now he saw one of the birds sitting on the nest; the other flew up as he watched and perched beside its mate. The sight reminded him that it was definitely spring.

He had been in high spirits all that morning, not only because such a beautifully warm spring day had affected him that way, much as it had affected Lord Dalmane on his walk to Summerhays Farm, but also because he had seen Susan. She had come into the

Estate Office just after nine that morning, when Jim had been there with Major Ambrose, at the start of the day's work. Susan had called there ostensibly to talk to Major Ambrose, but also, Jim was inclined to believe, so as to have an opportunity to talk briefly with him. As a result of her visit, his schedule of work that morning had been slightly re-arranged. Susan had suggested that the Major should give him some preliminary instruction in the work of an estate agent, so that Jim could take over this important job when Major Ambrose retired, which was going to be, probably, sometime towards the end of that year. This idea was not new to Jim; it had been talked about vaguely many times before, but so far nothing positive had been done about it. However, as a result of Susan's visit to his office that morning, Major Ambrose had given Jim his first lesson in the mysterious business of estate agency (as adapted to the requirements for managing the Rhodes Castle Estate). Afterwards Jim had gone outside to give the gardener a hand in the job of gathering up all the twigs and bits of broken branches from off the West Lawn, where they had been deposited by some recent days of high winds. Before Easter the Gardens did not open to the public until eleven o' clock in the morning, so that there was never any Guide work to do before that time; but that day, while he was working on the big lawn, he had met a couple of tourists who had asked to be shown around the churchyard and to see the inside of the church. Jim held one of the keys of Rhodes Church, which was usually in one of his pockets, as it was that day, and he had been delighted to stop picking up and loading twigs into a wheelbarrow, and instead to take that couple to see the Church and the Churchyard. He had only now come back from the Churchyard, meaning to take his lunch break.

First, however, Jim headed for the Estate Office door. Major Ambrose would not be there now, but it was Jim's usual custom to call there in the middle of the day in case any written messages or instructions had been left for him. That day, however, there were none. At that moment, Jim looked up sharply from Major Ambrose's desk on hearing the door open, just when he had been about to leave the office himself. He was a little startled to see Susan's maid, Samantha, standing in the doorway.

"Ah, Jim," she said at once. "I thought I might find you here. I've a message for you."

"Oh?"

"Lord Dalmane wants to see you in his study."

Jim was surprised to feel an automatic flash of fear go through his body on hearing this announcement.

"What? Now?" he said.

"Oh no, not right away. You haven't been in for your lunch yet, have you?"

"No, but I was just going to the kitchen now."

"Well, you do that, then. I had to tell you, Jim, that you'll probably find Lord Dalmane in his study up to three o' clock. Apparently he wants to talk to you about something important, so you'd best have your lunch first, and then go along to the study."

"Oh yes, of course." He felt oddly bothered by this most unexpected summons to the Earl's study. Can it be . . . ? he said to himself. No, surely it can't. He probably wants to talk to me about something quite different, not about that incident!

"Sam!" he called. The maid had at that moment shut the door behind her, but she heard him, and the door opened again for a moment. "What's it all about, Sam? Do you know what he wants to talk about?"

"No, I've no idea," said Samantha. "Honestly, Jim, I haven't the least idea why Lord Dalmane should have sent for you." She gave him a smile, waved a hand round the door, and disappeared. Jim followed her out into the bailey, not so quickly. As he shut the Estate Office door behind him he saw Samantha, who must have run across the courtyard, entering the Castle through the back door. Already trying to suppress some awful doubts which were arising in his mind, he followed her in, and went to the kitchen. At that time of the year the Cafeteria in the Visitor Centre was still closed for the winter, so Jim took his lunch in the kitchen.

A plate of cold lunch was waiting for him there as usual, but Jim did not enjoy eating it. Today the Cook had left him a particularly good salad to eat, with two baked potatoes and some slices of cold roast meat. He knew that if he had not just received that ominous message from Samantha he would have eaten that meal with a healthy appetite, but now he was too worried to feel really hungry. In the back of his mind there was a feeling that he was about to get the sack. The consequences of his crime with Susan, if crime it could be called, must have caught up with him. He could not quite see why this idea should feel so compelling in his mind, but he tried to pretend to himself that there might just as well be nothing at all sinister about a request from Lord Dalmane to meet him in the study. "About something important," Samantha had said, Jim reflected. Well, what else could it be if it wasn't to inform him that Lord Dalmane had somehow found out about the doings of that day on Batcombe Hill? Perhaps it's some good news, he thought. Perhaps it's to tell me that I'm to be promoted much sooner than I'd expected to Estate Agent duties because Major Ambrose has changed his mind, and is going to retire very soon, instead of at the end of the year. But Jim knew that such an idea seemed very unlikely to be true, and he ate his food mechanically, hardly noticing what he was eating.

When Jim approached the Earl's study door to knock on it his heart was beating rapidly, but he was still saying to himself, It'll be all right. Then he thought that what he was doing felt very like going to the Headmaster's study at school to receive a punishment; he remembered having to make such a visit to his Headmaster shortly before he had left school, just over three years ago, when he had indeed received corporal punishment for a minor misdemeanour.

He knocked on the door, as cheerfully and boldly as he could.

"Come in," said Lord Dalmane's voice.

For some obscure reason, perhaps because of the grave look on Lord Dalmane's face, Jim instantly felt less hopeful of hearing some good news. The Earl looked up as Jim came in; Lord Dalmane was at his desk, and had apparently been writing something.

"You sent for me, sir?" said Jim nervously.

"Yes. Take a seat, Jim," said Lord Dalmane, pointing to a comfortable armchair near the desk, which was positioned where Jim had seen it before, diagonally across the further window bay to face the door. "That's it, pull it up here, close beside the desk, so that we can talk comfortably. But I'm afraid that what we've got to talk about is not going to be too pleasant for you."

Jim knew at once as he heard Lord Dalmane say this that his call to the study was indeed to talk about his imminent dismissal. But, although he felt his spirits sinking, he managed to look fairly cheerful, and even to smile as he pulled the armchair up to one end of the desk, to face Lord Dalmane and the fireplace. There was a small fire of logs burning on the hearth, but the day had by now become so warm out of doors that it was quite warm enough in the study for comfortable sitting down without much extra heat.

"Yes," continued Lord Dalmane, as Jim made himself comfortable in the armchair, "I'll come to the point straight away, and not leave you in suspense any longer about why I asked you to see me. You may have to leave us, Jim. I've heard a very disturbing report about you today which concerns something which happened last summer, one day when you apparently went out with my wife for a picnic. Mind you, I only say that you <u>may</u> have to go because of what happened that day. I'd certainly like to hear an account from you of what happened the day you went to Batcombe Hill with Susan in her car; I believe it was while I was away in London. I'm sure you must remember very well what occasion I'm referring to." He looked straight at Jim; up until then he seemed to have been mostly looking at his pen and the letter he had been writing.

"Yes, sir," said Jim gravely. "I remember that day well. Your wife suggested to me, sir, that we should go out somewhere together in her car, and so I said Yes."

"I see; but before you tell me about it, Jim, I'd better let you know how I've been made aware of these things. I went over to Summerhays Farm this morning, you see, and happened to meet Robin Cottem. You know him, don't you?"

"Well, I know who he is, sir. He works for Mr. Challice, the farmer, at Summerhays."

"Precisely. Well, I chanced to meet him driving a tractor before I reached Summerhays Farm. Now, as a matter of fact, I had no intention at all of stopping to talk to him, because I'd gone that way to talk to Bob, not to Robin. But he insisted on stopping to talk; and he told me, Jim, something about that day we're talking about. He said that he'd met my wife having a picnic somewhere on Batcombe Hill. And he said that he'd seen Susan scantily dressed because, according to her, she was sunbathing. And then he said that there appeared to be someone hiding under the rug."

"That was me, sir," said Jim. He had decided by now to tell Lord Dalmane the whole truth about the affair in his answers to whatever questions were put to him, as it was evident to him that Lord Dalmane seemed to have found out most of the truth already.

"Yes, I realize it must have been you, if indeed there was someone else there," said Lord Dalmane. "When I came home from Summerhays I found Sue, and asked her what she remembered about that day; but she only told me that you were with her, because she'd asked you to come with her. And that, in itself, is fair enough." Lord Dalmane sighed and broke off his speech for a moment. Then he turned his desk chair sideways, so that he could sit facing Jim directly, without having to turn his head sideways, perhaps thinking that in this way their conversation might go more easily and more informally.

"You must understand, Jim," he continued, folding his arms and crossing his legs, "that I don't at all object to your going out with my wife for picnics, or whatever. I wouldn't think of dismissing you just because I hear a report that you two have been out together to some nice place in the country. The last thing I want is to feel that I <u>ought</u> to be telling you that you've got to leave us, and I still hope I won't have to. But—how should I put it?—I'm worried, Jim: worried by this report I hear of you hiding underneath Sue's picnic rug when Robin Cottem comes along. I, er . . . I fear that perhaps your behaviour with my wife may have, shall we say, 'overstepped the mark'? You know what I mean?"

"Yes, sir," said Jim seriously. He wondered whether he ought to go on to make a full and immediate confession of his part in that picnic, but was hesitant to do so.

"So perhaps you'd better give me a full account of this picnic," continued Lord Dalmane after a few seconds of silence.

"Yes, sir," said Jim again. I'd better come clean to Lord Dalmane about what we did, he thought quickly. I'll have to own up that we were making love: he seems to have guessed as much already.

Jim began his account of the doings of that day by telling Lord Dalmane of Susan's morning visit to his room to suggest the idea of a picnic together using her car, and then of how he had waited for her in the bushes in the back drive. He explained in some detail where they had gone to, and why they had sought out such a secret spot to have their picnic. Jim did not admit, in so many words, that he had felt sorely tempted to sexual misbehaviour by the arousing sight of Susan with most of her clothes removed; but by saying that she had taken off her blouse "because it was very hot" Lord Dalmane gathered that Jim was implying that he had found this action provocative and a great source of temptation to do what followed later. Then he told of Susan removing her bra, and saying, a little later: "Are we going to make love?"

"And I'm afraid I said 'Yes' to that, sir, and so we did make love." He was looking into Lord Dalmane's face carefully as he said this to see what reaction such a staggering confession might call forth, but he was a little surprised to see the Earl merely nod his head thoughtfully, hardly looking surprised at all; and not a hint of anger or resentment seemed to appear on his face either.

"I see," said Lord Dalmane quietly. "Yes, go on, Jim. When did Robin Cottem appear on the scene?" He had been saying little while Jim was telling him his story. But by now Jim was feeling surprised that he had found the courage to speak so frankly; it had not seemed to be as difficult as he had thought it was going to be.

"Oh, er, Robin didn't come along on his bicycle until after— after we'd finished, if you know what I mean." (Lord Dalmane nodded his head.) Jim then explained that the reason why he had hidden under the rug was simply because he had been naked, and that Robin Cottem had appeared so suddenly that there had been no time to put on any clothes: the main thing had been to vanish as quickly as possible. "And you see, sir, Susan only had her underclothes on at that point. And if anyone had seen me standing there—or even sitting or lying there—with nothing on, he'd have known at once what we'd been up to."

"Of course," said Lord Dalmane.

"Well, sir, that's really all there is to tell. After Robin had gone we both got dressed and came home again. But I think that we both thought that I'd been well enough hidden to give Robin no grounds for suspecting that there was anyone else there, except your wife."

There was quite a long silence of perhaps a minute or more. Jim was surprised to see that there was most decidedly a smile on the Earl's face, but he presently saw it fade from his features.

"Well," said Lord Dalmane at last, "the first thing I want to say, having heard your full and honest account of what happened, is that I can't find it in my heart to blame you. No, I don't think you deserve any blame for what happened. Believe me, Jim, I can understand just how sorely you were tempted under those circumstances to do what you did: and, of course, it must have been overwhelmingly tempting for Sue as well to invite you to be her lover. And I've long known about the great crush you have on Sue; and I know too that she's developed a considerable infatuation for <u>you</u>. You know, knowing that facts as I do, it hardly seems surprising to me that this has happened. To put it another way: I think that you two were <u>bound</u> to find some situation sooner or later in which you could go off together to some private place to make love. You perhaps, Jim, thought that I didn't understand about the depths of the feeling of love you have towards my wife. But I assure you, I <u>do</u> understand how you've been feeling. I understand that, having been invited by Sue to go with her to Batcombe Hill, you just couldn't help what happened when you found yourselves alone there."

He paused, and Jim looked at him hopefully. It began to sound as if he might, after all, be forgiven, and that perhaps the incident would henceforth be regarded as closed. But that was not to be.

"And there's another thing," continued Lord Dalmane. "I know it hasn't been at all easy for you to make this confession to me, Jim, and, if I may say so, I congratulate you and thank you for being so honest and frank in telling me about it."

"Thank you, sir," said Jim. "But will I, er—?" He hesitated to ask the question most on his mind at the moment.

"Yes?" said Lord Dalmane, after waiting a moment for Jim to speak. "But will you what?"

"Will I have to be dismissed because of this, sir?"

Lord Dalmane sighed deeply before he answered Jim's question; he seemed reluctant to give him his answer.

"Yes," he said at last in a quiet voice. "You'll have to go."

Jim hung his head and looked down at the carpet at his feet. For a moment neither man spoke.

"I'm very sorry," continued Lord Dalmane presently, "but I'm afraid that I must dismiss you after what you've freely confessed to. Believe me, it is very hard for me to make such a decision, and I'd love you to stay with us really, but I can see that my decision <u>must</u> be to ask you to leave—not right away, mind you, but you'll have to go."

"Yes, sir," said Jim sadly, and he again cast his eyes down to the floor, while a grim look came over his usually happy face, as he brooded quietly for a few seconds on the news of his dismissal. It was not at all unexpected, but all the same it felt shattering for him to hear this punishment pronounced on him. A little later he added: "I'm very sorry, sir, that I did it."

"So am I," said Lord Dalmane; "at least, I'm sorry that I've had to break this shocking news to you. But Jim, if you can, I don't want you to think of this as a punishment. By asking you to leave Rhodes Castle I really believe I'm not so much handing out a punishment as giving you the best possible chance you could have to make a fresh start in life. No doubt you won't see it that way: I suppose you're feeling so shattered by the idea of leaving that you can only think of it as a devastating sentence from me." He paused a moment, and Jim nodded his agreement. He was looking now past Lord Dalmane out of the window with eyes that hardly saw anything, although out there was still the same bright blue sky which only an hour earlier had seemed to him to be so spiritually uplifting.

Lord Dalmane continued. "Yes, in time I think you'll come to agree that what I'm doing for you now is really the best thing I could do for your own good. It'll give you the chance, I hope, to find a new job; and in time, probably, to forget your infatuation for my wife, and to find yourself a new girlfriend, although I daresay it may be quite some time before you can make yourself think along such lines. But, all the same, Jim, even though I've said that, I wish I could let you stay here. But I really can't do that. You see, apart from giving you a chance for a new start, as I've said, I must think about my wife's involvement in this affair: I simply <u>cannot</u> allow rumours to get around of Susan, my wife, having an affair with the Guide at Rhodes Castle. I don't know whether that really is being said already, or not, but such rumours certainly <u>would</u> spread, I'm afraid, if I were to allow you to stay here; so I feel compelled, much against my will, to dismiss you. But I feel fairly sure that I'm doing the right thing for you by asking you to leave, because this way you should have an opportunity for a fresh start."

"Yes, sir; thank you," said Jim weakly.

"Well, I think that's all we need say. You'd better get back to your work now, Jim."

Jim got up and walked slowly to the door, solemnly watched by Lord Dalmane. As Jim was about to disappear through the doorway Lord Dalmane suddenly remembered something he had forgotten to say.

"Oh—Jim!"

"Yes, sir?"

"I did say that I wasn't dismissing you right away, didn't I? Well, then, you can stay on, and continue in your job for another two weeks. After that—well, I'd better have a talk to Sue to see what <u>she</u> thinks, but <u>I</u> rather think that'll have to be the end of your job here; though Sue, no doubt, will want to plead with me for you to be allowed to stay longer. But if I were to say Yes, would that really do any good? I'll tell you what: as a gesture, if you like, of goodwill from me, I think you could stay on living here for a little longer, if you want to, after your job's ended. That way will perhaps give you a chance to sort out your affairs in some measure—perhaps even find a job to go to—before you return home to Cockermouth, if that's what you're going to do. Shall we say, you could stay here for a further week, if you want to, after your position here ends in a fortnight from now?"

"Oh, thank you very much, sir; that's very kind of you," said Jim.

"Right. You'd better go now."

As Jim walked down the corridor away from the study he was feeling dazed by the news of his dismissal, particularly as it all seemed to have broken so quickly and so unexpectedly. This is an awful bolt from the blue, he said to himself, as he directed his footsteps automatically in the direction of the back door and the Estate Office, where Major Ambrose would by now be back at his desk. He reflected that for this news to come on the very day when, only a few hours earlier, his promotion had been talked about, made it a cruelly ironical twist of fate. Yet for all this, he could sense that the full implications of his punishment—which Lord Dalmane had said he ought not to think of as a punishment—had yet to come home to his mind. I know what it is, he thought as he came to the back door, he thinks that if he were to allow me to stay here, sooner or later Sue and I would be tempted to do it again. I think that's really why he's said I've got to go. Of course, I can't say that a fortnight's notice isn't reasonable; and to be allowed to go on living here for another week after that, when I'm no longer the Guide, is even more reasonable. But to think that in just three weeks time I'll have to be saying Good-bye to Sue, and then knowing when I go that I'll never come back, and probably won't ever see her again. Oh, it's a really devastating, soul-shattering thought!—but I can't <u>really</u> feel it yet.

CHAPTER SIXTEEN

The private lawn at Rhodes Castle was indeed a very secluded, private place. It lay across the brook from the main part of the garden, and was reached from the Castle by crossing a rustic wooden footbridge, after which one approached the sloping lawn on a path which opened out from among the bushes. The lawn was entirely surrounded by screening bushes, so that it was very well hidden from sight from anyone strolling around in those parts of the gardens which were open to the public. It was an area of well-mown grass, of irregular shape. From the central part of it there were a number of re-entrants of lawn which twisted this way and that into the surrounding bushes—mostly rhododendrons—and in one of these grassy re-entrants, in the northernmost corner of the lawn, there stood a wooden summer-house of recent construction. In fact, the whole of this charming little self-contained garden was a very recent creation, the product of John Dalmane's imagination, and designed almost entirely according to his instructions. It had been almost complete by the time when Susan came to take up residence at the Castle when he married her, but she, like him, delighted in the place as somewhere quiet and beautiful in which to be alone. As well as rhododendron and laurel bushes, sapling trees had been planted here and there among the curves and islands of greenery surrounding the main lawn: there were little cherry, prunus, and laburnum trees, and others: and the positioning of each tree, and its type of blossom and leaves, had been tastefully and thoughtfully taken into account in the overall scheme of the place.

On the morning of the 12th of April, which was a Thursday, Susan and Jim came there together, walking hand in hand. It was going to be the fourth time that week that they had met there by mutual agreement. This time Jim had met Susan in the Great Hall at eleven o' clock, and then they had walked round together to the path which lead to the bridge over the Rhodes Brook and on to the private lawn. On this occasion Jim had found a written message from Susan lying on his bed when he had come back into his room after his breakfast; the note asked him to wait for her in the hall at around eleven o' clock. Jim, of course, had been more than delighted to comply with this request, and had been sitting in the hall, reading a book, for a quarter of an hour before Susan turned up, as she had promised, at eleven o' clock. He had by now become moderately accustomed to the strange idea that there was no work at all for him to do, so that the whole of each day was leisure time; the hours seemed to pass slowly, but he did not find it too difficult to keep himself occupied. However, he still found it odd and rather unpleasant each morning to feel that there was now no job for him to do, and nowhere to report to for duty after breakfast. Partly as a consequence of the necessary re-scheduling of his days, he had taken to having his breakfast considerably later than he had ever been accustomed to eating it when he had been reporting for duty to Major Ambrose at nine o' clock each working day. However, this new and dreary way of life which had come into force after he had done his last day's work had brought Jim one great bonus: during this week after his dismissal he had seen a great deal more of Susan than had ever been possible when he was working.

Outside it was sunny, warm, and altogether a delightful spring morning as Jim and Susan went out together through the front door and down the broad stone steps to the gravel of the main drive. However, it had but recently come out sunny and warm, the day having dawned in a thick white mist. But Jim had seen, when it was getting on for nine o' clock and he had come down to the kitchen for his breakfast, that the mist was rapidly thinning; by that time it had been possible to see a clear, cloudless sky appearing overhead. He confidently expected a fine, sunny day to develope, a day warm enough to sit out of doors; and when, a little later, he found Susan's message about meeting her in the Hall, he realised that she too was thinking along the same lines.

"I think it's warm enough for us to sit outside," said Susan, as she and Jim walked round the south-eastern corner of the Castle.

"I'm sure it is," said Jim. "Are we going to the private lawn again, Sue?"

"Oh, yes, of course; it's much the warmest and most private place to sit out of doors, and we could either be in the summer-house again or out on the lawn in deck chairs—I think it would be nice to sit out on the lawn today."

"So do I," said Jim. "You know, the sun came out quicker than I thought it would after such a misty start to the day."

"Well, yes, the mist did go fairly quickly, I suppose; but then by this time of the year there's plenty of power in the sun. I looked out of my window at about a quarter to six this morning, and the mist was really thick then—you could hardly see anything but whiteness from the window—but I thought even then that it'd get out really nice presently."

"And it has, and now it's getting beautifully warm. Yes, let's sit outside—unless we get too not, and have to move into the shade."

They walked round the outside of the Tower Library, keeping to the lawn path, but walking abreast, holding hands. As they passed the ground floor window of the library at the foot of the Tower Jim remembered that strange morning when he had been working on the inventory in there, and it had been very quiet, and he had quite expected to see the ghost of Beryl Buxton; but instead of meeting the ghost he had found a gemstone which had turned out to be the missing Great Beryl of Saint Helens. He reflected now that this seemed to have been an odd turn of events. And then quite a different thought struck him. It was indeed very pleasant to be walking hand-in-hand in the gardens of Rhodes Castle with his beloved Susan in bright, warm sunshine, and with the birds all singing heartily, and the flowers opening out their petals to the sun. It was very pleasant, but now it was almost over. This was his last full day at Rhodes Castle; tomorrow he was leaving, and that would be the end of it all. This idea was either in his thoughts or very close to his thoughts all that day: he could not for long forget that every minute of the day was precious to him, and none more so than these delightful minutes he was now enjoying together with his love. But they were minutes which were passing far too quickly; and that disturbing thought too Jim could not forget. It's all over, he said to himself. At least, it very, very soon will be—I know time's going far too quickly now that I'm with Sue. And by this time tomorrow I'll be in the "Pines Express" going north to Crewe, and then Carlisle . . . and then on home to Cockermouth. But I don't think it'll feel at all like going home . . .

"A penny for your thoughts, Jim," said Susan with a smile. She had seen the pensive, rather glum look on his face, and perhaps guessed at what sort of thoughts were passing through his mind.

"Oh, well, I was thinking about tomorrow. I'll have gone by this time tomorrow."

"Jim, darling," said Susan gently, "I think you'd do well to try not to think too much about that, if you can. You've got to go, I know, and I'm terribly sad about it, and I know you are too—but there's nothing we can do about it now. I say, isn't the old cherry tree there a gorgeous sight?"

"Yes, it's lovely," said Jim. They were looking up at the branches of a blossom-laden, tall, old cherry tree which grew to the right of the footpath close to the bridge on the Castle side of the brook. A moment later Susan and he were standing on the footbridge, where they stopped a while to lean over the wooden railings to look down at the clear water of the little stream. The Rhodes Brook was a silent, slow-flowing stream, except after heavy rain, when brown water would surge noisily along it; but at that time there was not a lot of water in it, and it slipped away under the footbridge without a murmur. Jim and Susan looked down and admired the reflections in the smooth water. Some branches of the cherry tree leaned out far enough that way to be reflected in the water against the brilliant blue of the reflected sky; while further away from the watchers the sun glinted off the quiet pools in a brilliance almost too bright to look at.

"It's such a lovely garden," murmured Jim, not so much addressing Susan as thinking aloud. But Susan answered him.

"Yes, indeed it is. You know, that tree's about at its best now, in full blossom, out with the leaves not yet out. I think the reflections in the stream are so beautiful—the branches bare of leaves, but with the white flowers floating against the blue background . . . Shall we go on now to the lawn?"

They walked slowly on, hand in hand as before. As soon as they were off the bridge they saw that the path lead through a narrow gap (which was not straight but had a kink in it) between the dense screen of rhododendron bushes, which came right down to the edge of the brook and hid the private lawn from view even from the footbridge, in spite of the nearness of the bridge to the lawn. They were walking uphill now on a gentle gradient, and a moment later they saw the lawn round the curve of the rhododendron bushes, an irregular-shaped carpet of smooth green which the gardeners kept mowed beautifully short. As they walked up the lawn towards the octagonal wooden summer-house, which stood in the northernmost bay between the bushes, Jim was feeling greatly moved. He was moved by the beauty of the garden and the day, and he was much moved by the nearness of his beloved; but perhaps most of all his deep emotions were stirred by knowing how fleeting these pleasures were. Tomorrow they would be gone; indeed <u>before</u> tomorrow the private lawn would be only a memory, for there certainly would not be time for him to come back there tomorrow morning, as he knew that he would have to leave early to catch the bus to the station. However, he was hopeful that he would see Susan again tomorrow morning to say Good-bye. Surely, he said to himself, Sue doesn't mean this to be our last meeting.

They stepped onto the wooden verandah of the summer-house, and Susan opened the door of the octagonal room in the middle of the house in order to fetch from it two deck chairs.

"Shall we have our chairs on the verandah or on the lawn?" she asked as they each picked up a chair.

"Oh, on the lawn, I think," said Jim.

"Right; and if it gets too hot sitting in the full sun we could move them back onto the verandah for a bit of shade."

They decided, after a little more discussion, that the best place for the chairs was close to the summer-house, so as to be at the top end of the lawn, facing nearly south-west, so that the sun would be on their left, where it would not bother their eyes. Susan set up her deck chair just in front of a laburnum tree, close beside the summer-house, and Jim put his down next to it.

"That's right, Jim," said Susan. "You must be right beside me so that we can talk comfortably. This is the last time we'll be able to meet, you know."

"Oh no!" said Jim in dismay, half rising from his deck chair, in which he had just sat down, at the shock of hearing this. "But Sue, I know I'll have to leave early tomorrow, and so I'll have to be in a hurry, and there won't be much time—but don't you think there might be just a chance that we could see each other tomorrow morning—just for a minute—before I actually go?"

"No, my darling," said Susan quietly. "I shan't be seeing you tomorrow." She smiled at him, put a hand on his lap, and paused a second or two. Jim waited anxiously for her to continue. "Jim," she said, "I thought it would be best—best for <u>you</u>, I mean—if I wasn't around tomorrow morning, and you didn't see me then, just when you're picking up your suitcase to leave the Castle and walk away for the bus. I think you're going to find it very hard to actually <u>leave</u> Rhodes Castle, when it comes to the point of doing that—to say Good-bye to it, as I know you've got very fond of the old place." She paused a moment, and Jim nodded his head thoughtfully.

"I am very fond of dear old Rhodes Castle," he murmured, hardly audibly.

"Yes," she said, "you are; and so I thought it would make your departing seem a little easier tomorrow, if you knew that you'd already said Good-bye to <u>me</u> today."

Jim considered this idea for a moment and then gave her his opinion on it.

"Yes, I believe you're right, Sue. It probably <u>would</u> make it seem easier to go if we say Good-bye today, and you hide yourself tomorrow morning."

"Well," said Susan, "what I've actually arranged to do is to go to Mrs. Beck's to spend a couple of nights there, so I'm off to Bournemouth on the train this afternoon. You see, Jim, I had this invitation from Norma to come and stay sometime for a few nights with her, and so I've deliberately chosen to go at this time with your departing in mind. I hope you won't mind, my love."

"Oh . . . no." Jim suddenly felt that he minded very much that Susan was going to go away that very afternoon, in spite of having just given his agreement to the idea of not seeing her in the morning. "What train are you going by, Sue?"

"The two-ten."

"From Stalbridge?"

"No, from Yetminster. As a matter of fact, there is a 12.38 from Stalbridge which I could have got; it would have got me to Broadstone in time for a latish lunch. That was what Norma really wanted me to do, but I said I couldn't do that. I pretended that I was going to be too busy today to set off until after lunch—but, of course, I really said that thinking that we could have a little longer together that way. If I was going by the 12.38 it would be just about time now to think of setting off in the car for Stalbridge."

"Yes, I see; but it was very sweet of you, Sue, to arrange it that way so that we could have a little more time together."

"Well, yes; unless you're already getting bored by having nothing to do except to sit here talking with me."

"Sue, darling!" exclaimed Jim reproachfully. "Of course I'm not getting bored. I'd <u>never</u> get bored with your company, Sue—never."

"Well, it's nice of you to say so," said Susan.

There was a short pause in the conversation. Jim saw that Susan was looking around almost absent-mindedly, perhaps studying the blossom on the small, young cherry trees which had been planted in the Private Garden here and there where there were gaps in the rhododendron bushes. He had noticed that these young trees were further on in their cycle than the big, old cherry tree; in fact the leaves were out on the saplings and their blossom was almost over, much of it having already fallen off or blown away. But Jim was hardly interested in the trees at that moment. He was still preoccupied with thinking of Susan going away that afternoon, his last afternoon at the Castle, so as to make his own going away next morning seem a little easier. Would it really work that way with him, or would it not, he wondered? And then, she was going from Yetminster Station: but would that not mean a rather complicated journey to Bournemouth?

"Sue," he said, "won't you have to change at Dorchester if you travel from Yetminster? Don't all the trains from Yeovil Junction run down to Weymouth?"

"I believe they nearly all do, but by luck the two-ten happens to be a through train to Bournemouth. Of course, I won't get to

Broadstone, Mrs. Beck's local station, on that line, but that won't matter. Norma's going to meet me at Poole, and drive me to her home, which is only quite a short way from Poole station."

"I didn't know that Mrs. Beck could drive a car," said Jim. "The last time the Becks came to stay here, last autumn, they came by train, and they had to be met at Staloridge, didn't they?"

"Yes, they did. But Norma said in her letter inviting me that she'd recently passed the Driving Test and now has a car of her own, and so I expect she'll rather enjoy this opportunity to show off her new skill. It means that she can take me out somewhere in her car tomorrow, if she wants to. She's ever so much better, you know, than she was when we met her and Nigel that time at Cockermouth Station, when I thought she was really ill—that day when I first met you. Anyway, it's all arranged about me getting down to her. I'm going on the two-ten, and leaving my car at Yetminster Station until I come back on Saturday."

"You're staying with Mrs. Beck until Saturday?"

"Yes, I am. John's due back from London on Saturday afternoon, so I reckon to come back home just before him." (Lord Dalmane had been staying at his London address all that week because of pressure of work). "But it only means that I'm stopping two nights with Norma, tonight, tomorrow, and tomorrow night."

"Yes."

"And another thing is: Yetminster's such a handy place to catch a train from, isn't it? You've been from there on the local train to Dorchester before now, haven't you?"

"Oh yes," said Jim. "Yetminster's a very handy station for the Castle. That time I went to Dorchester, I went on my bike by the Stable Road down to West Lodge, and so out onto the proper road by the bottom end of Knighton Lane, and then on to the station. It must be only about two miles to Yetminster that way."

"Yes, I should think it would be about two miles. So it'll only take me about five minutes, or little more than that, to get down to the station in my car, and then park it and lock it there in the station car park. Let me see: I'd better aim to be there not later than two o' clock, so I'd better be off at about ten to two—after lunch."

"That would be about right," agreed Jim.

"Well then, I'd better not stay here after twelve o' clock; that's about another half an hour. But don't think that you've got to stay here with me if you don't want to, Jim."

"But I <u>do</u> want to stay with you, Sue," said Jim with a smile at her.

"Bless you, my love, that's nice of you," said Susan.

After that they were silent for a while, enjoying the quietness and brightness of the Private Garden on that fine spring morning and listening to the songs of the birds. The sound of motor traffic did not disturb the peacefulness of the garden, for the only road which came fairly near the Private Garden was Knighton Lane which, although it was a public highway, carried only minimal traffic; and in any case, when a car or a tractor did go past in the lane, the screen of bushes surrounding the lawn baffled the sound to some extent.

Jim and Susan pursued their own thoughts in silence for several minutes. Jim had brought a book along with him, and now he opened it and tried to read; but it was no good, and soon he closed it again. It was a reasonably interesting novel, but he was quite unable to concentrate on it. It was nearly eleven-forty; at the most he had only just over another two hours to be with Susan before she left for her train; and then it would be all over: their happy relationship from that time on would be only a fading memory. Of course, it would surely fade only very slowly from his memory, but fade it would nevertheless. Jim, being honest with himself as he tried to explore in his mind the possibilities which the future might hold for him, could not see how it would be possible to come back to Rhodes Castle in order to see Susan again some time. He knew in his heart that having been dismissed, he would not really be welcome if he turned up again there to visit on some pretext. The thought that it would be a very long way to come, and therefore a very expensive journey in rail fares, if he did come back from Cockermouth to Rhodes Castle to visit Susan affected him much less than the thought that he would not be welcome there. Would Susan write to him, if he were to write letters to her, so that they would not altogether lose touch with one another? Jim wanted to know what Susan thought about that, but he dared not ask her for fear that she would say that it would be better if they did not write to each other. He remembered that Lord Dalmane had told him that he ought to think of this going away from Rhodes Castle not so much as a sad farewell to Susan as a chance for a new beginning in his life. Now he pondered over this, and could not help seeing the sensibleness of the idea: if a clean break with the past had to be made—and certainly it <u>had</u> to be so—then if he and Susan were to keep in touch by writing letters there would be no real break with the past in that all-important matter of their love for each other. What was more, Jim believed in his heart that Susan would incline to this way of thinking, and would not want to write letters to him. So it seems as if we'll just slowly have to forget about each other, he thought sadly. And then: But how much longer <u>have</u> I got with her? We'll have to leave this lovely garden all too soon. Then I suppose Sue will have to pack and get ready to go for this train, but maybe she'll have lunch with me today—surely she will, as it'll be our last meal together. (Susan occasionally ate her lunch with Jim and the other servants in the servants' common-room, next to the kitchen, when Lord Dalmane was away; in fact, she had done this on every day so far of this week with her husband away in London.) Our last meal together, Jim thought. Our last hour together! Oh dear!—but I suppose I'll get over it somehow, in time. But after Sue's gone it'll be my turn to pack my suitcase, to get ready to leave by the "Pines Express" from Stalbridge . . .

"Jim," said Susan presently, "I've been thinking about that day we had a picnic last summer."

Jim came out of his daydreams.

"That was a gorgeous day, Sue."

"Yes," she said after a pause, "but Jim, I am most awfully sorry about what happened. It <u>was</u> a lovely picnic, but I never should have asked you to come out with me. Oh, I know it was sheer heaven lying there in that hollow after our picnic, when we were making love—but we shouldn't have done it. If we hadn't, you wouldn't be leaving us tomorrow. But it's been all my fault, Jim, what's happened—entirely my fault."

"But Sue, it wasn't all your fault," said Jim. "After all, I said I <u>wanted</u> to come with you, when you asked me."

"Yes, but it <u>was</u> my fault," said Susan. "You've lost your job because I invited you to make love to me. That, I'm afraid, is quite simply the truth."

"Oh no! You can't say it was your fault, Sue, because of that: because you lead me on, and we—Sue, if Robin Cottem hadn't come along just when he did, all would have been well, wouldn't it? But you couldn't have known, and neither could I, what was going to happen. It was just bad luck—an ill stroke of fate, I suppose."

"Ah, but it wouldn't have happened if only I'd never asked you to come in the car with me to Batcombe Hill. Oh, Jim, I'd do <u>anything</u> to put that mistake right—but there's nothing I can do. And now it's all been found out about us, and you've got to go. You've lost your good job because of me, and I <u>am</u> most dreadfully sorry for you, Jim."

"Oh, don't say that, Sue," began Jim, beginning to feel distressed by her insistence on taking all the blame on herself for his dismissal. He was going to continue, but then found that he did not know what else to say. Then another thought came into his mind as he pondered over her words:

"You've lost your good job because of me". He remembered Mr. Ruddock, the train driver. On the day when he had first met Susan there had been that affair in the train in which Mr. Ruddock had been threatened with dismissal by the inspector. He had been faced with the sack also because of an involvement with Susan. Only his story, because of much help from Susan herself, had finished with a happy ending: Jim had heard of how he had got his job back. But he thought that the two stories ran strangely parallel, up to a point. Only the luck's run out with me, he thought.

"Sue," he said presently, "we both knew what we were doing that day. We both knew that we were running the risk that someone would see us making love, and that the word would get back to your husband, and now it has."

"What are you saying, my love?" asked Susan. "If I hadn't asked you to come out with me that day, you'd still be happily going about your work here today."

"Yes, but we'd probably have found some other opportunity by now to—to be alone together, Sue. I just can't think of it as a mistake, what we did. I'd do just the same if we had a chance to go back in time to that day to do things differently."

"Ah, but you can't alter the past anyway," said Susan, beginning to rise from her deckchair. "What's done's done; and what follows will follow. John says you have to go, and I suppose he's right really." She sighed and stood up. Wondering, Jim stood up too. "Mind you, I've pleaded and pleaded with John to change his mind and allow you to stay on as Guide, but it's no good: he's quite convinced that he's done the right thing in dismissing you. He said: 'If I were to allow Jim to stay here, then, sooner or later, you and he would surely find an opportunity for another picnic or meeting in some secret place, or else you'd end up in bed together here at the Castle sometime when I'm away.' And I daresay he's right about that, although I still don't think it's right to send you away. But it's going to happen anyway, so don't let's talk about that any more."

"All right," said Jim. "Are we going now?"

"Not just yet, out let's have a walk around the garden, Jim."

They began slowly to wander about the Private Garden, arm in arm, Susan pointing out to Jim things about the various little trees and shrubs. She seemed to know the proper Latin names and all about all of them, but in this garden the cherries and laburnums and, of course, the rhododendrons, were about the only tree species with which Jim was familiar. He was a little surprised to see that several of the pale-blossomed rhododendrons were already in flower, although it was only mid-April. "They're early flowering varieties," Susan explained to him. There was a great deal about that sheltered little garden which Jim did not know. He had hardly ever been into it before this past week of his dismissal, having preferred to think of it as out-of-bounds, a place only for the Family to visit. The conversation now seemed to be mostly about matters botanical until Susan unexpectedly changed the subject to something much nearer to Jim's and her own heart at that moment.

"Jim," she said in a voice little more than a whisper, "I wish I could come with you when you go back to the North tomorrow." They had stopped beside a white-flowering rhododendron, and had been examining its beautiful blossoms closely; their faces were very close together, but now, suddenly, Susan was not staring at the flowering bush but straight into Jim's eyes. "Almost, I'd like to run away with you, but not quite. I can't bear to think of you disappearing from my life; but you see, my darling, I love my husband too. I can't leave him, I really can't. I'm afraid I'm torn between the two of you . . ."

Jim gently put an arm round her shoulders.

"Sue, my darling," he began, and stopped, uncertain of what to say next. For a moment he looked straight into the black irises and pupils of her marvellous eyes. Even in very strong daylight those eyes were so dark that there could be no other way of describing them than "black" eyes. But were there tears in those eyes? No, he did not think so. Certainly there were no tears on her cheeks—not yet.

"I know you feel torn, Sue," he ventured, "but—but I'm sorry about it."

"Sorry? Why should you feel sorry, my love? Oh, Jim, I wish I could be wholly yours!"

"I love you, Sue," murmured Jim, "and I'll go on loving you . . . only you." He drew her lips a little closer, and then they kissed, and embraced and kissed for several minutes.

It seemed to Jim that hardly any time at all had passed, although really it was about five minutes later, when Susan, remembering the passing of time, looked at her watch. They broke apart.

"We must go now," she said simply.

*

As Susan and Jim walked together through the archway into the Castle bailey they saw someone who, by her mere appearance at that moment, was enough to affect Jim's whole emotional state, but not for longer than a few minutes. A woman came out of the Estate Office door and walked on briskly ahead of them towards the back door of the Castle. She was Mrs. Jean Grookes, the new Guide of Rhodes Castle, recently appointed to take Jim's place. She caught sight of Jim and the Countess behind her and cheerily waved a hand.

"Hello, Jim! Good afternoon, Lady Dalmane," said Mrs. Grookes.

"Hello, Mrs. Grookes. Are you getting on all right?" asked Susan.

"Yes, thank you, Lady Dalmane."

Jim despised this efficient-looking, brown-haired, middle-aged woman who had so hastily been appointed to fill the position left vacant by his dismissal; and he decided instantly, on seeing her at this time, that it would be best to say nothing. Almost he hated Mrs. Grookes, although he knew that his feeling of hatred was quite illogical. He had often said to himself: I hate her name. Mrs. Grookes, indeed! The Ghastly Grookes! Fancy being married to a man called Grookes! You could hardly expect a person to be nice with such an ugly name as that.

Mrs. Grookes was the wife of the man who owned and ran a garage in the nearby village of Yetminster. She came into work each day on a bicycle; Jim saw her bicycle propped up against the wall by the Estate Office. He did not at all object to her appearance which was, in his eyes, nondescript and harmless; but he did object to seeing her going around the place wearing the badge of office which had so recently been his own. The new name had, in fact, merely been a tape glued over the top of the old one, and the legend on the badge now ran: "Rhodes Castle: Official Guide, Mrs. Jean Grookes." Of course, what really upset Jim was simply the fact that she was there at all, doing his old job, while he was himself still living at the Castle. I do think, he said to himself as he now followed Susan into the Castle, that Lord Dalmane needn't have been so hasty in appointing that Ghastly Grookes to my old job while I'm still here. Why should I have to be so pointedly reminded that I've been sacked? Surely he could have waited a few more days until I've gone back to Cockermouth and <u>then</u> asked Mrs. Grookes to start work here.

Susan and Jim now went their separate ways, Susan saying that she had a few things to do in her room; but then she said: "I'll meet you for lunch, Jim, in the common-room at around one o' clock." That'll be good, thought Jim, if only the Ghastly Grookes isn't there too. But he was hopeful of not meeting the new Guide again at lunchtime or later that day: each day so far she had brought her own food with her, and had not eaten it with Jim in the common-room, but had taken it somewhere else.

Mrs. Grookes was not in either the servants' common-room or the kitchen when Jim came for his lunch rather early at ten minutes to one. Nor had Susan yet arrived there, but Jim did not worry: she had said "around one o' clock", and it was not yet that time. Clearly she would be busily packing the things she needed to take with her to spend two nights at Broadstone. Cook was in the kitchen, busy with final preparations for lunch, but Samantha was not there; however, she appeared a minute or two later, hurrying in to lay three lunch places at the common-room table.

"We're not quite ready yet," she said, seeing Jim already sitting waiting in an armchair.

"That's all right," said Jim. "I'm waiting for Sue. She said she'd be here about one. Can I help you, Sam?"

"No, thanks," said Samantha. "There's hardly anything more to do now."

Jim was beginning to feel a little worried when the time reached eight minutes past one and there was still no sign of Susan. He was still sitting in the armchair at one side of the room, waiting as patiently as he could, and feeling little hunger in spite of the wait for his lunch. But just then the door opened (the door in from the passage—the door between the kitchen and the common-room already stood open), and in came a slightly breathless Susan, who had just run down the stairs and along the passage, knowing that she was a little behind her schedule. She was carrying a small suitcase which she set down on a side table.

"Sorry I'm a little late," she said at once, "but I never find that packing a suitcase to go away is either a quick or an easy job, even with your help, Sam." Samantha had been helping her to pack when Jim had come into the common-room.

"I'm sure it isn't easy," agreed Samantha, "but the soup's ready now, if you're ready for it."

Susan came into the common-room, and Jim politely stood up for her before moving from the armchair to take his place at the table beside her. They had left the one place laid on the other side of the table for Samantha who, a moment later, came in bearing a tray with three bowls of hot soup. There was not a great deal of conversation during the meal, but most of it was between Susan and Samantha. Samantha waited on them, taking dishes in and out between courses. Jim was feeling very glum and ate mostly in silence, with little interest in his eating, thinking only of how dreadfully quickly his last minutes in Susan's company were slipping away. He noticed that she glanced at her watch from time to time, but she did not appear to be hurrying herself, but rather to be enjoying her meal as if everything was perfectly normal.

At the end of the meal they were each drinking a cup of coffee, but Susan was still in no hurry; she had seen that she was now, if anything, a little early. Samantha, however, drank her coffee as quickly as she could, as if she were impatient to move.

"Well, I must be going," said Susan a few minutes later as she finished her cup of coffee. "But first, I must just go and fetch my coat."

"I'll get it for you," said Samantha at once, springing to her feet. "Where is it, Sue? No, you stay there, Jim," she added under her breath, and caught his eye, and winked at him. She had seen that Jim had also made as if to move from his place.

"Thank you, Sam," said Susan. "I left the coat on a chair in the hall. Really I'd meant to bring it in here with the suitcase."

"I'll fetch it, and I'll put both the things into the car for you. There wasn't anything else was there?"

"No, I think I've got everything that I meant to take with me if I've got my coat and that case."

"Right." Then Samantha added, over her shoulder, as she came to the door: "But you needn't hurry too much, Sue. You're still rather too early to set off for that train, you know." She left the room with a quick grin at Jim, and closed the door behind her.

Jim looked round at Susan and smiled. He felt very grateful to Samantha for being so thoughtful as to see that they would now have a few minutes on their own.

The moment of farewell had come. But now that it had finally arrived, Jim unexpectedly felt that he was quite at a loss for words unless Susan should speak first. She rose from her seat, and her clear, dark eyes looked at him in silence for a second or two. Jim stood up too, but behind his own eyes he could now feel an unmistakable hotness by which he knew that his tears were not far away. Then he noticed that there were tears in the corners of Susan's eyes.

"Well, Jim, my darling," she said quietly. "I'm afraid the time's come when I've got to leave you. But I'll see you again some time. You must try not to be too upset, Jim. We're sure to meet again."

"Are we?" said Jim. "Do you think we really will meet again some time, Sue?"

"Oh yes, I'm quite sure we will." Susan sounded really quite cheerful. "Mind you, it could be rather a long time before I can ask you to come back here to visit me—I've got to think of John, haven't I?—so it might be a year or two, Jim—or longer."

"But we <u>will</u> meet again!"

"We will. And look here, Jim, I'll write to you, so that we can keep in touch."

"And I'll keep writing to you, Sue," said Jim eagerly. "Of course we must keep in touch by writing letters."

"We shall. Bless you, my darling. Good-bye!"

"Oh, Sue, darling!" said Jim rather breathlessly. "<u>Must</u> you go now?"

Susan nodded her head and spread out her arms. The next moment their lips met as they kissed each other, but their embrace lasted only for a few seconds. Jim felt a tear, one of Susan's tears (or was it one of his own?) touch his lips.

"Good-bye, my darling," breathed Susan huskily as she let go of Jim.

"Good-bye, Sue, darling!" But Susan was already hurrying for the door, almost running away from the room, the tears now streaming down her cheeks. She waved a hand and was gone, leaving the door into the kitchen open.

Jim remained standing where he was, as still as if he had been turned into stone, for perhaps half a minute. Then he sniffed once or twice, drew a handkerchief out of his trouser pocket, and dabbed at his eyes with it. He was not exactly weeping, but his vision had become so blurred and misty that until he had wiped the tears from his eyes he could see nothing clearly. Then, suddenly pulling himself together, he went quickly to the window and looked out. Samantha must have put those things into her car several minutes ago, he thought, but had the car gone yet? It had not. From the inside of that window he could just see where Susan's red car was still parked adjacent to the back door, further along that wall of the Castle. He waited there a minute, watching intently. Then he saw Susan come suddenly out of the Castle and step smartly into the driver's seat of her car. Jim waved his hand but, not surprisingly, Susan did not appear to notice that he was watching at that window. Within seconds he heard the engine started, and there was the car moving off across the bailey towards the archway: Susan had parked it facing the right way for immediate departure. Another second or two and the car with Susan driving it disappeared from his view where the back drive curved round to the right beyond the arch. Susan was well and truly gone. He thought for a moment of rushing off to his own room, which looked out from the other side of the Castle, over the front garden, so that perhaps he would get another glimpse of that departing car, but decided against it. He knew which way Susan would drive to get out to the Yetminster road: she would turn right at the North Lodge and go down the road which lead into the Car Park at the Visitor Centre, and then go straight across the Main Drive at the crossroads by Inner Lodge, just as he had done on his bicycle when going down to Yetminster Station. She would drive down the Stable Road past the Stables and West Lodge to the bottom end of Knighton Lane, and so out onto the public road; that way was a good short cut for Yetminster instead of going out by the Main Drive and South Lodge. But, even though it might have been possible, if he had hurried to his room, to catch glimpses of the bright red car as it moved down the Stable Road between Inner Lodge and the Stables, Jim decided that it would be futile to try it; he would not be able to see Susan anyway at that distance even if he did manage to spot the car.

She had gone. Jim looked glumly round to the table and noticed that there was still about a mouthful of coffee left in his cup, probably nearly cold by now. He ignored it and walked out through the kitchen, where there was no one at the moment. He had not bothered to bring his cup and saucer with him, as he usually would have done, or to attempt any clearing up of the dirty lunch things on the table. Samantha would be coming back at any minute to see to that work, but Jim at that moment did not want to meet anybody, not even Samantha. She had shown herself to be very kind and understanding about his unfortunate situation when, a few days earlier, she had invited him to her room, and he had poured out the affairs of his heart to her in a long talk. She had been very comforting to him, but just now he did not want to meet her. But luckily he met no one on the way to his bedroom.

When he had shut his door Jim sat down in the chair at his desk. He sat there for about half an hour doing nothing at all except allowing all sorts of thoughts about Susan, happy and sad memories, to pass in a long, unhindered procession through his mind. His head sank slowly downwards onto his chest, and he did not notice the sun shining in through the window from his right. Slowly his eyes again became misty with tears, but he did not know it. He only moved when, presently, the thought came to him that now that Susan had gone, and he would not see her again, there was nothing to make him want to stay in Rhodes Castle any longer. It was as if the Castle, and all its grounds, had suddenly become a very lonely place, or at least, somehow, a very empty place. It might still be full of people: Samantha, Major Ambrose, Mrs. Grookes, and many other servants, but its mistress was no longer there, and would not be coming back until after Jim had left. He had sometimes before felt that there seemed to be a peculiar vacuum in the Castle on occasions when he had been in residence and Susan had not, but now he had that feeling far more acutely than ever before. Damn it, he thought, now that Sue's gone I don't want to live here any more. I want to go home. I wouldn't mind if it were possible for me to set off for home straight away. Hurry up, tomorrow morning: I want to go home.

CHAPTER SEVENTEEN

The next morning, which was Friday, dawned even more foggy than the previous morning had been. Jim got out of his bed at just after seven and went to the window to look out. Fog, he said to himself. There was certainly no other word to describe such a thick general whiteness and dampness in the air; it was definitely more than mere mist. He could see nothing at all from his window that morning except pale fog, out he soon tired of looking at it. He took off his pyjamas and began somewhat listlessly to dress himself, feeling that he could hardly care less what the weather might do that day. In about two hours from now he would be walking out of the front door of the Castle for the last time, and setting off to walk down the Main Drive in time to catch the 9.40 bus from Leigh at the drive end by South Lodge. He expected that the day would become sunny and warm before midday, just as had happened yesterday when the mist had been clearing away while he had been having his breakfast; out yesterday he had got up considerably later than this morning, and besides, he believed that the fog today was in any case denser than it had been at the same time yesterday morning. But almost certainly it would clear away as the morning went on. However, fog or no fog, the state of the weather was hardly a consideration in Jim's mind as he dressed and then packed his pyjamas, slippers, and other belongings into his small suitcase which lay open on the floor. Even before he did so that room was looking less like his own room than usual. Most of his belongings had been packed into his trunk several days before, and the trunk had been sent off by rail to arrive at Cockermouth probably before he arrived there himself that evening.

Jim had been rather shocked when he awoke that morning at realising how depressed he was feeling as, even before he had had time to feel fully awake, the memory of his melancholy situation came most forcefully back to him. Susan had gone, and he would not see her again for years, probably, if at all. And that morning he was himself to leave Rhodes Castle to go back home to his father in Cockermouth. At first he found it hard to get back into yesterday afternoon's mood of wanting the moment for his own departure to come as quickly as possible. However, he made himself put on his clothes rapidly, as if hurry were essential, although he knew he was in ample time and had no real need of hurry; and straight away he slipped easily back into that mood of wanting to leave in a hurry.

Presently Jim left his suitcase still lying on the floor, and not yet completely packed, while he went off to have his breakfast. Samantha had promised him that a rather early breakfast would be ready for him by half past seven so that he would not have to rush to catch that bus. But Jim had still not calculated how much time he would have to allow to walk all the way down the Main Drive which was, as he knew, almost a mile long. He had vaguely thought of setting off walking at about nine o' clock and of arriving down at the road not later than 9.35; there he would hail the bus by the drive gates at South Lodge. As he walked along the corridor, and then began to descend the stairs, he tried to do an arithmetical calculation in his head: just exactly <u>when</u> ought he to set off walking? But he quickly gave up the problem. He felt too tired and depressed to bother about doing mental arithmetic, particularly so early in the morning. I'll start at about nine, he thought. It's probably allowing much more time than I really need, but I'd better get down to South Lodge early rather than late. You can't count on that bus to be punctual, and if I go and miss it, I'd have to stay here until tomorrow. If I miss the bus, I've missed the train. The timetable only says: "dep. Leigh 9.40", so I can only estimate that it should pass South Lodge about 9.45—or perhaps 9.43 would be nearer the mark. Anyway if I get down there by half past nine I'll be all right.

Just as Jim came to the kitchen door a more cheerful thought came to him. He remembered Samantha. Yes, here she is, he said to himself as he caught sight of her on entering the room. Yesterday evening Samantha had been very kind to him. At supper time she had invited him to come for a second time to her rooms after supper, and so Jim had gone there with her and had spent a happy time until half past eleven forgetting that he was not going to see Susan again, and forgetting that he was about to be sent home.

"Hello, Sam," he said, a smile appearing on his face as his thoughts became more cheerful. "Thanks for last night. I enjoyed it."

"Well, it was good for you, Jim," she said. "You shouldn't brood too much, you know, on what's happened."

"I know. I'll try not to."

"This fog's pretty thick isn't it? I hope your bus doesn't get delayed because of it. What time do you have to go for it?"

"The bus goes past South Lodge just before a quarter to ten, so I'm going to set off walking at nine."

"That's giving yourself plenty of time. And what time's your train?"

"It's the 10.38. The bus is supposed to get to Stalbridge Station at 10.17."

"Oh, well, it's a good thing that the connection allows quite a bit of time at Stalbridge. If your bus happens to be, say, ten minutes late, there's still nothing to worry about. Mind you, I think that the fog is already beginning to thin out a bit."

Jim went to the window and looked out carefully into the fog. He could see all the way across the bailey to the opposite walls and down to the archway in the mediaeval walls at the far end of the bailey, but the walls over there looked dim and insubstantial, and the back drive beyond the archway simply vanished into fog a yard or two further on.

"Yes," he said, "I'd say the fog is a little thinner now than it was when I first looked out at seven o' clock."

"Good," said Samantha. "It'll probably all clear away quite soon and become sunny like yesterday. Anyway, you'd better sit down now, Jim, and I'll bring you your breakfast."

Jim went through to the common-room and sat himself down at the one place which was laid at the end of the table. He was not used to being waited on at breakfast: normally he had to go and get things for himself. But today the idea of having Samantha waiting on him pleased him.

She brought him a bowl of porridge, and he began thoughtfully to eat it. But his thoughts were no longer of Susan and of his personal tragedy of being parted from her: instead he was reviewing in his mind the pleasant events of the previous evening.

"What about having a game of chess with me?" Samantha had said to him at supper time. "Do you play chess?"

"Yes," Jim had answered. "But very badly. I haven't played chess for ages, and I'm no good at it."

"Never mind about that. You come along to my room after you've finished your supper and see what you can do on a chessboard. And we can have a nice chat too, of course."

So Jim had gone along with Samantha to her sitting-room. She and Roger Burton, her fiancé, now had a suite of rooms on the first floor: as well as the sitting-room there was their bedroom, a kitchen, and a bathroom. The sitting-room was a large room at the front of the Castle, a room at least three times the size of Jim's tiny room, and it was very comfortably furnished. Unfortunately, however, soon after they had gone in there, and Samantha had brought out a chess set from a drawer, Roger had turned up. Jim had immediately felt that to have a third person present in the room was going to spoil the evening for him, because there would now be no chance to talk privately with Samantha about those matters which were weighing so heavily on his mind and in his heart. However, they had spoken of other things, and Jim had soon learned that Samantha and Roger were to be married in a month's time.

"We chose a date in mid-May because we both agree that May is the nicest month of the year," Samantha had said.

"And then, I suppose, you won't be living in Rhodes Castle any more?" Jim had said. He was unaware that the adjacent rooms had been converted into the Burtons' new flat within the Castle.

"Oh no," Samantha had said. "I'm not going to move out, but Roger's going to move in." Then she had offered to show Jim round her other rooms when they had finished playing chess. But when Jim had been shown into the bedroom, another pleasant front room, he saw the large double bed and was again uncomfortably reminded of his parting from Susan. However, Samantha had seemed to guess the thoughts that were in his mind, and after allowing him a quick glimpse at the bedroom had whisked him away to have a look at her kitchen. A little earlier that evening they had set out the chessboard on the carpet of the sitting-room and, squatting on the floor, they had played two games of chess, in which Samantha had beaten Jim easily both times. The first game had been a very short one, but in the second Samantha had made a number of deliberate mistakes, and so the game had lasted much longer. Roger had been squatting on the floor beside them, watching and making frequent comments, which Jim had found mainly irritating, although he had certainly been enjoying himself. Then Samantha had asked her fiancé to leave them so that she and Jim could have some private talk.

"Of course, I know you really want to talk about Sue," Samantha had said when her fiancé had gone, "so I've sent Roger away so that it'll be easier for you to tell me whatever you like." She had continued by saying that in her opinion it would certainly do no harm for Susan and Jim to keep in touch by writing letters until sometime he would surely be invited back to see Susan. She had, however, also recommended Jim to find himself a new girlfriend, preferably through finding a new job first; and in that way, she had said, he would be able to keep alive his close friendship with Susan while at the same time allowing the excess of his passionate infatuation to dissipate slowly and painlessly.

At this point in his daydream Jim started as he heard Samantha's voice, bringing him back to the present.

"There's a cooked breakfast for you this morning, Jim." She was looking in from the doorway. "Are you ready for bacon and eggs?"

"Yes," said Jim. "Thanks very much, Sam."

When Samantha brought Jim his plate of bacon and eggs she said: "Susan asked me to make a lunch picnic for you to eat in the train, Jim, and I've nearly got it ready for you. You mustn't go without it. Oh, and there's something else I've got to give you—which I haven't got with me at the moment."

"Oh?" said Jim. "Something from Susan?"

"Yes. I'll hand it over when you're setting off at nine o' clock. Look here, you'll be going out by the front door, won't you?" (Jim nodded.) "Well, there are a few little jobs I ought to do in the hall, so I could meet you there on your way out and hand over your packed lunch and the other thing that Susan said you were to have."

"But what is it?"

"Oh, you'll see. Nothing very exciting but—well, you'll see when I give it to you."

Jim decided to enquire no further as to what this thing from Susan might be. If Samantha wants to make a mystery of it, so be it, he thought. Keeping an eye on the time, and glancing occasionally out of the window at the fog, he pressed on with his breakfast.

At five minutes to nine Jim left his room, carrying his suitcase. Then he came slowly down the main staircase towards the

Great Hall. His mood of wanting to hurry away had completely evaporated now that he actually <u>was</u> leaving. He was feeling a very great reluctance to walk out of the Castle, feeling in his heart that it might well be a final action. True, there had been talk of his being invited to come back to visit some day, but nothing definite had been arranged, and Jim could not help believing that probably he would never return. Probably Susan would change her mind on that point, under pressure from her husband, and issue no such invitation. So Jim, as he advanced slowly, was looking studiously around at all the familiar surroundings and mentally saying farewell to everything. But side by side in his mind with his sadness and reluctance at departure there was a curiosity which amounted to a certain eager anticipation. What would this thing from Susan be? Some little parting gift, no doubt. And where was Samantha anyway? Oh, there she is, he said to himself, as he came down into the hall.

Samantha, an apron tied around her front, and a tin of metal polish and a cloth in her hands, was standing by the inner front door, polishing the brasswork on it. On the chair beside the door there was something in a string bag. As she heard Jim approaching she put down her brass cleaning equipment, turned, and dipped a hand into a pocket as if to check whether something was there.

"Well, Jim, so you're off," she said. "Have you said all your Good-byes?"

"Yes, except to you," said Jim. "I went round to Inner Lodge yesterday evening to say Good-bye to the Ambroses before supper. And Lord Dalmane's away, so—"

"So you can't say Good-bye to him; but you said Good-bye to Sue at lunch time yesterday."

"Yes." Jim felt a slight hotness in his eyes at the mere memory of that painful parting. But Sue was right after all, he thought: it <u>would</u> have been very difficult to say Good-bye to her <u>now</u>, when I'm actually going.

"Well, good-bye to you, Jim," said Samantha. "Here's your lunch picnic." She handed him the string basket in which there was one large parcel, carefully wrapped up in paper. "You can keep that bag."

"Thank you." Jim looked expectantly at Samantha who now drew an envelope from a pocket.

"Here you are," she said. "It's a letter from Susan for you. She asked me to give it to you as you were leaving." She handed the envelope to Jim, who looked at it. There was nothing at all written on it, but it was sealed: just an ordinary light-blue envelope with the Dalmane Crest on it, but clearly there was a letter inside it. "Don't open it now," continued Samantha. "Sue said you should wait to open it until you get home, or until you're well on your way home."

"I see," said Jim. He pushed the envelope into the inner pocket of his jacket beside his wallet where it could remain safely until he was ready to read the letter. Gosh, so Sue must have written this the night before last, probably, before she said I could write to her, he thought. Well, I'm certainly going to write to her this evening, if there's time, when I've read what she's put in her letter.

Samantha opened the inner and then the heavy outer front door, so that they looked out into the fog over the drive. "It still looks very foggy," she said, going out to the top of the flight of stone steps.

Jim picked up his suitcase in his right hand and the bag with his packed lunch in his left, and was following Samantha out to the steps when he checked himself. At that moment he saw a dim light appear out of the fog, moving towards them, and heard a sound of gravel scrunching under wheels. Then the next moment he and Samantha saw a woman on a bicycle, the headlight on, riding past them, on her way round to the western side of the Castle. Samantha waved a hand, and the cyclist waved back; but Jim hung back in the vestibule between the inner and outer doors and scowled. It's that

Ghastly Grookes arriving for work, he said to himself. He looked at his watch. And she's late too. It's just gone nine o' clock now, but Major Ambrose won't mind because of the fog.

He hung back for another few seconds to allow time for Mrs. Grookes on her bicycle to disappear; then he joined Samantha on the front door steps. He had argued to himself that as he hardly knew Mrs. Grookes it was not at all necessary that he should say Good-bye to her, and best that he should not be seen by her just as he was setting off to leave the Castle.

"Good-bye, Sam," he said, putting down the suitcase for a moment so that his right hand was free to shake the maid's hand. "Thanks for everything." His farewell to Samantha was taking up a lot of time, but he wanted to draw it out as far as possible.

"That's all right, Jim. Have a good journey home."

They smiled at each other and shook hands, but there was an unexpected pleasure in store for Jim, for Samantha immediately put her arms around his neck to Kiss him. Jim responded instantly and eagerly by embracing her to himself for a moment, looking into her green eyes as he kissed her on the lips, while she looked into his face. He realised in that moment that she was a prettier girl than ever he had fully understood, altogether a most attractive young woman; and he saw that her bluish-green eyes really looked decidedly green, a beautiful colour under the blue eye-shadow copiously applied to her eyelids. Heavens, he thought, however was it that I used to think of Sam as a rather plain-looking girl, not attractive, when I first came here, and for some time afterwards? But it's too late now to think of falling in love with her!

"Good-bye, Jim, my dear," she said as they quickly broke apart, and Jim again picked up his suitcase. "Write to Sue soon, won't you? You two should keep in touch—and I'm sure you'll get an invitation that way to come back to see Sue sometime. And, if you care to, you might like to drop a line to me too," she added with a coy smile. "I'd like to know how you get on after leaving us."

"That's a good idea, Sam; I will. But I'd better be off now." (He glanced at his wrist-watch: it was five minutes past nine.) "Good-bye!"

He descended the wide, stone steps to the drive with a broad smile on his face, having quite forgotten for the moment that he was leaving Rhodes Castle, perhaps not to see it again for several years; and, more importantly, even temporarily forgetting Susan. He turned round for a moment to wave a last farewell to Samantha, and saw her wave back to him. Then he saw her turn and go back into the Castle, closing the doors behind her. If I didn't know Sue, he was thinking as he walked away, and if I didn't love her so much, so that there's no room in me to be in love with anyone else, then I'd surely have fallen for Sam. And she's been so kind to me these last few days that it's really a bit of a wrench to have to leave her.

The air was not only rather damp with the fog still fairly thick, but also rather cold as Jim could not help noticing. At first he walked at a reasonably brisk pace, a smile on his face. When he reached the place where the drive passed between the two ponds he stopped and looked back. He had gone, perhaps, less than fifty yards from the stone steps by the front door, but already all that facade of the front of the Castle looked dim and shadowy in the fog. The front door appeared to be shut, but in the window beside it Jim could see an electric light burning: Sam was in the hall polishing the brasswork. There were no other lights showing through the gloom on that side of the Castle. Jim took one last look at the window of what had been his own room for more than two and a half years. "Good-bye, my room," he said to it. Just then he distinctly felt a breath of cold air on the back of his neck; he thought that he had detected a slight breeze on his face before he had turned round. He looked at the top of the Great Tower with its bare flagpole and at the more distant, broken towers and turrets of the East Wall where they could dimly be seen beyond the Great Tower: the further towers were no more than faint, insubstantial shapes in the white mist, like phantom towers, while the mist seemed to be moving past the top of the Great Tower, stirred by the light, southerly breeze. If there's wind coming the fog will soon blow away, he thought. He walked on, casting his gaze as he walked over first one of the ornamental pools, then the other. It was odd looking at the water with the fog hanging over it: the smooth, oily surface of the water might nave been hot and steaming to judge by the way that curls of white mist moved by the light air were floating over it.

Jim then looked as far down the drive as it was possible to see in the fog. He could see the pale outlines of the trees which hung over the drive inside the gate of the Inner Drive, but he could not make out either the gate itself or the outline of Inner Lodge beyond it. Looking to his left he could see the dark shape of the great cedar tree; the pale fog hanging in the air seemed to have the optical effect of emphasising the layered structure of its heavy branches. Rather further away he could dimly see the outline of the Maze, and between this and the drive there was a formless shape; this was the high hedge which cut off a view of the buildings of the Visitor Centre from the lawns of the Castle's main garden. He tried to see the Servants' Graveyard, and thought that a vague, dark shape to the right of the place where the gate must be, would be the screen of evergreen trees surrounding the little cemetry. He was reminded of the American tourist who had once insisted so enthusiastically on being shown the graveyard, and of his lively chatter about the ghost of Beryl Buxton and about the stealing of the Great Beryl of Saint Helens. Probably there is no such ghost, he thought. At any rate, I never saw it. He walked on, noticing as he went that the garden that morning seemed a strange, almost unfriendly place, not only because the fog blurred all the outlines of things, making them look unfamiliar, but also because there was a peculiar quietness with the fog. The light air was not a sufficient breeze to make any noise in the sycamore trees, in which the leaves were beginning to come out. Jim noticed, too, that there was very little birdsong to be heard apart from the occasional sounds of rooks in the upper tree branches. As he passed under an overhanging branch of the first sycamore tree by the driveside he noticed little drops of moisture falling on him, condensation of the fog on the young leaves. Before him now he could see where the gate stood open at the entrance to the Inner Drive, and beyond it the dim outline of a house was Inner Lodge.

Suddenly Jim checked, seeing someone (it was probably a woman, he thought) walking down the path from the Servants' Graveyard to the drive near the gate. He had not expected to meet anyone until he came out onto the public road. Was it Mrs. Ambrose from Inner Lodge? But Jim knew almost at once that this tall figure could not be the short and rather plump Mrs. Ambrose. Whoever it was, she presented a dim, blurred outline, seen through the fog, but she seemed to have black hair and to be oddly dressed: apparently she had on a black dress which came right down to her feet. Now she had reached the drive, and was coming quite noiselessly towards him. Jim walked on uncertainly to meet and pass the stranger, and perhaps exchange a "Good morning" with her; but he was wondering why she was there at all: the grounds were not yet officially open to the public. The silent figure drew quickly nearer to Jim, and a sudden fear siezed him as a thought came irresistibly into his mind: Beryl Buxton. This was no living woman, he realised, but a phantom presence—indeed the celebrated ghost of Beryl Buxton after all—unless what he saw was no more than a hallucination or a trick of the light in the misty conditions. No, it could not be that; but somehow he knew beyond doubt that he was seeing a ghost.

He stopped dead, his heart pounding loudly, and his legs felt weak with sudden fear, but he noticed that the figure did not appear to be <u>walking</u> to meet him; rather, it was as if it were floating along an inch or two above the ground.

"Stop!" he shouted a second later, finding his courage again, and at the same moment advancing a few steps towards the woman, his left hand held out in a clear gesture, having put down the bag with the food. But the apparition, if apparition it was, showed no sign of stopping. In a few seconds more it would have come right up to him. Then Jim's fear seemed to become completely submerged for a moment in a wave of rising anger. In a split second he decided on what to do, rejecting automatically any idea of turning back or running away. His eye had already noted some small sticks lying in the roadway, sticks which had probably been dropped by rooks building their nests in the tree overhead; there was one stick conveniently close to Jim's feet. He grabbed it and hurled it with all his might straight into the face of the approaching woman. The shot was well aimed in spite of his haste, and should have hit the figure right between the eyes, and perhaps have drawn blood; however, all that happened was that the stick whistled through the air, meeting no obstacle until it landed on the drive many yards ahead. At the very moment of his throwing the stick the shadowy figure had simply vanished into the air, as if it had never been. Jim stared ahead at his stick, lying on the drive, and blinked his eyes a few times, hardly liking to believe that the ghostly figure could have disappeared so promptly on being confronted by a missile aimed to strike it.

The next moment, without knowing what he was doing, he found that he had broken into a wild run, making for the gate of the Inner Drive, but still carrying his suitcase. He ran through the open gateway and pulled up, remembering that the bag with his packed lunch had been left behind on the driveway. He looked back. Very dimly now in the middle-distance he could make out the facade of the Castle, looming through the white mist, and nearer to him he saw that curling wisps of mist were blowing through the top branches of the trees; but there was no sign of that shadowy woman in black. It was hard, indeed, to believe that anything unusual had just happened. He walked quickly back the few yards to the place where he had set down the bag with his food, and again paused to look around for Beryl Buxton, if it had been her that he had seen, but now there was no sign of anything supernatural or, indeed, of anyone else in that part of the garden. He picked up the bag and walked back to the gate, saying to himself as he went: I must sit down for a minute; I'm still definitely on the early side for that bus. He had already seen that an electric light was burning in a downstairs window of Inner Lodge, which meant that Mrs. Ambrose was at home, but he knew that it was out of the question that he should go in there. For one thing he had already said Good-bye to Mrs. Ambrose yesterday; and for another, she would be sure to detain him for too long, and probably make him miss the bus and the train. So, having passed the white gate of the Inner Drive, he turned to the left at the crossroads onto the road leading into the Visitors' Car Park, and made for the bench beside the Car Park, and sat down on it. That morning the Visitor Centre looked quite deserted. There were no cars parked there, and the shop and the cafeteria were closed, although the shop would open later on, when the gardens opened at eleven o' clock. Jim only remained sitting on the bench for a minute or two, while he collected his thoughts and rapidly recovered from his shock. Had anything at all just happened, or had he simply imagined a dark, shadowy woman coming towards him? It would have been easy, he told himself, in such foggy conditions, to <u>imagine</u> that he had seen a ghost, when really he had seen nothing at all—or, at least, nothing except a hallucination in his own brain. Was that what had happened? Perhaps his distressed state of mind because of his farewell to Susan and Rhodes Castle had caused him to be overwrought, and had thus triggered a hallucination. But in his heart he did not believe this and, what was more, he felt secretly glad that he had seen the ghost of Beryl Buxton, as evidently he had. He had not really believed in that ghost, but now what room for doubt could there be? There had certainly been something of a joke about the whole episode coming, as it had, at the very last minute, before he left the Castle gardens, but he thought that it had been enough to change his mind: henceforth he would surely have to believe that he had met Beryl Buxton's ghost on the morning of his departure from the Castle.

Before Jim continued his walk he glanced up at the sky and saw that the fog was certainly clearing. Looking over his left shoulder he could see the sun now; indeed it was already nearly too bright to look at for long, although it was still a misty, red sun. But right overhead there was a patch of clear blue sky. It heartened Jim greatly to know that very soon the fog would have gone.

Within two minutes he was on his way again, feeling that he had got over his shock. He swung left at the Inner Lodge crossroads, having first looked nostalgically straight ahead down the Stable Road, the road which Susan must have used yesterday on her way to the station at Yetminster. Then at a moderate pace he began to walk down the Outer Main Drive to where the great iron gates, not yet visible, stood open beside South Lodge. It seemed to him to be a long way to walk, out the walking, far from making him feel tired, seemed to be helping him to feel stronger after the shock of seeing Beryl Buxton (he was reasonably convinced now that the woman he had seen <u>was</u> her ghost). Once or twice he looked back to see whether anyone or anything was following him, but nothing was, and so his thoughts slipped easily back to Susan, as he wondered when and how he would next manage to see her. As he made steady progress down the avenue of the Outer Drive he soon noticed how the left-hand line of trees were beginning to cast shadows in the sunshine: faint shadows at first, they were gradually becoming more distinct. Well before he came to South Lodge he realised that the fog had all but cleared, although it was still rather misty; but the sun was shining in a clear blue sky, and it was becoming warmer. Jim, thinking about Susan, was beginning to enjoy himself again, forgetting about Beryl Buxton, and forgetting too, for the moment, that he was leaving, and would perhaps not see Susan again for a number of years. He was noticing things in the Park with pleasure: there were masses of daffodils bordering the outer part of the Main Drive between the Inner and South Lodges, and these now made a fine sight in the misty morning sun. He saw that although the early ones looked more or less over, most of the daffodils were still fully in flower. Then, about half way down that stretch of the drive, he saw a group of hinds standing in the roadway. They ran off into the Park as he drew nearer. The Main Drive, like all the roads which ran through Rhodes Park, was unfenced, so that the deer were able to roam wherever they liked within the Park.

When Jim came to the black-painted wrought-iron gates where the drive opened out onto the main road he looked at the small house on his right, South Lodge, in the angle between the two roads. There were curtains or blinds drawn across all the windows, and Jim remembered that at the moment the lodge was untenanted. He looked both ways along the main road and consulted his watch; it was only just after half past nine, so he had arrived there with more time than he needed. He set the suitcase and the string bag down at the side of the road, and reflected that a warm, sunny day, such as it was rapidly turning out to be, was going to be completely wasted on him, pleasant though it was to see the sun again after the fog. Not that the mist had yet completely cleared away. Staring along the road to the right he could clearly see the signpost at the junction of the Yetminster road at Rhodes Corner, about a quarter of a mile away, but beyond that the road southwards to Totnell Corner, from where his bus would come, still faded gradually into the mist. Jim looked that way more and more intently as the time drew slowly on to twenty minutes, and then to a quarter to ten, trying to see a bus appearing out of the hazy distance; but a quarter to ten passed without a sign of the bus, and Jim could not help feeling anxious about it. I don't want to have to go back to Rhodes Castle now, as I shall have to, if I miss the train, he said to himself, because I'd have to say my Good-byes all over again tomorrow morning, and I probably wouldn't want to go at all. But right now I'm in the right mood—as much as I ever will be—to clear out. He turned from looking towards Rhodes Corner and instead stared back up the drive once again. Now he could see all the way back to the Castle quite clearly: there was hardly any mist at all. But just then he turned round sharply, having heard at last the sound he had been waiting for, and quickly picked up his baggage. The bus had appeared out of the haze beyond Rhodes Corner, and was rapidly approaching him. He boldly flung out an arm to signal to the driver to stop, as the South Lodge of the Castle was not designated an official bus stop.

The bus stopped, and Jim with his baggage clambered aboard. "Hold tight!" shouted the conductor, as Jim eased his way awkwardly forward along the gangway, looking for a seat on the rather crowded single-decker rural bus. The conductor rang the bell, and Jim almost lost his balance as the bus started with a jerk; but just then he saw an empty seat near the front. But in those few seconds of hectic bustle the distant view of Rhodes Castle up the splendid avenue of the Main Drive was left behind before Jim had a chance to turn his head for one last nostalgic farewell glance. However, in the few moments which were left before the bus turned off the Sherborne road onto the small road to Holnest, Jim had a view of the Great Tower of the Castle over the intervening Park, looking to the left. He mentally said farewell to the place which he had thought of as home since July of 1959, more than two years before.

CHAPTER EIGHTEEN

The "Pines Express" came into Stalbridge more or less on time, and left punctually. As the train started Jim was walking up the corridor looking for a good seat, preferably a corner seat in an empty compartment. Soon he found one, for the train seemed to be fairly empty, so he quickly settled down to make himself comfortable by the window. He was by now quite resigned to the idea that he was going home, although not resigned to the idea of living without Susan, so he told himself that he might as well take as much enjoyment as he could from the long train journey to the North. It was going to be a good opportunity too, he knew, whenever he was not actively interested in looking out of the window at the passing countryside, to indulge in extended and, hopefully, vivid daydreams. There was nothing for him to do now that his train journey had begun except, for most of the time, to sit in his seat, so why should he not let his fantasies about Susan take whatever course they would? At any rate, he would do that, alternating, as he pleased, in concentrating on watching the view, until the "Pines Express" had brought him to Crewe, where he had to change trains. Jim knew the route of the "Pines Express" just well enough to remember from his last journey north, for his holiday last autumn, that an especially attractive stretch of country came quite soon after starting from Stalbridge, as the line wound its way up into the Mendip Hills beyond Evercreech

Junction. The old Somerset and Dorset Railway ran through some lovely country up there and to the north of the summit of the line, between Midsomer Norton and Bath (but nowadays this route is an abandoned trackbed on parts of which one can walk). Jim always enjoyed long railway journeys, and saw no reason why today, just because he felt sad on account of his parting from Susan, should be any different from any other occasion in that respect: he was going particularly to enjoy watching that high part of the route before Bath. Further on, towards the Midlands, the scenery became much duller, so he reckoned to let himself do a great deal of thinking about Susan, and about his own future, as the train took him northwards towards Crewe.

There had been no mist or fog left by the time Jim had reached the station at Stalbridge. However, the bus journey from Rhodes Castle had not been entirely in the sun. Mostly the country roads had been quite clear of fog banks, but every so often, usually in a hollow, the bus had passed through an unexpected pocket of mist left behind after the disappearance of the main band of fog. That had been an interesting journey too in its own way, for that rural bus route wandered about strangely along many minor roads: starting from Yeovil, it went via Yetminster, Chetnole, and Leigh; then the bus had come from Totnell Corner (near Leigh) to the Castle South Lodge, where Jim had boarded it; and from there they had gone via Holnest and Bishop's Caundle to Stalbridge, where the bus was timed to connect at the railway station with the "Pines Express".

It seemed to take only a very short time before the train reached Evercreech Junction, beyond which point the line started the climb towards the Mendip Hills. Jim looked at his watch here and saw that the time was just after eleven o' clock. Suddenly he remembered what he had been doing at that same time yesterday. This time yesterday, he said to himself, Sue and I were just going out by the front door to go round to the Private Garden. What a beautiful little garden that is! Shall I ever see it again, I wonder? But it would be nice to be sitting there now in the sun with Sue. My word, it's getting almost too warm in here. And with that thought he turned off the heater in that compartment and opened the ventilators a little way.

It was twenty to four in the afternoon, and the train was approaching Crewe, passing the long sidings at Basford Hall. Jim, preparing to get out, took down his suitcase from the luggage rack. The day had turned out, as he had expected, warm and sunny, like the previous day. Far <u>too</u> warm and sunny, he thought; I'd be glad of a little fresh air here. However, once he had stepped out of the "Pines Express" at Crewe, he quickly became impatient to be continuing his journey in the next train, which was to be the "Mid-Day Scot" from Euston. But he had nearly forty minutes to wait until this train was due in. Crewe station in those days, before the re-building, was a very drab and depressing place, and he could find little of interest to look at, barring the trains. He sat in a dreary refreshment-room for much of this time, having bought himself a cup of British Railways tea, while he ate some of his own food from the string bag of provisions by way of a tea-time snack, but he kept something for later on. Samantha had put some good fruit cake in the food parcel, and as Jim ate it he thought about her with nostalgia. Write to Sam as well as to Sue? Well, why not? He would.

Jim boarded the "Mid-Day Scot" with relief at the thought of getting away from Crewe. It was fairly crowded, and he was unable to find a seat in an empty compartment, but he counted himself lucky to find a seat at all.

A few hours later Jim was looking out from the train window at a very different sort of country from anything else he had seen that day. The fields beside the line were no longer wide and flat, but sloped steeply upwards and were much smaller than the fields of the South; and mostly they had the characteristic dry-stone walls of the

Northern hills. The train had just passed through Oxenholme, the junction for the Windermere branch. The rising ground at which Jim was looking was the slopes of Hay Fell on the eastern side of the main line. Then, looking out the other way, he saw the wide panorama of the town of Kendal spread out in the valley below the line. He was back once more in the country on the edge of the Lake District, his native country, and it affected his mood considerably to see again the familiar hills of the North. It affected him with an odd mixture of emotions. There was certainly a feeling of coming home growing in him which gave a deeply felt sense of pleasure; but against this feeling were contradictory moods of doubt and worry. The effect of seeing these hills again had been, as it were, to make him wake up, as if out of a prolonged dream, for he had been paying but scant attention to the progress of the train since he had boarded it at Crewe. He had been thinking not so much of the future as of the past, happily living again in his mind through his adventures with Susan down in the South. But with the realisation, on seeing again the pleasant hill country around Kendal and Grayrigg, that he was once again on his home ground—was indeed not far now from Cockermouth—it became harder to continue to think about the past. Jim felt as if the sight of his native country was forcing him to sit up, to stop dreaming, and to take thought for the immediate future. But really there was little which he could plan at that stage: much would depend on what sort of job he might find for himself.

He now tried, with little success, to come to terms with the idea of life without Susan, while he considered some ideas about how he would like to be employed. Clearly the appointment of Jackie Rothwell as his father's secretary at the Leadthwaite Mine precluded any possibility that he might be able to take a job there himself. He thought that if his father had not advertised for a secretary he might have offered to do that work himself, even if that would have meant doing it as a voluntary job. But his father had met Jackie, and . . . Jim smiled, out only for a moment. Yes, he felt very glad for his father that the beginnings of a romance had been clear to see at the Mine Office—but it meant that there was no place for him there.

So what could he do? He now thought that he would rather have liked to be able to return to his old job in the police, but that, of course, was impossible. Oh, damn it all, he thought, if only I hadn't run away like a fool I'd have progressed by now from Cadet to Constable! But it's no good thinking about that, having deliberately thrown away my chances of a career in the police. Only, if I hadn't run away when I did, I'd never have met Susan. And that's something worth thinking about!

When the express reached Carlisle, Jim got out. He had to change at Carlisle rather than Penrith to catch the local train home because the "Mid-Day Scot" did not stop at Penrith. It meant a rather longer journey back to Cockermouth in the diesel train, but Jim did not mind that in the least. However, the time was only five past seven when he stepped down onto Platform Three at Carlisle station with his suitcase and his (now empty) string bag; and again he had to face a long wait for his connection.

He went at once to the Departures notice near the middle of the platform, and learned that, as on the previous occasion when he had made this journey, the 7.53 to Workington left from Platform Five. So without delay, although there was still much time to spare, he crossed the lines by the bridge and found the local train waiting in the short bay of Platform Five. He entered the two-car diesel unit near the front end as it was still nearly empty at not quite twenty minutes past seven, and took his favourite position, just behind the driver's cab. But there was now more than half an hour to sit there waiting for the departure, and Jim relapsed easily into his thoughts about Susan.

He was startled by a sudden voice.

"Hello, there, Jim!"

He looked up, and saw that the Driver, who had just boarded his train, had opened the door through into the carriage. Jim saw an elderly man with grey hair showing under his British Railways regulation driver's cap, and a kindly smile on his face.

"Hello, Mr. Ruddock," he said. "I didn't think you'd be driving <u>this</u> train. You weren't the last time I came on it, last September."

"Aye, but they've changed the shifts," said Mr. Ruddock, "and I'm on the late shift now, along with old Tim Blencow, my Guard. And how are you keeping, Jim?"

"Very well, thank you."

"And you're working for Lady Dalmane, so your dad told me the other day when I was chatting with him. Is she well?"

"She's fine, thanks." Jim, of course, did not want to let Mr. Ruddock know that he had just been dismissed from the Dalmanes' service, so he was thinking of being careful in what he said to the old Driver who, as he now remembered, had long been a friend of his father.

"Well, that's good," said Mr. Ruddock. "You're very lucky, I reckon, working at Rhodes Castle. It's a good job you got yourself there that day, I believe it was, when you and she were on my train together—that was the old 10.8 from Cockermouth that I'm not driving any more now. Aye, and she's a right gracious lady, is the Countess of Saint Helens, the Lady Dalmane. I'm very much beholden to her, Jim, as you may know, for she did me a great service. There was I threatened with dismissal, as I expect you know—I needn't go over the details of it again—but it was really very sporting of Lady Dalmane to speak up for me, and to get my job back for me. It was very kind of her, and I wrote to her telling her that I was very grateful for that undeserved kindness."

"Oh yes," said Jim, "she's very kind." He had been listening to this speech with increasing pain, not liking to be reminded of how Mr. Ruddock had been so lucky in being re-instated in his job, whereas he himself was clearly not going to have the same luck.

"You'll be on holiday, are you?" asked Mr. Ruddock, glancing up at the suitcase on the luggage rack.

"No, not on holiday."

Mr. Ruddock looked a little puzzled.

"Oh, I thought maybe you were coming back for a holiday at Cockermouth—at home."

"I am coming back to Cockermouth. But . . . but . . ." Jim allowed his sentence to falter into silence. Why the devil must he stay here asking me these awkward questions, he thought, when I'd rather be left alone?

Mr. Ruddock did not appear to notice Jim's awkwardness.

"Well, it's been a grand day," he said, "and now we've got a grand evening, and likely enough—eh, what's that, Tim?" The train had filled up with passengers by now. Mr. Blencow, the Guard, was standing just behind Jim in the gangway. He had been trying to attract Mr. Ruddock's attention, and now had managed to catch his eye.

"Almost time," he said, pointing to his watch. "We're signalled."

Jim glanced ahead through the driver's windscreen and saw that the colour-light starting signal at the platform end was showing the green light.

"Heavens, so it is!" said Mr. Ruddock. "Cheerio, Jim." He went back into his cab, shut the door, and sat down in the driver's seat.

"Hello, there, Jim Sandy," said Mr. Blencow. "Nice to see you again. Tom's retiring at the end of June, you know? Fifty years of service on the railways. Pretty good record, eh? But I must get this train started, and see that we're all safely aboard." With that he hurried off to the nearest door, his whistle in his hand.

Half a minute later the whistle was blown, and Mr. Ruddock started the train. But Jim began this last stage of his journey home feeling worried by the talk he had just had with Mr. Ruddock. He was sure to find out sooner or later that the reason why he was coming back to Cockermouth was because he had been sacked and was therefore no longer working at Rhodes Castle. Then ought he not to have told Mr. Ruddock that instead of pretending that he was still the Guide there? Oh well, it doesn't really matter, he said to himself, and presently he forgot about it.

*

The train had left the main line at Penrith and swung round the curve of the branch line, having passed the junction, and was now heading west for Keswick and Cockermouth. Jim looked ahead at the setting sun. The fiery circle was about to disappear; indeed it already <u>was</u> disappearing into a low bank of bright cloud stretched along the horizon of Lakeland hills which lay ahead. There was not a sign of any returning mist, but Jim wondered whether it would be getting misty again at Rhodes Castle as the sun went down. Probably it would get foggy again down there, he thought, but he was not surprised at seeing how clear the sky was over the hills of the Lake District. Jim, as a native of the region, knew very well that the kind of fog which often blankets large areas of the Midlands and the South of England and, indeed, of the North— particularly parts of Lancashire and Yorkshire—is very rare in the Lakes, where the nearest thing one usually sees to fog is the mist and low clouds which often envelope the fells. But it was nothing like that on this particular April evening. It was obviously going to be a marvellously clear sunset, with really striking colours lighting up the western sky. Certainly it was very different from the last time Jim had travelled on that evening train, coming home to Cockermouth for his holiday on that cold, damp, and windy night in September, when it had also been pitch dark on reaching Cockermouth at a quarter past nine. But this time it was still going to be more or less daylight when he finally left the train there. The sun had almost gone now. He could only see a tiny point of bright light, the top of a segment of the sun, which still protruded above the line of rose-red cloud. Watching it carefully he thought that he could actually see the brilliant point sinking behind the obscuring cloud. But within moments it was gone from his sight. He had for the moment forgotten his daydreams in watching the progress of the sunset so carefully. Not that the sun had in fact set yet: it had merely disappeared from his view, and he reckoned that it would set in about ten to fifteen minutes' time. The train was now coming in to Troutbeck station, having just passed the summit of the line; Mr. Ruddock was applying the brakes for the stop. Jim thought that the sun would be properly set before they reached Keswick; but the light would surely linger on for a long time thereafter on such a clear night.

Shortly after that stop Jim looked round. Mr. Blencow was coming up to the front to go into the cab to speak to the Driver. Jim remembered how on the day he had met Susan, travelling on the 10.8 train from Cockermouth, Mr. Blencow had gone through to the cab to talk to Mr. Ruddock, and he wondered whether they always did this. It put him in mind of that far-off day when luck had turned his way so remarkably. Why, Susan herself had been invited into the cab the better to admire the view. And with that thought he suddenly remembered that he now had with him a letter from her. He drew the envelope out of the inner pocket of his jacket. Should he open it now, or not? He hesitated a moment, and then remembered that Samantha had said that it was to be opened when he got home, or else when he was well on his way home. So, thought Jim, what I'll do is, I'll open it now, and read her letter through once, and then I'll put it away again. Then I can bring it out again tomorrow morning to read it again, as though the postman had just brought it. He tore open the envelope and took out of it the following letter. Susan had written it on two sheets of plain white notepaper.

Rhodes Castle,
Wednesday evening,

My dearest Jim,

By the time you read this letter you'll be at home, or
perhaps you'll be sitting in a train somewhere not far from
Cockermouth. My love, I know you'll be feeling very sad
because we've had to say Good-bye, but you must try not
to be <u>too</u> sad. We'll definitely meet again. I think, Jim,
that perhaps I could ask you to come down and stay here
for a few weeks in the summer of next year. I think it
would have to be next year, not this one, because John
wouldn't really approve of your coming back here too
soon after dismissing you.

You'll be in new surroundings now, my darling, and
I suppose it seems a strange thing to talk about getting
used to living in one's own home, but I expect you will
need time to get used to it all the same. I know you'd got
used to thinking of the Castle as Home, but of course
it wasn't that really. You know, in a way, I can't help
admitting to myself that John really was quite right in
saying that it would be good for you to leave us because
it's giving you a chance for a new start in life, and a new,
and perhaps a better job. I certainly hope you'll find
yourself something really interesting to do, my love,
and that it'll turn up quite soon. You must write and
tell me about how you're getting on in that way. But
write as soon as you can, won't you, darling, to cheer
me up—don't wait to write until you've got an idea of
what you're going to do. And I'll write to you again soon
when there's some news to pass on—of course, this time
there isn't any you don't already know.

As you know, I'm staying this weekend with Norma Beck at Broadstone, and I'll be back at the Castle probably on Saturday. Then I'll be hoping that on Monday morning the postman will bring a letter from you! You know, my real reason for going off to stay with Norma will be to make a diversion for myself, so that perhaps I won't cry too much because you've gone. But I expect I'll cry a great deal all the same. Oh, Jim, my darling, I love you so much! It's going to be absolutely awful in the Castle when I know you're not around any more; awful for me as well as for you. I'll still have John, of course, but that won't make up at all for losing you; and I love John too, but not in the way that I love you, my darling.

So all the best, Jim, and look after yourself; and remember, I'll always be interested to know how you're getting on.

With all my love, Sue.

Jim read the letter through carefully, and then resolutely folded it up, placed it in its envelope, and re-pocketed the envelope in his jacket. His face was looking serious and thoughtful, and now he hardly noticed anything outside the train, thinking over what Susan had said to him in her letter. Of course I'll write, he said to himself firmly. I'll write to her this very evening, or at any rate, I'll start a letter, and I'll post it tomorrow, and perhaps she'll get it on Monday morning. I hope so. But fancy; she wrote that letter on Wednesday—that was the evening <u>before</u> we had that lovely last talk in the Private Garden. So Sue thinks that I could come down to Rhodes Castle in the summer of next year, all being well. Oh dear, that's an <u>awfully</u> long time to wait to see her again, but at least we'll keep in touch with our letters.

Then a smile began to appear on Jim's face as he reflected how strongly Susan had expressed her love for him in her letter. "Jim, my darling, I love you so much," she says in it, he remembered. And she says she'll cry because I've gone. Yes, she's terrifically in love with me. Oh, Sue, my darling, my lovely darling, that's wonderful, simply wonderful . . . !

At this stage in Jim's thoughts a curious idea began to form in his mind. He looked dreamily ahead, past Mr. Ruddock and Mr. Blencow, who were sitting and chatting in the cab, at the sunset colours which were still blazing brightly in the west. The day was coming to an end, and his journey home was coming to an end. Then it seemed to him suddenly that the whole of his life since the day he had first met Susan had been very like a dream; not like a daydream, but like a dream during sleep at night: like one of those dreams which are so exquisitely pleasant that one can hardly bear the sensation of waking up and having to face ordinary reality again. This homecoming, thought Jim, really does feel <u>very</u> like that—as if it's all been some fabulously wonderful dream, ever since that day when I first met Sue. But if it's a dream, then I'm going to wake up from it very soon—when I get out at Cockermouth, in fact. Then it'll all be over: precisely then. It won't be like a dream any more after that. Even though Sue and I are going to keep in touch by writing letters, some magic is bound to disappear from our lives when we're living far away from each other. Life at home is going to seem very <u>ordinary</u> after living for so long under the same roof as Sue. But the dream isn't quite over yet. I can feel it ebbing away now, the last of this lovely dream, as the last miles go by, but I'm still in the dream . . .

However, it was at this point that Jim's train of thought was broken. The door of the cab opened, and out came Mr. Blencow. Jim pulled himself together and saw that the train was racing down the steep gradient towards Threlkeld station, which they would reach in about another minute. There would probably be passengers wanting to get in and out, which meant that Mr. Blencow would have to be on duty to see them on and off the train.

The journey home was very nearly over. Another minute or two and Jim would be stepping out of the little diesel train onto the down platform of Cockermouth station. But I hope dad hasn't come to meet me there, he thought, but I suppose he may be there as he must have come in from the mine two or three hours ago, and he must have finished his supper by now. Jim had tried to see his father's mine as the train had left Keswick, but that had not been possible. After leaving Keswick station the line headed west for a bit over level ground, before curving round towards the north by Braithwaite station; and from a train on that stretch of line, travelling west, it was possible on a clear day, if one had a view forwards, to make out where the Leadthwaite Mine lay amongst the hills to the west. But at this late hour on this particular evening those peaks looked almost black in the declining light of the sunset against the fiery red glow in the sky. What I'd like now, said Jim to himself as the train gathered speed, pulling away from Embleton, is to be able to walk back home to Lorton Road without being recognized by anyone who knows me, and there should be a fair chance of doing that as it's late, and there won't be many people about. Anyway, so long as I'm not seen by any of my old police colleagues, like last time, I won't really mind.

The train rattled round a bend by Strawberry How Farm, and a moment later Jim saw his home town of Cockermouth spread out before him in the dusk on the right-hand side of the line. Yes, and there, in particular, was the unmistakable outline of the spire of the parish church of All Saints, seen across the intervening fields. A few seconds more, hurrying along that straight stretch of track, they would come to that little bridge, numbered Eleven, over the Rudd Beck, the place where Lord Dalmane had been arrested by the Cockermouth police. The daylight was slowly fading from the sky, although ahead, in the west, the amount of light still lingering behind the departing sunset was surprisingly great, Jim thought: the buildings of the town were silhouetted in black against that light. There were street lights and other lights to be seen now; and in the train Mr. Blencow had turned on the lights some time ago.

Jim was watching for Mr. Ruddock to put out his right hand to the main brake lever. It seemed to him that they were moving at an almost excessively fast speed; but just as the train rushed across the Cemetry Level Crossing Mr. Ruddock reached for the handle and began to make a sharp brake application. Jim immediately stood up and held onto his seat while he pulled his suitcase down off the luggage rack. The poignant reminders of homecoming were all around him, and the feeling of awakening out of a happy dream became irresistible. A moment later (at least it seemed only a moment later) the train crossed the river and the station came into sight not many yards ahead. Jim took his place in a queue behind a few other passengers waiting to disembark by the nearest door on the left. The train was gliding smoothly and more and more slowly up to the platforms. It stopped.

The wooden mounting steps on the low platform had been carefully set in the right place by the porter, and now the passengers standing in front of Jim stepped down by it. But he was in no hurry, and was prepared politely to let others go in front of him. Then he stepped down onto the platform himself. He decided to wait a minute to see the train go on.

"Good night, Jim." Mr. Ruddock was leaning out of the window of his cab.

"Good night, Mr. Ruddock," said Jim. The driver waved a friendly arm at him, and then resumed his seat, shutting his window. The next moment the buzzer sounded in the cab, and the train started again, rumbling slowly away from the platform and passing under the road bridge on its way down to Workington. Jim, picking up his suitcase and empty string bag, went down to the subway to cross under the tracks. But then, instead of walking out of the station he stopped on the opposite platform, the one for eastbound trains. Something inside him prompted him to make this further delay, but he was not quite sure what it was. The beautiful colours in the afterglow of the sunset certainly had something to do with it. He looked up, first to the east, where it was getting dark; the brightest stars had already come out in the very deep blue over the hills to the east. Then he turned his gaze to that sunset afterglow in the west, fainter now, but still well worth pausing a moment to admire. The station buildings stood somewhat in the way of this view, but by looking right along the railway track westwards, in the bottom of the cutting Jim could see a small V-shaped segment of that spectacle. Faint pink along the horizon merged into pale yellow, and that into a wider area which was greenish, very pale lower down, but passing by imperceptible degrees upwards into the deep blue part of the sky. Jim felt as if he had woken up now from that dream he had been thinking about, but the magic of it still had not entirely passed away. A sensitive nature like his could hardly pass by such a sight without pausing to admire it. But if the sky was one of the stimuli which prompted him to delay for a minute or two his exit from the station, the other was simply a reluctance to leave the place. While he stood in the station within sight of the railway lines, it was almost as if his train journey were not really over because he was still in touch with the railway atmosphere of the place, which meant a lot to him. Then he remembered something else. Heavens, he said to himself, this platform is the very place where I first saw Susan! She was standing close to where I'm standing now, talking with Mrs. Beck, when Mr. Beck and I came running up along the tracks. And now I've said Good-bye to her. Well, no; it isn't Good-bye really, because we're going to write, and hopefully I'll be invited back next year to Rhodes Castle. Ah well, I'd better press on! That dream's over now, and I've woken up back in ordinary life. And there's the stationmaster waiting to collect my ticket.

So Jim picked up his baggage and walked out of the station, pausing a moment in the doorway of the Booking Hall to hand over his ticket (it was a through booking from Stalbridge to Cockermouth). But he stopped again in the yard outside and looked back at the old buildings, the place where he had met the Countess of Saint Helens on that momentous day. A ridiculous wave of nostalgia seemed to be coming over him, and for a moment he thought that he did not want to go home at all; he wanted to stay there, and would have liked, indeed, to step into a Carlisle-bound train, if there had been one, and go off travelling again. In his mind's eye he pictured Susan standing there beside him, her exquisite dark eyes staring dreamily into his own, and he wondered again how he was going to bear being separated from her until, maybe, some time in the next year. But then he seemed to hear her voice in his mind's ear, speaking to him: "Come on, Jim! This hanging about won't do. Let's go home."

Heavens, it's nine twenty-three! he said to himself, glancing at his watch. I must have wasted several minutes here already. But dad will have my supper ready, and then there's that letter I must write to Sue; I'm going to start it this evening. Oh, if only she could be walking home with me!

He was already walking towards the road. Yes, he said to himself, I mustn't wait another minute hanging about. I'm going straight home.

The End

The Guide of Rhodes Castle
by
Patrick Wetenhall

Lightning Source UK Ltd.
Milton Keynes UK
UKOW03f0823060314

227660UK00002B/140/P